The Far Land

The Far Land

Christina Green

ROBERT HALE · LONDON

© Christina Green 2009
First published in Great Britain 2009

ISBN 978-0-7090-8840-0

Robert Hale Limited
Clerkenwell House
Clerkenwell Green
London EC1R 0HT

www.halebooks.com

The right of Christina Green to be identified as
author of this work has been asserted by her
in accordance with the Copyright, Designs and
Patents Act 1988

2 4 6 8 10 9 7 5 3 1

Typeset in 10/13pt Classical Garamond
by Derek Doyle & Associates, Shaw Heath
Printed in Great Britain by the MPG Books Group, Bodmin and King's Lynn

ACKNOWLEDGEMENTS

My friend Viv Wilson, with her Teignmouth Wilson Archive, has been of enormous help to me when researching the setting for this book. My grateful thanks go to her and other people, books, websites, libraries and museums who have responded so kindly to my search for information. And I must also thank my writing friends, whose comments, interest and encouragement have helped me along the way.

CHAPTER ONE

The man, six feet two inches of bulk and stooping shoulders, stood in the log cabin doorway, flinching as the freezing wind hit him. His salt-stained reefer jacket was no safeguard against the icy spray that the howling wind scattered, neither could his dark breeches and canvas leggings protect him. But it was a cold that he had lived with for so long that it had little effect on him now.

Yet, automatically, he reached out a calloused hand to pull his fur cap further down on the straggling once thick fair hair and shrugged the coat tighter across his body as he stared into the whirling curtain of ice which engulfed the hidden landscape.

The far land . . .

Slowly, his weathered, lined face began to relax. Behind his eyes he saw visions of green trees and lush grass, felt the warmth of sun on soft, golden beaches, with a kindly sea lapping them, showing its other side, so different from the raging monster that battered this island, this hard, harsh rock of Newfoundland.

Thoughts raked him. The shoals of fish had stopped coming now and the centuries-old cod industry was dying. He could no longer make a living here. And these days, the old nightmares kept haunting him, only relieved by occasional dreams of bewitching, beckoning images of that far land he had once loved. And one gentle natured, slow-speaking woman and her child.

And he sensed himself changing. Wiser? Gentler? More in need of human warmth? A frown lifted his bronzed, lined face. Even guilt for abandoning them?

Was it too late to go back?

Loveday Jenkins walked along the beach, the hem of her grey stuff skirt damp and her boots forming squelchy imprints in the dark sand. The tide was ebbing and she walked as near to the untidy line of sea-washed flotsam as she could, eyes fixed on what she saw there. Sometimes there were things worth picking up – as a child she had dreamed of finding a floating bottle with a message in it, but never had. And today it was just strands of dark seaweed hiding a collection of intriguing things no longer wanted by the ocean – a black cuttlefish egg called a mermaid's purse, bits of driftwood that the river must have brought down from wooded valleys upcountry, and the usual piles of broken shells. Mussels, winkles, a pelican's foot – not often found – some tall razor shells, a couple of scallops and. . . .

She bent and picked up a tiny curling, sandy-coloured shell half hidden beneath seaweed. *A cowry. Mr Benedict says they're lucky. I'll take it to him.* She smiled to herself as she walked on. Frank Benedict's collection of curiosities was always fascinating. Maybe he'd like this small offering in return for all he'd done for her.

His cottage was in sight now, a small, lumpy thatched building, tucked away close to the church, looking almost part of the red sandstone cliff that rose above it. Loveday headed up the beach, the cowry clutched in one hand. She crossed the road, then, before opening the shabby white-painted garden gate, turned and looked out to sea.

What a day. A spring sun beamed down from sky as blue as a jay's feather, with puffy little white clouds blown in a neat line just above the hazy horizon. Taking a deep breath, Loveday stood there, lost in what she saw and felt. The brilliance, the warmth, the soft music of retreating waves, even the distant shrieks of a skein of gulls following a fishing boat just entering the harbour – all these were part of her life and she loved them.

She smiled, happiness warm and safe within her. And then thoughts expanded and her smile faded. For somewhere there was another land that she dreamed of, a rocky island that old Frank Benedict had told her about, a land of storms and icebergs, of native peoples wearing furs and skins, of bears and whales and strange birds. A dangerous land where he said men worked with enormous strength to earn a meagre living; where fish were currency for money, where the men from her Devonshire hometown had been sailing to for hundreds of years to catch the huge shoals of cod, dry them, salt them and then bring them home to sell.

The far land.

And then she remembered – faintly because it was so long ago – her father. *Lost at sea.* The remembered, haunting words from her childhood rang an unwelcome dirge and she frowned, steadfastly pushing them into the furthest corner of her busy mind. Think instead of the far land. Imagination prickled her spine then and she grew tense as the exciting images became more and more vivid. But Aunt Janet's common sense and practicality, handed down and resignedly copied from an early age, came to the fore, and so, from icebergs and wild seas, eventually Loveday forced herself to come home again, back here to Teignmouth, with her loved ones.

In her mind's eye she saw Aunt Janet with her upright posture, tight mouth and dark, dragged-back hair. There she was, sitting beside the window of the front room of the cottage which was not only home, but served as her dressmaking business premises. And Uncle Davey, slight, warm hearted, marching off to his accounting position in the shipyard and always ready to smile. No, no – forget the dream of the far land. She could never leave home. Could she? But why not? It was so dull here. . . .

'Mornin', maid. Got the sun in yer eyes?'

Dreams and images vanished. She turned, smiling at the small, wizened man who stood in his open doorway, a white cat sinuously rubbing against his legs.

'Morning, Mr Benedict. No, just looking. Thinking—'

'Day dreamin', more like. Time you was off to the big house, innit? Young lady'll be waiting fer you.' His faded, rheumy eyes squinted into the sun and he raised a gnarled hand to shield them from the glare, but she caught their warmth and smiled back.

She held out her hand. 'A cowry, Mr Benedict. Lucky, isn't it?'

The old man nodded and stepped closer. He shooed away the cat. 'Get on wi' ee, Crystal. Let the maid pass.' Then, nodding, he looked at the shell. 'Got plenty o' they on the shelf. Want to add this un?'

Loveday hesitated. If this really was a lucky charm, then she'd rather keep it herself. It might help the imagined dreams to become reality. But she recalled that lucky charms were a load of nonsense: Aunt Janet said so. The smile dying, Loveday nodded resignedly. After all, everything else Aunt Janet said was correct, and so she must be right about charms.

'Yes, please, Mr Benedict.'

'Come on in, then.' He stepped back and she entered the cottage, eyes blinking until she got used to the dim light and the shadows. Such a tiny room with an even smaller fireplace, where driftwood crackled and smouldered. Frank Benedict's rheumatic bones cried out for warmth, even on this April day. One armchair, sagging and lumpy, a table covered with a faded dark-red chenille cloth, still piled with empty plates and cups from the last meal, and there, leaning lopsidedly against the far wall, the old harmonium on which he had taught her to play hymns and songs he remembered from his seafaring days.

Where she had practised, with Aunt Janet's permission. The decisive voice still echoed – 'the child's got a gift. We must nurture it.' And so hard-earned pennies were handed out each week, first to Mr Brabner, the church organist, and then, on his retirement and recommendation, to Frank Benedict.

Music had become a much loved part of Loveday's life as she grew into womanhood. Slowly, but steadily, her talent had grown until she could play almost everything she heard. And now she was capable of playing the organ in church when Frank was unable to do so. Also, she had a weekly position as music teacher to Miss Eleanor, up at Sothern House, as well as her everyday work at Mrs Narracott's small hotel on the promenade.

Sunlight filtered through thin curtains at the window and fell on the cabinet opposite the harmonium. Loveday moved towards it, the cowry warm in her hand, while Frank Benedict stood and watched, pointing knobbly fingers at the crowded shelves. 'Put it where you wants, maid – jest move others around. 'Tis a praper conglomeration of they old things there.'

A conglomeration indeed. Loveday stifled her chuckle. Bits of this, pieces of that. Some old china, cracked and crazed. Brass artefacts that puzzled her as to their usage. Rough wooden sculptures made out of driftwood, shells of every size and variety, a faded flower and a long piece of something creamy white covered with etched lines.

She pointed at it. 'What's that, Mr Benedict?'

He moved nearer, narrowing his eyes, bending down to inspect the strange object. Then he straightened up, turning to look at her. His voice was slow. 'That there's scrimshaw. Whale's bone or tooth. Seamen used to fill up time when shoals were slow in comin' by scratching pictures on bits like this one. Then pressed soot or lamp black on the lines to show the pictures up. See, there's a praper picture, if you looks closer.'

She bent and, yes, once she got near enough, there were tiny images visible. A big man carrying something, a child . . . but then it all became letters and squiggles which curved into spirals and circles and swirls of rough decoration.

Fascinated, she nodded, stretched out her hand and carefully put the cowry beside it. 'What a funny old thing – I've never seen anything like it before.'

Frank Benedict was still watching her. 'Where there's fishing folk 'bout there's plenty o' scrimshaw, maid. Mebbe ee'll find some more, some-where.'

She smiled. 'I wouldn't know where to look, but perhaps one day, when I'm somewhere else—'

'Goin' places, then, are you, maid?' He grinned, following her to the open doorway and out into the sun.

'You never know! I want to go – oh, I don't know – places I've never seen, when I'm older, perhaps, when I've saved some money. I mean, Teignmouth is so dull and quiet.'

They smiled at each other. She looked at the roadway outside, which almost at once turned into a brown earth track, climbing the hill and following the contour of the towering red sandstone cliff. 'Shan't earn anything at this rate, shall I? I must hurry, or I'll be late, and Mrs Sothern won't be pleased.'

Another shared smile and a wheezy chuckle from Frank. All the town knew that Mrs Sothern, second and younger wife of Joshua, shipping merchant and owner of his family home, Sothern House, must never be kept waiting. 'Off you go, then. What's the young lady playin' now? Got to hymns, has she?'

'Not yet. Scales and arpeggios and a few simple tunes.' The breeze was playing with her wiry hair and she raised a hand to skewer her hat on more firmly, pulling the thin shawl tighter over her shoulders.

'Ah. Keep 'er at it. And don't fergit, maid, you'm at the organ on Sunday. Can't get there meself. Feet are too bad. Those ole frostbitten toes playin' up.'

She smiled back at him, a quick image of icebergs and frozen waste stabbing through her mind and then disappearing as fast as it had come. 'I'll be there. And put some of Aunt Janet's ointment on your feet, Mr Benedict. Oh, and I forgot to tell you – Miss Eleanor is learning to play that little tune I can remember my father playing on his fiddle. I picked it out for her and gave it a few easy chords, and she's got it off by heart. Pretty, it is.'

The tune arose, vibrant and clear as a bird, joining the space between them as she sang. He nodded, smile vanishing and a taut expression shad-owing his weatherbeaten face.

Then she was off, giving Crystal a last stroke, shutting the creaking gate, waving at the old man who watched her as she walked towards the path leading to Sothern House, perched further up on the top of the cliff.

Frank Benedict kept her in his hazy vision; tall and quick moving, chestnut hair straggling beneath her straw hat. Loveday Jenkins, so full of life, so needful of adventures and excitement, and so caught here in Devon in this small town by the sea where every day seemed the same.

He returned her final wave, saw her disappear behind the straggling bushes that climbed the hill, and for a long moment or two stayed in his doorway, looking out at the sea, thinking back to his past life in the far land and wondering how long mysteries and secrets were supposed to last.

Picking up the purring cat, he stroked her arching back and sighed. Well, he knew a few of both, didn't he?

Loveday paused as she reached the entrance to Sothern House, giving herself a moment to savour the grandeur of the building that looked so stern and precise with its tiers of windows and a large wing at either end, but which this morning was softened by the gleam of sunshine on the stonework. Relishing the fragrance of a small yellow early rose rambling along the nearest wall, she followed the path leading to the back quarters and knocked on the kitchen door.

Mrs Derby's resonant voice trumpeted 'come in' and Loveday entered. The kitchen was hot and full of baking smells. Roast beef, she thought with a sudden pang of greed. Beth and Mary, the kitchen maids, were talking in low voices as they put shining plates and dishes on the long dresser that filled one wall. Lou, the young skivvy, stood at the sink in the adjoining scullery, scrubbing parsnips and potatoes, while a pile of cabbages waited their turn to be washed. Inside the doorway, Loveday smiled at Billy, as he piled four pairs of boots of various sizes against his thin chest and clutched his box of brushes and polish in the other hand.

'I'll be listening, Miss Jenkins,' he said, grinning, his coarse, spiky hair made even more untidy by the sneaky wind that came rushing in from the sea, far below. 'I likes those tunes you'm teaching Miss Eleanor to play.'

Before Loveday could reply, a voice from the kitchen range slapped away the boy's grin. 'Get on wi' the work, Billy, else Mistress'll be on at 'ee.' The boy disappeared and the voice softened. 'Come on in, Loveday. She'll be waitin' fer 'ee with one eye on the clock, as usual.' Mrs Derby, arms white to the elbow as she rolled pastry, allowed herself a small smile before frowning and shouting across to Beth and Mary. 'An don't be all day with them dishes, you gels – there's washing to fold an' stack, remember, before luncheon.'

It was always like this in the kitchen, Loveday thought, warmth and life and shouting. She returned the cook's smile, caught a cautious grin from one of the maids, and then walked through the big room into the cold stone passages leading to the green baize door, the entry to upstairs and the quieter, more restrained company of Mr and Mrs Sothern and their daughter, Miss Eleanor.

Passing quickly through the dimly lighted hall with its vast bolted oak door and dark panelled walls, not pausing, thinking it a dreary space with a chill to it, she was glad to mount the elegant, curving mahogany staircase, with family portraits staring down from gilded, faded canvases. Upstairs, the carpeted passage took her to Mrs Sothern's boudoir. The door was ajar and she heard voices.

She waited a moment; there was irritation in Isobel Sothern's high voice, and Miss Eleanor was mumbling something inaudible in reply. What was the problem today, Loveday wondered? There always seemed to be something wrong. Determined to keep calm, she knocked and was told, snappily, to 'come in'.

The room was a delight, not too large, and furnished comfortably in pale colours, of which eau de nil was the pleasing background. Biscuit and gold-patterned wall paper toned well, and the two chintz-covered armchairs beside the decorative stone fireplace offered comfort along with floral cushions. Loveday particularly admired the pictures on the walls – seascapes and graciously arranged bowls of brilliant flowers.

Her mind flickered back for a moment – to Frank's tiny cottage and then to her own home in Market Street, which was reasonably sized but still dark and cold and lacking the comforts she saw here. At the end of the room there were two spacious windows that looked out over the garden and across the green turf to the cliff edge. She couldn't see it, but had an instant image of the ocean below, stretching away beyond the eye's vision. A swelling green, grey, blue, the horizon smudged with faintest indigo – Loveday's heart swelled. How beautiful it was, rolling away to far off lands.

The pettish voice brought her back to reality. 'You're late, Miss Jenkins. Is there any reason? Miss Eleanor has been waiting for at least five minutes.' Isobel Sothern was sitting at her bureau, the desk top covered with notepaper and envelopes. She sat there looking autocratic, pen in her right hand, left hand gesticulating as she spoke. Unsmiling, she looked at Loveday, her slightly tilted hazel eyes cold and questioning.

Her step daughter, Eleanor, stood mutely in the middle of the room and looked cautiously at Loveday, who saw the child's small hands were bunched into fists and the ten-year-old face full of distress. A quick surge of anger flashed through Loveday's mind and she had to bite her lip to avoid answering impolitely.

13

She took a deep breath. This was an unpleasant atmosphere, bad for the child and not conducive to a friendly and creative lesson on the pianoforte. Perhaps an apology would help.

Forcing her voice into quiet submission, she said, 'I beg your pardon, Mrs Sothern. I called in on Mr Benedict as I came.' Surely a small lie couldn't be counted a sin, considering the circumstances, could it? 'He has trouble with his health, you see, and so, on my way here, I like to make sure he is all right.'

'I see. Playing the Good Samaritan, are you?'

A frown marred Loveday's face as the unfeeling voice continued. 'He's the dour old creature who plays the organ in church, is he not? I wonder that the vicar allows him to appear – such shabby clothes, and I often hear a wrong note.' Isobel turned away, put down the pen and tidied the papers on the desk. She got to her feet and walked to the nearest window, stared out for a moment and then turned to look back at Loveday.

Abruptly, her pretty, heart-shaped face was transformed, and her voice rose a tone higher. 'I have a new lady's maid,' she said, a smile touching her lips. 'She's come from Cornwall with excellent references from the Treveryan family. Her name is Hunt – Margaret, I believe. I've told her that your aunt is a dressmaker with a shop in Market Street. No doubt Hunt will be visiting the shop when I need new ribbons, lace, or anything like that. Tell your aunt to expect her during the next few days, please. Hunt is very experienced and polite, and I'm delighted to have someone who knows her place and is light handed – and knowledgeable about hair styles, too, which is extremely useful.'

Turning away from the window she looked across the room. Her voice dropped and the smile faded. 'I got rid of that clumsy oaf Betsy Forder as soon as I could. A hopeless girl. She had no idea how a lady's maid should behave.'

Loveday nodded, remembering sad Betsy weeping when she was put off without a character, and said quietly, 'I'll tell my aunt what you've said, and I'm sure she will be pleased to welcome your maid, Mrs Sothern.' No doubt Aunt Janet would, indeed, be delighted to have a new source of trade, especially coming from the big house. Her small business might well increase once it got around that Mrs Sothern was patronizing her.

'Very well then.' Isobel walked to one of the fireside chairs, sat down and picked up the embroidery frame on the small table beside it. Stabbing a needle into the linen, she gave Eleanor a hard look. 'Off you go, child, and let me hear how well you do today. And, Miss Jenkins, perhaps we could have less of the scales and a little more of something tuneful, for a change?'

Loveday paused at the door as she started to follow her pupil into the passage, then looked back and said without thinking, 'But scales are the important part of learning to play, Mrs Sothern. All pianoforte players have to practise scales and arpeggios before they turn to more difficult study.'

There was a quick intake of outraged breath. 'I'll thank you to do as I say, Miss Jenkins. There are always other more polite and amenable tutors available, you know.'

Their eyes met. Loveday tightened her mouth as furious words spontaneously rushed through her mind. *I don't have to be beholden to you, you know. I have a good situation with Mrs Narracott – I can manage without your grudging shillings,* but she nodded and forced herself to be subservient. 'Yes, Mrs Sothern. I didn't mean to be rude. And I'll do as you ask.'

She left the room quickly, following Eleanor down the staircase, trying hard to control the feelings of frustration and resentment filling her. Really, what a foolish woman Isobel Sothern was! And how unpleasant – until the subjects of clothes and the new maid were aired. Well, Eleanor should play scales by the dozen before she attempted the piece by Mr Handel which had been her study this week, just to let her stepmama realize how much hard work was involved in developing her talent.

In the spacious, empty drawing room, Loveday sat the child at the upright piano against the side wall and said determinedly, 'The scale of C major, please, Miss Eleanor.' An eyebrow was raised, but Loveday met it with a smile. 'Let me hear it three times. I want to make quite sure you really are learning your scales.'

As Eleanor's small fingers grappled with the keys, Loveday went to the tall windows at the far end of the room overlooking the beautifully kept lawn and parterre flower beds. Ben Marten, one of the gardeners, was at work bending to remove winter weeds and give the emerging spring flowers space and newly forked earth. As if he felt her gaze, he straightened, looked up at the window and grinned. Loveday nodded and waved, remembering their days at school together and the small wickednesses they had enjoyed – scrumping apples, playing tricks on friends and writing huge letters in the golden sands of the beach. What days those had been. And now life was different. Sometimes more difficult but never as exciting. But she supposed it was the same for everyone.

Turning, she concentrated on Eleanor's playing and thought how lucky she was to live here in this lovely place, to have a position and to have Aunt Janet and Uncle Davey as well as all her friends.

Then Eleanor stopped playing. 'Well done,' said Loveday. 'You really do know those awful old scales!'

The child's face was wreathed in smiles. 'Papa likes me to play. He comes in at teatime. Yesterday I played the tune you wrote out for me. He said it was pretty and that I was getting on well.'

Loveday returned the smile as she sorted through the music on the top of the pianoforte. 'That's good,' she said, and then, suddenly her serenity was disturbed. *Lucky Eleanor had a papa.* It flashed through her mind with aching pain that she missed her father very much. But it was a momentary thought. She must control her feelings – other people had lost their parents and still lived contented lives. Firmly then, she opened a sheet of music and put it in front of Eleanor. 'Let's please your mama with some Handel, shall we?' She managed a bright smile and then made herself listen with a critical ear, forcing away the shadows that still loitered in her mind.

When the lesson was over, Loveday accompanied Eleanor upstairs to rejoin her stepmother and then, receiving Mrs Sothern's stiff smile and dismissal, went along the passage towards the staircase A woman came out of a room just ahead of her, holding an armful of clothes that smelled faintly of hot iron. She paused as Loveday approached, stood back and bowed her head.

'Good morning, Madam' The voice was low, polite and full of country intonation.

'You're Margaret? Good morning,' said Loveday quickly. 'Mrs Sothern has just told me that you will be calling on my aunt, Miss Jenkins, when you need anything to repair or renew her clothes. We live in Market Street.' She smiled, and Margaret smiled back.

'I know. Thank you, Madam.'

They looked at each other for a moment longer, then she bobbed a curtsey and walked rapidly along the passage, opening a far door and disappearing from Loveday's sight.

How could she know? Wondered Loveday vaguely, making her way out of the house.

But perhaps she had seen the shop when she first explored the town on her arrival here. It wasn't important, anyway. Then her thoughts took flight as she followed the cliff path, indulging herself for a few minutes to look over the edge, seeing the glint of sun on the railway lines below, hearing the surging lap of waves against the sea wall, and feeling, yet again, the intense love she had for the ocean and all its wondrous concealed mysteries.

She walked back towards the town, watching the brave holidaymakers frequenting the line of bathing machines situated along the beach beside the pier. She could hear their screams and laughter as they plunged into the waves, and then saw the inevitable photographer close at hand, immersed behind a black cloth, finally making himself known to his prospective customers. As she made her way along the promenade she passed him, a young man with twinkling eyes and a friendly smile. He lifted his hat to her and she smiled back. So the holiday season was definitely here – and the Beach View Hotel, where she worked as a chambermaid, would be filling up. Plenty of work ahead of her, then. So make the most of this walk in the sunshine, with a sense of happiness filling her, and as always, just that hint of excitement – for who knew when an adventure would come along?

Janet Jenkins, was, as usual, sitting as close to the window as possible to get what was left of the morning sun before it moved away, filling the narrow, busy street with shadows. On her lap, overflowing from the table at her side, was a large purple dress which her neighbour, Mrs Mutley, had requested should be turned and then enhanced with a new set of flounces, prior to a coming birthday party. The material was thin and worn and slightly odorous, but it was a piece of work and must be completed to her very best ability No one should ever say that Janet Jenkins's work wasn't the best in the neighbourhood.

She put down her needle, smiling as Loveday came into the shop. 'How was the little girl playing, then? Improving, no doubt, with you teaching her.' Her usually stern face was relaxed, a smiling lifting the tight mouth and allowing dark eyes to shine.

Loveday took off her shawl and hat and went to her aunt's side, watching the moving needle, quickly taken up again, as it shone in the beam of light coming through the window. 'Yes, she's doing very well. Her papa enjoys hearing her, but Mrs Sothern is full of complaints. I don't think they get on – poor child, she must have a strange life.'

Janet Jenkins put in a last stitch, stuck her needle into a large pincushion, and turned the dress over, looking at each seam with critical eyes. 'She won't be spoiled, that's for sure. An only child without a real mama is bound to feel unhappy. But once Mrs Sothern starts breeding, perhaps things will improve. With a baby brother or sister to care for, little Eleanor will have a new interest, won't she?'

Loveday chuckled to herself. Aunt Janet was always outspoken, not one to hide facts. Of course, the whole town guessed that Mr Sothern must have married again in order to have a son to inherit his fortune. And it also knew – not just guessed – that his young wife was more interested in living a busy social life than settling down to produce an heir. Betsy Forder, full of anger at being put off without a character, had told spiteful tales about goings on at Sothern House. Everyone now watched Isobel and made bets about how long it would be. . . .

'Can I do anything to get dinner ready, Aunt Janet?' In the dark kitchen, tackling potatoes in the stone sink, Loveday suddenly remembered the message she had been asked to give. 'I nearly forgot.' She went to the doorway, watching her aunt removing her steel spectacles and running a hand over her face. 'Mrs Sothern has a new lady's maid. Come from Cornwall with a good reference, and she'll be calling here when anything is needed – you know, lace, or ribbon, or some such. I saw her – a pleasant looking woman. She's called Margaret Hunt.'

About to return to the sink, she suddenly realized Janet had made no reply. Her aunt was staring into space, the purple dress slipping from her lap, spectacles falling to the floor.

'Aunt Janet, what's wrong?'

But Janet didn't appear to hear. Instead she just stared at the wall and muttered very low, so that Loveday could hardly hear, 'Oh, my good Lord. So Maggie's come back, has she?'

CHAPTER TWO

So long ago, but increasingly filling his mind: happy images, voices, the taste of salt, gulls' cries, children laughing and singing, sand between naked toes, warm enticing water with gentle waves creaming the beach. Boats lined up, rigging tinkling as the west wind blew a friendly breeze.

The other land, far away, yet close in his dreaming.

'Maggie?' Loveday was confused. 'Do you mean Margaret Hunt, Mrs Sothern's new lady's maid, Aunt? It sounds as if you know her – do you?'

Janet Jenkins inhaled deeply, meticulously placed her sewing tools on the table beside her, put the purple dress over her arm, and got up from her chair. She arranged the dress carefully over a hanger and then walked to the long curtain hanging at the back of the room, which opened into a small fitting room. There was a hook on the wall and there she hung the dress, pulling its skirts out and unfolding the creased sleeves.

Not looking at Loveday, she cleared her throat, and said quietly, 'Yes, I think I do. The name is familiar. I shall probably recognize her if she calls.'

Still bemused, Loveday returned to the potatoes, which she put in a pan on the hot range. But when her aunt joined her in the kitchen, preparing the fish for the midday meal, she asked, 'This Maggie – Margaret Hunt – was she a friend of yours then, Aunt Janet?'

'Yes. Many years ago.' Janet dipped the fish in flour, put it aside and then pushed a large black iron frying pan on to the heat.

'So, Miss Hunt—'

'Mrs' The word snapped out and Loveday felt even more curious. Clearly, Aunt Janet was not prepared to tell her the details of this unexpected arrival of the old friend. But curiosity was a prime fault, and she heard herself choosing words carefully, and saying, 'how did you know her, then, if she has been living in Cornwall?'

19

'Those potatoes need a good boil – your Uncle will be home very soon.' Janet's voice was controlled as she put a lump of dripping into the pan and then waited for it to heat up.

Loveday's lips tightened. This was obviously a secret that Aunt Janet wasn't ready to share. But why not? She glanced at her aunt, and said lightly, 'I expect you'll both have a lot to talk over when you meet again. I thought she was pleasant enough – she smiled at me and had good manners.' Looking at the expressionless face beside her she felt an inrush of irritation. Why this big secret? But then she remembered that, for a woman who could be very outspoken, Aunt Janet was also a hoarder of secrets. Many's the time the small Loveday had asked questions, only to be given a cautious and not very informative reply.

For instance, the first, all-important question that the toddler had asked, once the knowledge of her small friends having mothers and fathers but having none of her own had dawned on her, had been 'Aunt Janet, where is my mother? And my father?'

And the answer had been brusque and quelling. 'Your father was a seaman, unfortunately lost at sea. And your mother had to move away to find work, which is why your Uncle Davey and I took you in. Now, that will do, child. No more questions. Time for bed.'

And that had been that.

But now the memories refused to be put away. So Father had been lost at sea, no doubt a victim of a sinking ship, one of those many terrible disasters which the mighty sea demanded so frequently. *Drowned.* As she took plates from the dresser for dinner, Loveday blinked away threatening tears because the images were so awful. Drownings happened even here in the safety of this sheltered West Country bay, and she had seen bodies brought ashore, heard the mourning wives, sweethearts and families keening, realized that lives were broken up, thrown into chaos and the resulting often unrelenting poverty. Yes, she thought, returning to the range to make sure the potatoes were boiling well, the sea could be beautiful when it wanted, but sometimes it was simply a raging monster, devouring everything that challenged it.

A slight man with a pronounced limp, carrying a trusty stick to support him, Davey Jenkins arrived home at the usual, precise time of 12.40, after walking unhurriedly from the shipyard through the narrow streets to his house in the middle of town.

Timing him to the minute, Loveday was at the door. 'Hallo, Uncle. Let me take your hat.'

Leaning forward, he kissed her and surrendered his bowler and stick. 'A beautiful day. Let's hope it lasts.'

They moved together into the kitchen as Loveday said, 'I walked along the beach this morning on my way to Sothern House and found a cowry which I gave to Frank Benedict. And he wants me to play the organ in church on Sunday. I do hope I shan't hit too many wrong notes!'

His answering smile was warm. 'Of course you won't. You're a proper musician these days.'

Davey greeted his sister and then went to his customary chair. He sat down heavily, grimacing and stretching out his left leg to rub away the pain. Then he sat back, looking around the room and smiling.

'This sunshine,' he remarked as Janet began slicing bread, 'will be persuading our tourists to go on the pier, and try out the bathing machines too, no doubt.' An amused glance at Loveday then – 'and I suppose you'll be one of them, as usual, maid – how you can plunge into that cold sea I really don't know – but you were always a water baby.'

His pale eyes were on her, warm and loving as she took her place at the table and she was content. Until she remembered the piece of news about Margaret Hunt, the old friend and wondered if Uncle Davey remembered her, too.

The fish was excellent and made even better by parsley sauce. Taking a slice of bread, Davey reached for the butter and then pushed it away as Janet raised an eyebrow, reminding him of the need to eschew what she considered his natural greed. Silence reigned for a moment.

And then, 'Do you know someone called Mar—?' Loveday began, but stopped as Janet frowned across the table and shook her head.

Loveday's thoughts raced. Why shouldn't she ask Uncle Davey about Aunt's old friend? No reason at all that she could imagine. And then defiance, her constant companion, struck urgently and she heard herself asking, 'Do you remember Margaret Hunt, Uncle Davey? Only she's here now, working as lady's maid for Mrs Sothern—'

And then she stopped, guiltily aware that something was very wrong.

Uncle Davey's face had grown taut, his mild eyes suddenly keen and questioning, looking at his sister, while Aunt Janet was pursing her lips and staring furiously back at him across the table.

Loveday held her breath, watching as brother and sister exchanged looks and then slowly returned to their laden dinner plates. No one spoke, until Janet said in a determined voice, 'Davey, did you ever hear any more of the gentleman who wrote, asking for information about finding accommodation?' and Loveday realized that the subject – whatever it was, and however unpleasant – had been changed.

She pushed the parsley sauce towards her Uncle. 'More sauce, Uncle?' and saw his face relax as he nodded and helped himself to a large spoonful. One more mouthful, carefully chewed, and then he looked at his sister.

'Indeed I have, Janet. Mr Harvey spoke to me again today. He wondered if you might be willing to offer the gentleman a room and board. A well-educated person, a draughtsman, Mr Harvey believes, who is coming to the shipyard for a few months with a view to joining the staff, if all goes well. Or so I surmise – of course, Mr Harvey is very eager to retire . . . and this Mr Lennox Long is very interested in seeing plans of the old boats that sailed to Newfoundland for the cod fishing, apparently – well, we have plenty of material for him to sort out.' He sighed. 'Certainly, everything's got in a bit of muddle recently, you see. We're all getting old—'

Aunt Jane sniffed. 'All that ancient history? Whatever does he want to bother with that for?'

Davey smiled tolerantly. 'It's a very important part of Teignmouth's past, my dear. Apparently he's knowledgeable about sailing boats – extremely experienced, I understand – and I imagine he has plans to design something new perhaps, based on those old boats.' He paused. 'Well, what do you think of the idea, sister?'

At once Janet was enlivened. Finishing her meal, she put cutlery neatly together and smiled across at Davey. 'We could do with the money,' she said bluntly. 'Prices are all going up now that we don't have the revenue from the cod trade as we did in years gone by. And dressmaking never earns a lot, not here, anyway. Yes, tell Mr Harvey that I think I could manage to accommodate the gentleman.'

Looking thoughtfully at Loveday, she said slowly, 'I could put him in your bedroom, child – and you could go up into the attic.' Then, hurriedly, she added, 'Yes, I know, it's a tip at the moment.' A smile grew as Loveday's eyes widened. 'But we could do it up, make it cosy for you. I'll find something pretty for curtains, and I might even be able to get you a new mattress. What do you say?'

What could she say? Nothing, except, 'Yes, of course, Aunt Janet. I'm sure that I shall be happy up there.' Then memories of buckets and drips arose, and she added, 'As long as the roof doesn't go on leaking like it did in the winter.'

Janet tutted. 'I'll get Jem Brown in to make sure it doesn't,' she said. 'Not much good having a builder for a neighbour if you can't make use of him!' She turned to her brother. 'So that's decided. Yes, Davey, tell Mr Harvey that I'll be pleased to house the gentleman for as long as he needs accommodation. And if he cares to write I'll suggest terms.'

Next morning after breakfast, Loveday looked at the clock as she helped clear the table and said, 'I must get on. Mrs Narracott at the hotel said we had to prepare several rooms this week – she doesn't really like me having Monday mornings off, but I don't care.' She tossed her head, remembering Isobel Sothern's patronizing words and her own annoyance. 'I shall go on teaching Miss Eleanor as long as I can.'

Janet's face reflected her thoughts about such unseemly defiance, but she only said, 'Off you go, then. We'll talk about the bedroom when you come back, and I'll call next door and ask Jem to come in as soon as he can.'

Loveday bade them both goodbye, saw Uncle Davey putting on his hat, preparing to leave as Janet washed the dishes, and wondered if they had finally discussed the forbidden subject of Margaret Hunt. Shrugging her shoulders, telling herself that no doubt it would all come out in the end, she walked quickly down to the promenade and, entering the back door of the Beach View Hotel, found Mrs Narracott already in a state of impatience and bustle.

Loveday took off her hat and shawl, tied on her apron and picked up the box containing her cleaning tools and prepared for a day's hard work. 'What do you want me to do first, Mrs Narracott?'

'Make up the bed in the front number one, make sure the curtains hang straight, and then clean up all around. I'll do the armchair covers and the cushions – and then you can come down and help do the veg for dinner.'

Loveday tucked in linen sheets and plumped up newly covered bolsters and pillows, all the time wishing she was somewhere else. Out on the beach, perhaps, with the wind tugging at her skirts and the sea daring her to walk nearer the tide line. Then she cheered up as she began sweeping under the bed and around the bare floorboards, deciding that after work this afternoon she'd go on the pier, perhaps see Ben and his sister Daisy, and have a good gossip and laugh with them.

Thoughts jiggled around her head as she worked. What about the gentleman coming to lodge at home? Well, he didn't sound very exciting. Of course he would be old, grey-whiskered and dull and he was taking her comfortable bedroom away from her, which didn't exactly improve her thoughts of him.

Flicking her cloth out of the window, Loveday watched the dust motes float away, shining in the sunlight and saw the pier, stretching toward the hazy horizon. Towards dream lands and amazing adventures. She sighed. Another four hours and she would be out there.

Free from work, she paid her penny at the pier entrance and then found Ben and Daisy already sauntering along towards the machines that edged the length of the decking. *Not WHAT THE BUTLER SAW again*, she thought. *We've seen it so often.*

Ben turned, saw her and grinned. 'Want to get your fortune told, Loveday?'

'How much is it?' She was trying to save most of her meagre wages, just in case, one day, an adventure took her out of Teignmouth and to somewhere more exciting.

'Nothing, if we talks to the lady and tell her we'll spread her name around the town an' say how good she is.' Young Daisy was always practical, where brother Ben was just the opposite.

As if to prove the difference, he looked at Loveday with an expression of admiration, took a wilting flower from the brim of his hat and handed it to her. 'I knows you love flowers—'

'Thank you, Ben.' She took the half-dead stalk of blue love-in-the mist and held it to her nose, knowing that he had risked being told off for picking the Sothern flowers as he gardened. 'I'll put it in water when I get home. It's lovely.' She saw how his craggy face softened and his eyes shone. Yes, Ben had always been her admirer. He was such a good friend, but she knew she didn't feel the same way about him as he obviously did about her. What, have Ben for a sweetheart; marry him, live in a part of his old mother's cobwebby house, and forgo all her dreams about an exciting future?

Forget the far land?

Never, she told herself silently, and then considered what clever Daisy had suggested. A bit of advertising for a free reading? Such a good idea! 'Come on, let's go and see Madame Chance.'

The fortune teller's tent stood further along the pier, its faded red covering blown by the early evening wind, with the setting sun beaming bright shafts on to the strange figures that decorated it. Dragons, moons, stars, fairies – or were they angels? – all dancing over the tent and enticing customers to enter and learn what fate had in store for them.

Ben and Loveday knew from experience that Daisy, aged twelve, but with a businesslike head on her small shoulders, was the one who would best persuade Madame Chance to give a free reading. How many other times had they both waited while the little girl accosted shopkeepers, fishermen, old ladies, with a view to gaining favours? And most of the times Daisy had achieved her purpose. Loveday looked at Ben and they both chuckled silently as Daisy entered the tent.

For a few moments there was no sound. No voices arguing, no shouts of outrage. And then the tent flap opened outwards, Daisy appeared and, grinning triumphantly, said 'She ses as how she'll give one of us a reading if we spreads her name. You gotta come in and she'll chose.'

Narrowing their eyes in the stuffy darkness of the tent, Loveday and Ben crept inside and found themselves looking at a swarthy-faced woman with a bright scarf tied around her head and huge gold earrings that swung as she moved.

'Well,' she said sharply. 'Which one'll it be, then? Let's look at you.'

Loveday felt Ben stiffen, felt herself tense. They shouldn't be doing this – what on earth would Aunt Janet say if she knew? But she wouldn't know, so why not? And suddenly she knew that she wanted to be the chosen one. Because perhaps this Madame Chance would tell her about her future . . . *Let it be me. Let it be me.*

It was. 'You, the tall girl, the one with the carroty hair, come and sit down. And you two, out – and remember, I'll expect some results from you both.' The voice lowered into a growl. 'Or else. I can do charms, you know—'

Ben and Daisy fled with no backward looks, but Madame Chance was laughing, looking at Loveday with a friendly expression and telling her to sit down.

'Give me your hand, child.'

Loveday obeyed, her hand at once held by fingers encased in black mittens. She was nervous, but excited. What would the fortune teller say?

For a few stretching seconds, she said nothing. Loveday felt the strong fingers moving her own, and watched, wide eyed, as they explored every natural line on the palm of her outstretched hand.

And then, 'You have a destiny to fulfil. So much to do and discover. An important journey leading you on.'

A silence in which Loveday heard her heart beating a tattoo, then Madame Chance sat back, looked intently across the table and said slowly, 'I see you surrounded by water. The sea. It calls to you.'

'Yes.' Somehow she slowed her breathing. 'I've always loved it.'

'But it's not a true friend, child. It can be cruel.' The words were quick and hard and the mittened fingers moved to uncover something on the table. A crystal ball stood there. 'Now – what else can I see?'

Another stretching silence while Loveday felt her body grow stiff with expectation and even dread. She wished she hadn't come. What a silly idea of Daisy's this had been. Aunt Janet would have a fit. And, anyway, it was all a load of rubbish – wasn't it? This old gypsy probably told everyone the same stupid things.

The sharp voice spoke again. 'I see your journey going through life surrounded by water. And there's music – and something else; it's love. Ah yes, that's the mystical touch on the spider's web of your life that will take you where you need to go. The magic of love, given, and perhaps returned, but I can't say for sure.' Then the ball was moved away, quickly recovered with the black cloth, and the fortune teller sat back with a heavy sigh. 'That's all I can tell you. The gift comes and goes. I hope I've helped you.'

Loveday rose, wanting only to get away. But she saw how the elderly face was suddenly deflated and weary, and said quickly, 'Thank you, Madame Chance. Yes, I'm sure you have. And I'll make sure that we – the others and me – do what we can to bring you in some more customers. Goodbye.'

Wonderful to be out of the dry, clinging heat of the tent and the smell of candles and stale perfume. She walked rapidly to the rail of the pier and looked down over the edge. The sea was lapping the stonework with a soothing, monotonous rhythm, the sun slowly slipping down over the bruised blue horizon, and Loveday felt a great surge of gratitude rise inside her. She knew something important had happened in the tent, but for the life of her had no idea what it was. All she knew was that she must get away from Ben and Daisy and go home. She needed safety, and above all, the love the gypsy had spoken of. She needed Aunt Janet and Uncle Davey.

Voices followed her as she went rapidly down towards the pier entrance. She knew she should stop and tell her friends all that had happened, but her need was greater than theirs. She just waved and went on walking. And soon she was back on the beach, on the promenade, back in the town among normal people and ordinary houses and shops.

And then, there was Market Street and she was home. She was safe.

Back in the house, she heard bumps and scrapings and discovered Aunt Janet in the attic, her hair tied up in a duster and a sackcloth apron tied around her. 'I've never seen so much litter!' she said crossly as Loveday peered into the small room. 'How could I have let it get like this? Just look – all the old clothes that I thought Davey had thrown away, all stored up here just in case he might use them again . . . dearie me, what a hoarder that man is!'

'Let me give you a hand.' Thankful for the chance of returning to everyday tasks, Loveday took charge of the boxes of rubbish and old clothes and carried them downstairs into the back yard. There might just be a few things still useable – perhaps some of the poorer people down by the docks would welcome them. She was quite sure that Uncle Davey would organize something like that – if he was allowed to get his hands on them.

She made a pot of tea and persuaded her aunt to come down 'Just for five minutes, then I'll go up and finish it.' They sat at the kitchen table, both weary from their exertions. Janet sighed, removed the duster, fluttered it over the range and folded it in her lap. 'I didn't realize it was so bad. Are you quite sure, child, that you don't mind going up there to sleep?'

Loveday said stoutly, 'Just as long as Jem repairs the roof and I have that nice new mattress you talked about I shall be quite happy, Aunt. Now, why don't you sit here for a few minutes longer while I go and clear up the rest of the mess? You've done enough for today, and I don't mind working for a bit longer. Yes, really—'

'You're a good maid.' Janet sighed again, looked quizzically at Loveday and then allowed herself to smile. 'I'll see about that mattress first thing tomorrow. And some new curtains. You deserve a pretty room.'

In the attic Loveday stood and assessed the possibilities of turning this small, heavily beamed and sloping roofed space into a comfortable bedroom. The window was small and filthy. She found a piece of rag, spat into it, somehow managed to get her hand outside and rubbed hard at the ancient glass. A hazy view appeared – once the bird droppings and bleary rain spots were cleared – of next door's roof. Loveday shook her head, but smiled. Never mind, she'd only be here at night. And the gentleman at the shipyard wouldn't stay for ever – but then it came to her that she might not be here for ever, either.

'I shall be nineteen very soon. Isn't it time I decided what I really want to do? I do love Aunt Janet – as she does me – but I do so need to be free, to do something exciting.'

She left the window, took a last look around the shabby little room and sighed. Everything seemed dull and without the promise of better things to come. But, as she went slowly downstairs, Madame Chance's voice was there in her mind.

The sea. The magic of love. A journey . . . a destiny to fulfil . . . and although, at the time, Loveday had told herself it was all a load of make believe and nonsense, suddenly she began to think differently. Why shouldn't it *become* true? And she realized, with a startling sense of having stumbled upon the truth, that life is what you make it.

So yes – start the journey. Set out towards that predicted destiny. . . .

When she rejoined Aunt Janet in the kitchen, she was smiling, her head already full of amazing plans and therefore not prepared for her aunt's sombre face and slow words.

'You were asking about Margaret Hunt the other day.'

Loveday's smile faded as curiosity grew. She sat down on the opposite chair. 'Yes?'

'Well, she came to call this afternoon, bringing one of Mrs Sothern's gowns to be mended – the lady had tripped, her heel piercing the hem.'

'Good. A small commission, then Aunt. And the chance to see your old friend again. I'm so glad for you.' Sitting down by the banked-up fire, Loveday looked at the severe face on the other side of the table. If she hoped for a warm smile and enthusiastic reply, she was doomed to disappointment.

Janet Jenkins sat up even straighter, picked up one of Davey's socks which she had been mending, began weaving her needle in and out of the gaping hole and said quietly, without meeting Loveday's eyes, 'Margaret will be coming to tea on Sunday, which is her afternoon off. But you don't need to be here to meet her. She knows you are usually with your friends at that time.'

'I see.' Loveday thought hard. What was going on inside Aunt Janet's mind as she calmly darned the sock? 'But I'd quite like to meet her and to know how she's getting on with Mrs Sothern,' she said obstinately, and saw the busy needle suddenly stop in mid stitch.

'I don't think that would be a good idea,' said Janet firmly. And then, not giving Loveday time to argue, 'Goodness, I must start cooking. Your Uncle will be here at any minute, wanting his tea.'

No, it wasn't the time to ask why, and all the other questions that suddenly raced through her mind. Loveday watched the mending being tidied away, pans being put on the range, saw Janet's hands mixing pastry and for the first time in her life kept quiet so that she could think the more.

A strange feeling of elation filled her, and she sensed that the journey had started.

CHAPTER THREE

The woman looked at him across the counter. 'Thinking of leaving, are you, Amos? I heard as 'ow you've had enough of this cold ole place.' She smiled invitingly into his deep set blue eyes. 'Or p'raps jest lookin fer a new woman?'

He wavered for a second – two, three – yes, she looked warm and soft despite the skinny bosom beneath the soiled blouse as she boldly flaunted her body across the counter. He recognized the old weakness, but it was a dead thing now. He drank half the ale in his mug, wiped his mouth on his jacket sleeve and said coldly, 'I'm off to St Johns. I want work. No more women. I've had enough o' them.'

She stood back, thinking he looked dangerous. Everybody knew Amos Hunt was big and powerful with a mind all his own. Nobody willingly upset him – he had a maggot in his brain, stabbing him with thoughts of something he longed for but had never found. Keep clear of him, they said.

'We'll miss you,' was all she said and turned away to serve the next customer.

He drank the rest of the ale, banged the glass down on the counter and left. If he didn't find work in the capital, what would he do then?

Thinking yet again of the far land, he trudged back to the cabin. His belongings were few and, as he packed them into the old canvas bag which had seen so many dangerous journeyings and sailings across wild, cruel seas, memory began playing tricks. No more did he think of cold and danger, but of a small boy brought out from England by parents seeking work and brought up in this hard land.

Sunday – not a day of rest for everyone and certainly not in the Jenkins household. Janet was up early with Davey limping down the stairs not far behind her. Loveday knew she mustn't loiter so she, too, leaped out of bed and hurried down to breakfast.

'If you're playing the organ you must look your best,' said Janet anxiously. She stared disapprovingly at Loveday's frock of pale green linen with darker braiding. 'I think that's too dressy for church – you'd better change into your grey. And wear your dark coat. That will be far more suitable. And make sure your hair is well pinned up. We shall all be looking at your back, remember.'

Loveday sighed. Yet another whim of her aunt's that must, of course, be obeyed. She had thought the green linen was just the right dress for a lovely May day, but perhaps Janet was right. A church organist must, at all events, appear respectable, so up she went and changed. And pinned her best hat on very securely, wishing she could add a flower or two to the dull straw.

'No, don't bother with the dishes,' said Janet, waving her away. 'Just go along – you mustn't be late. Everybody will be wondering about you playing, and you must be there in time to welcome them as they come in. Your uncle and I will follow in a few minutes.'

'Really, Aunt, you're making a great fuss about it,' said Loveday, slightly irritated. 'I've played in the church before, you know, and the world didn't end because of it.'

Janet frowned at the sarcasm. 'Yes, but I understand the Sothern's are entertaining a guest who will be there. And so of course you must look your best, and play as well as you can.' She hung the tea towel above the range, and went upstairs to get ready, calling from half way up, 'Davey – have you polished your boots?'

Loveday smiled to herself as she heard his muffled reply from the back yard, where the shoe cleaning box was stored. Did he never rebel against his sister's bossiness?

Leaving the house with time to spare, she walked unhurriedly down the street towards the harbour, deciding to give herself a few calm minutes before going to the church.

From the far end of the beach, the summoning bells pealed and suddenly all the peaceful beauty of the scene rushed into Loveday's mind: the sun shining on the quietly lapping sea, and here, in the harbour, looking upriver, the view of Dartmoor blue and hazy against the skyline in the far distance. On the quay she stopped, watching the gulls lazily flapping up the estuary towards the sand flats, and looked at the huge, moored ships along the docks awaiting tomorrow's unloading. She relished the quietness, with all the customary noise and shouting of men around the harbour absent today. But there was still the familiar, ever present smell of size and resin, paint and the stink of fish and she realized that living around the harbour, as many of the fishermen did, life must be far less pleasant than living in Market Street and the Jenkins household.

She continued walking along towards Polly Steps and watched a couple of small boys sitting on the quay edge, baiting their homemade rods and hopefully waiting for the John Dorys to bite. Watching them also was a tall boy with shaggy fair hair and untidy clothes, leaning against the wall. Their eyes met as she strolled the length of the quay and she smiled. 'A lovely day.'

The boy, aged, she guessed, about fourteen, nodded, but said nothing. Abruptly he turned towards the moored ships, looking at them with a wide, intent gaze. Again he turned, walking alongside the river as it flowed past and she saw him staring at everything around him – the lumpy shape of The Salty in the middle of the harbour, the boats lined up on Shaldon beach on the opposite side of the river, and then back again at the moored ships. Searching for something, or someone, she wondered idly?

And then, hearing the carillon of bells cease and knowing she must hurry, she walked back towards the promenade and the church at the far end of the beach.

She was early and so able to relax in the quietness of the familiar silence and candle scent. The verger nodded at her as she entered and then she heard a familiar voice behind her. 'Well, maid, ready with those hymns, are you? Good of 'ee to take over for me,' and there was Frank Benedict in his Sunday-best dark suit, shabby shirt and well-worn embroidered waistcoat, smiling at her with his old, rheumy eyes.

'Hallo, Mr Benedict. I'm feeling a bit nervous – all the Sotherns are coming, I think. Mustn't play any wrong notes, must I?'

He came to her side as she stood beside the organ in the sanctuary. 'Don't take no notice of they, maid. What do they know 'bout music?'

Loveday opened her hymn sheets and put them in place. 'Well, no – but I don't want them to think I'm not qualified enough to teach Miss Eleanor.' She smiled at the old man. 'After all, I haven't taken any examinations, or anything like that. I only know what you taught me.'

'An' that's enough to get by. Why, other folks give pleasure by scraping on ole out o'tune fiddles, and playing squeaky accordions and things. When I were a boy the fishermen all played something.'

Loveday was silent for a moment or two. Then she said quietly, 'You mean like my father did with his fiddle. That pretty tune he played – I can't ever forget it.'

Frank Benedict looked at her and nodded. She thought he was about to say something more, but he just sighed, then turned and made his slow, limping way down the nave and to a pew at the back of the church.

Still standing by the organ stool, Loveday looked around her. People were filing in at the main door, their voices suddenly lowered and only the swish of the ladies' skirts and loud footfalls of men breaking the quietness. She saw the gentry arrive, with Mr and Mrs Sothern and Miss Eleanor at the head of them with a stranger, a man with bright hair – their guest, of course. They settled in their pew at the front of the nave, and Eleanor looked up, meeting Loveday's gaze and lifting a gloved hand to wave. But Mrs Sothern, looking in the same direction, frowned and slapped down the child's hand.

Loveday felt resentment rise and wished she was well born enough to ignore Mrs Sothern's frown and wave to the little girl. *But I mustn't. I know women are trying to gain more freedom these days, but if I cause trouble Aunt Janet and Uncle Davey will suffer because of me.*

So she turned towards the organ, sat down and opened the music on the stand in front of her. Removing her gloves and rubbing her hands together she prepared to play the opening notes – this waiting was awful. Inside her a short, selfish prayer announced itself – *please let me play well.*

She gave one last look around the filling church, saw Aunt Janet and Uncle Davey kneeling in the benches behind the gentry pews, and then, at the far end where the servants sat, had a glimpse of Frank Benedict rubbing his knees as he endeavoured to kneel.

And suddenly she saw, right beside him, Margaret Hunt, her dark hat and plain dress making her an almost anonymous figure among the crowded benches. But Loveday's eyes remained on her for a long moment and for some unknown reason she found it difficult to look away, until the signal came from the verger and she knew she must start playing.

The notes came easily, rolling grandly around the church and calling an echo from the stone walls and ceiling. And at the same time, came the procession of choir boys from the vestry, looking angelic in their white surplices and ruffs, followed by the vicar and his attendant curate. And then Loveday's thoughts were centred completely on her fingers and her feet and the glorious music she was making, which seemed to be taking on a life of its own.

She played hymns, psalms, accompanied the choir's well-rehearsed anthem, bowed her head in prayer, and then sat quietly while the vicar climbed into the pulpit, adjusted the spectacles on his plain, angular face, and preached for the requisite half hour.

Fidgetting, coughing, even an occasional sneeze, were the only sounds overriding his voice and Loveday saw one or two heads nodding. But at last the sermon was over, she played a final hymn while the collection was made, and then, after the choir had processed back to the vestry, the congregation began to stir and the church was again full of sound and movement.

An organ voluntary was the custom at this time, and although Mr Handel's piece which she had been teaching Miss Eleanor was on the stand facing her, Loveday found herself playing her father's tune instead. It just came from nowhere, its haunting melody and simple chords whispering around the church and turning a few heads as if they wanted to question the organist's right to play anything but religious music.

But as they all dispersed, one head still looked in Loveday's direction and one face alone expressed a deep emotion. As Loveday finished playing, gathered her music and stood up, she faced the back of the church, and saw, to her surprise, Frank Benedict talking to Margaret Hunt. And now Margaret's head was bowed, she held a handkerchief to her eyes, and Frank had his knobbly hand on her shoulder.

Loveday felt a pang of something that startled her: not just pity for a weeping woman, but an urgent sense of having to help in some way. How, she didn't know, but perhaps if she went to them – beside Margaret, beside Frank – some good might come of it. What was it that Aunt Janet said when disaster struck among the community? 'Do what you can to help, even if it's just to be there, picking up the pieces.'

Putting her music under her arm, she walked quickly down the nave, watching the verger trying to get rid of the last of the lingering congregation. She hurried, hoping she could join Frank and Margaret Hunt outside before they went their separate ways.

The sun shafted down on the churchyard where groups of people still stood and chattered. She saw the Sotherns waiting by the main gate for their carriage to come down the Exeter road. Miss Eleanor looked back, again waved at her – secretly this time and with a mischievous smile – while Mrs Sothern nodded peremptorily at her husband and then turned to look up at her guest, giving him a smile from down-tilted eyes.

Loveday turned her back on them. Frank and Margaret Hunt were far more important and there they were, by the small gate leading to the beach. She hurried towards them and then stopped. What should she say?

Frank Benedict came to her rescue. In a quiet, slow voice, he said, 'Here you be, then, maid. They hymns sounded fine to me. Well done.

Now – this is Margaret Hunt, who works up at the Sothern's house and who has to hurry back there, so she can't stop.'

He paused, watched the woman's face as he added, his voice sounding strangely tender, 'This is Loveday Jenkins, Maggie.'

Loveday saw a flash of charged emotion on the tearstained face as she met Margaret's startled eyes. She felt uneasy, not sure what to say next, but just nodded quickly, wondering what was happening as she watched the gloved hands clutch the handkerchief more tightly, saw the rapid sideways glance at Frank as if to ask for reassurance – or was it help?

The moment dragged on, and panicking, knowing it must end, but not understanding how or why, she smiled and made herself say politely, 'We've met before, haven't we? Last Monday, in the big house, when I was on my way home from teaching Miss Eleanor.'

'Yes. Yes, of course—' The subdued, uneven words died away and Margaret Hunt bowed her head, but not before Loveday had seen a rapid, hastily concealed, expression of pain spread across her face.

She tried again, this time her voice bright and friendly. 'You're coming to visit my aunt and uncle this afternoon, Mrs Hunt, aren't you?'

'Yes. Yes, I am. It's my afternoon off. But I have to go now – to help Mrs Sothern change her gown before luncheon – and—' A pause while Margaret Hunt and Frank exchanged glances. And then, turning, already walking rapidly away, there were a few last words over her shoulder. 'I look forward to seeing them. And you?' But the question was lost among the gulls' cries and the noise of horses' hooves pounding along the road as churchgoers returned home.

Loveday watched the small, darkly clad woman walking away up East Cliff and then met Frank Benedict's wary eyes. She saw how cautious he looked, as if he was afraid of what she might say. *Why?* Was there some strange mystery attached to this meeting? Was it a friendship? Had they met before? Or had he just offered sympathy to a disturbed stranger who happened to sit next to him? And then, why was Margaret crying and why was Frank so clearly awkward about introducing her? Loveday decided it was a mystery, and she must ask him about it.

But here her upbringing reminded her that personal questions should never be asked. Yet she needed to know so, walking beside him as he turned towards his home, she said very quietly, 'Mr Benedict, how nice for you to meet an old friend – you obviously know Margaret Hunt – I mean,' she floundered, hoping he wouldn't resent her being so personal, 'I saw you were comforting her—'

She slid a glance at his lined face and read obstinacy in every wrinkle.

'A weeping woman needs a word o'comfort,' he said steadily and avoided her eyes.

'Yes.' She dared to go on, stumbling a bit over the words. 'I suppose she's an old friend – just as she and Aunt Janet were once.'

Frank Benedict reached his garden gate, opened it, went inside, closed it again and looked at her over the paint-stripped wood. 'You're a deter-mined maid,' he said, and allowed the hint of a smile to brighten his faded eyes. 'Yes, Maggie and I were friends a long time ago. An' that's all I can tell 'ee.' He turned and limped towards the door, one hand out to Crystal, a bundle of sun-burnished fur, who got up from the window ledge, stretched and ran to greet him.

At the door he looked back at Loveday. 'So now you can go home and eat Janet Jenkins's good roast dinner while I put the ole pot o'soup on the fire.' There was amusement in his croaky voice. 'So off you goes, maid, and keep practising yer hymns. You played well.' He disappeared into the darkness of the cottage and Loveday was left, knowing that Frank would always keep his secrets.

She walked back along the beach, asking herself what the mystery about Margaret Hunt could be. Why had Aunt Janet been so silent and forbidding?

The music of the gentle waves scalloping the golden sand was comfort-ing and calming, and before she turned back on to the promenade she came to the conclusion that there was only one way of discovering more about Margaret Hunt's return to Teignmouth. She must definitely be there when the guest arrived for tea, this afternoon.

Janet Jenkins said nothing as they ate their dinners except to remark on Loveday's playing. 'You did very well. I was proud of you. And you looked respectable from the back.'

Davey smothered a laugh by putting a napkin to his mouth, but Loveday picked up the bait.

'So, Aunt, it didn't matter to you that my foot slipped on the G pedal in the first hymn and caused a chord to sound all wrong? Not as long as my hat hid my awful red hair and my coat concealed the rest of me?' But she laughed and was glad to see that Janet's mouth lifted, hinting at wry amusement, though she said firmly, 'You may think appearance isn't important, child, but believe me, it is. And if you are going to better your-self, as you keep telling me you will, you must always be neatly dressed and in possession of good manners. Now, have another potato and stop being so saucy.'

It was while they washed the dishes, with Davey safely half asleep in the parlour – only used on a Sunday and therefore cold, cheerless and unwelcoming, thought Loveday resignedly – that she dared to make the all important suggestion.

'I'm so looking forward to meeting Margaret Hunt that I've decided to stay at home this afternoon.'

Janet's back stiffened and her busy hands paused among the hot water and dishes.

'But you always go out on a Sunday afternoon and meet your friends. You know that Ben and Daisy will be waiting for you. Much better that you should be out in the fresh air – I mean, working in that hotel all the week isn't very healthy. No, go along as usual, child. I should be happier if you did.'

'No, Aunt Janet, I'm not going.'

Janet turned, looked with shocked eyes at her, and said flatly, 'You're disobeying me.'

Loveday sucked in a big breath. 'Yes.'

They stared at each other and she saw on Janet's face a flurry of emotions not usually released in public and so was emboldened to add, 'Aunt Janet, I know there's something mysterious about your friend Margaret, and I want to know what it is.'

The tight lips pursed further and Janet returned to the dishes in the sink. 'Such nonsense,' she said brusquely. 'Of course there's no mystery. You and your imagination – I've always said it'll be the end of you. Now, go along – leave me to finish here; get your hat and go and enjoy yourself.' She gave Loveday one last, compelling look. 'You heard me, child. Let's have no more argument.'

Loveday dried the glasses already rinsed on the draining board, then put down the towel and carried them to the dresser, put them in their appropriate places and looked again at her aunt. She knew, with a knot in her stomach, that this was a huge moment of decision. So far, her life had been spent giving in to Janet's orders, but it had to stop. And now was the time.

'I'm sorry, Aunt – I'm staying here. I'll go out for ten minutes just to please you, but I'm coming back for tea. I want to see Margaret Hunt. Can't you understand? I'm not a child any longer. I earn wages, I'm capable of making my own decisions. I'm a grown woman—'

'And a wayward one,' growled Janet, rinsing the last dish and stretching up to put it on the plate rack over the draining-board.

'No,' Loveday retorted, 'just someone who wants to live her life independently. Please don't try and stop me.'

Perhaps their raised voices had awoken Davey, for suddenly he appeared in the doorway, mild face clearly anxious. 'What's all this about?' he asked and Janet snapped back, 'Loveday insists on meeting Maggie.' and then blinked and set her mouth into an expression of annoyance for having clearly said the wrong thing.

Davey looked at Loveday, standing by the kitchen dresser, her face taut and her frown demonstrating her own disturbed feelings. He said quietly, 'Perhaps it's for the best, Janet,' nodded, and then went back to the parlour.

Janet Jenkins's outraged sigh was a loud one. She glowered at Loveday, took off her apron and hooked it behind the door. 'Well,' she exploded, 'what with the two of you telling me to do things I think are completely wrong, I wish I'd never asked the wretched woman to come and visit. But she'll be here soon, so I suppose I must make the best of it.' She disappeared down the passage, towards the parlour, and as Loveday went upstairs to her bedroom, she hear her aunt whispering to Davey, 'Keep quiet, if you can, you foolish creature.' There was a pause before hardly audible further words. '- keep it secret – I just won't let you tell—' And then the door shut and she heard no more.

Upstairs, Loveday sat on her bed willing the tightness in her chest and the quick anger raging through her mind to still. She hadn't wanted to upset Aunt Janet but somehow it had happened; as if, she thought numbly, *something inside me was wanting to get out. And now I've not just angered, but probably hurt her too. But did she think I was always going to be a child who obeyed her every word?*

The minutes passed. She heard Uncle Davey go out to the yard, filling the coal bucket and guessed the parlour was being made ready for Margaret Hunt's visit. Cushions would be plumped up, Uncle Davey told to go and make himself look more presentable, and then Aunt Janet would be in the kitchen again getting out the best bone china tea set and opening the cake tin, ready for her unwanted guest.

Suddenly Loveday knew what she must do. Go out, as she had promised her aunt, for a short stroll, chat to Ben if she met him, and then wait for Margaret Hunt who, no doubt, would be walking down East Cliff and along the promenade as she made her way to Market Street.

Downstairs, she encountered her aunt in the passage and felt regret at their altercation spreading through her. 'Aunt Janet,' she said impetuously, 'I'm sorry I upset you. You know how I love you and Uncle Davey . . . but—'

She stopped. Janet's implacable face was stony. She met Loveday's eyes and nodded. 'Very well, child. We'll try and forget it. Now – going out for your walk? Good. Breathe in the sea air and just think about teaching your pupil tomorrow morning. I'm sure the Sotherns will have been impressed with your playing this morning. No doubt they'll recommend you to their rich friends and then you'll certainly better yourself, as you seem to be so keen to do.'

Turning away, she went upstairs and Loveday knew that her aunt would be making sure her dress was tidy, and that she looked neat and respectable in order to greet her guest. She smiled, accepting that nothing in the world could upset Aunt Janet for long, and that she would always remain obstinate, dogmatic, and very loving – in her own curious way.

The afternoon felt warm and relaxing as she slowly walked towards the promenade, watching the people enjoying the spring weather. There were already plenty of holidaymakers. The donkeys were on the beach, plodding along with their small riders perched on their backs, the pier was alive with visitors, and a Punch and Judy stall was just opening up beyond the bathing machines. And yes, there was that photographer again, setting up his tripod – she thought there was something slightly familiar about him but then he disappeared behind a black cloth and her thoughts took a different direction.

She felt an overwhelming urge to forgo her wish to meet Margaret Hunt and instead take a dip in the appealing blue-green sea. The water would be cold as yet, so early in the season, but just to feel it around her would be the usual dose of sheer contentment. She pondered as she walked on that there was something about the sea which spoke to her, and she knew that when immersed in its slowly rolling waves she felt more truly in her element than here, out in the open air.

Yet what had Madame Chance said? '. . . not always a friend – it's cruel . . .' and suddenly Loveday's spine prickled. Yet again the haunting words flashed through her busy mind, staying all enjoyment and for a long second, bringing a darkness that dismayed her. *Lost at sea. . . .*

And then, into this darkness, a welcome light shone as a quiet voice said, 'Loveday Jenkins – I'm just on my way to visit your Aunt and Uncle. How very nice to see you again.'

Blinking away her fears and distress, Loveday looked into brown eyes that were full of something that was comforting and warm. And then, slowly, she was able to smile, and to say, quite simply and with sincerity, 'Mrs Hunt – yes, we're all looking forward to your visit. Shall we walk back to the house together?'

CHAPTER FOUR

Memories. Long ago now, but filling his mind. Father who died soon after reaching the rock. Father who he had trouble remembering. Mother working, working, with never a moment for him because life was bitter and hopeless with starvation waiting around every corner, and then the coming of the stepfather who brought the stability of work and better living.

Stepfather. The word narrowed his eyes as he recalled those times. The shouts from the small, wiry man with the bald pate, fierce weather-blown face and huge fur cap, as they offloaded the cod, heaving it on to flakes beside the wharf where the boats rocked in the menacing waters. 'You, boy, get on wi' it.'

The reek of oil as the great fish were split, sliced, the livers flung into barrels, then the cod spread out to be dried before salting. His small hands raw and frozen. Sea birds shrieking overhead and the wind singing its usual wild chant. The small man shouting even louder – 'What you waitin' fer, then? Get on, or I'll give it 'ee. . . .' Never a word of praise or help or sympathy.

He hated what he was made to do. He wanted a proper house, to sit at a laden table, watching a loving mother make soup and dole it out into steaming bowls with chunks of bread. Someone to dry his clothes and rub his hands and feet warm. He wanted security. He needed love and knew he'd never get it here, not with this new man of hers who was rapacious and violent, shouting at him, whacking him around the shoulders, and letting him know beyond all doubt that he wasn't wanted, save for being an extra pair of hands to help offload and process the bloody fish.

Janet must have been looking for them – she stood in the open doorway and Loveday saw the tension on her unsmiling face 'So here you are – both of you! I suppose you met Loveday on the way here – well, Maggie, you'd better come in.' There was no hint of welcome in her voice as she stepped backwards and Loveday felt the itch of slow resentment. Surely Aunt Janet could have said something warm to her old friend? Watching Maggie's pale, uneasy face as they walked through the hallway and into the parlour, Loveday decided she would do her best to make the afternoon visit a success, no matter what the mystery might be.

So – 'Shall I take your coat, Mrs Hunt?' she asked with a smile.

'No, thank you. I'll keep it on. I shan't be staying long.' There was unsteadiness in the quiet voice.

Janet Jenkins stood by the long Chesterfield beside the fireplace and looked at her visitor. 'Sit down,' she invited coldly. 'Davey's getting some more coal in – he'll be here in a minute.'

Maggie Hunt obeyed, sitting on the edge of the sofa and looking away from Janet's taut face. Loveday perched on a rocking chair by the far wall and her aunt settled stiffly into her usual winged chair opposite her guest. They sat in silence, until footsteps sounded along the passage. Then the door swung open and Davey came in carrying a hod of coal.

He stopped just inside the room, put down the hod and smiled warmly. 'Ah, Maggie! How good to see you again after all this long time – keeping well, I hope? And with a good situation, I hear . . . well, well, isn't this fine, being together again—'

Janet made a muffled noise which Loveday interpreted as a snort politely concealed and wondered how her aunt would deal with Uncle Davey's friendliness. She thought it would help if somehow she got things moving. 'I'll put the kettle on, shall I?' she suggested brightly. 'We need a cup of tea after our walk, don't we, Mrs Hunt? The sun's warm, but there's a cold wind—'

What nonsense I'm talking. She slipped out of the room with a smile, thankfully noticing that the visitor looked slightly more relaxed, watching Davey as he placed the hod beside the fire, then turned and seated himself on the sofa beside her. Clearly, his presence had broken the horrible atmosphere that Aunt Janet had evoked, and Loveday sighed with relief.

She heard voices as she prepared the tea tray and, when, she returned to the parlour with a plate of scones, a dish of cream and some of last year's raspberry jam, she was glad to hear a warmer, although still hesitant, conversation beginning.

'Let's think,' said Davey, with a quick glance at his sister before smiling warmly at Maggie. 'Must be what – fifteen years – since we last saw you, Maggie?'

'About that.' Maggie sat further back on the sofa and looked less unhappy. Loveday set a small table in front of the sofa and then put plates, knives and linen napkins on it. She glanced at her aunt, who was sitting very upright in her chair and watching Davey with suspicious eyes.

Keep talking. 'Will you pour, Aunt Janet? Or would you like me to do it while you talk to Mrs Hunt?' Loveday was determined to help things along, and saw the expression on her aunt's face swiftly change from cold resistance to irritated recognition. *She knows just what I'm doing – but I don't care. I want poor Maggie to feel more at home. After all, they're old friends.*

Davey solved the situation by slowly getting to his feet, settling his painful leg into a more comfortable position and saying, 'You pour, maid, and I'll do the handing out. Now, Maggie, help yourself to a scone. And that jam is excellent. Janet was always a dab hand at preserves, as I'm sure you recall.'

Slowly the atmosphere began to clear. Aunt Janet managed the hint of a smile when Maggie said carefully, 'You don't look very different, Janet, from the last time we were together. No grey in your lovely dark hair. Just look at mine—'

Wryly she put a hand to her head but Loveday said at once, 'It's a good colour, Mrs Hunt. Silver, not grey.'

The quiet voice grew a degree more confident. 'Do you remember, Janet, how we used to imagine what our futures might hold? You wanted a dressmaking business and lots of children and I thought I'd just like to live quietly with a loving man and enjoy life.' A wistful smile spread, and her voice rose slightly. 'You always thought you'd be fat and unsteady on your feet – I can't think why – and I was sure I'd be thin and ready to be blown over by the first blast of wind! My goodness, what sillies we were then? Didn't know anything, did we?'

Janet spread cream on her scone very slowly before she said, equally slowly, 'We were young then, Maggie. We had a lot of living to do. A lot of mistakes to make.' She stopped, staring across at the sofa and Loveday thought she saw recrimination in her aunt's taut expression.

Maggie's teacup hovered in mid air and then was replaced on the table, clattering slightly. Loveday saw the hand holding it tremble.

But when Maggie spoke, again there was a faint ring of resolution. 'Mistakes are better known perhaps as challenges, Janet. Yes, I made mistakes, but I've worked my way through them. And now I'm living a different life.' She paused before adding, almost defiantly, 'Not the one I hoped for, but it's not ended yet, is it?'

41

Another silence, with Davey breaking it by scraping the spoon against the side of the bowl of cream as he took a second helping. Cheerfully he asked, 'And what was Cornwall like, Maggie? Different from Devon, so I've heard.'

'Yes, indeed. I must say I missed Devon when I left. But my situation was a pleasant one with the Treveryan family and I got used to it being so different down there.'

'And now you're back again.' Janet nodded at Loveday to refill the guest's empty teacup. 'Are you happy with your situation as Mrs Sothern's personal maid?'

Loveday saw a quick nod and a slight compression of the lips and wondered just how happy any servant could be working for demanding and autocratic Isobel Sothern. But Janet was still probing. 'And where are you living now? That is, when you're not at Sothern House? On your days off, for instance?'

'We've rented a place down by the harbour. It's small and run down, but Jack is trying to improve it.' Maggie met Janet's questioning eyes and stopped.

'Jack?'

Loveday watched a flush rise on pallid cheeks, but also saw a new determination in the pursed lips.

'Yes, Jack is my son.'

'Your – son?' Janet's shocked surprise was full of accusation.

'Yes.' Maggie's head lifted. 'He's fourteen, and he's working as handyman for Jem Brown, the builder who lives next door to you. I wouldn't be surprised if you haven't seen him passing your door.'

Davey turned to her, smiled placatingly as he passed his cup to Loveday for a refill. 'Building's a good job. Has the boy ambitions to start up on his own when he's older?'

'No. Definitely not. It was hard, getting him to agree to work for Mr Brown. All he's ever wanted to do since he was a child is to go to sea.'

Janet hissed in a loud breath and suddenly Loveday felt all her hopes of a reconciliation disappearing. Anxiously, she looked from face to face and saw Janet's mouth set like a trap. Even Davey had lost his smile and looked worried.

What can I say? I must say something. 'Well, if he's so keen, why doesn't he ask one of the local boatmen for a job? Maybe one of them would be glad of an extra hand.' She heard her words slowly dying away and realized that somehow she had made the situation worse.

Maggie set her empty plate on the table, stood up and put a trembling hand to her hat. 'No, I won't let him go. We argue about it all the time, but – I won't have him go to sea. It's cruel and dangerous.'

Madame Chance's exact words. They ran through Loveday's mind and she shivered.

Maggie was looking down at Janet, who sat there like a stone statue. 'You must remember what it was like in the old days when we were young? How all the young men went away, fishing for cod in that terrible place? How so many of them never came back?' Her voice broke. 'No, I'll never let my Jack go.'

Janet looked up and Loveday watched Maggie meet her cold stare. She felt as if war had been declared and was thankful when Davey coughed awkwardly and broke the oppressive silence. Uneasily it came to her that an old wound had just been reopened and she felt the tension and the pain that now hung around the women regarding each other with such hostility.

But Maggie was doing up her coat, her face set. 'I must go now. I have so little time with Jack – only one afternoon a week off and perhaps an hour one evening if Mrs Sothern can spare me. I won't stay any longer.'

She walked to the doorway and, turning, gave Janet a last look. Resentment? Pleading? Loveday felt confused and helpless.

'Goodbye.' Maggie's voice was high and disturbed. 'I won't bother you again. No don't see me out.'

But Loveday was opening the front door. 'Mrs Hunt' she whispered as Maggie stepped out on to the street. 'I think Aunt Janet is very upset – I don't know why, but please do come again – I'm sure things will work out all right in the end—'

'Do you? Do you really?' Maggie looked at Loveday, her mouth tilted down, eyes moist, ageing, lined face full of unhappiness. Her voice was unsteady. 'Then I must warn you, child, that you have a lot to learn about life. No, I shan't come again – but perhaps I'll see you somewhere. I – I'd like that. Goodbye.' She walked rapidly down the street towards the harbour, turned the corner and disappeared.

As she closed the door, Loveday relived the awkwardness of what had just happened, letting those last words linger in her mind and reluctantly agreeing with them. *Yes, I have a lot to learn.*

Returning to the parlour she saw Uncle Davey standing beside his sister, hand on her shoulder. Abruptly Aunt Janet turned away, hiding her face. Nothing was said and Loveday, feeling the charged atmosphere and not knowing how to deal with it, collected cups and plates, took the tray into the kitchen where she washed, dried and then replaced them in the cabinet beside the dresser. Her thoughts tossed and circled but she could make no sense of them. *Maggie Hunt, Janet and Davey. Jack, her son . . . and what was all that about going to that terrible place? Where was that?*

Then, hearing the clock chime five times, she sighed with relief. Soon she must go to St Michaels and play for Evensong. At least it would take her out of the house and away from whatever it was that had turned her home into a place of inhospitable gloom and sadness.

In the church, she noticed that only Mr Joshua Sothern was in the family pew. So Mrs Sothern and Eleanor had somehow managed to escape the weekly ritual. And where was the guest? Loveday tried to force her thoughts into ordinary ideas about ordinary people who seemed to live happily and without conflict. The music helped, but she was glad when the service ended, the vicar complimented her on her playing as she left, and she paused outside Frank Benedict's cottage to enquire about his afflictions.

He held Crystal in his arms, sitting on a rough bench in the tiny garden, letting the last of the sun warm him. 'Not gettin' any younger, that's my trouble, see, maid. Not like you, bright and lively with things to look forward to.' But his smile was warm and Loveday returned it with affection.

'Yes, I'm always looking forward to tomorrow,' she confessed, stroking the purring cat and scenting the fragrance of early cottage pinks in the bed beside the white picket fence. 'And hoping that something exciting will happen – were you the same when you were my age, Mr Benedict?'

He considered. Then, 'In my day all we had to think about was how to make a living. That's why we went off fishing, see. Gone fer months, we was. But coming back, why then things got better. Back to our families, money in our pockets, tales to tell—'

'Mr Benedict—' She had to tell someone. 'Mrs Hunt visited us this afternoon. She talked about men going to sea and—' Loveday paused. Was this telling him too much? Aunt Janet wouldn't want anyone to know personal things: but she needed to know. So, 'Mrs Hunt said something about "that terrible place". Do you know where she meant?'

Carefully, Frank Benedict lowered the cat on to the bench beside him and raised his head to look beyond her, his eyes squinting into the fading sun as it began to dip towards the horizon. For a long moment Loveday thought she had said something offensive; he wasn't answering. Guilt surfaced. Why did she keep asking things no one wanted to talk about?

And then he said, slowly, 'I reckon 'er meant Newfoundland. That's where we young uns went to catch the cod.'

Excitement overtook uneasiness and she said quickly, 'That's the place you've told me tales of? Icebergs, and whales and – the place I call the far land – where your toes got frostbitten?'

'That's it, maid. Where all me troubles began.' But now he was smiling, raising himself painfully off the bench and hobbling towards the open doorway. 'But you don't want to know 'bout that – think of sunny places instead and of all the adventures you'll have one day.'

So near, yet so far. Loveday sighed, walked to the gate and looked back at him. 'Will I? I'm not so sure. Life seems to go along without much happening.' But at once she knew she was wrong. Something had happened this afternoon that would stay at the back of her mind for ages. Until perhaps she discovered why Janet disliked Maggie, and why Maggie was clearly so unhappy.

She gave him a last smile, closed the gate, and started walking home, thinking that what she really wanted was for lovely, exciting things to happen. Perhaps tomorrow?

'Miss Jenkins!' Eleanor Sothern appeared, her face pink and happy, ringlets bobbing on the shoulders of her dark green coat, running along the promenade, followed at a short distance by her mother and a man.

Loveday stopped at once, smiled at the child, and said, 'Hallo, Miss Eleanor – what are you doing here? No church this evening?'

'No, Mama thought we should show Uncle Ned the beach and the boats in the harbour because he's going to take photographs tomorrow.'

Loveday watched the approaching figures. Mrs Sothern looked most elegant in a striped black and white skirt topped with a figure-hugging jacket of black wool, beneath which a high-necked blouse showed. Her hat, Loveday saw, with admiration and a hint of envy, was one of the very fashionable straw boaters, perched on the bun of her swept-back hair. *How smart she looks, and me in my old grey stuff coat.* But envy became curiosity, for beside Mrs Sothern walked a young man whom Loveday thought looked vaguely familiar. Then, as they came nearer, she saw twinkling eyes and a friendly smile and knew she'd definitely seen him before. *Where? Oh yes, on the promenade – so he was the photographer – and in church this morning.*

Eleanor looked over her shoulder and smiled proudly. 'Uncle Ned goes all over the world. He's been telling us about the desert and the camels.'

'Eleanor, don't rush about like a gutter snipe. I told you to keep at my side. Good evening, Miss Jenkins.' Isobel Sothern's voice was tart, and despite the greeting, Loveday felt her presence here was being questioned.

'Good evening, Mrs Sothern,' she replied, and noticed how the man was looking at her. She met his eyes, hazel brown with lighter flecks, saw sandy hair curling around neat ears, and sensed his smile was a real one, not just switched on for politeness's sake.

Mrs Sothern said crisply, 'This is my cousin, Ned Kerslake. He's down here for a short visit. Ned, this is Miss Jenkins, who is teaching Eleanor to play the pianoforte.'

At once, a hand stretched out and Loveday put hers in it, smiling as she did so. Warmth and strength pleased her, and she saw something in the shining eyes that banished all the misery about Aunt Janet and Mrs Hunt, and instead filled her with hope and excitement.

'G-good evening, Mr Kerslake.' Her voice was quiet, but inside she was strangely excited.

'And good evening to you, Miss Jenkins. I admired your playing in church. You have a light touch.'

'Thank you.' She looked down at her feet, feeling curiously young and ignorant. What on earth must Mrs Sothern's worldly cousin think of her? If only she could find something really interesting to say.

'Uncle Ned, shall we have a race?' Eleanor's voice broke into her confusion, and at once Ned Kerslake took up the challenge.

'Certainly. We'll run to the church gate. I'll give you a chance because my legs are longer than yours. Start up there, by the bench by the wall – do you see it? And I'll stay here. Now, Isobel, please say one, two, three, go—'

Mrs Sothern's face was stiff with horror. 'Ned – really! Eleanor – don't you dare!' Her voice rose shrilly and Loveday hid her smile.

'Hurry up, Issy – you only have to say one, two, three, go.'

'I'll do no such thing!'

Ned Kerslake sighed loudly, held up a finger to Eleanor who fidgeted by the bench a few feet ahead of them, and then turned to Loveday. 'Miss Jenkins, will you be our starter, please? My cousin seems to find it quite beyond her.'

Loveday could hardly contain her laughter. 'Of course,' she said at once. 'Are you both ready? On your marks then, one, two, three, GO!'

And off they went, Eleanor giggling as she rushed along, and Ned Kerslake pacing himself and keeping a step behind her. The church wall was soon reached. Eleanor turned and shouted back, 'Mama! I won! I won!' before looking at her antagonist and grinning wildly at him. 'I beat you, Uncle Ned! I ran faster!'

'You certainly did. But now I think we had both better apologize to your stepmama for making such exhibitions of ourselves. Otherwise, it's sure to be something nasty like early bed and no supper.'

Still giggling, Eleanor took his hand, while Loveday, spellbound, just stood staring and wondering how on earth Mrs Sothern would react to such wild behaviour – and in public, when all the inhabitants of Teignmouth were taking their Sunday evening strolls and so witnessing the wickedness of her stepdaughter.

Isobel Sothern walked rapidly towards them, ignoring Loveday and holding her parasol close above her head as if it might well form a disguise. 'We must go home at once! Really, Ned, such behaviour – and persuading Eleanor to join in – but there, you were always a hobblede-hoy when we were younger. And you haven't changed a bit! Now – Eleanor – hold my hand, no, don't look at your wicked uncle, but walk along with me. And, let me tell you, when we get home I shall inform your papa—'

The high, irate voice continued as Mrs Sothern and a by now contrite looking Eleanor, marched down the promenade towards the East Cliff, soon out of hearing and then out of sight.

Loveday began walking in the opposite direction, laughing to herself, but feeling worried about Eleanor's impending punishment. And then Ned Kerslake caught her up, his face bright with amusement, his steps slowing to match hers.

'What a to do,' he said wryly. 'You'd have thought we'd been caught pilfering the church alms box, wouldn't you? But there, Issy was always far too prim and proper, even as a child. Not like me.'

Loveday glanced cautiously at him as they continued to walk towards the pier. *Issy*, she thought, laughing beneath her breath.

But he heard. 'Yes, she was the darling of the family and I was the black sheep. Still am, I fear.'

Their eyes met as they slowed to avoid the groups of strolling families with their children and dogs. Ned said, more gravely, 'But at least she was right about me being a photographer. I work for Mr Frith, taking pictures all over the world.'

'Really? Of camels, in the desert?' Loveday's imagination was instantly at work.

He grinned. 'Certainly camels. And tomorrow, if I can arrange it, groups of holiday makers in Teignmouth, and even one or two interest-ing people who live and work here. Like you, Miss Jenkins. A church organist who is young, talented and extremely pretty.' He looked deep into her eyes and smiled.

She blushed and then, aware of it, blushed an even rosier colour. *Don't be ridiculous. Mr Kerslake is only amusing himself. Of course he won't photograph me.* With enormous strength of will, she ordered her cheeks to return to normal and turned her head away from his admiring gaze. 'You're joking, and – and anyway, I'm afraid you won't be able to do that, Mr Kerslake, for I am at work every day, and it's only on Sundays that I'm in the church, and . . . and. . . .'

His eyes were laughing at her now and she took a deep breath. Oh dear, why couldn't she behave in a more sophisticated fashion? But still the words rushed out. '. . . and not every Sunday, you see – so it won't be possible—'

She stopped because he was touching her arm. 'Miss Jenkins,' he said gently, his fingers warm on her sleeve, his hand drawing her into the shelter of the covered shelter at the end of the promenade. 'I wasn't joking. As a professional photographer my job is to observe everyone I meet – and I've met you, a young woman with an unusual talent. Believe me, you, seated at the organ, will make an interesting and memorable photograph. You see, the aim of Mr Frith, my employer, is to record for posterity people and their occupations. This will be an archive for the future. It's very important.'

Loveday sank on to the hard bench and he sat beside her. She hoped desperately that no one would tell Aunt Janet about this young man, with his wide smile and those warm eyes. And yet, what harm was there in sitting here and talking? After all, she was a woman, no longer a child; she could do what she liked.

But he had been laughing at her – so, yes, she would tell this forward young man a thing or two. She looked into Ned Kerslake's amused face and said firmly, 'I am not just a church organist, but I am also a maid of all work. I make beds and clean rooms and carry slop pails – does that interest you, too?'

She watched keenly, hoping he would realize she wasn't just a young girl he could play games with, and saw the twinkling eyes narrow a little as the smile faded. His voice, when he answered, was quiet and, to her surprise, sounded most respectful. 'Miss Jenkins, I apologize if I offended you. And yes, I would be even more interested to photograph you in your work place.'

'Oh.' She hadn't expected this, and frowned at him. 'But the hotel isn't very beautiful – it's small and rather crowded and definitely a bit old fashioned, and I doubt if Mrs Narracott, who owns it, would want you to take photographs—'

He removed his hat and she saw how his sandy hair sprang upwards from his broad forehead, catching the dying sunlight and making a sort of halo around his head. And then she understood that she was wrong; he wasn't making fun of her; he was a professional man who cared for his work and had seen something interesting and worth recording in the idea of a maid of all work appearing in his employer's archive.

'Well—'

He was looking at her again, his elbow close to hers. He smelt of hair pomade and tobacco and something else that she quite liked. His own smell, perhaps.

'Well, I suppose I could ask her—'

'I'm so glad you agree, Miss Jenkins. Where is this hotel – on the front?'

'Yes. It's called The Beach View Hotel. So shall I ask Mrs Narracott tomorrow afternoon, when I get there?' Already she was imagining the fuss and horror with which Mrs Narracott would receive the idea of one of her staff being photographed.

Ned Kerslake shook his head, and put his hat on again. 'I'll call on her in the morning. Mr Frith is very particular with regard to our manners as we ask for interviews and photographs. Don't worry.' Again a twinkle in his bright eyes, and a big smile. 'I'll charm her into saying yes.'

She could well imagine it and laughingly pictured the scene. He joined in and she felt better now; he was respectful and well mannered and she liked him. Even Aunt Janet couldn't possibly object to her talking to him. And then suddenly she realized how the time had fled. She was expected back at Market Street for supper.

She rose quickly. 'I must go. My aunt will be worrying about me. Goodbye, Mr Kerslake.'

Following her out of the shelter, he stood watching as she walked away very fast. But she heard him say, 'Until tomorrow then, Miss Jenkins,' and felt herself fill with excitement. Expectation, or just anticipation? Whatever it was, she felt suddenly older and happier. Perhaps, as Maggie had told her, she had at last started to learn about the world and its ways.

CHAPTER FIVE

Young Amos decided then, when his brain thawed and thoughts again began to spin around, that when he had a son he would treat him better than Mother's new man. He would teach him to live a better life. He would not shout but explain. He would love his boy. He longed for a son.

At home again, Loveday found everything very quiet. In the parlour, Uncle Davey, sitting reading the newspaper, looked up and smiled rather wanly as she entered.

'Where's Aunt Janet?' she asked. The house seemed wrong and empty without her.

His smile died. 'Upstairs. Said she had a headache. Gone to lie down.'

They looked at each other and Loveday nodded sadly. She understood just how Aunt Janet must feel after that distressing tea party and felt the disturbance mirroring her own thoughts, indeed, so much so that the words came out in a rush. 'It was dreadful, wasn't it? Aunt Janet and Mrs Hunt—'

Davey nodded, carefully folded the newspaper but made no reply.

Loveday sat down on the sofa, not knowing what to do or what to say next, but in her mind Maggie's remembered tearful face caused great surges of emotion to billow through her. At last, again, words forced themselves out. 'Uncle Davey, there's some sort of trouble – isn't there? I heard Aunt Janet talking to you.'

And then, as he still gave no answer, she moved to the edge of the sofa, her body stiff, her face tense, and said unsteadily, 'Please tell me. I'm not a child, you know. I love you both very much and I can't bear to see Aunt Janet – and you – so upset.' She paused, looking at him searchingly, and added, 'And Maggie Hunt seems so nice: I'd like to know her better, but Aunt Janet won't let me do that, will she?'

Silence. Davey sat up straight, rubbed his painful knee and avoided her intense stare.

'Why, Uncle Davey? WHY?' She stared at him. 'Please, I need to know.'

Slowly he sank back into his chair, his expression uncharacteristically disturbed. His mild eyes were narrowed, soft mouth pursed into a hard line and his fingers tapped the arms of the chair. Seeing how worried he looked, Loveday suddenly felt ashamed of her outburst. Was she making things even worse?

But he forestalled any apology by saying, in a more than usually forceful voice, 'My dear girl, every family has troubles.' A long pause. 'And you're right, your aunt and Maggie share one. It's an old, painful business, and quite honestly I think you should be told the ins and outs of it, but, well, your aunt . . . you know what she's like.' He stopped, shrugging his shoulders.

Loveday eased back into the sofa and let the pent-up breath sweep out. 'Whatever it is,' she said unevenly, 'surely it would be better to talk about it. Poor Mrs Hunt was so unhappy when she left.' She sat forward again. 'Uncle, please will you persuade Aunt Janet to tell me what it is that she holds against Maggie?' She stopped, unaware of what she was going to say next, but the words erupted. 'She thinks Maggie has done something wrong. It's that, isn't it, Uncle?'

Another long drawn-out silence before he nodded. 'Yes, maid, that's it. But I can't tell you.'

'No. But you can ask Aunt Janet to tell me, can't you?'

A coal slipped in the fireplace, sending sparks glittering over the hearth rug. On her knees, Loveday brushed them away, then, sitting back on her heels, she looked into Davey's troubled eyes and whispered, 'You will – won't you, Uncle?'

Davey nodded, sighed and said in a low, reluctant voice, 'I'll try.'

The coal collapsed in embers, Loveday returned to the sofa and watched the flames licking the fireback. She felt she had won a small victory. Eventually, this wretched secret would be revealed, Aunt Janet and Maggie would renew their old friendship and—

Davey's voice interrupted her dreams. 'While Janet's resting I'll just go into the attic and see what happened to those clothes I stored there last year.' Standing up, he put the paper on the table and stretched his legs.

Loveday was thankful to see the old relaxed expression return to his face. 'I'm afraid we moved them, Uncle, when we were clearing out. They're in the outhouse in the yard. I wondered if you might give them to one of those poor families living around the harbour.'

Davey's voice held a hint of vexation as he said, 'I see,' but then the old, easy smile returned. 'Your aunt says I'm a hoarder. Well I reckon I am, but I hate to throw things away. So I'll just go up anyway and see if there's anything else there before she throws it out.' Chuckling, he disappeared into the hallway.

Loveday rose, deciding to start getting supper ready. At least she could knock on Aunt Janet's door offering her a bowl of soup. But before she reached the kitchen she heard voices on the stairs and looking up, saw Davey and Aunt Janet meeting halfway. Davey at once retraced his steps downwards, and Janet followed, her voice filling the stairwell. 'I'm quite recovered, thank you, Davey. So weak of me to have a headache. It's gone now. And I'd like to talk to you about Loveday's new bedroom being completed – I expect to hear very soon from Mr Lennox Long, about him coming to lodge with us, and we must get on with things. Now, out of my way, if you please – and goodness, the fire needs making up. What *have* you been doing all the afternoon?'

Davey followed her into the parlour and Loveday, in the kitchen, smiled. Life seemed to have returned to normal. *Thank goodness*, she told herself.

'And how did you play this evening?' Janet sat by the fire in the parlour, hands for once idle in her lap. No sewing on a Sunday; this was the Lord's day of rest. Of course these days, sadly, the old traditions were dying away, but not in Janet Jenkins's world. She would resist change for as long as she lived.

Loveday said modestly, 'I think I did quite well. And the vicar said he liked the last thing I played – that little tune that I remember my father playing on his fiddle. The vicar said he thought it melancholy, but none the worse for that. I just think it's pretty. And it keeps going round in my mind.'

'Hm.' Janet gave Davey a quick glance. 'And was the church full?'

'About half full, I think.'

'And were the Sotherns there again? They usually set a very good example.' Janet nodded. Mrs Sothern might be a flighty lady, but she went to church each week, which said a lot for her.

'Only Mr Sothern.' Loveday paused. She longed to tell them about her meeting with Ned Kerslake, about his amusing race with Eleanor and Mrs Sothern's high and mighty disapproval, and then, of course, the idea of being photographed: but knew the time inappropriate. Aunt Janet would certainly not relish such chatter on a Sunday evening. So she opened her book and buried her head in it, even as images of a certain suntanned face surmounted by a halo of sandy hair flashed behind her eyes. And then, as quietness fell and the gas light was lit, she realized she was creating yet another secret – so this is how mysteries grew, was it? So easily. And without really thinking about them.

Later that evening, about to go up to bed, clutching her candle – no gas in the bedrooms – and seeing the shadows creep up the stairs, Janet called her back.

'With all the trouble this afternoon, Loveday, I quite forgot to tell you that Mr Lennox Long has written, and we have agreed terms for his accommodation. He's coming this week, so Jem must do the roof tomorrow and you will have to move your belongings up there very quickly.'

'That's all right, Aunt. I'll help you when I get back from the hotel.'

'Thank you, child.' Janet frowned 'He sounds a very pleasant gentleman, but he's added a postscript which I don't feel at all comfortable about. Let me read it to you.'

She drew the candle nearer, opened the sheet of paper, screwed up her eyes and read slowly, 'I hope you will not mind me bringing my dog with me. Floss is well behaved and affectionate. She can sleep outside and be no trouble to anyone. We shall arrive on Wednesday late afternoon.'

'A dog! What sort, I wonder? Floss sounds like an old lady's lapdog!'

Janet tutted. 'All very well for you to laugh, child, but I'm not used to animals in the house. Well, we must just wait and see – and hope for the best.'

In bed that evening, Loveday relished, for possibly the last time, her comfortable and safe, pretty room. Tomorrow the repairs would be done and Aunt Janet would hurry to organize the delivery of the promised new mattress. Already the curtains – pale and flowery – were cut and waiting to be sewn. Before slipping into welcome sleep she visualized Mr Lennox Long who would be old and perhaps slightly intimidating, with a small, furry little dog that slept on his lap by the fire. And then, as the images blurred, she smiled to herself, remembering that tomorrow she and Ned Kerslake would probably meet again.

'I shall take my bathing costume, Aunt, and have a dip on my way home from teaching Miss Eleanor. Now, where is my towel?' Next morning Loveday felt the seduction of the new day – the sun already shafting down into the street outside her bedroom window, the gulls being more than usually noisy as fishing boats unloaded in the harbour, fishy smells vying with the evocative smell of ozone drifting over the town as the calm sea lapped the golden sands. Definitely a day for swimming, for finding that wonderful element in which she felt so at home.

She left Market Street after breakfast, carrying a small carpet bag and promising Janet that she wouldn't go out too far into deep water, and that she would dry herself properly when she came out. *Oh, and dear child, make sure that you're very private as you dress.*

Sothern House was awake and noisy when she arrived. Eleanor was playing chopsticks on the piano with her Uncle Ned in the drawing room and Isobel Sothern was standing in the doorway trying to stop them. 'For goodness sake, Ned – please don't teach the child such terrible tunes—' She turned. 'Oh, Miss Jenkins. Just in time to remedy things, I trust. Ned, will you come with me? Eleanor has her lesson now, and I want to talk to you about photographing the garden.'

Ned Kerslake looked at Loveday as she approached the piano. 'Very well. I give way to the practised teacher, Issy,' he said and bowed deeply, but not so deep that his twinkling eyes didn't catch Loveday's.

She looked down at the floor but kept a half smile on her face. *Issy* again. How lovely to have Mrs Sothern put down to where she belonged – in the world of a small, spoilt child.

'Good morning, Mr Kerslake. I think I can teach Miss Eleanor something prettier and more acceptable than that noise you were just making.' She put the usual hymn sheets on the piano and prepared to ignore him.

He wouldn't be ignored. At the door, presumably following Mrs Sothern to her boudoir, he turned and looked back. 'I shall be listening, Miss Jenkins – and I hope very much that you will be teaching your student the lovely little melody you played at the end of the service in church. It has stayed in my mind, but I'd like to be reminded of it. If you please?'

He couldn't have struck a cleverer note. Loveday at once looked up, met his smile and returned it, her heart quickening slightly. 'Yes,' she said, 'Miss Eleanor will play it for you – but not yet. First we have scales and arpeggios.'

His grimace was amusing. 'I shall be waiting. Upstairs with Issy. I look forward to it, Miss Jenkins.' Another bow, another twinkle of the smiling eyes and he disappeared.

The lesson was enjoyable. Eleanor sailed effortlessly through the exercises and then pleased Loveday with her attention to the classical pieces she was learning. And then, 'Can I play your pretty tune, now, Miss Jenkins? The one Papa likes so much.'

'The one your uncle would like to hear – yes, Eleanor, please play it.'

Loveday stood at the side of the piano watching her pupil's fingers as they struck simple chords and picked out the plaintive little melody. And once again, as it always did, the tune returned her to childhood days and that faint memory of Father scraping away at his squeaky old fiddle and someone – it must have been her mother, she supposed, though she had no memory of anyone in particular – saying, 'stop that awful noise!' And then laughter, loud, happy and drifting over the years into her ears now.

He must have been a cheerful man, her father, thought Loveday; but then the memory faded and Eleanor was slipping down from the piano stool. 'Thank you, Miss Jenkins. I'll practise the new piece and have it ready for next week. Now I'll go and find Uncle Ned.' She skipped from the room as Loveday collected the pieces of music, found her bag where she had left it out in the passage, and then went downstairs.

As usual, the kitchen was warm, scented and full of ringing voices. Cook smiled and waved a red hand, Billy grinned as she went into the yard, and Ben came round the corner just as she walked down to the gate. 'Daisy an' me wondered what the gypsy told you last week, Lovey.'

His grin was warm and she smiled back. 'Just the usual things, Ben. About going on a journey, finding my destiny – that sort of thing. Rubbish, really. But I can't stop now, I'm off to have a swim before I go to work.'

He watched her go, calling after her, 'See you this evening? Down on the river beach? They'll be seine fishing there – come and watch?'

'Perhaps.' She waved and went quickly down East Cliff, arriving at the nearest bathing machine with her face warm from the sun and her breath coming fast.

Ma Rounsell greeted her. 'Mornin', maid. I was wonderin' when you'd come fer a swim – water's cold yet, but you don't mind, do 'ee? Not like they holidaymakers – what squeals and shouts we get when they steps in! But no one here at the moment, so in you goes.'

The bathing machine was damp and musty smelling, but in no time Loveday shed her clothes, pulled on the bathing dress, pushed her knotted hair into the accompanying cap and emerged into the sunlight. Ma Rounsell held the spreading tarpaulin that stretched from the door around her, providing privacy from the eyes of any possible Peeping Toms, and then Loveday felt the cold, clear water embracing her toes, her legs, her body. With a deep exhaled breath of pleasure, she pushed forward, arms and feet working effortlessly, and swam out towards the swelling waves beyond the shore.

Janet Jenkins looked at her brother, her body stiffening as she said tightly, 'I don't agree, Davey. I won't tell her. It would be quite wrong – she would be confused, unhappy even – and I love her too much to want that. No, Loveday doesn't need to be told.' She stood by the bare table in the front room and spread out the length of floral cotton she was working on. 'And now please let's forget the whole sad business. I want to get these curtains finished – only the hems to do now and then I'll be able to hang them.'

'No, Janet. You must tell her.'

Slowly she turned. This was a Davey she rarely saw, determined, quietly sure of himself. She shook her head and felt emotions stirring and immediately straightened her shoulders. Ridiculous! Over the years she had schooled herself never to give way to uncomfortable and unnecessary emotions. And she would not do so now. But, the way he was looking at her . . . she sighed, put down the scissors and sank into the chair behind her.

'Davey, do you know what you are asking me to do? To go back over all that grievous pain we suffered so long ago?'

He moved slowly, coming to her chair, bending and putting an arm around her shoulders. His mild eyes were resolute, his voice stronger than usual. 'Sister, believe me, it's time to let the secrets go. To open them up and to see how we can make the best of what's happened as a result of them.'

Tears pricked her eyes and were instantly blinked away. Such memories, and not just herself, but others, too. Such recurring pain. No, no, she could never go back into all that.

'I promised the child I would ask you to tell her.' He stepped back, went to the window and looked out on to the busy street.

Janet felt her cosy, secure world unsettling around her. She took a long breath and slowly realized that what he said was right. Loveday must be told. But perhaps not everything. A glimmer of light appeared and she brightened. Why not just tell her the secret between herself and Maggie? But not the whole truth. Would Davey be content with half a secret being revealed?

She tried him. 'I will tell Loveday about Maggie and me. But that's all. The rest can wait.' And then, because he looked at her with almost comic dismay, added sharply, 'Don't ask for more, Davey. You've forced me into this, and it's enough.'

'For the time being, perhaps.' Turning from the window, he smiled down at her and once again he was the familiar Davey – easy smile, bright eyes, the younger brother she had always dominated.

'Very well. I'll tell her this evening – or tomorrow.' Standing up, she returned to the curtain length and began measuring and then pinning up the hem.

Davey nodded. He'd done his best. This would have to do. For now.

Bending, he pecked her cheek, found his hat on the hallstand and left the house. He was already ten minutes late for work and would have to make up the time by working on later today. And he hadn't found those old clothes and various other things up in the attic, after all. He sighed as he walked. Life had suddenly become very complicated.

Loveday swam without measuring the time. Enough that she felt in her rightful element, supported by swelling, lapping water. The exercise soon warmed her, and it was with regret that she at last knew she must turn back. Life had to go on, even if she felt she could stay here for ever, drifting onwards, towards that distant horizon which was the open door to other lands. To the far land, perhaps.

Heading back towards the beach, she allowed herself to dream, to remember, to imagine, even to hope. Frank Benedict had said the sea over there, in that cold Newfoundland, was cruel and dangerous. Men were lost as they fished the shoals of cod which brought them their living. Men like her father . . . had he, too, sunk with his fishing boat? Had an iceberg crushed the small, vulnerable craft? Frank had suffered such a fate, but had survived, though frostbite had taken the tips of his toes.

As she felt sand beneath her feet and slowly waded back to where Ma Rounsell stood with her waiting towel, Loveday found herself thinking more realistically. Did she really want to find such a cold, hard land? Wouldn't a place full of sun, camels and desert be much more pleasurable? And then, suddenly, she realized that all her dreams of the far land were tied up with the loss of her father.

Lost at sea. If only he were here perhaps she would forget the dreams of that cold, far land.

Again the darkness and hurt until Ma Rounsell's loud, indignant voice broke into the sad thoughts. 'Off with 'ee! No pictures allowed 'ere.'

Startled, Loveday looked up the beach to see a familiar figure waving at her as he unfolded his tripod, set up the camera he held, fished a large black cloth out of the bag at his feet, and then called down to her, 'Hold the pose, Miss Jenkins – just half a second and it'll be done. And please – please – smile, will you?'

Ned Kerslake. She dithered for a few seconds, her mind rapidly registering what the requested photograph would look like if she allowed him to take it – a fast young woman dressed in a wet and possibly revealing bathing dress – and then ran towards Ma Rounsell and the welcome, concealing towel, not bothering to answer the wretched man's cheeky call.

'Friend o' yourn, then?' Ma Rounsell held the tarpaulin around her until she was in the machine, and then handed her a dry towel.

Loveday removed her cap, shaking out her damp hair and avoiding the suspicious eyes regarding her. 'No, just one of those nosey photographers that we get every summer.'

But he wasn't, was he? Not just a cheapjack with a camera who had to take everything he saw in order to live. She stepped out of her bathing dress and let it lie on the sandy floor as her thoughts took flight. After all, his appearance, wanted or not, had come at a moment when she was slipping into memory and sadness. So really, with that in mind she couldn't possibly ignore him, could she? He would cheer her up – he had tales to tell of his own far lands. And he was good looking, had a charming way with him, and was Mrs Sothern's cousin. She began to smile as she continued drying herself. He wasn't just anybody. And yes – the towelling stopped as she reached for her clothes – she found him, well, quite attractive.

It was a mind-filling moment. Loveday stood still, looking into the flyblown mirror hanging rather unevenly on the wooden wall, allowing herself to remember those bright, amused hazel eyes and that lovely warm smile. And, most of all, his very clear interest in her.

By the time she was dressed and had dried and combed her hair into something more respectable than the fiery tangles the sea had caused, soaking through the thin cotton cap, she picked up her bag and left the machine, knowing just what she was going to do.

'Thank you, Ma', she said, emerging into the sunlight and smiling at the big-boned woman busily stretching out wet towels on the sunlit sand. 'I feel all the better for that swim – I'll come again when I can.' She put a hand into her skirt pocket. 'How much, Ma?'

'Nought fer you, maid. Keep yer pennies. I'll take a copper or two extra off the next fine lady who comes fer her swim.' The treacle-dark eyes glinted with amusement, and Loveday set off up the beach smiling her thanks.

Now, she thought bracingly, *now to find Ned Kerslake and tell him just what I think of him and his saucy ideas.* But she was smiling.

Seeing him waving at her in the distance as he packed up his camera and tripod, she waved back and waited as he walked rapidly towards her.

His expression held a hint of accusation. 'You didn't pose for me, Miss Jenkins – now, why was that?'

She looked into his bright, candid eyes. 'I'm not the sort to want to appear in my bathing costume, Mr Kerslake. My family and I have our reputation in the town to think of.'

'Ah.' He shifted the large shoulder bag he carried and readjusted the folded tripod beneath one arm. 'So everyone knows that you're the lady organist, the lady pianoforte teacher, and – I don't really believe it, you know – the lady who cleans all the bedrooms in the Beach View Hotel. Am I wrong?'

Slowly Loveday fell into step with him and they walked together down the promenade. She hid her smile. 'No, that's quite correct. But please don't make fun of me. I enjoy my work, all the different things I do, and I hope to find even more pleasant sources of earning my living in the future.'

He threw her a glance, standing to one side to avoid a family out for a morning stroll in the sunshine. 'I wouldn't dream of making fun of you, Miss Jenkins – I have far too much respect for you.'

Her heart took an uncomfortable leap. 'You may call me Loveday – if you wish.' *Was this too bold? No, Mrs Sothern had formally introduced them.*

Abruptly he stopped, removed the tripod from beneath his right arm, and took her hand. He bent, kissed it, then looked into her somewhat shocked eyes. His voice was quiet, the amusement gone, and Loveday heard only a friendly and welcome warmth as he said, 'I am honoured to do so. But only if you agree to call me Ned?'

Her hand pulled away and moved to her throat. Suddenly, for a moment, she was at a loss for words. She could only nod and then manage to say, with a tremor of unsteadiness in her voice, 'This is where I work – Ned. I have to go now.'

'But you'll see me again, Loveday? If I arrange with your employer for a staff photograph, you'll be there, won't you, making my photograph come to life with your beautiful smile?' No one had ever said such things to her before. Or looked at her in such an intense, exciting way.

Loveday turned quickly as fright added wings to her heels. But she stopped again at the entrance to the hotel, looked back at him, and managed one of those smiles he so obviously admired. 'Yes, I'll be there, Ned. Tomorrow, perhaps—' Then ran up the back alley and into the servants' quarters of the hotel.

Mrs Narracott looked at her severely. 'You look all flushed – too much sun, my girl, too much playing about on the beach, I shouldn't wonder. Now, bedroom number four needs a good going over. And don't forget to bleach out the slop pail.'

CHAPTER SIX

The fish making went on and on for years. Cod haunted the fog-laden waters of the Grand Banks and the industry flourished. But at some point – when he was about twenty, Amos reckoned – he'd had enough. By then he was independent, no more living with Mother and the small bald, leather-faced man, who glowered at him whenever they met, but bunking up with whatever girl of the moment smiled at him and gave herself in return for a few kisses and a hurried fumbling on the fur-laden cabin bed.

There had been children of those uncaring unions but always daughters. Never the longed-for son. And then, suddenly, he'd had enough. He and Addie, the latest woman, had been together for over a year, but in the end she disappointed him again. 'A daughter's no good to me.' How well he recalled telling her when she gave birth to the mewling scrap who was to die so soon afterwards. There were months of struggle, of argument and a touch of rough stuff when she caught him on the raw.

'Want a son, do you, Amos? Someone to grow like you – big and strong and powerful? Selfish?'

And then the answering words that had erupted so fast he had hardly heard them. 'Just a son to love. A son to give everything to. A son who'll have love and safety, like I never did.'

Jem Brown and the boy, Jack, arrived promptly at eight o'clock the next morning, finding Janet already preparing breakfast and calling to Davey to hurry up.

'Mornin', Miss Jenkins. We'll get on wi' it, all right wi' you? Here, Jack, carry this stepladder – I got enough wi' me tools.' Thump, thump up the stairs and much banging about in the attic. Janet resignedly made a large pot of tea and wondered if Maggie's boy ever got enough to eat. She'd only seen him briefly, shouldering the stepladder and following in Jem's footsteps but he looked thin. Not a happy looking lad – she saw sullen boredom filling his lean face. And those clothes! Gangly wrists shooting out of sleeves halfway up his arms, and trousers that revealed bony ankles. What was Maggie doing, letting her son look like this?

Lips pursed, thoughts flying, she found a mutton chop left over from Saturday's dinner and put it in the frying pan with slices of streaky bacon and two eggs. Then she made toast – Jem or no Jem, that boy should have something to eat and help get him through the day.

Davey cocked an eyebrow as voices sounded above and a tool fell to the floor with a loud bump. 'Is Jack there?' he asked, finishing off his breakfast and leaving the kitchen table.

'Yes,' said Janet, 'the boy looks half starved. I'll give him a bite before he leaves.' She watched her brother go into the hall, find his hat and stick and prepare to leave the house. 'Davey?' she called, bustling after him. 'Those old clothes I found in the attic – would you object if I offered the jacket to the boy? It was still in good condition – just a bit worn around the cuffs, and Maggie could mend those.'

He looked at her, smiled and nodded. 'Do whatever you think right, sister. Just make sure there's no five-pound notes left in the pockets. . . .'

Janet tutted. 'I'm not as daft as that. Go on with you.'

It was a good two hours later that boots again thumped down the stairs and Jem appeared in the doorway. 'All done,' he said, dusting down his baggy corduroy trousers and then running a huge hand through his straggly brown hair. 'No more rain comin' in. I've left the boy to clear up – got to get to another job, see. I'll send the bill at the end of the week. Good day, Miss Jenkins.'

Janet saw him out with a nod of approval. He did a good job and, living next door, he wouldn't risk her disapproval by overcharging. And the boy was still up there. She paused at the foot of the stairs. 'Jack? Can you hear me?'

Footsteps and then a head appearing in the dim landing above. 'Yes, Miss Jenkins?'

At least he had some manners. Her voice softened. 'I've got a cup of tea and a bite to eat down here when you're ready. Don't go rushing off.'

'Thank you.'

There was some awkward manipulation of the stepladder, Jack manhandling it outside and propping it against the wall, but at last he appeared in the kitchen, cap in hand, looking uncomfortable.

'Sit down, Jack.' She thought orders would be better than sentimental overtures.

He did so, avoiding her gaze, putting a hand to his mouth as he coughed.

'Well, how do you like Teignmouth? Nicer than Cornwall? And what about that place you live in . . . where is it?' She poured tea and dished up the plate of bacon and eggs, then produced the toast, and noted how he cheered up immediately, stirred sugar into the cup and started eating.

He's really hungry, Janet thought, watching. After a couple of mouthfuls he said thickly, 'Yes, I like it here, but the house isn't very good – down in Carpenters' Row, number three. But it looks up the river.' She saw his eyes brighten, watched the hint of a smile lift his bony face, relieving the sullenness that had marred it.

'You like the water.' Not a question, not to Maggie's son. Images from the past suddenly filled her mind, but firmly she banished them.

'Yes. I want to go to sea.' The last piece of toast lay on the plate and he looked at her, silently asking for permission to eat it.

She nodded, suddenly feeling emotions that she'd long ago dismissed surging through her. Such a tall, nice-looking boy, with his father's fair hair and vivid blue eyes. The past harassed her, but she was strong and denied it. Think of something practical. Clothes.

'Jack, would you or your mother object to me giving you a jacket of my brother's which he has no more use for? Clearly you're growing very fast and you'll need a warm coat if you do manage to get out on the water. What do you think?'

Suddenly his smile almost blinded her – a ray of sunlight flashing across the table. He chewed the toast and gave her the full radiance of his bright eyes. 'That's kind of you, Miss Jenkins. Yes, thank you, very much.'

Janet felt faint. *Maggie's boy.* She sat down quickly and forced herself to be sensible. What did he know? Anything? Nothing? Never mind. *Just give him what you can. A meal, an old jacket, a word or two that would let him know she was always here, would always be here if he needed her.*

She got up and went to the back door. 'It's outside in one of the sheds. Have you finished?' She watched him nod, wipe his mouth on his thin sleeve and follow her. 'Somewhere in here.' The shed was damp and musty but she found the jacket at once and, true to Davey's amused comment, fished around in the two pockets but found nothing. 'Here, try it on.'

It fitted him nicely. A little long in the sleeve and perhaps a bit loose around the shoulders, but he would grow into it. Something inside her turned over and helped her smile. *Maggie's boy.* But she mustn't be silly and sentimental. The boy had work to do, Jem was waiting for him, and at least he'd had a meal and would be warm, enough to stop that nasty cough perhaps, when the easterlies blew. 'Well, off you go.'

She watched him go out through the front door and begin shouldering the stepladder He carried it down the length of the busy street, pausing to accommodate passers-by, and then turned the corner and was gone.

Closing the door, Janet went back to the kitchen and cleared away the dishes. She wouldn't think about Jack any more – goodness knows, she had enough to do today. The attic must be made ready for Loveday. Davey must help carry the new mattress up, then there was the bed to make up and the curtains hung and then, this afternoon, she had that dress to repair for Mrs Sothern. Maggie would be calling for it in a day or two.

But, even as she worked through the list of tasks ahead, a part of her still saw Jack eating a good hearty breakfast. Saw him put the old jacket on and look pleased about it. And then, going up stairs to the attic, her arms carrying the new curtains, she had an amusing thought.

Foolishly she hadn't checked that the inside breast pocket of Davey's jacket was empty, had she? A chuckle brought her, breathless, to the top of the stairs as she considered how wonderful it would be if Jack, looking in it, found one of those fairytale five pound notes!

Tackling the attic with a smile lifting her usually straight lips, Janet found herself unexpectedly and immensely glad to have met Maggie's son and to have been able to so something for him. It felt like a sort of gift. Warmly, she thought that clearly the lad was in need of help, and also, equally clearly, that Maggie was unable to provide enough of it. A good thing she was here, really.

Mrs Narracott was in a whirl. 'Oh my, why did I ever say yes?' she thundered, as Loveday returned to the kitchen, ready for the dinner break. 'But there, he seems a nice young man, ses as how he's working for some chap or other up country, and this would make a good photograph for the . . . arch . . . archives, or summat.'

Loveday, putting away her cleaning equipment and untying her apron, realized that it was Ned and his camera that was causing such havoc. So he'd done exactly as he had said he would do, clearly having charmed Mrs Narracott into agreeing to the ordeal of being photographed.

She smiled to herself and said quietly, 'I expect it'll only take a minute or two, Mrs Narracott. And how lovely to have Teignmouth put on the map – and another thing, if people see us outside the hotel, they'll want to come and stay here, won't they?'

'Oh my – I hadn't thought o' that.' Mrs Narracott paused in the middle of taking off her crisply starched white apron and pulling down her turned-up sleeves. She looked at Loveday helplessly. 'What shall us wear?'

'I think the idea is to show us as workers, Mrs Narracott. So aprons and brooms and things like that.' Another smile. 'Slop pails, perhaps?'

'You wicked girl! Just try and take this seriously, if you please.' She shouted up the stairs. 'Susan? Are you still up there? Come down, quick. An' make sure your cap is on straight.'

Susan appeared, as muddled as ever, carrying her bucket and scrubbing brush, having just cleaned the bathroom. 'What is it, m'm?'

'Just do as I say. Tidy your hair and come outside . . . go on, maid, get a move on. You'm as slow as an old dog.'

'Sorry, Mrs Narracott.' The girl followed obediently as they all trooped out of the kitchen, and into the yard where Ned Kerslake awaited them.

He smiled broadly as he picked up his tripod from where it leaned against the wall, and slung the large satchel carrying his camera on to one shoulder. 'Ah, there you are – good morning, Miss Jenkins. Mrs Narracott, this is really very kind of you to stop work and let your staff be my models. I think it will make a very good photograph – the sun isn't too strong today, and you all look very efficient in your aprons.'

He caught Loveday's eye and winked. 'Brooms, buckets, scrubbing brushes? Everything that you use everyday. Yes, that's what we want. A good picture of hotel workers outside their place of work. So, what do you think of the idea to come out into the road, and stand by the hotel entrance? With the name right above you?'

Mrs Narracott started arguing, but was quickly tamed. 'No, it will all look very respectable, Mrs Narracott, and extremely pleasing.' He led the way on to the pavement in front of the hotel entrance. 'So, that's it, just here, against the wall. Mrs Narracott, you in the middle, please, with the two young ladies on either side of you. . . . Miss Jenkins, a little more to the right, please, and hold your broom straight, and the other young lady closer to Mrs Narracott, with the bucket in one hand. Ah yes, that's splendid. Now, stand quite still, will you? This will only take a second or two.'

He disappeared behind the black cloth and the little group stood, breathless, staring at the spot where they imagined his face might be, somewhere in the middle of the equipment.

And then he reappeared, clicked a bulb that he held in his hand, and smiled charmingly at them. 'Good – just a couple more and then all done!' Another stiff breathless moment and then, 'Excellent. Thank you so much.'

Coming across, he offered his hand to Mrs Narracott. 'I shall process the plates this evening in my dark room – the actual prints, of course, must wait until I return to my workplace. But you will certainly receive a copy of the finished photograph eventually. Thank you again, Mrs Narracott. And you, too, young ladies.'

He bowed, and Loveday saw the usual twinkle in his bright eyes before he turned away to busy himself packing away the camera and the plates, and then refolding the tripod.

'Well,' said Mrs Narracott, looking gratified, even if a bit bewildered, 'that were quick. Well, best go back and get on with the cooking, I reckon. And you girls, off to dinner an don't be late back.' She gave Ned a last regal smile and disappeared, heading for the kitchen entrance.

Susan deposited her bucket and brush in the yard, along with her untidy apron, giggled and ran off, mousy hair flapping out of her cap as she did so. Carefully, Loveday put her broom in the shed reserved for the outdoor tools, and then looked back at Ned. He was still busy and not seeming to notice her at all. She hoped he would look up in a minute and smile at her.

He did so, but it wasn't quite what she had been hoping for, more self-satisfied than friendly. 'That'll be a good one, I think.' He nodded. 'I'm sure Mr Frith will be delighted. I've got quite a few plates ready for developing, so I'll soon be able to go back home and let him see them.'

Loveday's smile faded. Going back? But they'd only just met – and she had thought – had hoped. . . . She caught her breath. 'You mean – you're leaving Teignmouth?'

He turned, gave her a look that she didn't recognize – quizzical, impatient, amused?

'Loveday, my work matters to me.' Even his voice was different, clipped, hurried. 'Of course I shall be leaving – but not today; not tomorrow; not even this week. I only told Mrs Narracott she'd have a print in due course to keep her quiet.'

She thought about it. 'To . . . keep her quiet? What do you mean, Ned?'

He was at her side, a step too close, his eyes bright and full of laughter, once more the uncomplicated Ned she thought she was getting to know. Lightly he brushed her shoulder and smiled at her surprised expression. 'What a child you are! Of course to keep her quiet; to stop her asking me when the photographs will be done and when can she see them. They're all the same – can't wait to admire themselves, you see.' His voice lowered and his touch became a caress. 'Not like you, Miss Jenkins, who didn't want to see herself in a bathing costume with dripping hair—'

Instinctively she stiffened. Yes, this was in the back yard where no one could see them but he was taking liberties. It was too soon for him to touch her. Even though, of course, she had to admit to herself that she was enjoying the feel of his fingers through the stuff of her print dress. She drew away, avoided his amused expression and said hesitantly, 'I have to go now, Ned. Dinner will be ready at home and then Mrs Narracott will expect me back here.' She walked quickly out of the yard, not looking back but knowing he watched her. Once safely distanced, she turned indecisively and met his eyes.

He stood there, smiling, one hand shifting the strap of the shoulder bag. 'When shall I see you again, Loveday?'

Her mouth was dry – so it was all right; she had been mistaken; he was still eager to meet her. Quickly she said, 'Why don't you come and watch the seine fishing this evening? Lots of people will be there. It would make a wonderful photograph.'

She waited. He nodded, raised his hand in a wave and then turned away. But his words reached her, ringing in her mind all the way home to dinner.

'I'll be there if you are, Loveday. Make sure you are.'

'Loveday, hurry home when you've finished this evening – we must move your things into the new bedroom tonight so that I can clean out Mr Lennox Long's bedroom tomorrow. He comes on Wednesday, if you remember.' Janet stood at the sink, washing the dishes and issuing orders over her shoulder.

As if I can forget, thought Loveday resignedly. *Already he is Mr somebody-Long as if he owns the house and we are mere tenants. Well, I hope he'll be satisfied with my old room. One thing, it hasn't got the view that I have from the attic.*

But it was no good feeling resentful. Aunt Janet had hung the new curtains and they looked lovely, rippling as the breeze off the river beach sneaked in through the small window and fluttered them. And the bed – she had been up there, sitting on it, trying it out – felt very good. Firm, but soft. Yes, the attic looked surprisingly pretty really, considering what it had been before all this clearing out.

And yes, she would take up her clothes and the few small pieces of decoration that she had collected over the years. Dried lavender from last summer, picked by Ben at Sothern House and secretly given to her with the widest, hopeful smile possible. A small cardboard star, painted when she was at school and always arranged on the top of the Christmas tree. And her collection of shells gathered over the years and arranged on the old piece of ecru lace that Aunt Janet had given her. Razor shells, pelican's feet, cowries . . . Loveday thought back to the cowry she had found recently and given to Frank Benedict. And strangely, at the same time she saw again the piece of ivory-coloured scrimshaw with its black pin people and patterns in his collection. Such an unusual, foreign thing.

Then she heard the clock strike the quarter hour and knew she must hurry back to the Beach View Hotel or else Mrs Narracott would shout at her for being late. And that brought Ned back into her mind and she went off up Market Street with a smile. They would meet this evening – after she and Aunt Janet had done all the removal jobs. Perhaps he would walk her home after they'd watched the seine fishing – what would Aunt Janet say when she introduced this handsome, cheery young man?

Such thoughts helped her through the busy afternoon and it was with a light step that she returned home to find supper already on the table, a brief meal of soup and fruit.

'Oranges are good for you, child. Eat up.' Loveday obeyed, wondering where they came from. Some far off land, where they grew in sunshine and everlasting warmth, where people had black skins and talked in different tongues. Where she would love to go, one day. One day. . . .

'We'll leave the dishes. I want to get that room cleared as quickly as possible.' Janet was already halfway up the stairs and Loveday followed with a sigh. No time for daydreaming. With Davey's help they carried everything that had to be removed from Mr Lennox Long's bedroom. Then the windows were cleaned, the floorboards swept and polished, the one big, dark red-patterned mat arranged carefully where his feet would emerge from his bed. Clean towels, clean water in the jug by the basin on the washstand, clean bedding, even a small vase of flowers from the market.

Janet stood in the doorway and beamed. 'It looks a treat. I'm sure he'll be pleased.' Something inside Loveday rebelled and she said slyly, 'What about the dog?

'Outside,' said Janet briskly, turning and going downstairs. 'He said it would sleep in the outhouse. I've put some straw there, and the door has a lock on it. The little thing will be very comfortable, I'm sure.' She turned to Loveday still standing at the top of the staircase. 'Well, child, are you pleased with your new room?'

Her smile was warm and rebuked Loveday's selfish thoughts. 'Yes, thank you, Aunt. You've made it look really lovely. I shall be happy up there. I'm just going to arrange my shells before I come down. And then . . . I . . . I'm going out for a little – they're seine fishing and I want to watch.'

Not easy to tell even a white lie, but until her aunt actually met Ned it would be sensible not to mention him. And even then he must be introduced as Mrs Sothern's cousin.

Janet frowned but then shook it off. 'Very well. But don't stay out late. You need your beauty sleep, working so hard . . . and now I must put the final stitches to that dress. Davey, please leave the newspaper when you've finished – Mr Lennox Long might find it interesting to read the local news.' She disappeared into the front room and Loveday heard the gas purring as it was lit.

A shawl around her shoulders, hat firmly skewered on – sure to be a wind blowing. Before she left, Loveday looked around her new bedroom and nodded. It would always be just an attic, but it was comfortable and even pretty. Aunt Janet had been very kind in sewing new curtains and buying another mattress. She must go and thank her properly on the way out. Ned could wait . . . for another few minutes.

Downstairs, she opened the door into the front room and saw her aunt sitting very straight at her worktable, Mrs Sothern's lovely gold taffeta dress spread out on her lap. She didn't look up as Loveday entered but stared at the wall opposite, her face tight and her eyes unblinking. One hand still held a threaded needle and a long flounce of matching satin ran down from the chair over the carpet at her feet.

Loveday's smile died. Something was wrong. What had happened?

'Aunt Janet?' she said, her voice rising uneasily.

The stiff figure slowly eased around to look at her. There were tears shining in Janet's eyes and her breathing was too fast. 'I've been thinking about Maggie,' she said in an uneven, strained voice. 'She'll be coming to collect this dress tomorrow. And Davey insists that I tell you about her. About us.' She looked at Loveday and carefully removed the dress from her lap, putting it on the table, making sure no part of it dropped to the ground.

Then she got up, swaying slightly. For a moment, silence opened up and the room seemed to be waiting. Then, 'Maggie and I are sisters,' she whispered. 'Yes, she's my sister.'

Her eyes bored into Loveday's. 'My . . . sister,' she said again, her voice touched with bitterness. 'My half sister, who was born out of wedlock. Davey said I had to tell you, so I have.'

Loveday was stiff with shock. And then, almost at once, realization came; this was the secret! And now it was told, and surely all the unhappiness could be resolved?

She went up to her aunt and put her arms around her. 'Sit down, Aunt Janet,' she said softly. 'And thank you for telling me. I knew it was something, but I couldn't really imagine . . . and it's not so bad, is it? You and Maggie being sisters – even half sisters?'

She coaxed Janet back into her chair and bent over her. 'Why, she's my Aunt Maggie, isn't she! How lovely, a new relation in the family. And I know you'll be happier to talk it all out when she comes tomorrow.'

Janet sighed, put on her spectacles, picked up her needle and began arranging the dress in front of her. She stitched slowly, fingers working expertly and her face gradually losing its tension. After a few seconds she looked up at Loveday.

'You're a good child. And yes, I should have told you before, but the shame was too much. I mean—' Once more the stitching stopped and she picked her words. 'Maggie was my mother's illegitimate baby. My father knew, but took her in. We grew up as sisters. But it was a hard time. People talked, well, you know how they still do. But at that time having a child out of wedlock was a shocking thing. And I had a difficult time at school, called names, stones thrown at me, even. I always held it against her.' She hesitated, mouth trembling. 'But I got over it. And then I tried to build my little business, but still Maggie's reputation was bad and people associated me with her. And then she married some one else.'

'What was he like, her husband?' Loveday pulled out a stool from the fireplace and sat down. The secret was coming alive; she couldn't leave yet. What else was there to learn?

But Aunt Janet said no more. 'I won't talk about that,' she said shortly. Then she looked across the room, managed a tearstained but recovering smile, and Loveday knew that was all she would learn today. 'Now, child, off you go. You've heard enough of my troubles. Go and find your friends. And don't come back smelling of fish, if you please. We must keep things fresh and clean for our lodger's arrival tomorrow.'

On the beach, Loveday found Daisy and a few other children watching the men row the seine nets out from shore. Ben, at one of the oars, grinned at her.

It was a warm, benign evening, with the lightest of breezes moving the air around. Oars creaking in the rowlocks, gulls calling, and the chatter of people echoing all around, as they walked, sat down and watched.

Loveday looked around her expectantly. This was a marvellously evocative scene – and one that she knew Ned would appreciate. The age-old ritual of rowing out with the seine nets to form half a circle, and then rowing back again, with hands on shore pulling in the nets, sure to be full of wriggling, gleaming, fish. What a photograph it would make.

She looked again. But Ned wasn't there.

CHAPTER SEVEN

The men at the oars were shouting, cursing, encouraging. 'Pull! Pull. C'mon, b'y, what you waitin' fer, eh?'

And slowly, inevitably, the two ends of the net came together in a half-circle as the rowers touched shore and the group of men hauling on the other end of the net met them. Then the half-circled length was yanked out of the water and deposited on the beach. Fading sunlight glistened on writhing iridescent bodies, fish gasped, contorted, jostled and then fell back, limp and dying. The watchers came nearer and the gulls hung lower, still shrieking.

Once the boat was grounded the men leaped out of it, joining the throng busily handling the catch. She saw Ben there, hands deep in the wriggling mass, shouting at his sister Daisy to 'Get the baskets – up there, by the wall – where's yer little cart? Go on, maid, get a move on.'

Loveday sat on the warm sand just below the huts, watching the gatherers of the fish. Old men who had been sitting quietly in the doorways of their huts smoking pipes, mending nets, now limped down and joined the increasing band of gatherers.

'Like ole times,' one of them said, grinning. 'Unloading the fish, save that these 'ere aren't from that those foggy ole Grand Banks and that demmed rock.'

Baskets appeared, boxes, buckets, barrels, dishes and yes, there was Daisy, pulling a little cart down to her brother's side.

And there was a boy, fair-haired, tall, surely the one she'd seen on the harbour on Sunday, she thought, who was being drawn towards the heap of fish, with Ben saying, 'C'mon then, Jack, take some back to your mother – praper supper, that'll be.'

Thoughts whirled in her head. *Jack. My son, Jack.* Unexpectedly a shutter snapped open and her intuition flashed. This was Maggie's boy, Jack. No, she must call her Aunt Maggie from now on. And Jack was her cousin. . . .

Gone was the disappointment of not meeting Ned and the dull pain of rejection. Now she recalled one of Aunt Janet's maxims, 'blood is thicker than water', and although at the time the words had been meaningless, now, as she watched him crouching beside Ben, industriously scooping the still wriggling catch into Daisy's cart and a box she held out to him, Loveday immediately understood them.

She smiled. Life had taken on a new dimension. She now had a real family. Two aunts, an uncle, and this cousin. And, even as the haunting words returned briefly, *lost at sea*, recalling her absent father, she was able to quickly overcome them as she ran down the beach, eager to speak to Jack, to introduce herself, to get to know him.

It was a truly wonderful feeling.

Once the fish were all stored and carried away, the nets pulled up over the beach and stretched out to dry, she edged herself between Ben, Daisy and Jack as they stood with their spoils, discussing the evening's catch.

Ben was grinning. 'Jack Hunt, eh? Well, I'm Ben Marten and this l'il maid's me sister, Daisy.'

'And I'm your cousin, Loveday Jenkins.' The words leapt out and her smile grew brilliant as she held out a welcoming hand.

Ben's jaw dropped, Daisy's sharp eyes widened, and Jack stared into Loveday's eyes. 'Cousin?'

He frowned and she thought, too quickly, that he looked almost stupid: as if he didn't understand the word. Surely he knew what a cousin was?

'Yes. Your mother and my aunt are sisters,' she said quickly. 'Aunt Janet has just told me.' She stared at his thin face, willing him to smile back and show some emotion.

But he just stood there, expressionless, meeting her stare and returning it with his own. Slowly, automatically, he began brushing off fish scales from his hands and arms, and then, equally slowly, he said, 'No, you're wrong. We're not *cousins*—' the words finished abruptly and he coughed.

She heard the emphasis and her smile dredged away. 'But I've just told you – we are!' Her voice was sharp and full of irritation. This stupid, gangling boy was spoiling her warm and comforting dream of a reunited, happy family.

'No!' He stepped back, face suddenly alive, animated by something she didn't recognize. 'No!' Again the one word shouted over the chatter of voices around them, over the gulls' calls, above the pulse of the waves throwing themselves up the beach as they washed away all signs of dead

71

fish, sloughed off scales, and the flurries of wet sand pounded by heavy boots.

She held her breath, watching as he broke away, almost running up the beach, the box of fish clutched in his arms. By the steps leading up to the promenade, he picked up something hanging on the end of the wall – Uncle Davey's old jacket, she saw – and then walked rapidly away.

Beside her, Ben grunted. 'What were all that about, then?'

Loveday's face was pale. She swallowed to relieve the dryness in her mouth and stood quite still for a long moment. Yes, what was it all about? Not her cousin, he'd said. But he was – *he was*. Then the sound of the sea, the stink of fish all around her, and Ben's eyes boring into hers returned her to the present. She turned away.

'I don't know. Maybe I made a mistake.' No one, not even Ben, her friend, must know about Aunt Janet's secret. Not until it was made more public – if ever it was.

'See you termerrow, Loveday? Come out in me boat?'

He was grinning at her, not understanding her confusion and disappointment. Daisy stood at his side, hands on the little cart full of fish. Her bright eyes were steely sharp. 'Thought that ole photograph man'd be ere to see this. He be all over the town . . . I tole him 'bout this but he didn't come.' A grin filled her small, sallow face. 'Somethin' better to do, mebbe. Someone else to see.'

Loveday scowled. The wretched child knew a thing or two, didn't she? 'Mind your own business, Daisy. And take those stinking fish away from me – I was brought up to be clean and not smelly, even if you weren't.'

But even as she heard herself, the childish, cross words made her wince, and she smiled apologetically. 'Sorry, Daisy. But why don't you mind your own business? We don't all want to hear your gossip, you know.'

Turning away, she realized, too late, she'd said the one thing that would incite the child to even more prying and mischief making. But there, it was done. Words came out too easily. She must learn to control them. And then it was Maggie's words that suddenly filled her mind. 'You have a lot to learn, child.'

Yes, Aunt Maggie was right. Slowly, Loveday trailed home, felt a quietness about the place with Aunt Janet and Uncle Davey not meeting her eyes as she went into the kitchen. 'I'll go to bed now.' She managed a grin. 'Try out that new mattress. Goodnight, Uncle Davey. Goodnight, Aunt Janet.'

Their kisses were as warm as usual, but she knew something had changed. Secrets could be unwieldy once they were out, and so hard to get used to. She went upstairs with her head held high and her thoughts firmly concentrated on something different from what had happened this evening.

The bed was comfortable, the small, sloping-roofed room more friendly than she had imagined it might be and if the gulls outside sounded louder than usual, it didn't disturb her. Loveday slept well and in the morning faced the new day with a feeling of having changed inside herself; she felt more grown up. More of an adult woman, no longer a young girl chasing her dreams.

Janet and Davey seemed different, too. The warm kitchen was full of a closer intimacy. They ate breakfast with only desultory remarks, but beneath it Loveday sensed a feeling of relief and of hope. She left for work with a warmer hug than usual from her aunt and a huge smile from Uncle Davey.

She ran along the road, finding a few precious minutes to walk around the Point, to watch the river forging its grey-green way out into the deep blue-washed ocean. There were small fishing boats sailing out of the estuary, and beyond the sand bar a cargo ship at anchor, waiting for the pilot to arrive to steer it into harbour. A fresh wind blew her hat askew and flirted with her skirt. She revelled in everything this morning – but then, aware of the time, she smiled to herself, turned and ran back along the promenade, arriving at the Beach View Hotel with only seconds to spare.

Mrs Narracott frowned. 'Not on that ole beach again, was you? Look at you, maid, hair all twistin' round yer ears.'

Loveday didn't care. She had a new aunt and a cousin – bother Jack, she knew she was right and he was wrong and it would all come out soon – and perhaps today Ned would come looking for her. Surely last night he must have had a very important appointment somewhere else that had made him miss the seine fishing? But it didn't matter. Today was today and anything could happen.

What happened was that she worked extra hard, ignored Susan's flibbertigibbet remarks and giggles, and went home for dinner with her mind full of new dreams. The family. The aunt and cousin she would welcome and soon get to know.

Aunt Janet dished up boiled mutton and turnips and said crisply, 'I would like you to go to the station when you leave work this afternoon, Loveday. I told Mr Lennox Long in my letter that you will meet him. His train arrives at a 5.40, so you should be there in good time if you leave the hotel promptly.'

Loveday dropped her fork on to her plate. 'Meet him? Mr what's-his-name Long? Oh, must I? I had thought I would—' She stopped quickly as Janet's dark eyes sparked at her across the table.

Janet piled potatoes on to Davey's plate. 'Please do as I ask. The poor man will have no idea where we live, and it would be a nice welcome to have someone waiting to direct him.'

They looked at each other very keenly until Loveday picked up her fork and stared down at her plate. She had planned to walk on the prom-enade in the hope of meeting Ned – just casually, of course. But she understood her aunt's reasoning. So, 'All right, then. I'll meet him.' Amusement touched her lips and she looked up again. 'And his dog – Floss, isn't it?'

Janet sighed. 'I'm afraid so. But he insisted that the little thing was well trained.'

Before Loveday left to return to the hotel, she said very quietly, 'When will Aunt Maggie be coming? I'm looking forward to seeing her – and cousin Jack, too. Do you think—' She stopped. Janet turned in the act of pouring a kettle of hot water into the bowl in the sink, giving her a look of determined obstinacy. Loveday sighed. How well she knew that look.

But she could be determined, too. Bravely she went on. 'Do you think, Aunt, we could have a tea party on Sunday? All of us? To welcome Aunt Maggie and Jack—'

A long pause with Janet concentrating on adding soda to the hot water. 'Perhaps,' she said grudgingly at last. 'We'll see. After all, we have our lodger to consider now.'

Mr Lennox Long – oh dear. Loveday went off to work deciding that his imminent arrival really did upset things. Just when she had foreseen a lovely family party with all secrets revealed and a new feeling of happi-ness prevailing, this old man and his wretched dog had to be considered. Well, perhaps he would take the dog for a walk on Sunday afternoon and so keep out of the way.

The afternoon was busier than usual with new guests arriving and all the soiled bedding to prepare for the wash. A woman from the docks came in twice a week to take it home, wash and iron it and then return it and Loveday, shaking her duster out of an open window in a front bedroom, was thankful for small mercies. Washing meant red hands and damp aprons. At least up here she was dry and comfortable.

She paused at the window and thought she saw Ned coming around the corner. Was it him? He didn't carry anything, but his straw hat was worn at the familiar jaunty angle, and was he coming to find her? For a second her heart jumped – and then slowed again.

No. Not Ned. Just another holiday maker who looked a bit similar. She shut the window with a bang and flicked more dust off the chest of drawers before closing the door and making her way to the next room where sand was all over the carpet and slop pails awaited her. Nearly time to finish. And then she must meet this old man.

Henry Lennox Long – he shook his head impatiently, abruptly deciding to drop the Lennox, the old family name, he'd never enjoyed using. With the twentieth century only a decade away the world was freeing itself from restrictive traditions and gentlemen no longer needed to brandish their titles as a means of earning a living. He straightened burly shoulders and smiled wryly at his thoughts; entrepreneurism was in the air, thank God, and one could freely make use of experience, talent and ambition.

As he was about to do.

The train rattled along beside the estuary of the River Exe in Devonshire and he looked through the window, idly watching a family of shellduck – careful mother and eight ducklings, spuddling about on the sand flats – and unexpectedly experienced a sudden awareness of the lack of something in his life. That word – family – touched a nerve.

Now that Uncle Stephen Lennox Long had died, he, Henry, had no family. He recalled his early life in Newfoundland, living with his parents in the lighthouse at Cape Thunder. There had been storms, monster seas, ice and danger, exciting and character forming and tempered with love, providing a human warmth he no longer experienced. Uncle Stephen had been formidably reserved, spending his last days stalking about his Dorset shipyard, irritating the new partner, so recently engaged, suggesting impossible ideas and finally dying in his bed, muttering a few sad last words for his nephew, impatiently sitting at his side.

Sail has given way to steam.

Henry thought about his past as the train jolted and went under a tunnel, blacking out the scene of river and birds and far horizon. The old shipyard had been left to the jumped-up and manipulative partner and so he was in search of a new life. But at least Uncle Stephen had been help-ful, giving him the name of an acquaintance in Teignmouth who might well require a new manager to a neglected business. Henry was full of hope that this might be a new life to which he would bring new blood, new energy and new, amazing ideas.

He knew about ships, having watched them rolling at the mercy of impossible waves, relentless currents and impenetrable fogs, crashing on unmapped reefs, sinking with all hands – and then, working as an apprentice in Uncle Stephen's shipyard, he had learned about their construction, their maintenance and their need to move forward into the future; yes, he knew enough to bring his plans to action. Somewhere, he also knew, there was a need for his expertise and he hoped it was here, where he was about to disembark and look around, in Teignmouth. This small sleepy seaside town had a history of building boats for the cod fishing industry in Newfoundland and would surely be a suitable place to try and build up a yard where he could use all his plans and release his ever growing ambition. Or even, as recent correspondence with the owner, Kenneth Harvey, had suggested, bring that new blood to an already well-known and respected old business.

His hand dropped on to the huge black head of Floss, lying happily, like a black rug, at his feet, as the train rocked slowly to an imminent halt. She was his only link with the land of his birth and upbringing, the Newfoundland dog he had brought back to England after his parents died tragically in that wild storm. She had been the one loving creature to help him accept the offer of home, education and training that his uncle had reluctantly given. Indeed, Floss was his one source of affection.

Henry shook his head, no longer having time or inclination for sentiment or memories. Now the train was stopping and he must disembark. He rose, let down the window, looked out and shouted for a porter. 'You – my luggage in the van – name of Long – a couple of bags.'

With Floss on a tight rein in one hand and his briefcase held safely in the other, Henry got out of the carriage as the train squealed and steamed, and started walking rapidly down the platform. Too many people with children and luggage, in his way – he must get on, so much to do. Someone to meet him, Miss Jenkins had written – but if not, he would find his own way.

He strode along, Floss at his side, porter and trolley running behind, until they reached the ticket barrier and entrance. *Hmm, no one there.* And then he saw her, a tall girl with untidy auburn hair creeping from beneath a shabby straw hat. A girl with huge eyes, a rather charming snub nose and a face that expressed everything she thought. And as she saw him, so he watched awareness turn into amazement. He grinned briefly, put his briefcase under his arm and removed his hat. She was clearly the one sent to meet him; well, he hadn't expected a woman, but still. . . . He walked towards her and held out his free hand. 'Henry Long. Good day to you.'

The train was three minutes late drawing in at the station and Loveday was already tapping her foot impatiently. She wanted to get home, to know if by any chance Ned had left a message for her – but how could he? He didn't know where she lived. But surely, if he really wanted to see her again he would find out . . . wouldn't he?

Groups of people emerged from the train, making their way through the steam from the noisy engine. Several old ladies, bundled in black, three noisy families, a young boy, whistling as he ran down the platform, and a big man, at the far end of the last carriage. Loveday stared. Was this him? This tall, broad shouldered, impressive-looking man wearing a dark suit and a soft-brimmed felt hat, signing to the porter to carry his luggage?

And the dog. . . . *Oh! Surely not.*

Now the man had stopped at the entrance, where she stood. He spoke, briefly smiled, and held out his hand. 'Henry Long. Good day to you.'

Taking in the unusual slatey grey eyes and the lean, chiselled face, she held out her own hand and then snatched it away as strength and a sort of shock tingled through her body. 'G-good day, Mr—' She stopped uncertainly. 'I mean, we thought you were called Lennox Long.' Aware that this wasn't exactly the polite greeting Aunt Janet had had in mind, she felt her cheeks start to colour.

'Sure, that's my name, but I don't use the Lennox bit. Long is short and good.'

'And sweet?' The foolish ending was out before she thought about it. Flushing, she watched a dark eyebrow tilt upwards ominously, and the curiously drawling voice said sharply, 'I guess that remains to be seen.'

She stared, bemused, into eyes that unexpectedly revealed a glint of silver as the sun shone into them, and felt her surprise grow even further. What sort of voice did this unexpected Mr Long have? Certainly a drawl, but his voice was beautiful; low, vibrant – the words coming out very fast and already she was aware of something about him that made her just want to stare and listen.

'And you are?' Quick words and again that glint in the watchful eyes.

She shook her head to banish wayward thoughts. What must he think of her, standing and staring like a dimwit? Quickly she said, 'I am Loveday Jenkins. My Aunt Janet asked me to come and meet you.'

'And how very good of you, Miss Jenkins. Floss and I are very glad to make your acquaintance.'

Loveday looked down at the huge black dog and began chuckling as she thought of her aunt's amazement. 'We thought Floss would be a lapdog,' she said lightly.

'Not in my lap,' said Henry Long. 'She's a Newfoundland water dog – large, web-footed, with a waterproof coat. Very affectionate. They use them for pulling in the boats on the rock.'

Loveday looked at the intelligent black eyes regarding her, and said uneasily, 'Does she bite?'

'Try her.' Again, that hint of dry amusement.

She did. Floss seemed to smile up at her, a huge black paw lifted to gently nudge her hand and Loveday was caught by the dog's obvious friendly overture.

But Henry was impatient. 'Let me see about my luggage.' He moved aside to consult the waiting porter before tipping him and then returning to her side. 'The carter will deliver my bags to Market Street very soon. Now, shall we walk? Is it far? Would you prefer me to call a cab?'

'No, it's only a short distance, Mr Long. And you can see something of the town as we go.' She stepped forward, crossing the station yard. 'This way.'

Out of breath although she had no more than walked a couple of paces, her mind whirling, Loveday knew that this man was so different from what she had imagined. Young, energetic and with little time for anything else, it seemed, than doing what came next. She pulled herself together, and, remembering the need for polite conversation, asked, 'Do you know Teignmouth, Mr Long?'

He swung along at her side with Floss padding sedately between them. 'No. I've lived in Dorset since I came back from Canada about four years ago.'

'Canada?' Her voice rose. If that wasn't a far land, what was? 'Is it very cold there? Full of mountains?'

He looked at her and again brief amusement tilted his lips. 'Sure it is. Up north. Which is where we lived. And where Floss comes from.'

She gasped. 'You mean – you come from Newfoundland?'

'I do. But I shan't be going back. Too cold. Too rocky. Too smelly.' She was captivated. 'All those fish and barrels of oil.'

Loveday felt liberated. Someone who actually knew the far land she craved for! She said quickly, 'Frank Benedict, who lives here, had his toes frostbitten when he was there,' and felt Henry Long's arm carefully holding her elbow as they paused to cross the road leading into Orchard Gardens. 'He's told me about the whales, and the icebergs, and . . . and

. . . I would so love to see them all.'

'I'd like to meet him. But don't bother to go there, Miss Jenkins.' A pause and then the drawling voice went on, 'Devon is a far nicer place, no frostbite here, it's warm and green and full, I guess, of contented inhabitants.'

'I don't think *I'm* contented—' The words rushed out before she thought what she was saying and instinctively she stopped.

Still holding her arm, Henry Long looked down at her and said, eyes narrowing slightly, 'I wonder why? You would appear to have everything you want – a good place to live, fresh air and the sea, your youth and your beauty.'

Everything stood still. Even the horse and cart plodding up the hill wasn't there as Loveday's thoughts exploded. No one had ever said such things to her before. Not Ben – of course not! – and not Ned. But Henry Long had . . . and suddenly she realized how right he was. She *should* be contented. So why wasn't she?

They walked on in silence until they reached Market Street and Loveday sensed her companion taking in everything around him. She thought guiltily that she should have shown him the interesting buildings – the Assembly rooms, the Wintergardens and the market – but her mind was swirling with chaotic thoughts.

'This is a quaint old street,' he commented, stepping aside to give her room as they walked down narrow Market Street, looking at the numbers on the house fronts. 'And you live here with your family, Miss Jenkins?'

Her heart quickened as all the confusing images of the recent few days came together in a blurring veil. *Ned, Aunt Maggie, Jack. What am I to tell him? Is he really interested, or just being polite?*

Stopping at the front door of number 6, she gave the knocker a rap and then turned to him, standing just behind her. 'Yes, I live here, Mr Long. I'm—' She stopped as the truth suddenly came. 'Yes – I'm the adopted daughter of Janet and Davey Jenkins. They took me in when I was a small child.'

As the words erupted, in Loveday's mind words and voices and pictures circled. Was she adopted? Had Aunt Janet ever said so? But how else did she come to live with them? All she knew was that her mother had gone away . . . that was what she had been told and what she had always believed, without any further thought or questioning. But now, abruptly, she had grown up and facts needed to be made clear.

But the door opened before she had time to sort it all out, and there was Janet, smiling in her cool way, stepping back and holding out her hand to welcome the new lodger. 'Mr Lennox Long. How do you do? I am Miss Jenkins. We have corresponded.'

Loveday stood inside the hallway and watched numbly as Henry Long shook the offered hand, said he didn't use the Lennox name and gave his warm, brief flash of smile. He and Aunt Janet talked for a few moments, and she saw Janet's change of expression upon seeing Floss, but she didn't hear what they said. It seemed that all around her new ideas – new, disturbing ideas – were assaulting her confused mind.

Why had she never asked Aunt Janet for details of the mother who had 'gone away'? Why couldn't she remember her mother, just as she remembered – although not too clearly – the father with the squeaking fiddle who played the tune that haunted her? *If only she knew what had happened.*

Aunt Janet was taking Henry Long upstairs, saying that brother Davey would bring up the luggage when it arrived, and Floss was definitely not quite the small pet she had envisaged from his letter, but no doubt the animal would be happy in the back yard.

Voices floated around Loveday in a bewildering cacophony of sound as she slowly took off her hat and went towards the kitchen where the kettle already sang on the hob, and a tray of cups and saucers waited on the long table. She wished dully that she could resolve all the problems crowding in on her, but then footsteps told her Aunt Janet was coming downstairs and so she did her best to smile and say, 'He seems very nice, Mr Long, I mean.'

Janet closed the kitchen door and pulled the kettle nearer the flame. 'Indeed. Younger than I imagined and a colonial, too, which I was not prepared for.'

'He comes from Canada.' Loveday helped arrange biscuits on a plate and had a brief vision of whales and icebergs. But he hadn't liked living there . . . too cold . . . too rocky . . . her mind sharpened. Perhaps, once he was used to being here and his severity had lessened, he might be persuaded to describe the hard world in the north. He might even have a picture of it . . . a lithograph, perhaps, or even a photograph.

Aunt Janet looked at her. 'You're very quiet, child. Not your usual talkative self at all.'

'I'm – just surprised. I mean, he's not old. And he seems quite friendly, except that he doesn't smile much. But he was telling me very interesting things as we walked. And then, the dog—' Loveday ended up grinning, remembering the smooth, powerful paw reaching for her arm.

'Yes,' said Janet, making the tea. 'One thing after another, indeed. And that reminds me, I have a message for you.'

Loveday lifted her head. 'Yes?'

'A young man called after dinner today. A Mr Kerslake. He came from Mrs Sothern. I understand he's her cousin, here for a few weeks. And he told me he had met you.' Janet looked querulously over the tea tray. 'I suppose that was when you were at Sothern House, teaching Miss Eleanor?'

'Yes, yes, that's right.' Loveday looked away. *She must never know he saw me in my bathing dress.* 'And then I met him again when he was with Mrs Sothern and Miss Eleanor, walking along the esplanade.'

'I see. Well, Mrs Sothern is inviting you to join them when they visit the Wintergardens on Friday. Probably a concert, or a play, or something. So kind of her to invite you.' Janet checked the tea tray. 'Everything there, I think. No doubt Mr Long will be glad of some refreshment after his journey. And I must explain that although supper tonight will be a hot meal, we usually eat at dinner time.' She frowned. 'I hope he won't object to that.'

Loveday said impatiently, 'I'm sure he won't. But, Aunt, tell me about going to the Wintergardens. What else did . . . er . . . Mr Kerslake say? I mean, what shall I wear? What are we going for? A concert would be nice – are you sure he didn't say?'

'Mr Kerslake didn't inform me, Loveday. Now please be good enough to take this tray upstairs. Tell Mr Long that there's no hurry about supper – we generally have it at seven o'clock. And – oh yes, what about the dog? I mean, it's upstairs at the moment – will he feed it? Will it sleep in the outhouse? Oh dear, it's extremely upsetting to have that huge animal here.'

Loveday told herself to stop thinking and just to accept what was happening. Clearly Aunt Janet needed calming down over the arrival of Floss, and yes, she would give Mr Long the message about supper. As she went up the stairs and knocked on her old bedroom door, she also suggested to her busy mind that it would be time enough to think about going to the Wintergardens on Friday with the Sotherns when she was in her own room later tonight. But the glow that had built inside her at the mere mention of Ned's name stayed warm and, reassuring as she knocked and then entered, put the tray on the small table in Henry Long's room, and saw him looking out of the window. Floss, she saw, lay quietly on the mat beside the bed, lifting her head as she entered.

From his viewpoint by the window, Henry Long watched her pouring the tea and came to her side. 'You don't need to wait on me, Miss

Jenkins,' he said impatiently. 'I'm a grown man, you know.'

She thought he sounded sharp, and replied equally sharply, 'I can see that, Mr Long.'

They looked at each other and she felt suddenly outraged that this comfortable familiar room, hers for all her life, now belonged to this brisk, difficult stranger.

Holding the cup of tea, he said casually, 'I shall be out of the house most of the time I'm here, and will cause you and your aunt little trouble. And Floss will always accompany me. We'll try not to inconvenience you in any way.'

'I'm sure you won't, Mr Long.'

They looked at each other. He drank his tea, put the cup back on the tray and nodded at her. 'Thank you.' Clearly it was a dismissal.

Loveday tightened her lips, lifted her head an inch higher and took the tray out of the room. She was confused; this man was very authoritative and would always want his own way. Clearly, he had few social talents and he even found it hard to smile.

Halfway down the stairs she realized guiltily that she hadn't told him about supper.

What was happening to her? She was going to meet Ned on Friday, but at this moment all she could think of was how important it was to make Henry Long learn to smile.

CHAPTER EIGHT

It was at the end of October when they saw the last of the cod, and the start of the inflowing ice pans which heralded the seal killing, that he knew he must move on. He had packed up, counted his money and worked his way back to England on one of the schooners that regularly made the long trips and it was then he had discovered the far land – the land of his birth.

England, Devonshire, Teignmouth – a small, unhurrying village spread along a wide beach with green hills behind it, and an estuary that wound down through fields and hamlets into the hinterland of wild moorland. Boats in the harbour here, men working, children laughing and playing and one particular woman who took his eye as soon as he saw her.

Maggie was soft and warm and welcoming. Before Amos knew it he was courting her, forgetting the harshness of his past life, but revelling in the sunshine, in the soft burred dialect of the fishermen, the shopkeepers, the women. Marriage? He thought and was shocked at his change of heart, his longing.

This time his loving was careful, gentle and full of shared pleasure. He met Maggie's family, worked happily in the shipyard beside the river beach and believed that at last he had found the life he had been looking for. There would be a son, he knew it. And then, nine months after their wedding Maggie had a child.

Jack scraped the last bit of fish from his plate then wiped it clean with a hunk of bread. He sat back and thought hard. It had been good, watching the seine fishing, seeing the men at work, envying them, wishing he was one of the crew. Remembering, he screwed up his face into an expression of longing. What his mother used to call 'that awful look of yours' and which always resulted in a telling off.

'No good looking like that, my lad, you'll do as I say and that's it.

You're delicate – no sea going for you. I'm not having you go off like your dad did. Oh, that wicked, cruel sea.'

She was still at it, almost daring him to even think of the sea. Now he worked for Jem Brown the builder and already, after just a few weeks, was sick of it. Hammers, chisels, screwdrivers, wheelbarrows full of heavy stuff which was always his job to move along. The only good thing that had come out of labouring for Jem had been the meal that Miss Jenkins had given him. A nice lady. He thought of her with approval.

He got up, rinsed his greasy plate in the stone sink and left it to dry in the rack above, before going to the open door of number 3, Carpenters' Row, and looking up the river. He smelled size and grease and resin coming from the shipyard, fish from the cellars along the harbour and perhaps a hint of something sweet and unfamiliar drifting down river from the distant moorland. A cargo boat, unloading, lifted and swayed heavily at anchor, cranes manhandling the timber and depositing it in big piles along the quay. Rigging rang as the wind touched it, masts swung at angles, gulls swooped and squawked and Jack knew, with an even greater explosion of decision than usual, that he couldn't go on any longer being Jem Brown's labourer.

He must go to sea. Somehow. Soon.

But how? He left the cottage, shutting the door and hiding the key under the flowerpot outside because Mother would be coming later tonight. A smile lightened his tense young face. He'd left her a couple of fish, gutted and ready to cook. She'd be pleased. Maybe she'd listen more carefully to what he had to say to her.

The evening light was low and golden, shining with mellow softness on the lapping waters of the river as it flowed serenely onwards, gathering strength for its final onrush into the ocean. He walked along the narrow passage of sand, passing the inn and the shipyard, making his way to the Point. And knowing that in his pocket was the piece of crumpled paper that had turned his world upside down, and which might – somehow, but he wasn't sure how – make it possible for his dream to come true.

A dream of himself on a ship. Pulling ropes, climbing to the heights, barefooted and lithe, balancing like someone on a tightrope, scanning the ocean. Heard himself call down, 'Land ahoy!' and the captain's heavy voice reaching him in return, 'Well done Jack, lad.'

Just a childish dream of course; reality, as he knew, would be harder, dangerous, even brutal. But he could deal with it, once he was there. Reaching the Point he sat down, watching the ferry slowly making its way across the channel to the village of Shaldon on the far side of the river. There were groups of holiday makers in bright clothes and parasols, chattering children, some free-running dogs, voices echoing: all humanity enjoying itself, he thought with a tinge of bitterness. But this paper he'd found could change everything.

Taking it from his pocket, he undid the creases and read it slowly. The school in Cornwall had instilled a degree of knowledge of letters into his unwilling mind, but it took him a few minutes to decipher the message on the paper. And then he remembered the girl's voice – Loveday – calling him 'cousin' and his own wild denial of the title. She didn't know, did she? Had no idea of who he really was? Should he tell her? Should he show this paper to Mother this evening? Would it make her even more worried than she always was? Would it – here he sucked in a huge breath and looked longingly back into the harbour where the cargo ship was still being unloaded – help him to get what he wanted? Make his dream come true?

Slowly he walked home, to find his mother frying the fish he'd left her and greeting him with her usual loving smile. He felt it was the right time to tell her; again he took the paper from his pocket, cleared his throat and, laboriously began to read.

Henry Long soon became a part of the daily life at number 6 Market Street. He made no demands, was no trouble, and, indeed, was rarely in the house. He was punctual in his arrival at Harvey's shipyard every morning; he called on the harbour officials, explored the town and its environs with a map in his hand, thin wire framed spectacles on his aquiline nose and said little. Floss accompanied him everywhere – but not to the kitchen. Janet Jenkins demurred strongly at that, but Loveday saw her give a cautious smile to the dog as it obediently withdrew into the back yard and its strawfilled outhouse-kennel.

Loveday herself was too excited about visiting the Wintergardens on Friday evening and seeing Ned again to think too much about anything else. Yes, she had found the lodger curiously interesting, but a good night's sleep in her new bedroom – the mattress was firmer than her old one – found her with frustrated thoughts of clothes.

What would she wear? The green linen was a day dress, not at all suitable for evening excursions. And definitely not that old best dress which was already too short in the sleeves? Aunt Janet looked at it, thought and then offered to add bands of some matching material to lengthen them, but Loveday was offended at the idea. 'I want to look really nice!' she said crossly. 'Not in this old made-up thing.'

Janet sighed and came to a difficult decision. 'I'll see what I can do,' she said obliquely, and disappeared into her sewing room. Later that afternoon, when the house was empty and she had given the matter considerable thought, she looked in her purse and ensured she had sufficient money – thank heavens for the new lodger's rent paid in advance – and set out to look in the windows of the shop in Fore Street which went by the name of MODES, but which, as everybody in the town wryly accepted, was just another title for second-hand clothes. Respectable, clean ones of course, but not new.

Returning to Market Street with a large box under her arm, Janet told herself firmly that the money was spent on a worthy cause – showing Loveday exactly how loved she was. And this at a time when the dear child might well experience surprise, not to mention shock once all the secrets were revealed. Janet sucked in a supportive breath as she settled again to her sewing. It certainly wasn't her wish to reveal them, but who knew what Maggie might decide to do?

The dress lay on her bed and as she entered the little room, weary from her day's work, Loveday's mind soared into realms of delight. So pretty, so elegant, so *new*. How had Aunt Janet come by such a beautiful thing? But never mind the whys and hows ; Loveday tore off her dull print workaday dress, washed hands and face and then slowly, infinitely carefully, took up the soft muslin garment and put it on. Then she looked in the small, flyblown mirror but could see nothing except her excited face. For a moment she hesitated; then went downstairs to Aunt Janet's sewing room, paused inside the door, smiled excitedly, and said, 'May I look in the mirror, please? To see . . . if it fits . . . if it looks as lovely as it feels . . . if I look nice in it—'

Janet nodded and allowed a smile of loving gratification to ease her face. Indeed, the child looked beautiful. The choice of the pale butter-coloured muslin with the big sleeves at the tops of the arms, softening down into close fitting cuffs, and the sweeping décolletage filled decorously with high necked ecru lace, was perfect. And the band of even paler yellow flounces on the wide skirt, matching the broad armlets and the wide sash around the waist, was the finishing touch. She let out her breath, and knew the money had been well spent. 'Dear child, you look very well. Very well indeed. And it fits – perhaps a touch long in the sleeve, but I can easily remedy that.'

Loveday moved fast, fell upon her aunt, arms warm around the solid, upright body that sat so straight, her tears of happiness sprinkling Janet's lined face, and bringing an unfamiliar warmth to her disciplined heart. 'Thank you, oh, thank you, Aunt Janet – it's wonderful, and you're so kind to give it to me – oh, I shall look just as well as anyone there—'

Janet stood up and shook herself back into normal life. 'Yes, well, there's no need for vanity. Now, let me pin up those sleeves.'

Loveday passed the next day in a dream of excitement. The new gown, Ned taking her to the Wintergardens; a faint blur of quick anxiety – would Mrs Sothern approve of how she looked? Not above her station, surely? But worth looking at twice? And would Ned do the same? The dream grew even rosier. A photograph of her, perhaps – one to treasure for always as a reminder of the first time she and Ned had met publicly. And oh yes, *of course* he must think of her with a certain fondness, having made all these arrangements.

She dusted, made beds, cleaned washbasins and slop pails with her mind far removed. Her usual best summer shoes must be cleaned. Her only summer hat garnished with flowers. And should she take a shawl, or not? Loveday was away in her own land of dreams-coming-true when she almost bumped into Jack Hunt as she hurried back home at the end of Friday afternoon.

'Loveday.' It was a hoarse demand to stop.

She did so, staring up into his vivid blue eyes, wondering for a moment who he was and then remembering. 'Oh – cousin Jack.' She allowed him a quick smile and would have passed on but he stepped in front of her.

'I need to talk to you. Where can we go?' His voice was hurried and anxious, his cough an extra irritation.

She paused, thinking what a nuisance he was, coming upon her when she needed all her attention on this evening. She frowned. 'Can't stop now, Jack. I'm in a hurry. What about Sunday? You and—' She stopped and then smiled. 'Aunt Maggie are coming to tea, aren't you? You can talk to me then.'

She saw his expression change into determination. His voice grew stronger and harsher. 'That's no good. I need to tell you *now*.' He stepped closer and instinctively she flinched. He was suddenly a man, no longer the rather annoying boy whom she had bumped into. 'Just listen, it's to do with what I found in the pocket,' he said rapidly, and took her arm, almost pulling her towards him.

Afraid, annoyed, Loveday jumped back. 'Stop it! Leave me alone! I don't want to talk to you. And don't think you'll get me listen to your nonsense when you come on Sunday either . . . as if I cared what you found in your pocket! Fish scales and bits of building rubbish, I expect! Go away, Jack.' She fled, running down the narrow street and looking back over her shoulder in case he was following.

But he stood quite still and only when she disappeared into the house halfway down Market Street did he turn and slowly slouch his way through Northumberland Place and head for the Point. And there he sat beneath the sea wall, watching the ships, dreaming his dreams, furious at having lost the opportunity to tell her the truth. Well, no matter what she had said, it would have to be on Sunday. He'd get her on her own and tell her.

'Your shoes have come up well – and I've put new trimming on your hat. I used the white feathers and fern leaves that Mrs Bridges told me to remove from her old one. Now, let me see – yes, you look very well, child.' Janet stood by the mirror in her sewing room and admired the reflection.

She thought that Loveday seemed taller, more grown-up in the voluptuous pale gown, her glowing hair neatly coiled behind her head, hat pinned securely into position, shading her wide, brilliantly shining eyes, and a shawl arranged over one arm. Janet felt a lump in her throat. What a lovely young woman the small child had grown into. And not just physically attractive, but with a disposition to match.

She turned to Davey, standing in the doorway. Their eyes met and she knew he felt the same stomach-turning knot of apprehension that she was experiencing, despite his strong determination to open up the family secrets.

On Sunday Maggie and Jack were coming to tea, and she was very afraid that Maggie would decide to reveal the other half of the secret. Davey had finally made her understand that it was time to be open about everything, but she feared the loss of Loveday's love which had been, and always would be, the mainstay of her life.

She sighed. Well, no doubt she would somehow deal with it when it happened and nothing must stop this happy evening's outing. 'Mr Kerslake should be here at any minute,' she said firmly. 'I hope you will introduce us. Your uncle and I would like to know what sort of young man he is. Ah, there's the door.'

Loveday stiffened. This was the moment she had been imagining – Ned calling for her, charming both Aunt Janet and Uncle Davey into realizing how delightful he was, how suitable an escort to take her to the Wintergardens. As Janet went to open the door, she moved to the back of the hallway, her eyes wide, her mind wondering exactly how to greet him.

He stood in the doorway, his quick, easy voice bringing smiles and even a chuckle from Aunt Janet and Uncle Davey, and she knew everything was falling into place. It was Ned she was growing fond of; Ned who had come to escort her to the Wintergardens. Ned for whom the dress had been bought and was being worn.

'Hallo, Ned,' she said brightly and moved out of the shadow of the stairwell, until she stood in front of him, basking in his obvious admiration and feeling thankful that he had worked his usual charm on both Janet and Davey.

Looking down at her, Ned smiled broadly. 'My word, what a picture,' he said. 'And perhaps this time you won't mind me photographing you, Miss Jenkins?' He winked and Loveday felt her cheeks colouring as she avoided Janet's questioning eyes. For a moment she was cross with him for alluding to that awful moment of the wet bathing dress, but then he was offering her his arm, they were waving goodbye to the little group in the open doorway, and then they were on their way up the street.

'How nice to get you to myself, Loveday,' he said, holding her arm and smiling down at her. 'I've been looking forward to seeing you again – oh, and I nearly forgot to tell you, poor Issy has become ill; just a chill I think, but said she wouldn't risk coming out this evening.'

Loveday stopped. She stared into the flecked hazel eyes looking at her so intently, and said 'You mean, we're alone? Just you and me? No one else? But—'

'I know, you thought it would all be rather formal and stiff, but now we've got this chance to be on our own and get to know each other. Don't you think that's a good idea, Lovey?' He was hurrying her along.

Lovey? No one had ever shortened her name before and at first she didn't think she liked it. But the way he was smiling at her, the charm in those twinkling eyes – well, it was just Ned's way of speaking, of course. No harm to it. So she smiled back, and allowed him to lead her towards the entrance to the Wintergardens.

'I just hope no one sees us together, that's all,' she said hesitantly. 'You don't know what this town is like for gossip. And my Aunt Janet will be very upset that Mrs Sothern isn't here to chaperone us.'

They paused inside the wide doors, and Loveday looked around, suddenly more aware of the spacious, high-ceilinged building than the disturbing circumstances in which she found herself.

Ned laughed lightly. 'It's time you grew up a bit, Lovey. You're a sweet girl but so naïve – and there's so much to learn about life, and to enjoy. You must realize that there's lots more freedom in the world now and all sorts of new ideas to think about. Of course we're doing no harm coming to a concert together. Let's just have some fun, shall we? Think of this outing as your first step into the adult, sophisticated world!'

His laugh reassured her. He was right, of course he was. She was very inexperienced and yes, she loved the thought of gaining more freedom in her life. So she would just enjoy this evening, and forget about Aunt Janet's tight lips and frown when she discovered what had happened.

The concert held her attention throughout the hour and a half that they spent in the huge pavilion. The scent of flowers, the light from the tall windows, other people's voices and clothes, all assailed her senses, but the music was the most powerful gift of all. She sat very still beside Ned on a hard gilt chair three rows away from the platform on which a fine concert grand piano dominated her vision. She thought of Frank Benedict's wheezy old harmonium and could hardly believe what she saw.

The orchestra played well and the soloists were splendid. A thin, dark-haired, foreign-looking man with huge hands played a rhapsody which had Loveday holding her breath and hardly believing in the beauty and expertise of the performance. Then, after the interval, during which she and Ned strolled about the big hall and had ice creams, a large lady came on to the stage and took her stance in the bow of the piano.

A different man – slight, younger and anxious looking – came on with music sheets and seated himself ready to play, while the lady, dressed in a purple gown that swung and swayed as she moved, told the audience what she was going to sing.

Loveday was enchanted. The recital lasted some ten minutes, during which she felt she had entered heaven. All this music, these tunes, the rich voice soaring effortlessly through the warm air of the pavilion, the hush of the audience as the songs ended, and then the noisy, enthusiastic applause. All this was manna to her thirsty soul.

Until Ned nudged her. 'You look as if you're somewhere else,' he teased. 'Come back to earth, Lovey. The evening's not finished yet, you know.'

She sighed, nodded, even laughed a little but found it difficult to think straight. All she knew at that moment was that Madame Chance had been right – music was such an important part of her life. And even as her mind whirled around, she heard the plaintive little tune on the scrapey old fiddle, and thought again of her lost father.

But Ned was standing up, taking her arm, joining the crowds who slowly, chattering the while, moved towards the exit door and then out into the quiet, dim lit street. 'Let's take a stroll,' he murmured.

Loveday was still overcome by what she had just heard and seen and allowed him to link his arm with hers and slowly walk into the maze of dark, empty courts that led off Brunswick Street. But at last she came to her senses, drew her arm away from him, looked about her and said anxiously, 'Where are we? This isn't the way home, Ned.'

He had moved closer, and she could only just make out his face in the dusky light. But she saw his eyes gleam as he said, very quietly 'No, it isn't, Lovey, but it's a fine place in which to teach you how to take another step into a grown-up life. Come here, sweetheart.'

He reached out for her and suddenly his arms were around her, strong and unexpectedly demanding, and Loveday gasped. She felt the prickliness of his jacket on her cheek, saw his head lowering, nearer, nearer and then he put his lips on hers and at once she was lost in a confused world of touch and excitement that was fast becoming distaste.

She had never been kissed before. All her girlfriends had giggled and hinted that it was a pleasurable experience, and at first she thought this was. His mouth was warm and she savoured the taste of ice cream and lingering tobacco. Until slowly she felt his arms pulling her closer, his hands stroking her back. He must be crushing her beautiful gown. He was being too intimate. And at once she knew she wasn't enjoying this any longer.

Instantly she pulled away. 'No,' she said fiercely. 'Don't do that. Let me go.'

But he held on to her and she began to feel herself unable to resist any longer. His big hands were too powerful and she was about to scream for help, when a shape appeared from the far end of the court, walking towards them, and at once Ned released her.

Loveday wiped her mouth on her sleeve and looked thankfully at her deliverer. She knew him, even in the semi-darkness – it was Ben Marten. But he mustn't see her, so she turned her head and waited for him to pass. He grunted something inaudible as he went and she realized that he had probably seen her, but had decided to pretend that he had not. He was her friend, and she sighed with gratitude.

It was easy then to slip away from Ned, running back into Brunswick Street and heading for home She heard him call her name, but didn't look back. And then someone else called, not *Lovey* but her proper, respectable name.

'Miss Jenkins.'

What a relief to recognize that voice, gravelly, quick, not Devonshire but pleasant to listen to all the same. Slowly, she turned and looked at the man approaching her and at the huge black shape by his side.

'Mr Long!' Suddenly she wanted to rush to his side, to ask for reassurance, to hear him tell her everything was all right, but of course she couldn't do that. She hardly knew him. So she took a deep breath to quell her fear and smiled through the gas-lit semi-darkness, saying quietly, 'Yes, it's me. I'm on my way home from the concert at the Wintergardens.'

'Alone? At this time of night?'

She heard the disapproval and thought quickly. 'Er . . . yes. My . . . friend . . . was unable to escort me back. And anyway, it's only a step.'

A wet nose thrust itself against her hand and she looked down into Floss's deep eyes. Again, reassurance and the welcome start of relaxed amusement. Slowly the turmoil of her evening shifted, becoming instead a host of memories, some of which were worth keeping, others that she would banish from her mind.

Politely, Henry Long offered his arm and she took it gratefully. He told her they'd been walking on the beach, and then they continued in silence through Northumberland Place and up the street towards Market Street. Until he asked, 'And did you enjoy the concert, Miss Jenkins?'

'Yes, it was . . . wonderful. The music . . . well, I shall never forget it.'

'Hm.' She heard a note of new interest in the sound and wondered what would come next. 'Good,' he said. 'Art is a great gift and one we should all cherish. Do you paint – or sing – or write, perhaps?'

Loveday found herself chuckling. 'No, Mr Long. I play the pianoforte a little and mostly I just clean rooms in an hotel, but I do love music.'

There was a pause and then he said tentatively, as if uncertain whether she would be interested, 'Where I come from – Newfoundland – there's some fascinating folk music. Sailors always sing, you know – as they work, usually, but they sing and dance when off watch, too. Some of the ditties are very appealing.'

Something deep inside Loveday brought a new awareness. She looked at him, walking along beside her, his customary rather severe expression almost invisible in the half-light, but she was certain that he was smiling and this made her smile, too.

'I would love to hear them, Mr Long.' They turned into Market Street and she saw Uncle Davey standing outside the open door of number 6, looking up and down, clearing waiting for her to come home. But before they reached him, she said quickly and with growing pleasure, 'I know one of the songs. I heard my father play it and I play it on my pupil's piano when I'm teaching her. And I have played it in church, too.'

'You play the organ, Miss Jenkins?' He looked down at her from his greater height and she saw the slatey eyes reflect the shafts of light as the moon sailed through the clear sky above.

'Rather badly.' She smiled.

The evening was ending, she was safely home and her confused thoughts were slowly simmering down, waiting to be sorted out later when in her bed. But at the moment she was only thinking of telling Henry Long about that plaintive little tune, because – was she wrong? The new-found inner awareness told her she didn't think so – because she had a feeling that he was interested in her life. In her.

CHAPTER NINE

'We'll call her Loveday cos we Jenkins come from Cornwall and that's a good Cornish name. What do you say, Amos?' Her smile was brilliant, but he had said little, just nodded and turned away, appalled at his thoughts.

Another girl. No boy. But it had seemed so right. The months turned into years and his sadness grew. No more could he tell Maggie how he felt. He watched the bright toddler dance as he scraped away at his fiddle and wished it was a boy to whom he could teach the hornpipe.

Until, one morning when the fishing boats were leaving harbour and the wind blew his bleached hair over his eyes, he knew what he must do.

Saturday, Sunday – how quickly the days passed. Loveday met Ben Marten as she hurried home for dinner on Saturday and didn't know what to say. But he did.

'What you doin' wi' that chap last night, Loveday?' His voice was hard, his frown disapproving and Loveday braced herself. What she did was no concern of his.

She lifted her head an inch higher. 'He took me to the concert. And it's none of your business, Ben.'

Footsteps, and Daisy came running along behind them, her face eager and her words sharp. 'Someone said as 'ow you and that photograph man were together last night, Loveday – and you had a new dress, lovely, all pale yellow—'

Disturbance hit Loveday. Did everyone gossip like this? She knew they did, but never before about her. It was a horrible experience. She didn't like all this personal curiosity. 'If I did, it's nothing to do with you,' she said sharply. 'And I can't stop for any more silly talk,' and she walked away, leaving them standing together, watching and – she was quite sure – gossiping even further.

On Sunday she went to church as usual, anxious about seeing Ned in the Sothern pew, but he wasn't there and although she missed his handsome face and observant eyes, she was relieved. Last night still lived in her mind. Mr and Mrs Sothern and Eleanor were present and Loveday, looking for signs of the chill Ned had spoken of, saw nothing. Obviously it had been a very minor chill.

She saw Maggie at the back of the church and began imagining how the tea party would go this afternoon, but then she noticed that Frank Benedict wasn't in his usual place, and this thought overcame all others. Leaving the church she went around to his cottage where Crystal was asleep on the windowsill and the door was ajar.

Inside she found Frank half asleep in his chair by a nearly dead fire, a half-empty cup of soup on the hearth. He looked exhausted, old and very pale, and he coughed incessantly. Loveday was alarmed.

'Mr Benedict, you're ill. Shall I ask the doctor to come?' Looking around the small stuffy room she saw neglect and dust and was shocked.

Wearily, as if any move was too difficult to try, Frank Benedict shook his head. 'No, no, 'tis only the ole cough. I've had it before. It'll go' He smiled at her with a hint of the familiar wry mirth. 'Or I will. 'Tis a race between us, I reckon.'

Loveday put kindling from the pile of driftwood on the embers and encouraged a fire to burn, heating water in the blackened kettle on the overhanging trivet. She made a fresh drink while Frank watched her. 'You're a good maid. Make the right man a proper wife one o' these days.'

She got to her feet and turned her head away. Why should she at once think of Ned? Ridiculous. Instead she recalled that casual remark of Mr Long's as they had walked from the station. 'We have a lodger,' she said, 'A Mr Long. He would like to meet you as he lived in Newfoundland once.'

She saw the rheumy eyes brighten and Frank tried to sit up straighter. With an arm around his shoulders she helped him, plumping up the cushions behind his back. 'Knows the rock, does he? Mebbe he knows people I knew. Ask him to visit, if he'd like to.'

She was relieved to see the unexpected burst of recovery and smiled warmly at him. 'I'll come again tomorrow, Mr Benedict, and bring some of Aunt Janet's cough medicine. And some soup. Can you manage on your own?'

' 'Course I can. Off you go, and don't forget to ask this chap to visit.'

'I won't, Mr Benedict.' In the doorway she gave him a last smile. She wasn't quite sure what he muttered in reply as she left him, but it sounded uncomfortably like, 'An' he better come soon. I'll not be here much longer.'

Jack pounded down the beach, shaggy hair brilliant in the afternoon sun, his voice loud and urgent as he shouted after her. 'Loveday . . . wait for me . . . I got to tell you something.'

She was walking slowly along the tide line, automatically looking for shells, but thinking all the time of meeting Aunt Maggie who would be coming down from Sothern House for her Sunday afternoon off. It would be a difficult tea party to follow, with Aunt Janet having to tell Maggie what she had revealed of the family secret, and now here was that nuisance, cousin Jack, yelling at her. She turned and stared at him crossly.

'For goodness sake, stop shouting. Do you want the whole world to hear?' She gestured at the people on the beach around them, at the toddlers building sand castles and the few men coming out of the beach huts and swimming away from the shore.

Jack reached her side, swallowed, snatched a paper from his pocket and waved it under her nose. 'Read this,' he demanded hoarsely, voice croaking with urgency. 'Then you can understand what I'm trying to tell you – you're my sister, not my cousin.'

'What?'

He nodded. 'I know you don't believe me, but go on, read it.'

She did. The sepia-coloured words were carelessly written, the paper cracked and brittle and it took a few seconds to make out what it said. But there it was – a fact she must make herself believe, like it or not. She gasped. 'My birth certificate. Where did you get it?'

'From that jacket Miss Jenkins gave me. It was in the inside pocket – I s'pose they forgot to take it out.' He had calmed down, was looking at her with intent eyes, willing her to accept the truth.

As surprise mounted into shock, Loveday felt a slow banking up of something knotted and uncomfortable moving inside her. She turned the paper over and saw another hand had written something on the back in faded black ink and more readable writing. She read slowly once, and then again, and the knot in her stomach tightened.

I give my daughter Loveday Hunt to my half-sister Janet Jenkins and my half-brother Davey Jenkins to have as their own and to bring up as best they can. Margaret Hunt, 17 October 1869.

For a few seconds Loveday thought the world had gone mad.

Suddenly she was dizzy, unsteady enough to grab Jack's arm to keep her footing. The sun was too bright and hot, the gulls' cries too loud, Jack's vivid blue eyes were looking into her mind and she wished wildly that this wasn't happening.

'I've got you, don't be afraid. I won't let you fall.' His voice was quiet now, the hesitant smile on his face telling her he understood how she felt.

He's my brother. Slowly things settled themselves around her. She was on the beach, and Jack was beside her, his arm around her shoulders and they were brother and sister. She gasped as a new thought touched her, the sound turning into a painfully bitter chuckle. 'So Maggie's not my aunt – she's my mother.'

'And mine.'

Carefully, Jack led her away from the bathing huts and their squeaking winches. He headed for the wall beyond the families sitting in deck chairs on the beach, and said, 'Sit down. Go on, sit down.'

She was thankful to do so. Her legs had turned into jelly and she imagined her face must still be a tight mask of surprise and disbelief. But Jack was being helpful. She felt the warm wall at her back and his lanky body seating himself beside her. She looked at him, managed a weak smile and knew he deserved the best she could give him. *My brother.*

She was still holding the birth certificate. Now she looked at it again and studied the details. After her own name there was her mother's name, Margaret Hunt. And under Father was Amos Hunt. Raising her head she met Jack's eyes. 'Our father,' she began unsteadily, 'this Amos Hunt – he was lost at sea, I was told. Did you know that?'

He nodded. 'Mother told me. She said he went back to Newfoundland to earn money which he would send to her, but nothing came and after a few years she reckoned the boat must have sunk – lots of them did up there in that wild place – and he'd been drowned.' Staring out to sea, which was calm today, showing no sign of the fearful storms which caused such tragedies, he began digging fingers into the sand beside him, making small piles and then pushing them down again.

Loveday watched in silence, understanding all that he felt. That cruel ocean. A shared mother and no father. And then suddenly something else struck her. Why had her mother – no, not Mother, still Maggie in her mind – given her to Aunt Janet and Uncle Davey?

And then came the insidious, creeping niggles of rising anger. *She gave me away. My mother. How could she do that? I was her daughter.*

And then another thought, darker, crueller, more painful still. *She didn't want me.*

97

Her breath came faster now and she felt her body tightening as the awful truth hit her. Her own mother hadn't wanted her, so had given her away. But mothers always loved their children, didn't they? And Maggie had kept Jack, so why hadn't she kept her daughter, too?

Loveday shook her head to try to clear away the unanswerable, churning thoughts that filled it. She said wildly, more to herself than to Jack, 'I'll never forgive her! Never. To give me away – how could she? No, I won't forgive her, not ever.'

'No, you mustn't say that—'

She turned, stared into his suddenly unhappy face and heard the anger erupting as she snapped, 'I do say it. How can I possibly forgive her for not keeping me with her – and you – and my father?' Slowly the enormity of it overtook the confusion and one thought remained, strong, irrevocable and almost unbelievable.

My mother gave me away.

The church clock struck half past three, interrupting the darkness in Loveday's mind and bringing back the ordinary world. They would be waiting for Maggie to arrive at Market Street so she must go back and face them. Never mind meeting Maggie as she'd wanted to, now she would hurry back and tell Aunt Janet what Jack had told her. Show her the birth certificate. Ask why it had happened, demand reasons, let out some of this rage which was swirling so uncontrollably around her bewildered thoughts.

And then a shadow fell on her and looking up, she found Maggie smiling down at them. 'Well, you two sitting together. That's nice. I thought I'd walk along the beach on my way, but I didn't expect to—' Words tailed off and the smile became apprehensive. 'What's happened? What's wrong?'

And then, as if by instinct, the whispered, accusing question, 'Jack, you've told her?'

Loveday slowly looked from her mother's anxious face to that of her brother, still sitting at her side, sifting sand through his fingers. She saw dismay in his bright blue eyes, a tremble in the generous mouth and knew she shared all his feelings. It came to her that he was so young, so vulnerable, and she must help him. Maggie mustn't blame him.

She got to her feet, facing Maggie and said unevenly, 'Yes, he told me. I know that you're my mother and that you gave me away.'

'But I can explain—'

'Explain? Giving away your baby?' Her voice grew in strength and anger. 'Well, I don't want to hear. You left me and that's all there is to it.

You said that, on the back of the birth certificate. Here, look for your-self.'

Maggie took the paper and stared at it, her face contorted, her hands shaking. 'Yes, I know, Loveday. But at the time it was the only thing I could do. You see, I was—'

'Don't bother.' Loveday cut in, sharp as a knife. 'You did it and that's all I care about. And now I'm going home to tell Aunt Janet and Uncle Davey that I know this wretched secret at last.' She turned, looked back over her shoulder at Jack, scrambling to his feet, staring at her, and then at her mother's tear-filled eyes. 'I don't want to see you again, Maggie. Not ever. Goodbye.'

Feet slow and clumsy in the loose sand, she walked as fast as she could towards the steps leading on to the promenade and then almost ran back to Market Street, rushing into the house and calling out, 'Aunt Janet! Where are you? Oh, please come here.'

Janet appeared in the kitchen doorway. 'What ever. . . ? Is something wrong, child?'

'Yes! It's all wrong. She should never have given me away. I'm her daughter – she's my m-mother and . . . and—' Loveday could no longer speak. Hot tears pricked at her throat, making her eyes swim, and then she was in Janet's arms, weeping on that broad, loving shoulder, and wishing that she could relive the last half hour and forget everything that had happened. And realizing at the same time, that she could never do so.

What happened then was something Loveday could never quite recall. There were voices, trembling at first, soft and growing loud, her aunt and uncle arguing. She sensed pain and outrage, and then she was being half carried upstairs into the attic bedroom, told to lie on the bed and try and be quiet.

Another voice, strong and quick, broke through her throbbing thoughts as Aunt Janet closed the attic door behind her and went down-stairs. 'Can I be of any help, Miss Jenkins?' and Janet saying rapidly, her voice shaky, 'No, thank you, Mr Long. But . . . but if you wouldn't mind not using the parlour this afternoon. You see, my sister is coming and we have to talk about certain things.'

That quiet yet vibrant drawl. 'Of course. I'll give Floss a good long walk. Like me, she gets stiff with too much sitting about, writing up my notes. We'll be back in time for supper, if that's convenient?'

'Thank you, Mr Long. So understanding of you,' and then no more.

Loveday lay on her bed and re-ran that wretched scene on the beach until blessed sleep claimed her and the pictures and voices and emotions disappeared. But when she awoke it was to hear more arguments down-stairs. Muted voices, but the arguments and pain and anger reached her just the same and she knew Maggie was here. She forced herself up, tidy-ing her dress and hair, splashed cold water on her face and then slowly went downstairs. The parlour door was shut and she paused for a long moment, gathering strength, knowing that she was about to enter into what would be a distressing and harrowing scene.

I've just got to face up to it. I'm not a child any longer. I'm a woman and I don't need to be protected with secrets any more. They must tell me everything.

Opening the door, she went in.

It was a long and painful afternoon. Maggie was in tears, sitting on the chesterfield and facing Janet on the opposite side of the hearth. Davey sat beside her and Jack sprawled awkwardly on a hard chair, making up the circle. When Loveday came in they all looked at her and there was a diffi-cult silence.

Until Davey said quietly, but with enough emphasis to make all eyes turn towards him, 'Come in, my dear. It's time you learned the truth. Maggie will tell you why she gave you to us, and all about your father and Jack. Now come and sit down beside her and let's all try and forget how angry we've been – yes, angry and hurt and disappointed. How much better it would be if we could forgive each other, don't you think?' He smiled at them, eyebrows raised, and seemed to be waiting for a reply.

Slowly they all nodded. Loveday stayed standing within the door, her gaze on Maggie, the woman who'd given her away. She couldn't possibly talk to her. She would never forgive her. But then she saw Maggie shift-ing on the sofa to make space for her and Jack fidgetting on his chair and knew she must somehow manage to make peace with them both. What good was this awful, hot anger?

Janet remained straight and stiff, but her face was slowly showing less misery. Uncle Davey's gentle eyes were watchful, and Loveday waited for the silence to end, but it went on, and then she knew she must somehow try to understand . . . but not forgive. She could never forgive.

Swallowing to relieve the sudden dryness in her mouth, she turned to Maggie and tried to find the right words. They were slow in coming. 'Why did you go away? Why did you leave me with Aunt Janet and Uncle Davey?' Her voice broke. 'Why didn't you take me with you?'

Maggie heaved in a huge sigh and looked into Loveday's eyes. At last: 'It's a long story,' she said brokenly, hands gripped in her lap, her body a picture of stiff unhappiness.

'We've got the rest of the day,' said Uncle Davey quietly.

'Yes. But it's hard to tell her why I left her here. With you. But, you see,' Maggie turned towards Loveday. 'I was younger then. Foolish. Full of anger because Amos had gone away.'

'Amos? My father?'

A nod. Maggie's lips trembled. 'We were happy together for a while, though he was so badly disappointed—' She stopped, shook her head. 'Disappointed that you were a girl. You see, he wanted a son.'

Loveday's head was spinning; more rejection. She stared across the room at Jack, almost enviously. 'But he has a son—'

'Yes, he has, but he doesn't know. How can he?' Maggie was growing pink with emotion. 'He was drowned – he must have been – I never heard from him any more. And he said he'd send money back but none came. Oh, that wicked sea, that terrible place – I wished so much he hadn't gone. But he did. And then, weeks later, I found I was with child again and he would have stayed if he'd known. But he didn't. And so I knew I had to bring the boy up as well as I could, just in case Amos came back. And I had no money. So I would have had to go into the workhouse – with you, Loveday. But someone offered me a home and a job in Cornwall, and so I asked Janet and Davey to take you in, and I went away.'

Davey cleared his throat and said very quietly, 'And I hoarded the birth certificate your mother gave me, Loveday, putting it in that old jacket, feeling I mustn't throw it away, although Janet wanted me to do so. And then I forgot it was still there.'

The room was alive with feelings of overwhelming pain. Loveday sat rigidly by her mother's side watching the tears flow and the hands being gripped even harder. She looked across at Aunt Janet and saw a hint of sympathy loosening the tight lips. And she wondered what to say about all she had just heard.

The words came out of the blue. 'Did you love him?'

Maggie turned her head abruptly. Her eyes were wet but she smiled weakly and at once Loveday thought something more gentle and kindly began to flow through the room.

'Yes,' she said, and the one soft word seemed to bring an end to what had been a terrible scene. 'I loved Amos, and he loved me. But he wanted a son. That's what it was all about, you see. And now he'll never know.'

Later, empty teacups littered the table and the plate of scones had all been eaten; it all seemed to have come to an end. Loveday heard Maggie and Jack say goodbye and somehow managed to nod her head and force a smile. Then she helped Aunt Janet take the tea things out to the kitchen. When everything was washed and put away, she said carefully, 'I'd like to go out, I can think better out there. I'll be back in time for supper.'

Janet looked at her across the room and it came to Loveday that she wasn't the only one who had been so terribly hurt, learning Maggie's story. Janet's memories must be haunting her as she recalled being given the small toddler to bring up. So what must she feel now, when the child's real mother had returned? Did she think Loveday would turn to Maggie and forget all that Janet had done for her?

Spontaneously, she put her arms around the older woman and held her very tight, burying her head in the capacious bodice of the dark dress. 'Aunt Janet, I'll always love you,' she whispered. 'You're my real mother.' And then she turned and left the room, snatching up her hat from the hall and going quickly into the sunlit narrow street and heading almost instinctively for the beach.

There was so much to think about. So many different feelings to look at, to experience and to either welcome or push away. Loveday walked along the promenade in a trance, not seeing or hearing the Sunday crowds enjoying themselves on the beach and all around her. Her head spun with the wounding facts. Maggie, her mother, had given her away because she needed to give all her time and money to bringing up Jack. All for the sake of the father who was no longer here. Whom she would never see. What a muddle it all was.

And then, oh, what a sudden relief to hear a familiar voice, to shake herself out of the encapturing trance and look up into twinkling eyes and a huge smile.

'Hallo, Lovey, I was hoping I might see you. Shall we go for a stroll, or would you like to sit down?' At once she forgot the fear in that dark court last night. This was the acceptable Ned Kerslake himself, self confi-dent and attractive, a man who knew where he was in the world, and seemed only too happy to spend time with her.

Loveday sighed and let out some of her inner anguish. 'I'd like to walk,' she said, her voice a little unsteady. 'Down there, by the sea. Let's get our feet wet, shall we? And look for shells.'

If Ned was surprised he didn't show it. Instead, he slipped her arm through his and said gaily, 'Good idea. And then I'll tell you what I've got lined up for tomorrow – and please, Lovey, be sure to be there, up at Sothern House.' As they went down the steps on to the beach he gave her a searching, quick look. 'Forgiven me for last night, have you, sweetheart?' His voice was low and tender. 'A bit quick, was I? But you're such a lovely girl . . . all right, all right' as she coloured and tried to speak – 'I won't do it again. At least, not for a while. Not till you tell me you want me to.'

And then he started running, with her tight beside him, running down towards the sea where finally they stopped. He put his arm around her, said wickedly, 'Never mind what anyone thinks, Lovey, I can see you need a bit of cheering up. So let's find some shells and then we'll have an ice cream on the pier before I take you home. Is that all right?'

It was. Oh, how very all right it was. Loveday pushed away the afternoon's emotions and persuaded herself to start enjoying the peace of being beside the sea, of feeling damp sand beneath her feet, of pushing aside the detritus of the tide line and searching for what ever might lie there.

'Look!' she cried triumphantly, bending to pick up a tiny shell. 'A cowry, Ned. Put it in your pocket for luck.'

He took it from her, turning it over in his big hands and then returning it to her. 'Let's share it,' he said quietly. 'Let it make luck for both of us, shall we, Lovey?'

A capricious wind fluttered tendrils of hair beneath her hat and he gently tucked them away beneath the brim, looking into her eyes. 'I've been lucky already,' he said. 'I didn't know when I came down here that I'd meet someone like you, Lovey. But you know that, don't you?'

She nodded. Of course she did. And already she knew herself half in love with him.

But then memories sparked. Maggie said she loved Amos; and Loveday knew now that love didn't always bring happiness. So she said nothing, but walked away from him, her eyes on the tide line, hoping for something else to bring good fortune back into her life.

CHAPTER TEN

Go back to Newfoundland. Save money. Send it back to his wife. She was a good woman, she deserved everything he could offer her. But the passion still within him was urgent – he had to move on. Go back to the rock and his old friends, make a new life for himself. And then, perhaps one day when he was older – and maybe no longer in need of a son, he would return. He caught his breath. He was still young, there was still hope. Another woman, maybe? The decision was made. He left Teignmouth feeling ashamed of doing so, but driven to go.

'I'm sorry, girl, but I can't stay no longer. If the cod's still there I'll soon find work and send you money. I'm sorry, sorry—' They kissed and she wept and the small girl waved goodbye.

'Come back soon, Father. Come back—'

On Monday morning Loveday awoke with heart-sinking awareness of all the disturbance of the day before. To the shattering thought that she now had a mother and a brother. That she would never forgive Maggie for giving her away. Bad thoughts, unhappy ones that she knew instantly she must try and forget – at least for the moment. Time now to get up, to go to Sothern House, to meet Ned, to go on living as if nothing momentous and disturbing had ever happened. Difficult: almost impossible, but she would do her best to try to forget.

Yet, dressing, she couldn't forget yesterday. And then, amid all those troublesome memories, something else rushed into her mind, and she was shocked at her forgetfulness, for Mr Benedict had asked her to give a message to Mr Long, and she hadn't done so.

Running down stairs she paused at his bedroom door, wondered if it was respectable to try to speak to him before he was properly up and dressed, but then was relieved when no reply came to her hesitant knock.

In the kitchen Aunt Janet looked at her very carefully and said in a more gentle voice than usual, 'Did you sleep properly, child? You look a little weary.'

'Yes, I did sleep,' said Loveday, making her words bright, intent on reassuring her aunt. 'The new mattress is splendid. And I'm looking forward to going to Sothern House this morning. Miss Eleanor is working hard on her practice and—'

The door opened and Henry Long came in, followed by Floss who looked around at everybody with a smile on her large, black face. Water dripped from her coat and huge paws and Henry Long said quickly, 'I'm so sorry, I'll clean it all up. She had her usual morning swim, and I guess didn't quite shake it all off.'

Janet tutted, reached for a cloth and handed it to him. 'Down by your foot, Mr Long, and there, in the doorway, if you please.'

'Sure. Yes, thank you.' He bent and wiped very efficiently. Then, straightening up, 'I'll put her outside, give her clean straw and some water. Excuse me for a moment longer, will you?' He didn't wait for an answer but rapidly took the dog outside.

Davey glanced across at Loveday and shared a smile. Janet pursed her lips tighter and refilled the kettle.

Henry Long came back and sat down beside Loveday, who looked at him apologetically and said, 'Mr Long, I meant to tell you yesterday, but, but—'

'Yes, Miss Jenkins?' He had caught a touch of the sun and his eyes seemed brighter than usual. He looked at her – a bit stiffly, but definitely with a hint of a smile – and Loveday thought that his usual severe expression seemed a little less severe, slightly warmer and even almost approachable.

Firmly she pushed these odd thoughts out of her mind. *Never mind how he looks, tell him about Mr Benedict.* 'Well,' she said, 'I told you that Mr Benedict was in Newfoundland years ago and you said you would like to see him – I saw him yesterday, he's not at all well, but he's invited you to visit him.'

Henry Long stirred honey into his porridge. He looked at her thoughtfully. 'I remember,' he said. 'Yes, I'll go. Perhaps this evening.' He took a large mouthful of porridge.

Loveday felt the subject was closed, but heard herself say, 'You could come with me if you like.' As ever, the words came out without thought and she felt a blush creeping up her cheeks as she looked down at the toast on her plate. But it was such a good idea. 'I walk along the beach on my way to Sothern House on a Monday morning, and I could take you to Mr Benedict's cottage at the bottom of East Cliff,' she offered. 'That is, if it's convenient . . . I mean, if you think—' The toast split into crumbs and one landed on his lap.

Sitting side by side, they looked at each other, Loveday scarlet, Henry Long clearly feeling he was being inveigled into something alien to his wants. He frowned. 'That's kind of you, but—' Then he stopped, thought, allowed his mouth to curve upwards and added unexpectedly, 'Sure, I'll be glad to come with you.' He gave her another enquiring look. 'And what's wrong with this Mr Benedict, may I ask?'

Janet, watching all this, came to Loveday's aid. 'Old age,' she said wryly as she refilled the empty teacups and offered further porridge to the lodger. 'Frank must be getting on now, and all that sailing to and fro to Newfoundland for the cod did him no good at all.'

'Frostbitten toes,' murmured Loveday, on safe ground again.

'I see.' Henry Long said *no thank you* to more porridge but *yes* to toast which Loveday passed to him. After a moment he added, 'It was a hard life out there, and not at all a healthy, or even a long one.'

Loveday's spine prickled He knew about the far land. Again the unthinking words rushed out, 'My father was lost at sea going back there—'

A taut silence filled the room. Henry Long methodically spread butter, then looked into Loveday's shocked eyes. 'I'm so sorry, Miss Jenkins,' he said, his voice surprisingly gentle. 'You must miss him a lot.'

She nodded, staring down at her crumb-littered plate, thankful when Aunt Janet said firmly, 'Now, Loveday, hurry up – give yourself time to introduce Mr Long to Frank and don't be late reaching Sothern House.' She reached across for empty plates. 'I don't want Mrs Sothern thinking badly of you.'

They walked briskly along the esplanade and down the steps, Loveday suggesting that a walk on the beach was preferable to being above it, with Floss and Henry beside her. The huge dog bounded in and out of the surf and Henry looked at ease with the wind blowing his rather long hair and forcing him to remove his hat. Loveday's curiosity bloomed and she heard herself asking, 'When did you leave Newfoundland, Mr Long?'

He paused for a few steps as if thinking back. Then, 'Quite a few years ago. I came to England when my parents died, finished my education here, then did an apprenticeship in my uncle's boatyard in Dorset.' The low voice was hard and tight.

'Oh.' She wished she hadn't pried into his life. How difficult it must be for him to tell a stranger all these private things. A quick glance at his set face revealed just how difficult it had been. Loveday thought and then said quietly, 'My father was lost at sea – I told you – and I only had my mother for a few years . . . so I – I know how you must have felt when your parents died, Mr Long.'

'Thank you.' Turning his head, he looked into her eyes and she saw a new depth in their guarded darkness. Strange, she thought, how everybody has troubled family memories. Stranger still that she and Mr Long both had parents who had been in Newfoundland.

Again, curiosity pushed her to ask, 'And were your parents in the fishing trade, Mr Long? My father was.'

He looked past her, out at the horizon, a distant indigo blur, and for a moment she thought he resented her question, but then he smiled rather faintly, and his voice lightened. 'My father was a lighthouse keeper. We lived at Cape Thunder until his death in a particularly wild storm. And my mother died soon after. An uncle adopted me and then educated me – and now he's dead too.'

Listening, Loveday understood that he was still trying, perhaps unsuccessfully, to accept life's hardships. She drew in a deep breath. 'So you're all alone?' she said spontaneously.

'No. I have Floss.' Suddenly the tense, sharply angled face softened and spread into a grin, new warmth in the eyes hinting at amusement.

'And now you're here with us, in Teignmouth.' What on earth had made her say that? It wasn't as if she was part of a happy family. She felt the colour grow in her cheeks and at once started walking more quickly. 'That's Mr Benedict's cottage, over there.' She nodded up the beach and headed for the steps on to the promenade. 'I do hope he's feeling better today.'

As usual, the door was ajar, and Crystal still slept on the window sill, until Floss nosed around the small garden, making the cat rise and arch her back, hissing.

'Floss,' said Henry, 'come here, girl. Sit down and wait. Just there.'

The huge dog obediently sat on the path beside the door, then lay down, head between paws, black eyes pools of interest, watching as Loveday and Henry entered the cottage.

'How are you, Mr Benedict?' She went to his side, taking in the ashes in the grate and the empty bowl on the hearth beside his chair and at once producing the cough medicine and pan of beef tea Janet had carefully packed into the small bag she carried.

'Same as ever, no need to worry. My word, that smells good.' The old man looked brighter and struggled to sit up straighter in the chair, smothering a cough.

'Let me help.' Henry was at his side, arms around the bony shoulders.

'So you're the chap Loveday tells me about? Know about the old rock, do you, then? Sit down, b'y, sit down.' Frank's voice was stronger today, and as Loveday kindled the fire and put a pan on the trivet over the flames, she realized that this expected visit had been enough to bring new energy into the failing body.

Henry Long pulled up a stool and sat opposite the chair. He and Frank Benedict looked at each other assessingly, and then Loveday saw smiles spread and voices meld as Frank began asking questions and Henry Long obligingly answered them.

'I can't stay,' she said, reluctantly. 'I have to go – my lesson with Miss Eleanor, you see – goodbye, Mr Benedict. I'll come again tomorrow. Goodbye, Mr Long.'

Outside the door Floss's unblinking eyes, half hidden beneath the shaggy fringe, watched her run down the path, on to the road and up East Cliff, hearing the church clock strike the hour and knowing that she was late. But somehow she didn't much care today about Mrs Sothern's certain reprimands.

Life was full of other, far more important things. One of them was that she hoped desperately that she didn't encounter Maggie, her mother, while she was in the house.

The kitchen was noisier than usual. The fire and the new gas stove radiated heat through the room and Loveday heard voices raised in argument as she passed through, exchanging smiles as everyone stopped talking for a few seconds, suddenly seeing her.

Mrs Derby, red cheeked as she pounded dough, said, with a chuckle, 'Watch yer step this morning, Miss Jenkins. Herself don't feel well disposed towards anyone – not that it's ever any different.'

Loveday paused, recalling Ned's words about Mrs Sothern being ill. 'I'm sorry to hear that,' she said. 'I do hope Mrs Sothern is recovering from her chill?'

'Chill?' Mrs Derby's scornful voice trumpeted through the room. 'She's had no chill.'

'But on Friday evening—' Loveday was frowning.

A great hoot of laughter greeted her words. 'Her went to a supper party over to Dawlish. New friends. Lots of young men, so Sharrow, the coachman, told us. Didn't get home till all hours – and you think she was ill?' More laughter, and Loveday was thankful to close the green baize door behind her and go up to the drawing-room.

But Ned had said Issy was ill – and yet she hadn't been. So Ned had lied. And why should he lie? She paused at the top of the staircase. Because he knew she would never have gone out with him – alone – if he hadn't told her Issy would be there.

So Ned is a liar. And I thought he was well-intentioned. Nice. Honest. But he's not.

And then she looked around her anxiously. No sign of Maggie, thank goodness. Her mind was suddenly full of yesterday's revelations and the anger that had surged through her. Today it was still there, but different, somehow. But this was no time to think about it.

When Ned's voice sounded from a distance, coming down the stairs from the upper floor, with Eleanor's giggles weaving in and out of his cheerful words, Loveday rapidly went into the drawing room, busying herself putting music on the stand and not looking around when Eleanor came in, saying, 'Uncle Ned's going to arrange a picnic, Miss Jenkins. Won't it be fun? Would you like to come?'

'I don't think so, thank you, Miss Eleanor. Now, please settle down and let us start our lesson, shall we?'

Eleanor pouted, looked towards the door and called out, 'Uncle Ned! I want to come into the garden with you and be in the photograph. Please wait, will you?'

And Ned's light, easy voice answering back, 'No hurry, Eleanor. It'll take me a while to get the staff together and arrange things. Oh, and when you do come, bring Miss Jenkins, please. Tell her it's important.'

Eleanor sat at the piano, looking pleased with herself. 'Did you hear what Uncle Ned said, Miss Jenkins?'

'I did,' said Loveday sharply. 'Now will you please play me the scale of C major – with both hands? And Miss Eleanor . . . kindly concentrate. This is important.'

'So is the garden photograph,' muttered Eleanor, but then sighed as her hands touched the keys and the familiar notes began to fill the room.

Mrs Sothern appeared at the end of the lesson, looking at her step-daughter with a frown and then at Loveday, who was putting music sheets away into her bag. 'Miss Jenkins, my cousin, Mr Kerslake, is very eager to take us out for a picnic one day soon – something to do with his photography. He suggests we go to Labrador Bay, which means either taking a boat or forcing the horses up those terrible hills. My stepdaughter is adamant that you must accompany us. Of course, you will agree to come.'

Loveday thought she had never received such an unwelcoming invitation. She felt herself disliking everything about Mrs Sothern – *Issy* – especially the fact that she was dressed in a particularly becoming morning dress of pale pink and carrying a beautiful hat to match. But then the idea of a picnic overcame her irritation, and she said calmly, 'Thank you, Mrs Sothern. I should like to come very much, but I fear my work doesn't end until four o'clock in the afternoon. So I don't think—'

'Nonsense, you can easily tell your employer that I have invited you.' Mrs Sothern's voice was full of the usual hauteur. 'I shall need you to help with the picnic basket, and to stop Miss Eleanor climbing the rocks.' She paused. 'Will there be rocks? I don't know the place but Mr Kerslake has heard about its attractive scenery.' She sighed, rearranged the artificial flowers around the brim of her hat, and then added, 'I shall tell him that he must organise the outing – perhaps you can recommend a reliable boatman – and then inform me of the details. Now, Eleanor, come into the garden and let us see what your Uncle Ned is doing.'

Eleanor gave Loveday a meaningful stare before following her stepmama down the stairs, through the hall and out into the garden. Slowly, Loveday also followed, wondering at several things. Why had Ned lied? Why did he want to go to Labrador Bay, which was a difficult little bay to land on from the sea, and even harder to climb down to from the road above. Was it just photographs? Or could it be – she walked thoughtfully down the gravel path towards the cedar gazebo at the bottom of the long border, where she saw the garden staff assembled, with Ned arranging them into a group – that it was another plot to have her beside him? And yet, this time, not alone? But he would be sure to have an idea to somehow avoid being too much in the view of picnickers. In which case, of course, she wouldn't go.

But she knew she would.

'Stand together, please, with your tools. That man on the right – yes, you, with the bowler hat – come forward a bit.' Ned Kerslake was too busy organizing his group of garden staff to notice at first the arrival of his cousin and her stepdaughter. Loveday watched from the shade of an overhanging lilac bush and saw Mrs Sothern and Eleanor enter the gazebo. Eleanor wouldn't sit still and her stepmama chided her loudly, but when Ned turned, his encouraging smile persuaded the child to run to his side.

'Did you bring Miss Jenkins?' he asked, looking around as he slotted glass plates into his camera, already positioned on the tripod.

'She's over there.' Eleanor nodded towards the lilac bush and Loveday saw Ned look around at her.

He was smiling in the way that she knew was special. Not just an encouraging smile for Eleanor, or a saucy one for Issy, but that warm, twinkling-eyed smile that she was sure was just for her alone. Of course, she smiled back, forgetting her previous doubts about him. And then a feeling of pleasure began to spread through her. Suddenly the day was brighter, the sun shone, the lilac fragrance enclosed her, birds sang, and Ned and she would meet again very soon. She had been wrong to think he was anything other than friendly and warm. And next time, she told herself forcefully, next time they were alone, she wouldn't be so naïve. So childish. If he wanted to kiss her, then . . . then. . . .

'Are you all ready?' Ned's voice was full or authority now, as he prepared to take the photograph of the group in front of him.

Loveday saw that Mr Sharp, the head gardener, stood in the centre looking even more pompous than usual, while beside him stood Ben Marten, a tweed cap on his head and a scowl on his face, while the other undergardener, Jim, and the garden boy, Dickie, completed the group. A wheelbarrow stood in front of Dickie, hoes and spades were clutched hard and the group stared as if the camera might be about to shoot rather than photograph them.

As Ned disappeared behind the black cloth and the seconds mounted up, Loveday saw Ben's scowl grow ever more fierce and when the photographs – for Ned insisted on taking two more – were successfully completed and the group walked away to their neglected duties, she heard him growl at his companion, 'He'm a man to watch, that chap is. Wouldn't trust him further than I could throw a bad 'tater.'

But Ned was putting away his plates, folding the black cloth, dismantling the tripod and then stacking all his equipment in the large shoulder bag on the ground. He nodded to Mr Sharp, still watching, said casually, 'I'll send the developed prints to your master and no doubt he'll let you have a view of them. Thanks for your help, and good day to you.' He shouldered the bag and walked towards the lilac bush at the side of the garden, where Loveday stood.

She met his smiling gaze, but looked anxiously behind him at the gazebo. 'Mrs Sothern and Miss Eleanor are over there.'

'I know that. But it's you I want to see, Lovey. So what about this picnic I've suggested? Apparently Labrador Bay is interesting and worth a trip. So if you tell me the name of a boatman who can take us there I'll make the arrangements.' He came a step nearer. 'Wear that pretty yellow dress and see Issy's eyes go green.' His laughter soared and Loveday at once moved away.

'I have to go now, Ned.' But how could she meet him again to suggest

111

a likely boatman? Inspiration came quickly. 'Ben Marten, he's one of the under gardeners here – well, his father takes out holidaymakers in his boat sometimes. Why not get him to take us? Ask Mr Sharp if you can have a word with him. I really must go.' And she went rapidly, not looking at the gazebo where she felt sure Mrs Sothern would be fuming, having seen her conversation with Ned, then thankfully running out of the garden and heading for the safety of East Cliff and home.

Loveday tapped at the parlour door and was told to enter. Henry Long sat on a hard chair at a card table Janet had put beside the window to hold all his books and papers. Floss lay at his side, full length on the dark hearthrug, so that dog and rug seemed one large black mass.

He looked up, spectacles pushed to the end of his nose, pen in hand, and got to his feet. 'Miss Jenkins.' No smile as the pen was put down on the table. Floss also rose, coming to Loveday's side and pushing a damp nose into her hand.

'Dinner is ready, Mr Long.'

They looked at each other. She was very aware of the difference between him and Ned Kerslake. Much taller and bigger and eye-catching but thinner, far more elegant and imposing, in his dark suit and white shirt, the collar neatly arranged and a sober tie beneath completing the gentlemanly look. She hesitated. Of course, Mr Long was older than Ned – perhaps in his late twenties? Ned was still so obviously young; very charming, but a little prone to forget manners and expectations. That business of taking her into the dark court and then. . . .

In confusion, she said again, 'Dinner is ready, Mr Long,' and then turned quickly because his slatey eyes were watching her almost too intently.

'Thank you.' His voice followed her. She heard the parlour door close and Floss being told to wait in the hallway until the meal was over.

Dinner was quiet, with Janet's stew and dumplings rapidly disappearing off the plates.

Loveday, though, had little appetite and had to force the meal down. She felt thoroughly upset and not at all her usual bright self. How could she act normally, she wondered miserably, helping Janet to remove plates and set a raspberry jelly on the table. Her life had been completely changed. Too much had happened. First of all Ned, then Maggie and Jack, and now poor Mr Benedict ill and needing looking after.

A sob suddenly erupted and she put down her spoon with a clatter. Janet sucked in a quick breath. 'My dear child,' she said, 'please don't be so upset.' Her anxious, loving glance moved from Davey to Henry Long and back to Loveday. 'Perhaps if you went to your room to compose yourself?'

Loveday shook her head, wiped away the tears and sat up straighter. 'I'm sorry,' she said unsteadily, avoiding all the eyes looking at her. 'It's just that . . . with Mr Benedict so ill, everything seems to get worse and worse.' She sniffed hard, cleared her throat and stared at the plate holding a spoonful of wobbly pink jelly.

The low, vibrant, drawling voice was very close to her as a hand reached out, unobserved, to touch her own, clutched hard in her lap. 'Miss Jenkins,' he said quietly, 'never apologize for suffering such feelings. We all have them.'

Surprised and strangely comforted, she looked at him, seeing that his eyes, guarded as ever, actually had a warmth that gave his lean face a softer look, and then as she nodded slowly, saw a hint of amusement soften the straight mouth. 'Even Floss. Do you know, when I first had her, she used to howl when she was on her own. But no longer, because she knows for sure I won't ever leave her, or let harm come to her.'

Eyebrow raised, Janet glanced at Davey before watching Loveday who was somehow managing to smile. Slowly things returned to normal. 'Some cream with your jelly, Mr Long?' And an extra spoonful because of his perception.

Henry's hand slipped away as he gave his hostess a brief smile before enjoying the rewarding sweetness. Beside him, Loveday trifled with her jelly and, surprising herself, managed to eat it all. So he knew about feelings. About being left alone and being afraid. And she had thought him a strange man who had no feelings at all. How wrong she had been.

With such thoughts filling her head and beginning to make yesterday's awful scenes a little less haunting, Loveday returned to the Beach View Hotel, where she obtained Mrs Narracott's grudging permission to be absent for a day to be named by Mrs Sothern for the proposed picnic.

'Well, I s'pose I can't say no to 'er – but you'll have to make up the time later,' she grumbled, and Loveday went up to the bedrooms, to sweep up sand and toffee wrappers, to tidy away clothes, make beds and open windows to let the fresh, sweet air in while her thoughts circled in great, puzzling clouds, varying between deep unhappiness and a whispering, unexpected hope for something not yet known.

When she left the Hotel, just after four o'clock, it wasn't Ned who waited for her on the pavement as she had hoped, but Henry Long who removed his hat, pulled Floss closer to his side and said quickly, 'I thought I might meet you here, Miss Jenkins. I've just come from Mr

113

Benedict. I fear that he's no better today, but he asked me to give you this.'

Out of his jacket pocket he took the piece of carved scrimshaw which Loveday recognized at once. It was from Frank's cabinet of curiosities, where her cowry was, the one she had thought might be a token of good luck. That seemed so long ago, and so much had happened since. She turned over the bone piece and felt the carvings against the palm of her hand. Saw the tall figure holding something, the woman's blurred face and then the smaller one running away, and then – just indistinct letters, spirals and flowers.

'Thank you,' she said at last. 'But . . . but why should he give it to me now? I mean—' She guessed that poor Frank was dying, but was too wretched to say so.

Henry Long's voice was low. 'Why don't we take a walk? And sit down over there in the shelter? I have something important to say to you, Miss Jenkins.'

In a daze, she went with him and Floss into the shaded pavilion, happily empty of other people, and they sat side by side with the dog lying at their feet.

Henry Long turned to her. 'Miss Jenkins, have you never thought that your father may not have been lost at sea? That he might have survived and even be alive today?'

She shook her head, staring into his eyes and wondering at the interest she saw there. 'I . . . I . . . no, I hadn't thought.'

But now she did. Father, perhaps alive. Why, he might even be coming home – to his family. To Maggie, to Jack and herself. But then she knew it was just a dream. Just another of her imagined far lands – the happy family of stories and hearsay. But it could never be for her. Slow anger began to kindle inside her and she looked at Henry Long suspiciously.

'I don't know if you mean to be kind,' she said, 'but all you're doing is raising my hopes. And I can't do with that.'

Again, Henry Long's hand found hers, his long, hard fingers strong and somehow reassuring. 'I understand how you feel,' he said, 'but believe me, all we have to do is to find out the truth of the matter.'

She caught her breath. 'And how do we do that?'

'Ways and means, Miss Jenkins.' The brief, rapid smile surfaced for a second as he pressed her hand very firmly. 'Ways and means. Leave it to me.'

114

CHAPTER ELEVEN

At first, after Loveday learned that Maggie was her mother, she had felt
torn apart, thinking wretchedly that she would never be the same again.
And she was right, for each new day she discovered something new about
herself.

When the growing light and the sounds of life outside in the street
awoke her in the morning she watched the June sunlight stream through
the new curtains and slowly bring fresh energy into the little room which
was now her refuge and felt, just for a moment, excited and almost hopeful.

On the dressing table her shell collection basked in the filtered rays,
each small, curiously shaped piece evoking happy memories and briefly
removing the recollections of the awful scene last Sunday afternoon. She
looked at them fondly. There was the pelican's foot Uncle Davey had
found for her years ago. Next to it a long razor shell she'd dug out of the
wet mud, thinking it looked like some sort of ladder going down into the
depths of the world. Then, among the variously shaped cowries she'd
found on the beach, was a huge coral-coloured conch shell which the
kind owner of the shell shop had seen her looking at through his window
one cold winter's day and given to her, saying. 'Listen to it, maid – 'tis
full of sunshine and hot sand.' Loveday smiled. That was probably the
start of her dreams about other, far lands.

But on this particular morning it was the piece of scrimshaw that
caught her waking eye. She was curious about it; the long piece of bone
with its black pictures inscribed. By whom? What did they mean? And
above all, why had Mr Benedict asked Mr Long to give it to her? As she
got up and dressed, Loveday's thoughts centred on the sick old man and
she knew she must go and see him sometime today. As soon as work was
over she would come home, collect whatever kind Aunt Janet could spare
in the way of food and medicine and then walk along the beach to his

115

cottage. She had questions to ask; her mind darkened. He was clearly very sick and she knew she must get there before it was too late.

And then she recalled what Henry Long had said, that maybe her father was alive. That extraordinary and hardly believable idea, together with Henry's quick, brief smile at breakfast, brightened her and as she hurried along the esplanade to the Beach View Hotel, she began wondering. 'Ways and means, Miss Jenkins.' What had he meant? Could he really find out about her father?

About Amos Hunt?

Then suddenly, pausing as she tied her apron around her, before gathering the box of cleaning equipment and climbing the stairs to the messy bedrooms, she knew she must acknowledge her proper name. Not Miss Jenkins any longer.

I am Loveday Hunt and everyone must call me that now.

Mrs Narracott and Susan were the first to know. At dinner time she said, very determinedly, 'I've just found out who I really am – please call me Loveday Hunt. That was my father's name, you see.' She heard a ring of pride in her voice. Susan giggled and Mrs Narracott gave a bemused frown. 'But I thought as you was Janet and Davey's adopted girl.'

Loveday, preparing to leave and go home, looked back over her shoulder. 'Well, I'm afraid you were wrong. I'm Maggie and Amos Hunt's daughter.'

Returning to Market Street, she marvelled at the easy manner in which all that had come out. As if she were proud of the fact. As if she had been waiting all these nineteen long years to know who she really was. Well, now she had a father and a mother. And then the old rage ignited again.

She gave me away. She never loved me. No, I won't see her, not ever.

After tea, when she had changed from her working dress to the old faded pale-blue linen, too short in the sleeves, and a bit tight over the chest, but still good enough for a summer's evening outing, she carried her basket of Aunt Janet's soup and a small bowl of junket, together with another dose of horehound and honey cough syrup, along the beach to Frank Benedict's cottage.

He was slouched in his chair, eyes closed, with Crystal purring on his lap, when she knocked at the door and entered. 'Come in, maid, come in.' The words were slurred and his voice was so quiet she hardly heard it, but the old eyes brightened as she smiled and unpacked the basket.

The cat stretched and jumped to the floor and she helped the old man to sit up straighter. 'You'm a good maid. An' that b'y, that Henry Long, he's all right. Had a good old tell we did; he and his family living near where we made the fish, that headland we called Cape Thunder. Lighthouse people they were, so he knows 'bout the hardships and the sea and the wind.'

The soup was going down easily and Loveday, sitting on the stool opposite, wondered if this was the moment to ask about the piece of scrimshaw. But before she started, suddenly Frank looked at her with a new light in his eyes, spoon poised above the bowl. 'Tell 'ee what, my bird, heard a chap playing old music yesterday. Someone with a squeeze box – not far away. Outside the church I reckon – wanted to get up and have a look, but no, I couldn't.'

Seeing the question hovering over his mouth and knowing what it was, she nodded. 'If I see him along the promenade, Mr Benedict, I'll ask him to come and see you. What sort of music was it?'

The soup forgotten, Frank slumped back in his chair and Loveday caught the bowl just before it spilled. She saw memories being evoked, small pleasures relived. And then he said slowly, 'Sea music, it were. A jolly sort o' song we used to sing when the work were done, when we could warm up, have a drink and think of anything but cod; when an ole fiddle scraped and someone else blowed his pipe or whistle. Why now . . . it's comin' back . . . something 'bout *come all you jolly fishermen.*'

She watched his eyes closing, saw the disappointed tightening of the mouth. 'Damme, can't recall it now. Old age, what a curse it be.'

'Never mind, Mr Benedict, finish your soup before it gets cold. If I find the man who was playing, I'll definitely bring him along here.' With bright, hopeful words and a smile she tried hard to bring new cheer into his sunken face and when she left he was stroking the cat which, once again, was on his lap.

'I'll jest have a l'il nap, now, maid . . . you go along, and thanks for coming, and thanks to your aunt for all her kindness.' He was yawning, and she left with a feeling that maybe, after all, the sickness was getting better. There would be another chance to ask him about the scrimshaw in a day or so.

Ben Marten shouted to her across the street as she crossed Northumberland Place. 'Loveday, I got a message for 'ee.' He caught up with her and she saw a certain gleam in his usually mild eyes, which broke into her thoughts and alarmed her.

'What is it, Ben?'

'My dad's agreed to take Mrs Sothern and her lot in his boat over to Labrador on Tuesday next week. Ses he reckons as how the weather'll be good and he's got time to clean out the boat ready for her ladyship to get in it.'

Loveday smiled. Yes, she knew what the town thought of Isobel Sothern's high and mighty ways. 'That's good, Ben. So it's all arranged? Then I only have to tell Mrs Narracott that I'm taking the afternoon off.' She paused. 'And Mr Kerslake? Does he know? Have you given him the message, too?'

Ben's sunbronzed face tightened. 'What would I want to be talkin' to that smarmy geezer fer, then? No, went to the kitchen and asked Mrs Derby to tell Mrs Sothern and she did and came back and said all right. 'Er'll be at my dad's boat at three o'clock sharp. And you'll be in charge of the picnic basket, she said. Tell 'ee what, Loveday, I might jest have the afternoon off, too.' He grinned and she saw the hardness in his eyes soften into laughter. 'Reckon that picnic basket needs two lots of hands to get it off the boat, eh? Yes, I'll be there, maid, you can count on me. Mr Sharp, why, he'll jest have to do without me for a coupla hours.' The grin grew large and sunny. Ben slipped his hand over hers and stepped closer. 'All right, then, Loveday?'

She smiled, amused at the proposed mischief, quite ready herself to make the most of Mrs Sothern's expedition. 'Yes, Ben. I'll be there.'

At the top of Market Street he pulled her to a stop and looked intently into her eyes. 'Something diff'rent 'bout you today, Loveday.' He frowned. 'Not that Kerslake feller, is it?'

'Don't be silly, Ben.' For a moment she paused, but then said slowly, 'It's just that I've learned who I really am. My name's not Jenkins, but Hunt.' Just for a second pain stabbed but she took a deep breath and went on. 'My mother has come back after a long time away, and I have a brother too. Jack – I think you know him.'

Ben stared. 'So he's yer brother? B'y who wants so bad to go to sea? Well, dang me . . . but if you've got a new name, then that's why you'm different.' He frowned more deeply. 'Seems like you're goin' some other place, Loveday, an I don't like it. An' I reckon it's not jes the name, but that smarmy Kerslake chap. Oh yes, I seed you an' 'im, that night . . . well—'

The hardness was back in his eyes. She watched a scowl slide across his face and felt her stomach turning over. She didn't need more trouble, especially not with her old friend Ben. Carefully, choosing her words, she said, 'Don't be silly. I'm not different and I'm not going anywhere. And as for Mr Kerslake—'

'*Ned.*' The word was full of hatred.

'Yes, Ned.' Quick annoyance flooded through her. 'And if I do have any feelings for Ned, well, it's nothing to do with you, Ben. Just remember that. And now I must get on. I've got nothing more to say to you, so goodbye.'

Rapidly she walked away, aware of him watching, and then hearing his voice shouting after her, 'I'll see you on Tuesday then. An' tell that feller he better mind his manners in future. I'll be watchin'.'

After supper the next evening, Henry Long went into the parlour, tidied his notes on his day in Kenneth Harvey's files of past and present boat-building plans and designs and then came out, folding his spectacles and putting them in his waistcoat pocket as he walked into the kitchen where Janet and Loveday were putting away the remains of the meal.

He was becoming aware of some sort of disturbance in the household which had seemed so quiet and peaceful when he arrived last week and this wasn't at all what he needed. He had much to do and think about. Old man Harvey was turning out to be a ditherer in his failing years, and though friendly and possibly inclined to relish Henry's tactful suggestions about possible future designs, was taking his time to decide.

'Yes, Long, well of course you're very progressive and modern ... hmmmm, I really must try and catch up with things. But give me time, boy, give me time.'

Which was anathema to a busy and fast mind. And – a final annoying thought – this domestic disturbance in number 6 Market Street was clearly all to do with the girl, Loveday.

At the kitchen door he paused, watching the two women tidying up. He approved of Janet Jenkins – a good woman with a strong mind, which was something he instinctively admired. And the brother, Davey, nice enough: a good worker and clever with his accounting work. Getting on in years, of course; for a moment Henry considered whether Davey would retire when Kenneth Harvey did, which, with luck and some further intense discussions, would be in the fairly foreseeable future.

But then his eye fell on Loveday and the feeling of unease strengthened. She had almost broken down at dinner the other day; well, women, of course, were of nervous disposition and quite unable to meet the natural hazards of everyday life with their weaker strength But his first impression of this young woman had been to embody her with capability, resolution and strength. When they met at the station he had immediately felt her spirit; but now she appeared almost a victim of whatever it was that upset the family, and he had no wish to become involved.

119

He found himself pushing away a grudging smile, thinking as he did so that those wide eyes and friendly charm had upset his idealistic and masculine ideas more than he liked to consider. There was no time or place for a woman in his life; of course, there had been slight dalliances with various feminine charmers as he grew up, but now – now that ambition and determination powered his life – those memories and needs were blanked out and had no further hold on him.

So why was he saying, 'Miss Jenkins—?' in an enquiring voice.

Janet looked across the room. 'Yes, Mr Long?'

He blinked, frowned. 'So sorry – of course you're both Miss Jenkins, aren't you?'

At once, wide grey-green eyes stared into his from where Loveday was stacking plates on the dresser. 'No, I'm Miss Hunt.'

She spoke without thought, then paused and looked at Janet, wondering fearfully what her aunt must feel at this painful declaration of independence; then, receiving a nod and a warm smile of understanding, she looked at Henry. Her cheeks started to flush but it didn't matter. Everyone must know who she was now. She chose her next words carefully, aware that her aunt was watching. 'My family has just come together again after some years, Mr Long. And—' She swallowed the lump forming in her throat. 'And things have become clearer. So I'm not Miss Jenkins any longer, you see.'

Henry gave an acknowledging half-bow, which gave him time to consider before replying. So this was it, was it? Family problems. Well, he didn't want to know. 'I'm sorry for my mistake, Miss Hunt. But thank you for telling me.' He moved away, ready to leave the disturbance behind him but suddenly Loveday was laughing and he turned back.

How ridiculous this was, she thought. *Better to make light of it.* She smiled. 'So who do you really want to speak to? My aunt, or me?'

They looked at each other across the room.

'Both of you, I guess.' Henry looked into those wide eyes, watched Loveday's feelings chase each other over her beautiful young face, and, for a moment, had an amazing thought that he should do what he could to help things along. Why not take her out of the house and its sad atmosphere? Would it help her to reclaim her good spirits, to smile again with the freedom he recalled from their encounter at the station?

As usual, with ideas, he had to put them into action immediately. He cleared his throat. 'Let's get this straight – I would like to invite you, Miss Hunt, to walk along the beach with Floss and me, but I would also like to ask Miss Jenkins if she has any objection to the idea.'

Janet's face cracked into the hint of a smile as she walked slowly towards him, putting her hand on the door latch, her dark eyes inspecting him very intently. 'My niece must answer for herself, Mr Long, but I think the idea is a good one. She needs some fresh air after working all day, and even some company, perhaps.' A pause, then she nodded. 'And I know that she will be safe with you.'

Henry bowed again, feeling slightly out of sorts. What was he doing? But this nice woman must be reassured. 'No harm will come to her, Miss Jenkins – I will care for her.'

Janet nodded, gave him an approving smile and went out of the room, leaving Loveday looking at Henry Long and wondering at his choice of words. No harm – I will care for her.

She met his deep-set eyes, wondered if he had really meant to give such an invitation and then decided to accept it. She had a wry thought that something had forced him into it, and then her customary curiosity persuaded her that it would be interesting to try to find out why he had done so. She smiled, trying to mask such feminine wiles. 'I'd love to come, Mr Long. And please call me Loveday.'

'Thank you. And you know my name – Henry.'

A moment's silence as they looked at each other. And then, 'I'll get my shawl,' she said, moving towards the door.

'And I'll tell Floss she has a treat in store.' As he went into the back yard she heard his voice returning to that easy, casual drawl.

In the hall, she put on her hat and considered Henry's invitation. In spite of his authoritative manner, he had certainly brought a new feeling into the house. He moved fast, spoke fast, made decisions, she was sure, with equal rapidity, and altogether, in some strange way, was spreading a more positive atmosphere. Aunt Janet was impressed by him, that was quite clear. Uncle Davey, nodding sagely, had said that Mr Harvey found him clever, helpful even if a bit masterful. 'A good chap,' he told them, 'but I'm not sure what game he's playing. And Mr Harvey isn't saying – not yet.'

So, thought Loveday, waiting outside the front door, if he plays games, what sort of game is this, asking me to walk with him and Floss? Does he want something? *Surely not. He's a man who is completely self sufficient. But – how intriguing. I must try and find out more.*

As they walked they talked about the chattering holiday makers, watched Floss swimming strongly in the ebbing tide, heard the concert blaring out from the pier, and slowly Loveday grew easier in her mind. Suddenly she drew a quick breath and looked at her companion. 'I'd almost forgotten. Mr Benedict told me he'd heard an accordion player near the church yesterday and he recognized the music that was being played. A sort of sea shanty, I suppose. I said I would try and find the man and ask him to visit. I wonder—?'

He nodded, called Floss out of the water. 'Sure. I think I can help. Someone was playing outside the Jolly Sailor when I passed by before supper. Shall we go and see if he's still there?'

Gus Andrews was his name, a huge, thin man with grizzled hair and a skin like tanned leather. But his fingers worked magic, persuading amazing music out of his worn old accordion.

Loveday was thrilled. For a few moments they stood outside the inn, listening to the tunes. Gus sat on the bench with his cap on the pavement, half-full of copper coins. She turned to Henry. 'Do you think he might go and play for Mr Benedict?'

'Why not? I'll ask him.' Henry frowned. 'I guess I know that song. The seamen often sang it when they were waiting for the tide.'

Loveday watched as he dropped coins into the cap and looked down at Gus. She didn't hear the conversation because of the noise coming from the inn, but saw how the old musician grinned and nodded. Henry turned, looking at her and smiled. 'He says he remembers someone called Benedict. He's going there now – shall we join him?'

They walked down the esplanade with Gus Andrews, and found Frank Benedict's front door ajar as usual. Henry knocked, heard a faint voice and nodded at Loveday. 'Go in,' he said. 'Tell him about the music. Or if he's not well enough, we'll come back tomorrow.' His thoughts, as he gestured Gus to sit on the garden bench, and told Floss to stay, were busy. Something about the old boy inside the cottage had taken him back to Newfoundland; they had talked about storms and the beauty of the spring in that hard rocky place. And now he felt that the music would unite them even further. He hadn't reckoned on ever having to think back to his boyhood, but the memories were being hurled at him and, strangely, in this one instance, he had no strength to deny them.

And again, of course, it was the girl who had brought him to this. Loveday Jenkins – no, Hunt. What was it about her that he found so difficult to ignore? He was frowning when she appeared in the doorway, smiling, saying 'he wants you both to come in,' she nodded towards Gus, 'and to hear some of your old songs.'

Inside the cottage Frank Benedict was a small, frail figure in the dilapidated chair by the half-dead fire, but his smile was a welcome. 'Good of you to come,' he wheezed. 'Thought as I 'eard your music – like to 'ear more.' He nodded at Gus who was shouldering his instrument and flexing large calloused fingers.

The notes began squeezing out in a fast, rhythmic tune that set Loveday's feet tapping. She watched Henry, standing behind Frank's chair, watching Gus play, and looking very different from the autocratic man she had met at the station nearly a week ago. Could he be thawing a bit? Did the music do to him what it did to her? Make her forget troubles, set her fingers snapping, entice her legs to dance?

And then – Frank's thin voice was singing and Henry was taking it up. Gus Andrews was grinning and playing even faster. Loveday watched and listened in amazement as the words became clear, and she knew instinctively that she was hearing a song born in that rocky far land of which she had always dreamed.

Henry's voice was clear and true and he sang without embarrassment, smiling over Frank's head and fixing his eyes on Loveday's surprised face.

Come all you jolly fishermen who sail the mighty sea,
Come sing and dance, with heel and toe,
And bring back fish for me.

And then Loveday heard the change into a minor key and held her breath as the music saddened. Henry's voice faded and Frank's gasping words were almost inaudible, just loud enough for her to understand that the sea was a monster who always wins.

But when waves leap and storms do blow, forget your jolly glee,
Lash tight your spars, tie hard your knots,
And come back safe to me.

Silence as the accordion wheezed to an end and no one spoke. Gus spat into the fireplace and Henry put his hands on the back of Frank's chair as the old man closed his eyes and lowered his head to his chest.

Loveday moved to the harmonium in the far end of the room. She had no idea of what she was doing, for the music and the images had taken hold of her and all she knew was that she needed to hear that other little tune. The sad little piece that Father had once played on his scrapey old fiddle, so many years ago.

Seated, her fingers moved without thought and the plaintive notes filled the room. When the tune was finished she still sat there, her back to the watchers, her eyes staring at the blank limewashed wall behind the harmonium, but her thoughts far away.

The far land. My father. . . .

It was Gus Andrews who brought her back to reality. He was on his feet, unstrapping the accordion, looking down at Frank Benedict, and saying in his rough, wheezy voice, 'Reckon I'll stop along you, Frank. See to yer fire and yer food if as how you'll give me a sleeping place for the night.'

Loveday got up, turned, saw Frank smile and nod. Henry came to her side. 'Seems a good idea,' he said in a low voice. 'A bit of companionship is what he needs. And we'll come again tomorrow and see how things are.'

We, thought Loveday, returned from dreams to the reality of the situation. She blinked. *Yes, if Gus stays Mr Benedict will be looked after. And I'll come tomorrow as Henry says. We – will he really come, too?* She nodded, whispered 'Yes' and then, smiling goodbye to the old man, moved towards the door.

Outside the sun was setting, its fiery rays lighting a stormy sky half-filled with pale apricot clouds tinged with deepening grey and indigo. The tide was nearly full, waves already lapping against the sea wall, foam hissing as it struck stone and then fell back. She shivered for no reason and was glad when Henry came to her side. Floss brushed against her and lifted dark eyes as she put her hand down to stroke the huge black head.

Henry stood silently for a moment or two, and then said quietly, 'There's an old tradition that seamen go with the tide, but Frank isn't ready yet. Something more to be done, I guess.'

She looked at him and saw something in his angled face that moved her to say, 'You're being so helpful. I'm grateful – and I know Mr Benedict is, too, though he can't say much.'

'He's said quite a lot already.' The quizzical smile had a touch of humour.

'About what?'

Henry looked down at her. 'You. And your father.'

She drew in a quick breath. 'Tell me.'

'Only what you already know. That your father worked on the rock, was friends with Frank, then decided to come back to England, but left again years later. And his ship was sunk.'

Loveday pulled her shawl tighter about her suddenly chill shoulders. 'And you're going to find out about that,' she said sharply. 'You said you would. Just in case . . . in case he survived.'

Henry put his hand beneath her elbow. 'I will,' he said crisply. 'But right now I'm taking you home. Your aunt will have the hide off me if I keep you out too late.'

They walked back to Market Street in a silence caused by busy minds. Loveday was thinking about the power of music, and of Henry's surprising pleasure in it, and he was cursing himself for offering to find out about Amos Hunt.

As if he didn't have enough on his mind without all that – but tomorrow, or perhaps tonight, he'd write that letter. Yes, all right, then, he would do it tonight. For Loveday's sake.

For Loveday's sake? The thought jolted through him uncomfortably. God in heaven, what was happening to him?

CHAPTER TWELVE

The ship on which Amos found a berth left England on a high, wicked tide. The weather for the first leg of the journey kept up its warning gusts and waves and current. Amos denied his thoughts by thinking of what lay ahead, not behind. Maggie had a family, she would be all right until he sent money back.

And the girl – bright as a button and already independent – nothing could go wrong for her. And although a stab of guilt pierced him, he was still able to smile, remembering how she had sung the old tune he played on his fiddle. She was a pretty child, with a true, sweet voice. They had made music between them, and now the old air came into his dreams, into his mind as he worked with the other crewmen to hoist sails, to pump bilges, scrub decks and climb the ratlines when ordered.

But when the bank of ominous black clouds ran towards them and the waves thrust up into thirty-foot monsters, he, like everyone else on board, thought only of how to survive the coming storm.

Henry sat at the long table in the upstair room of Harvey's shipyard with charts and blueprints and plans littering the space all around him. The sun shining through uncurtained windows reflected too brightly on the papers he was examining and he removed his spectacles to rub his eyes. His suit was too thick, too hot, and Janet Jenkins' tasty dinner lay heavily on his stomach. Cleaning the glasses, he looked at Kenneth Harvey opposite him, supposedly searching through yet another pile of ancient documents, but showing signs of dozing off, and envied him the means of escape from this overwhelming heat.

Kenneth Harvey eased into soft, deep breathing, awoke, gave a snort, cast a hurried look around and made the decision to go home, find his chair in the shady garden with no one to stop him having an afternoon nap. This young man, Long, was too keen, too eager – not at all a chap to spend a hot afternoon with peering through all these musty old records and trying to pick his sleepy brain.

He sniffed loudly. 'Too hot, b'God, Why not take time off? Tell you what, how about you taking a trip round the bay? Jest the day fer it, seas not too choppy, wind's coming round, d'you fancy it, Long?'

Henry stretched his legs beneath the table and with rising enthusiasm allowed his mind to change direction. 'You won't come? Well, I'm game for it, sir. Perhaps a run around to that nearby smuggling bay you told me about? Labrador, I think you called it.'

'Aye, Labrador. Called that because they landed the fish there coming back from the Grand Banks in the north Atlantic. I'll get one of the apprentices to row you out there.'

He rose stiffly, carefully. The rheumatics were getting worse and the vague idea of retirement became a bit more compelling each day. He walked to the door, opened it and shouted down the stairs into the yard, 'Tell Briggs as I wants him.'

Henry smiled to himself as he tided away the papers and watched the old man standing at the top of the staircase. The foreman, Briggs, came clumping up and was given instructions. 'Get the old dinghy out – one of the apprentices can row Mr Long round the Ness to Labrador.'

Henry joined the old man as he slowly descended the stairs. 'The pram dinghy? One of the old boats? Well, I'll be interested to see how it manages, sir,' he said and was given a sharp stare over the shoulders as Harvey replied fiercely, 'Not so old that it can't run better'n all this steam nonsense that everyone's using nowadays.'

Henry knew better than to argue, but as he waited at the wharf in the yard below, his interest grew. There was something about the elegant lines of old craft that, as a draughtsman, fascinated him. And as for steam – well, of course, it was vital to commercial progress and helped the world's trade revolve faster and easier, but he still had a yen for the silence and power of sail. The notebook he carried in his pocket was half full with detailed sketches of old-time schooners, ketches and brigs and he had a strange feeling that there might still be a future for them – somewhere, somehow. But that was for tomorrow – not now. Quickly he collected Floss from the cool spot in the yard where she spent her afternoons being spoilt by the men who seemed to be mostly idle. He smelt the familiar scents of resin, wood, size and grease with relish, saw the hands standing gossiping with no new work to return them to the usual routines. This neglected old yard had clearly had its day, but it could be renovated. Someone could breathe new life into it. Someone. . . .

127

Once in the boat, Mick, the apprentice, rowed through the harbour and out over the bar into the open sea, nodding his head as they passed the newly forested headland of the Ness. 'Celebrated the old queen's jubilee,' he shouted, and grinned. 'Us had a good time – cider and ale and dancin' an' lots o' girls.'

Henry nodded, only half listening. He was more interested in the old dinghy's performance. Not as useless as he had imagined, but with a primitive power that swept through the current with surprising strength, reminding him of the classical galleys of the past. Something to be reckoned with. He took out his notebook and added words to a page already nearly filled with information garnered from all he had read and seen so far at the shipyard.

'Labrador.' Mick nodded towards the bay which had just come into sight as they rounded the headland. 'Smugglers here once, they say. An' fish . . . I'll drop 'ee and then go back. Collect 'ee – what time?'

Henry consulted his watch. 'Give me a couple of hours. I'll have a good look around – maybe a swim. The dog would enjoy that.'

Mick grinned. 'No one to see 'ee here – no ole ladies sayin' as how you shouldn't swim naked. We gets it all the time when we jumps in off the end o' the pier.' His eyes raked the shore. 'Ah, no, there's someone there, see? You'll have to keep yer breeks on after all, mister.'

There was a larger boat already approaching the attractive small bay. As Mick headed for the beach, Henry narrowed his eyes against the sun and looked around at the rocky outcrops, and the steeply wooded cliff with a small café at its foot. Floss was scenting land, standing up and having to be restrained from plunging in and swimming ashore. Henry grinned and kept his hand on her collar.

He watched the big boat grounding and passengers being helped to disembark. There was a child, a young man and two women. One of them – he frowned and looked more keenly – was surely Loveday Hunt. What on earth was she doing here? Why wasn't she still cleaning bedrooms at the Beach View Hotel?

Loveday sat in Daniel Marten's boat beside Ned Kerslake, opposite Mrs Sothern and Eleanor. Baggage – lots of it, canvas chairs, umbrellas and parasols, blankets, the picnic hamper, complete with spirit stove – was stowed in the stern behind the two rowers. Ben had given her a wink as he helped her into the boat and his father Daniel had nodded his shaggy head. She felt in safe hands and for once allowed her thoughts to concentrate on what was happening now, instead of reliving all the dramas and problems of the recent few days.

Water lapped the sides of the boat in a lazy rhythm and she dipped her fingers into it as they rowed out of the harbour and towards the open sea, while the old joy of being in her element slowly spread through her mind. Here, with the ocean all around her, the hot sun beating down on her bare hands and neck, with Ned beside her and the memory of his smile when they had met on the quay, she felt inexplicably happy. And then the longing idea came: *wouldn't it be wonderful to dive in, and swim to the shore? But of course not . . . Issy would be horrified.*

Laughing aloud, she caught Ned's eye and smiled, receiving in return that special smile and the quick, slight touch of his hand, reaching out to hers. For this moment all the troubles in her life had faded into the background and she was content to let it be so. An afternoon off, a picnic on Labrador beach, with Eleanor to look after and to help enjoy the outing, and a chance to smile, unseen, at the memory of Mrs Sothern's horror at the way the boat rocked and the wind flirted with her stupid hat fashioned like a bird's nest with huge flowers rising out of it.

The atmosphere was pleasant. Again, she felt Ned's presence at her side and half turned her head to glance at him. Again that smile. That nod. Those eyes that promised such pleasure.

And now they were on the beach, Eleanor leaping ahead excitedly and her stepmama's shrill voice echoing around the cliff enclosed little bay: 'Eleanor, come here – Miss Jenkins, for goodness sake, look after her—'

Loveday walked rapidly up the beach, knowing that Ned was organizing the off-loading of all the luggage. His voice followed her. 'Take that hamper up to that space below the café. And the rugs – and don't forget the chairs – you, what's your name? Ben? Well then, come on, man, put your shoulder into it.'

At last they were all settled. The chairs were unfolded and Mrs Sothern seated herself nervously on the biggest one. 'It feels very insecure – what if it folds up with me in it?'

Ned laughed loudly. 'You're quite safe. Just sit still, girl, and stop being so silly.'

Already Eleanor was somewhere else: Loveday, recalling her duties, scanned the beach hurriedly. There she was, climbing the rocks and looking back with a triumphant smile on her face.

'Miss Eleanor, wait for me – careful you don't slip on the seaweed.' Reaching her, Loveday found a usefully flat rock and persuaded her lively charge to sit down and look out to sea.

'There's another boat, Miss Jenkins. Is it coming here, do you think?'

Loveday looked and was surprised. Henry Long. Floss. And in one of Kenneth Harvey's old dinghies – was it still seaworthy, she wondered, recalling Uncle Davey's condemnation of old neglected craft lying unused in the failing shipyard. She watched the boy at the oars skilfully land the boat alongside the one they had all arrived in, her thoughts running in circles. So what was Henry doing here? Just a coincidence, surely? He couldn't have known she was there – quickly she reprimanded her imagination that he might have come because. . . . *Don't be so stupid! He's far too busy at the shipyard, caught up in his everlasting papers and notebooks and charts to think of picnics – even if he had known.*

'Miss Hunt!'

She stood up, holding Eleanor's hand, wondering what to do. What to say.

Eleanor looked up at her. 'Is he calling you, Miss Jenkins? He's got your name wrong, hasn't he? Oh, and look at that enormous dog!'

At once all the old muddles flew back into her mind as she watched Henry, with Floss bounding ahead of him, start walking towards them. She almost wished he wasn't here. This was the part of her life that had to deal with the Sotherns and with Ned. How could she manage Henry as well? Really, how complicated everything was. But reassurance came with rising irritation, and her voice, when she answered was sharp.

'Hallo, Mr Long. What are you doing here?'

He stopped on the beach just below them, flinty eyes catching the sunlight and gleaming with amusement. 'Having an afternoon off – like you, Miss Hunt.'

'I'm here in my capacity as tutor to Miss Eleanor,' she said primly. 'Mrs Sothern – over there,' nodding towards the group setting out the picnic at the far end of the beach, 'Mrs Sothern's cousin, Mr Kerslake, is a photographer and wanted to see what possibilities there are here.'

'I see. Can I help you down?' He held out a hand and smiled up at the little girl fidgeting beside her. 'Miss Eleanor, you resemble an elegant mountain goat – safe and energetic on these dangerous black rocks—'

Eleanor giggled, took the offered hand and jumped down to the sandy beach. Bravely she touched Floss's silky head. 'Is this dog your pet?' she asked.

'Yes,' said Henry, catching Loveday's eye. 'My pet – and my friend.'

'Oh.' Eleanor considered the matter, and then, 'We're going to have a picnic,' she said. 'I expect there'll be enough for you, too. Would you like to come?'

Henry bowed. 'Thank you. Sure, I'd like that.' He lifted one dark eyebrow and glanced at Loveday. 'That is, if Miss Hunt, who is clearly your companion for the afternoon, thinks that it wouldn't be too rude of me to butt into a private tea party?'

More giggles, and then Eleanor started tugging him up the beach, one hand on Floss's head, with Loveday following, still unable to decide how she could manage this unlikely intrusion.

'She's my piano teacher, not my companion,' confided Eleanor. 'And my stepmama is always glad to receive new people – especially if you're a man.'

Really, the child was far too knowledgeable. Despite her worries, Loveday smiled and caught Henry's backward glance at her. He looked as if he was enjoying himself, which surprised her. And how charming he was with Eleanor. Henry – charming? New thoughts flew about. How little she knew him.

And then Ned's voice across the beach. 'Loveday! Come and help me – how do you light this wretched spirit stove?' His smile faded as Henry, Eleanor and Loveday approached. 'Who's this? I don't remember inviting anyone else.'

There was a long moment while both men stared at each other assessingly. Ned frowned but Henry's face remained expressionless, and, her heart sinking, Loveday felt the atmosphere become charged.

And then Isobel's high-pitched voice broke the awkwardness. 'Introduce us, please, Miss Jenkins. A friend of yours, I imagine?'

Loveday took a step forward. 'Yes, Mrs Sothern. The gentleman who lodges with my aunt and uncle, Mr Henry Long, who is spending time in Mr Harvey's shipyard.' She turned, met Henry's intent gaze. 'Mr Long, this is my employer, Mrs Sothern, and this is Mr Kerslake, her cousin.'

She watched Isobel Sothern eyeing Henry with something approaching approval, heard her voice growing warmer than usual. 'How do you do, Mr Long? Come and join us, won't you? My husband has contacts with the old shipyard. Do tell me what you are doing there.' She turned to Ned who was staring with obvious dislike. 'Where are your manners, Ned? Pray make Mr Long welcome.'

Ned nodded a dismissive head. 'How do you do, Long. I just hope we've got enough tea for an extra guest.'

Loveday took in a long, reflective breath as she helped Eleanor sit down on the rug beside her stepmama with Floss spreading herself in a black mass at the child's side. A horrid feeling began to grow that this tea party could well end in tears, and they wouldn't just be the result of Eleanor possibly slipping on the seaweed.

131

But the business of unpacking the hamper banished her fears. Henry and Isobel chatted while the boxes of sandwiches, sausage rolls, meringues, scones, and cakes were placed on the white tablecloth spread on the sand, and Ned at once took Loveday aside, whispering conspiratorially, 'We'll need to light this in a sheltered spot. Look, behind that big rock over there. Come along, Lovey, I can't manage without you.'

She was glad to be alone with him, even though she knew Mrs Sothern was probably watching with an eagle eye, but Henry's arrival had been a surprise, upsetting the comfortable feelings the boat trip had engendered, and now, with Ned beside her, she was glad to feel the old warmth between them being established once again.

Quickly she arranged the equipment. 'Like this – give me the matches.' They watched the kettle settle into place on the top of the flame and then Ned took her hand. 'Got you to myself again, Lovey. What a good plan, wasn't it, coming here? I knew we'd find a quiet spot.' He faced her, looking deeply into her eyes. 'Where have you been lately?' His voice lowered and his grip tightened. 'I've missed seeing you, talking to you . . . and then that funny little scrap, what's she called, Daisy, the child who's always around, said as how I ought to come here and take photos and I thought . . . well, you know what I thought, don't you?'

Loveday nodded. Yes, she knew. He wanted to take her in his arms, just as he had done last week. He wanted to kiss her. And she wanted him to do so. Didn't she? So what on earth made her step back, shake her head and say rapidly, 'We must go back, Ned. They'll wonder what we're doing.'

His frown returned. 'We're boiling the damned kettle,' he said sharply, 'and I don't care who wonders anything.' He grabbed her arm. 'Lovey, something's different about you – you've changed. Why?'

'Of course I haven't.' She raised her voice, forced a smile. 'You're imagining things, Ned, I'm just the same.'

For a moment he held her captive. 'Not that other feller, is it? Who is he, this Long chap?'

She pulled away, dismayed at his disapproving expression. 'He's a draughtsman. I hardly know him. Let me go, Ned, I don't want—'

Eleanor appeared, red faced and smiling, Floss at her heels. 'Mama says isn't the kettle boiling yet? Someone's come down from the café with strawberries and cream. Isn't it lovely? And, Miss Jenkins, I want to build a really big sandcastle after we've had tea – will you help me, please?'

Relief flooded. 'Yes, of course, Miss Eleanor. And look, the kettle's just started singing, so in a minute we'll collect the teapot and make the tea –

let's go back and fetch it, shall we?'

Back at the spread tablecloth, with Isobel smiling at Henry and saying, 'But I do believe my husband used to know someone in Dorset called Lennox Long – what a strange coincidence that you're here now! I'm sure Joshua would love to meet you. You must come to dinner – one evening next week, perhaps?'

Loveday bent down to pick up the teapot and the caddy and couldn't stop herself looking at Henry as he replied politely and with a smile that showed just how charming he could be when it paid. How manipulative he could be. A fierce thought struck. *I don't like that about him.*

She scowled, hearing the lazy drawl and the casual, charming voice. 'I should be delighted, Mrs Sothern. Sure, I look forward to it. Now, can I spread one of these scones with this amazing Devonshire cream for you? And perhaps some of those strawberries?'

Loveday marched up the beach and made the tea, took it back to the tea party and poured into bone china cups with saucers. 'Sugar, Mrs Sothern?'

'No, thank you.' And then a coy smile, directed at Henry. 'I hope I'm sweet enough.'

This time Loveday made no effort to watch his reaction. Instead, she looked across the beach to where Ben and Daniel sat on some rocks, smoking and lugubriously watching the gentry amusing themselves.

Anger rose high inside her. 'Ben,' she called loudly. 'I'm sure we can squeeze two more cups of tea out of this pot. Would you and your father like some?'

'Oh aye, thank 'ee, miss.' Daniel's deep voice was respectful as he got to his feet and, with Ben, slowly came across the beach.

Isobel Sothern protested. 'Miss Jenkins, what ever are you doing? I don't think that is a good idea,' but Loveday pretended not to hear her. She hated the fact that she was forced to be part of this privileged gathering, while her friends were ignored. She poured the cups, handed them to the two men and smiled warmly. 'You deserve this, bringing us here.'

'What's this, feeding the work force?' Ned's voice sounded behind her and she turned quickly.

Her reply was quick and sharp. 'Why not? They've worked hard, bringing us here, with all this baggage.'

'That's what they're for, isn't it? Working for their betters?' Ned was laughing, his face full of smiles, but she heard the careless contempt behind them and felt her anger grow.

But before she could answer, Ben said quickly, 'Somethin' in the good

Book 'bout the labourer being worth his hire, isn't there?'

Ned's voice was heavy with annoyance. 'You'll get your fee when I'm ready, my man, but not a penny more. Your strength may be necessary, but I don't like your manner.'

Daniel was pulling at Ben's arm, tea slopping down on to the sand. 'C'mon, b'y,' he muttered, 'watch that tongue of yours – gettin' us into trouble, as ever.' Then he gave Ned an obsequious smile. 'Sorry, sir, don't take no notice of him . . . got a temper, he has, but don't mean nothin'.'

Ned snorted. 'All right, I'll let it pass. This time.' He looked at his watch. 'Be ready to take us back in about an hour's time.'

Daniel turned. 'That's a bit late, sir – better go with the tide, if you don't mind. 'Nother half hour, say?'

'Nonsense. I booked you for three hours and that's what we're having. It's up to you to cope with the tide, whatever it does. Now, Loveday.' He left them to walk down the beach, and looked at her, smiling at her dismayed expression, the old Ned, twinkling eyes, saucy words for her alone. 'Come on, let's go and explore the rocks over there – you and me together.'

But of course they couldn't be alone. Mrs Sothern's high voice made Ned turn back. 'Ned, where are you going? I thought we were here for the sole purpose of you planning your photographs?' Another of those coy laughs and Loveday guessed Issy was glancing up at Henry from beneath her parasol. 'And I put on my new hat specially!' The tone changed sharply. 'And Miss Jenkins, where are you off to, pray? Miss Eleanor wants you to build her a sandcastle.'

Henry helped tidy away the remains of the tea party, listening as he did so to Isobel Sothern's monotonous little voice telling him about her husband's interest in the old shipyard. 'He gave Kenneth Harvey financial help when Mr Harvey took it over. Even now he has a share in it, though, goodness knows, there have been no profits for several years.'

Her small hands managed to touch his as they piled plates into the hamper and she smiled artlessly up at him. Quickly he moved aside; he wanted no flirtations with this pale, trivial woman. But the husband could be a different matter. So when she returned to the dinner invitation, 'Shall we say Friday evening, Mr Long? Shall I send the carriage for you? It's such a steep hill up from the promenade,' he was ready with his answer.

'Thank you, Mrs Sothern, but I would prefer to walk. I spend enough time sitting and looking at Mr Harvey's old records, you see. And yes, Friday would suit me very well.' He regretted the slight warmth in the

next few words – 'I look forward to it' – but there, all was fair in business, love and war actually, but he had no time for either – while business
was definitely on his mind.

When Ned Kerslake finally rather reluctantly started walking around
looking for photographic sites, Henry saw Loveday, sitting on the sand a
little lower down, helping Eleanor build sand pies and occasionally glancing back over her shoulder. Was she looking at the uncouth Kerslake man,
or – he raised an eyebrow unbelievingly – at him?

He bowed to Isobel Southern, fiddling with that ridiculous hat on her
piled hair, and said politely, 'Forgive me, but I think Floss needs a little
exercise.'

'Oh yes, your dog—' He felt her eyes on him as he walked away from
the rugs and the canvas chairs, Floss already charging ahead into the lace-
edged waves. The tide had turned, he noticed – the trip back to
Teignmouth would be choppy. Perhaps that wretched hat would finally
fly away. A smile tugged at his taut mouth, and then he put Isobel Sothern
out of his mind. Loveday Hunt, sitting there, with a wooden spade in her
hand, was a far more attractive subject to think about.

He joined in the digging, finding pebbles and shells with which to
decorate the grand castle that Eleanor was regarding with such pride and
was ridiculously pleased when Loveday said, 'This is where your background of art comes in, Henry – I didn't know you were an architect as
well as a draughtsman.'

'You know very little about me, Loveday'

Their eyes met and for a moment her fingers stopped pressing deco-
rations into the wet sand. 'No, Henry, I don't. Any more than you know
about me.'

He heard the sudden lowering of her voice, the light fading from those
brilliantly green eyes, and the turning away of her lovely face and
suddenly he wanted to console her, to say that life could be terrible but
that it was also wonderful, but the words refused to come. Instead he
looked away, towards Eleanor. 'We're too late to let the tide come in and
wash away your castle. Shall I fill a bucket so that you can do the
honours?'

'Yes! You can help, but I want to do it myself.' She was dancing along
at his side, one eye on Floss, gambolling in the waves, and one back at
Loveday, still sitting by the castle. Henry held the small, sand-sticky hand
and wondered at the pleasure he was abruptly feeling. Children, women,
homes – families.

And then Ned Kerslake shouted down the beach, 'Come up here, will you, Long? Tell me if you think this would make a good shot.'

No more time for filling the moated castle, for watching the child's wide-eyed pleasure, for wondering about Loveday and the extraordinary feelings she created in him, but the wearisome need to politely accede to Kerslake's demands. He half wished he was back in the shipyard.

Ned was scribbling down ideas in a notebook. 'This view from here, I think, and one of the café. And then, of course, the boat moored down there.' He took no notice of Henry's polite agreement, but called Loveday to join him. 'I think a photograph of you and everybody else – we'll have another picnic and I'll bring all the equipment with me.' He turned and looked out to sea. 'The light isn't good today, but another time.'

At his side, Loveday wondered if she dared suggest he should consider putting the boatmen in one of the photographs, but when she did so Ned frowned. 'I don't think so. But I'll get them to stop rowing once we're a bit off the beach so that I can get an idea of the bay from a distance.' His voice dropped. 'Lovey, when can I see you again?'

Something made her turn away without replying, saying hurriedly that she must help pack up the baggage ready to load the boat, her thoughts full of confusion. *I like Ned, even though he's a bit nasty sometimes. I suppose it's his privileged upbringing, and yes, I do want to see him.* And then she was back in the family problems; her dead father, Maggie's excuses for abandoning her and the awful, freezing feeling of rejection.

She didn't want me. Slowly the darkness faded . . . *but Ned does.*

So she smiled at him as she followed Ben and Daniel, whom Ned had called up to carry the baggage down to the boat. Once Isobel Sothern and Eleanor were safely out of the way she would quietly suggest that she and Ned should meet tomorrow, after work.

The business of getting everybody and everything back on board the boat took its time, and when, finally, Daniel pushed off from the beach, the water was lapping quite fiercely at the gunwales. Isobel proclaimed herself to feel sick, Eleanor anxiously tucked herself into Loveday's side and grabbed her hand, while Henry, watching on shore, exchanged looks with Ben. The turning tide had brought currents with it and the wind had sharpened.

But nothing was going to stop Ned from planning what he thought might be a small masterpiece. Some yards out from the beach he stood up uncertainly and frowned at Ben. 'Keep the boat steady, man, can't you?' He shifted his position, as the boat rolled on the waves, and Loveday, with trepidation, saw how Ben scowled and took a firmer grip of his oar.

The next few moments were confused. A sudden fierce swell swept a powerful wave to rock the boat and somehow – Loveday, afterwards, could never be quite sure whether Ben purposely brought the oar out of the rowlocks, or whether Ned was momentarily unbalanced – but somehow he received a shove, his unsteady legs gave way and with a shout he disappeared over the side.

An enormous splash covered everything with spray. Isobel Sothern screamed, Eleanor hid her face in Loveday's side, and a yard away from the boat, Ned, gasping for breath, with his mouth half full of seawater, shouted incoherently, 'Help! I can't swim!'

And then as Loveday stood up, ready to jump in and rescue him, she heard Ben shout, 'Man overboard!' and, with anger instantly sparking inside her, saw satisfaction on his face, realized that this was no accident.

CHAPTER THIRTEEN

A gusting wind and a mounting swell. The boom lashed down, hatches battened, the helmsman injured and the wheel spinning and the ship riding side on to the waves thundering down and then mounting again. Spray drenching bodies and terror filling minds. And then a crack as the mast broke, the ship wallowed, slid sideways and water rushed in. Voices shouting, the passengers screaming, hands launching the boats, bodies jumping from the rigging as below them the vessel capsized.

Amos was one of the last to jump – into frothing, furious water. He watched the boats slowly drawing away from the drowning ship and made an effort to catch up and climb aboard. His breath giving out, his body stiff with cold and unable to swim any more. And then a huge piece of broken timber appeared, making straight for him. He grasped it, pulled his body on to it, felt his lungs heave in more breath.

It was twenty minutes later that a passing coaster saw him, picked him up, delivered him half dead to St Johns in Newfoundland. He and three other crewmen survived, but the small boats with their praying, terrified passengers foundered. Amos knew he was lucky to be alive.

Loveday saw Ned struggling, his head suddenly immersed beneath the waves, then coming up, gasping, with another feeble shout for help. She must do something. He needed her. Thrusting Eleanor aside, she stood up, but Ben's hard voice hit into her racing thoughts, stopping her from jumping.

'No need to do that, maid, let 'un make his own way out o' it.' Roughly, his hand pulled her back on to the bench beside Eleanor. And then, with enormous relief, she saw help was already at hand. Majestically, Floss swam out through the waves, huge black head rising and dipping rhythmically and heading straight towards Ned, while on shore, Henry was shouting encouragement. 'On, Floss, on – good girl, bring him in.'

Then she heard a shout from a dinghy coming alongside, and saw the shipyard apprentice, Mick, shipping his oars and producing a boathook. 'I'll get'un,' he called, and they all watched anxiously as the dog pulled Ned towards Mick's outstretched hand and the boathook caught at the back of his sodden jacket. Between them they got Ned into shallow water, where he floundered like a beached whale.

Henry watched as Floss relinquished her quarry, shook herself, spraying him with water, and then stood looking up at him. 'Good girl,' he said, patting her wet head. 'Good dog.'

Mick grounded the dinghy and leaped out to help Henry heave Ned on to the wet sand above the water line. 'Good thing I were here,' he said, grinning. 'Didn't think as 'ow I'd have to fish someone out the water, did I?'

Henry stooped over Ned's body as he lay in a waterlogged heap, face down on the sand, spitting and coughing. *Drunk half the ocean, has he? Well, we'll see to that.* Taking off his jacket, he rolled up his shirt sleeves and then knelt down, arms massaging Ned's back. *Drowned men.* The images came crashing back from his family days at the lighthouse. Always bodies on the beach after a wreck, some of them brought back from the brink of death, others carried up to a pit dug in the hard ice-bound soil and buried. This one, Henry thought with a wry grimace, would live. He applied more pressure with his hands and was rewarded by Ned spluttering through his coughs and vomit, 'What the hell are you doing? Let me be—' Half turning on one side he caught the full force of another shake by Floss. 'And take that bloody dog away.'

'That bloody dog,' said Henry between gritted teeth, 'just saved your life. Stop complaining and be thankful for the fact that you're here and not at the bottom of the ocean. For God's sake, why did you have to play tricks when the sea was obviously too choppy to be safe?'

Painfully, Ned turned and sat up, looking into Henry's face, standing above him. 'It was that fool boatman's fault – couldn't keep the boat steady, could he? And I swear he pushed me. Well, he'll be sorry about that. Undergardener, isn't he, when he's not mucking about in boats? Not much longer, he won't be.'

Henry rolled down his shirt sleeves, looked up and saw the larger boat rowing out of the bay, its occupants clearly relieved at Ned's escape. Then he put on his jacket and stared at the wet mass of still-shaking body that now climbed to its feet. 'Revenge gets you nowhere,' he said shortly, watching Ned pull off his coat and squeeze water from his sleeves and trouser legs. 'Anyway, Mick'll take us back to harbour and then you can dry out. Can you walk to the dinghy?'

Somehow Ned managed it, allowing Mick and Henry to help him board the rolling little craft. He sat, shivering, as the boat turned and headed home. No one spoke until, well past the Ness and about to enter the harbour, Ned pulled his wet coat closer about him and looked down at the dog. 'Clever,' he said grudgingly. 'Special breed, is it?'

Henry nodded. 'Newfoundland.' He dropped a hand on to the dog's head, Floss looked up and Henry had a sudden, new feeling of warmth.

Silence again. He stared at Ned. *We're miles apart,* he thought; *he and his photographs and me obsessed with design . . . yet there should be something mutual between us, men of the same new, exciting generation.* And then it came. Loveday was the link. *Clearly Kerslake has an interest in her; as I do. As I do?* He pushed away the thought because it came not on its own but bringing other, painful memories and hopes and fears with it. And at the moment he must concentrate on his ambition; on the ideas swirling around his brain every time he saw Mick feathering the oars of the dinghy and felt the sturdy power of the old boat; on the vague yet certain feeling that here was a connection that might just bring his dreams to fruition. *Dinghies, racing gigs, racing craft of other sorts, perhaps.*

The boat halted, Mick leaped ashore and secured it, offering his hand to Ned. 'Take it easy, mister, an' you'll be all right. 'Tis only sea water.' Then, as Ned clumsily disembarked, he added, 'You was lucky, me an' that dog being at hand.'

Henry watched Ned's immediate reaction of searching his wet pocket for change, and grinned to himself. *The man of breeding about to tip his rescuer.* Climbing out of the boat, Floss at his heels, he pointed Ned in the direction of the waiting carriage down by the New Quay. 'There's your way home, Kerslake. Have a hot bath and you'll feel better. And don't worry, Mick and I will sort out the fare.'

Ned, shivering, running a hand through his soaking hair, followed his gesture and saw Isobel and Eleanor sitting in the carriage, while Loveday stood beside them, a rug over her arm. Henry fancied there was anxiety on her face and watched as she walked quickly towards them. Was she fond of this patronizing, superior idiot? The thought irked him, but then Ned was turning towards him, saying slowly, 'You've been helpful. I'm grateful,' before walking rapidly away, dripping as he went.

Henry and Mick looked at each other as money changed hands. 'What a fool, eh?' said Mick.

'Yes. But he's learned a lesson.'

And, Henry, thought, so had he. That the unpredictable sea and his past were still there in his memories, no longer banished because of pain and lack of love, but slowly infiltrating into his daily life. Walking back towards Market Street, knowing that Loveday was with the Sotherns, with that chap Kerslake, he wondered at his feelings and allowed himself to think into the future. Not just the boats and the neglected shipyard, but perhaps something warmer; more stable – more long lasting? An image of Eleanor's bright eyes and the sound of her uninhibited giggles brought a smile to his thoughtful face. Families. Perhaps, after all, not quite so unattainable and unwanted as he was used to thinking.

How the days spun by. Loveday, rising next morning, found her head full of intrusive thoughts and memories. Life was busy, too busy, perhaps, but it had to be faced and dealt with. This afternoon she must do an extra two hours' work for Mrs Narracott to make up for yesterday. Somehow she must make time to meet Ned who, having dripped all over everybody in the coach, had left her on the quay with a grudging smile and not a word of hope that they might meet again soon. And then there was Frank Benedict to be visited. Brushing her hair, she looked at the reflection of her sober face and knew there were things she wanted to ask him before he died. *Before he died.* She shivered. Life and death were things she had never really thought about before. Life just went on and death was something eventually happening to other people. Not to loved ones – and yet – Father was dead. And dear old Frank was on the way there. Her mind did a somersault.

A step on the passageway below her room alerted her to Henry Long's descent to the kitchen for breakfast. She would tell him he must come with her and see Frank. And she would ask about the scrimshaw. Suddenly, she had a feeling it was important in some way that was strange and, as yet, hidden. But she had to know.

So – 'Good morning, Mr Long.' He could only be Henry when Aunt Janet wasn't around.

They exchanged greetings and brief smiles. Loveday took a deep breath. 'I shall be seeing Mr Benedict again this evening. I wonder – you said you might come—'

Janet tutted. 'My dear child, Mr Long has better things to do than go and gossip to Frank.'

'They don't gossip, they talk about things they both remember. And I want to ask—' She bit her tongue and looked down at her plate.

Loveday paused and frowned across the table, but Henry said quietly and in an agreeable way that made it easy for Janet to continue pouring the tea, 'Certainly I'll come with you, Miss Hunt. And what do you want to ask? Can I be of any help, I wonder?'

'It's the piece of scrimshaw he gave me.' Loveday sat up straighter and met his calm gaze. 'It's got carving on it, and some letters. I thought Mr Benedict might know what they meant.' She frowned. 'And I don't understand why he gave it to me. I've seen it before, but now it's mine, and I want to know—'

Janet exchanged glances with Davey and then said quickly, 'No doubt it's the old man's way of getting rid of his possessions before he dies. I shouldn't think too much about it, child – just respect his wishes and put it with your shells.'

Breakfast continued and Loveday thought about many things; why Aunt Janet had no use for a piece of scrimshaw, why she had so clearly ended the topic of conversation, and why Henry should imagine he could help in any way. And then something else burst into these teeming thoughts. Was Henry actually going to have dinner with Issy Sothern on Friday? And then all the rest of her private world swirled away, leaving her agog to know what might happen; what Issy would wear; how Henry would behave and – finally, just as she helped Aunt Janet clear the table – whether Henry would, afterwards, tell her all about it.

The muddle stayed in her mind throughout the day and it was with relief that she came home from the Beach View Hotel and welcomed the idea of Henry accompanying her to Mr Benedict. She began forming words in her mind. 'Where did you get this piece of scrimshaw? Why did you give it to me? And what do the letters mean?'

After tea, it all happened rather differently. Aunt Janet said carefully that a neighbour had told her that Frank Benedict had been taken to hospital, his bronchitis having turned into pneumonia. Apparently an old friend of his, an accordion player, had made all the arrangements. Poor Frank was said to be very ill and few visitors were allowed. 'So child, don't go traipsing all over the beach to his cottage. Just rest here and we'll wait for better news.'

Loveday felt life growing darker. Of course she had known Frank was dying, but this seemed too brutal, too hopeless. She could do no more for him. And now she had lost the chance of learning about the scrimshaw. Now, with all her heart, she longed to be able to tell someone of her confused and sad feelings. Ned hadn't appeared. Henry had gone rushing off to answer a summons from Kenneth Harvey and Aunt Janet was busily turning shirt collars for a neighbour.

I wish I had a mother to talk to.

The idea was startling, even shocking, and made her sit up on the edge of her bed. She had escaped upstairs after tea to try to battle with her charged emotions, but this was something she had never expected to be thinking. For a long few moments she sat there, staring into space, ideas, images and voices flowing all around her. *But I have a mother. I have Maggie. Talk to her? But. . . .*

Such an unwanted, unbelievable thought, but it brought with it a tiny twist of change of heart. She knew now that she had been unkind, cruel even, to the poor woman who had been brought to the edge of despair and, as a consequence, had done what she considered best by giving her daughter to a kind and responsible sister. Now Loveday recalled the hateful words she had hurled at poor, weeping Maggie and wondered how she could have said them. But she had been in pain, rejected, afraid to believe all she was told.

And now, days later and in some way years older, she knew she needed to make reparation for the anger that had forced her to discard her mother. Now she was able to think about her without that overwhelming pain of rejection. Now, perhaps, she could start to understand. Slowly, she rose, looked in the mirror and saw a new light in the surprised green eyes. Downstairs, she put her head around the door into Janet's room and said casually, 'I'm going out. I might see Jack – or Ben – or someone. I won't be late back.'

Janet put down her needle, saw how Loveday looked – older, wiser, less confused – and nodded. 'All right, child. The air will do you good.' She might have said more, but the door closed and she heard footsteps walking fast down the street towards the harbour. Towards Carpenters' Row, she dared to wonder? Resuming her sewing, she hoped fervently that this unexpected outing might be a step towards a reconciliation of some sort, but then sighed and shook her head. Life was hard, and families often stayed at odds for generations. Her needle stabbed and pierced the worn linen neckband as her thoughts continued. What right had she to hope that Loveday's life would be any different?

Loveday walked slowly, her mind too busy to observe what went on around her. She knew that all the emotions of the past weeks had mounted and become a hindrance to her normal everyday contentment. She was learning – what had Maggie said? that she had a lot to learn – well, it was happening and she wasn't enjoying it. And yet, with that unwelcome knowledge also came the feel of a new self confidence, a supportive strength denied to her up till now. She walked on, towards the harbour, down the street leading to Carpenters' Row, following her instincts and not making any plans. What ever she did next would be right. Although, of course, it might well end in more tears and emotions, if Maggie was at the cottage, but the thought had suddenly run around her head that having a family meant you had responsibilities and duties. It meant that, come what may, you had to learn to love.

The door of the cottage was open with sand blowing in over the threshold. Loveday paused, uncertain what to do next. She took a step and looked into the small room opening out before her. No one there. For a second relief took the weight off her shoulders and her mind cleared. But she must go on. She called, 'Anyone in?' and heard her voice echo through the cottage.

There was a creak in the floorboards above her head, and then a sound of footsteps coming down the stairs. She held her breath and let it out slowly, with a sense of anticlimax, as Jack came into the room.

'Oh,' he said, 'it's you. Mother's not here, I suppose you wanted to see her.' His voice was dull, his expression even duller, his cough wheezy and irritating.

'Hallo, Jack.' She thought he looked uncared for, untidy and unhappy. They looked at each other until Loveday broke the awkward moment. 'I wondered if Maggie might be here.'

'It was her evening off yesterday. She won't be here till Sunday afternoon. Did you,' he paused, frowned, 'want something?'

'Well,' said Loveday, recovering her poise. 'I just thought I'd come and see what you are doing.'

He nodded, slumped down into one of the two chairs at the table and put his head in his hands. 'Nothing,' he mumbled. 'Nothing to do 'cept work.'

Loveday pulled out the other chair and sat in it. She felt the boy's wretchedness, saw the expression of hopelessness in his thin face and was at once moved by it.

'Jack, what's wrong? I mean, you have a job and I'm sure Maggie,' she paused for a second, hesitating before using the new, unfamiliar word – 'our mother – does her best for you. So why are you feeling like this?'

He dropped his hands and stared at her. 'I want to go to sea and she says no. I'd have to get her permission before anyone took me on. But it's not fair. I'm nearly a man, I'll be fifteen soon, I want to go.' He got up, the chair almost falling behind him. '*I shall go!*' he shouted. 'I don't care what she says.'

Loveday watched him turn and stare at the hearth behind him. She saw his body shake, heard him swallowing and knew the anguish that filled him. But decision came with instinctive certainty and the words erupted without any thought save that she knew Maggie didn't deserve any more unhappiness. 'You have to wait, Jack. Wait until Maggie . . . Mother . . . is ready to give her permission. You love her, so try and think how she must feel when you go on about going to sea – all her memories of losing Father must come back. Oh, Jack, no – she'd be so miserable if you went, worrying about you, missing you. You can't leave her. Please think again.'

He turned and she saw his eyes swim with unshed tears. She thought he looked at her with something close to hatred, but knew she must go on, for Maggie's sake. 'You're the man of the family, now, Jack. It's your duty to stay here and look after Mother, to find a good job that will help you live in something better than this wretched old cottage. Where's your pride?'

She wondered if anyone had ever said these hard things to him; probably not. But now it seemed right to upbraid him, to encourage him, in some odd way to help him. She watched him across the table. 'How about a cup of tea? Is that water boiling?'

He seemed almost stunned, she thought, but slowly he nodded, pushed the kettle closer to the slow-burning flame and then went to the dresser behind the table to collect two mugs. He found milk in the meat safe on the wall near the door, and then produced the tea tin. Then he looked at her, his face perplexed, still tense with only half-suppressed anger, but with a new expression that suggested her words had reached him and made sense. 'If you're so keen to look after Mother, why don't you do it yourself, then?' His voice was surly, his movements as he poured water into the teapot clumsy and awkward. He pushed the filled mug towards her and then sank down into his chair. 'Why are you saying all these things to me? I don't hardly know you.'

'But it's time you did. I'm your sister, remember?' Loveday managed a smile and sipped her tea. 'Look, Jack,' she said, 'I think our mother might come round eventually if you proved you could manage your life properly without her help. She knows we all have to grow up. Give her time, can't you?'

He slurped his tea. They looked at each other in a dragging silence and then, at last, he nodded grudgingly. 'All right. I'll try. I reckon you're right. But I'll go in the end; see if I don't.'

Loveday heaved a sigh of relief and said quietly, 'Of course you will. But until then, let's be friends, shall we?'

Another pause, then a reluctant smile and a nod. 'All right.'

'Good. Why don't you come to tea on Sunday? Uncle Davey would love to have a man to talk to, and Aunt Janet always makes cakes then.' She felt she'd won a victory, a small one, but something that made the future seem happier and more positive.

They drank the rest of their tea in silence, Loveday looking around the small room with its stained, damp walls and sandy, littered floor. She wondered how Maggie coped, living here in squalor and then working at Sothern House amid such comfort and opulence. And then her eye was caught by something familiar standing on the mantelpiece above the hearth and everything else went out of her mind.

She got to her feet, went to the fireplace and reached up. 'What's this?'

Jack turned in his chair. 'That? Dunno. Something Mother's always had. Says it the luck of the house or something. Daft, I think.'

'It's a piece of scrimshaw. It's like the piece Mr Benedict gave me. It's got figures on it, and flowers, and letters.' Loveday stared raptly at the object in her hand as if it held the answers to all the problems in her life, and into her mind raced the ridiculous thought that perhaps it did. Why did Maggie have this piece, and why had Frank Benedict given her his? What was the connection? It couldn't just be coincidence, could it?

She sat down again, still holding the scrimshaw, trying desperately to decipher the clumsy, tiny letters carved into it. Suddenly she thought that perhaps the two pieces might make better sense when they were seen together. 'Can I borrow this, Jack? I'll bring it back again, but I want to see if—'

'Reckon so. Mebbe we could go and watch the fishing boats come in tomorrow evening?' He looked at her with brighter eyes.

'Perhaps, but I can't promise. Now I must go – goodbye then, Jack.'

She left Carpenters' Row slowly, instinctively heading for the harbour and then around the Point, the scrimshaw warm in her hand, and her thoughts involved with the carvings on it. Somehow, the sea lapping along the warm, empty beach, with the sun setting in its usual majesty made her feel quite different. She would go home soon, but, coming as it did, without warning, this moment of serenity and inexplicable new hope must be enjoyed as long as it lasted.

Henry came back late from visiting Kenneth Harvey, his mind overflowing and excited. The old man had suffered a seizure in his office this morning and was now in his bed at home. His housekeeper had taken Henry up to the room that overlooked the river, pulled the bed covers neatly up to the patient's chin and said firmly, 'Doctor says no excitement,

Mr Long. Mr Kenneth's had a bad turn, he needs rest, so I'll thank you not to stay too long.'

'Of course. Ten minutes and I'll be away.' Henry had pulled a chair to the bed and sat down, looking into Kenneth Harvey's puffy, slightly lopsided face and wondering why he'd been called here.

'I need to talk to you.' The weak voice was slurred and the words slow in coming. Henry nodded patiently, but the prescribed ten minutes had lengthened to a good half hour before the matter was clearly sorted out. Kenneth Harvey slouched back on to his pillow, closed his eyes and breathed heavily as his last words slid out. 'I reckon I can trust you – you're young and you're a good draughtsman. The bank can see to the figures, while you get the business going again. I'm finished.' Then his pouched eyes opened wide and he stared at Henry. 'But I want your word that you'll keep the old hands on. What do you say, boy?'

Henry said, 'Yes, sir, thank you, of course,' in an unnaturally quiet and obedient way, while his heart raced and his mind grew busy with plans, designs, ambitions. He held out his hand and the old man reached across painfully and they shook on the deal.

'Now I can sleep easy. Come back tomorrow and mebbe I'll be brighter. I'll get Hutchins, my solicitor, to come and we'll put it all on paper. Now, I must sleep.' The hard moments of forcing his bewildered brain to make sense were over and Kenneth Harvey was already snoring slightly as Henry left the room and said goodbye to the watchful housekeeper.

He walked back through the town in a heady trance of dreams come true and then decided to give Floss a last run before going to bed. Sleep? He couldn't sleep, not with so much going on inside him. Turning back along the esplanade, he went down the shadowy steps on to the beach and headed towards the Point, where the river flowed into the ocean, and where Floss always enjoyed a swim.

The sand was dark and gritty beneath his boots and behind him the town had become a grey, shadowy blur, but the flaming western sky held a promise of another good day ahead. Another day, when perhaps his dream of becoming master of the neglected shipyard would come true. Just let Kenneth Harvey get his solicitor to write it all down, let the money work itself out, let his plans come to fruition. . . .

Suddenly he saw a figure ahead of him and blinked. A woman, tall, slender, carrying a hat and letting the capricious breeze play with her glowing red hair. Loveday, with darkness descending, and on her own.

Calling Floss to heel, he strode rapidly towards her.

CHAPTER FOURTEEN

She heard his footsteps, saw a large, shadowy figure approaching and stopped, alarmed. And then a wet nose butted her hand and relief came, driving away the uneasiness. 'Floss!'

'Loveday, what on earth are you doing out here so late?' Henry was close to her, the fading sun lightening his deep-set eyes into silver grey. He put out a hand, touched her shoulder and Loveday thought warmly that this was what he had promised Aunt Janet – to care for her.

'Just walking,' she said. 'Thinking.' No answer, but she sensed interest in the way he stood quite still, looking at her. 'I've been talking to my brother, Jack. I . . . well, I persuaded him not to leave our mother. Not yet. He wants to go to sea, but I know she would be terribly unhappy if he did.'

A nod and then his arm moved, turning her towards the harbour. 'You're fond of him?'

Loveday thought. Then, 'I've only just met him.' She drew in a steadying breath. It was good to let it all out. 'I think you know that our family has only come together again after a long time. And that my father is dead.' She frowned. 'Fifteen years. So it's hard to get to know each other now.'

Henry made no reply as they walked back slowly, reaching the river beach with its moored boats and spread out fishing nets. Some of the boat huts were still open with their owners inside, talking, smoking pipes, watching the water as it swirled past. He stopped suddenly, drawing her towards him. 'I know nothing of families,' he said gruffly. 'My parents were too busy to bother much with me. So I can only imagine your feelings now.'

The fading light left his face in shadowy darkness. All she could see were angles and hollows, that strong chin and, beyond her vision, she knew those perceptive flinty eyes were watching her. His quiet words had stirred up her feelings; now emotions billowed through her and she said unsteadily, 'I don't know how I feel, really. At first I was furious to think that my mother had abandoned me. And then today, for some reason, I began to understand. But I still can't forgive her. And of course I have to meet her – she's Aunt Janet's half sister – and it's all so difficult.' Her voice broke and she bowed her head.

Henry's arm moved to encircle her waist, drawing her closer. 'You're not alone, Loveday, you know that.' His low voice was strong and gave her a feeling of warmth. 'You have your Aunt and Uncle, and now your brother, and your friends.' He stopped, before adding abruptly, 'and I hope you think of me as a friend, too.'

'Yes.' Words drifted away then and she was conscious only of his nearness. Of his vibrant words echoing through her mind like calming music. She closed her eyes. 'Thank you, yes, you're my friend, Henry.' And then, without thinking, she raised her face towards his, needing to be held, to be touched, to be cared for. To be loved. Perhaps to be kissed.

Henry held her in his arms and tried to deny the insistent urge to give her everything she was so clearly asking for. Thoughts flashed through him like a lightning strike. He was on the verge of achieving his long-held ambition, and once Kenneth Harvey had legally made him manager, or who knows, even a partner in the failing shipyard, business matters would fill his life. There would be no time for anything save work. Nothing could matter more than what was in front of him. But another idea rose, foolhardy in its demands. What, commit himself to loving this sweet, beautiful but lonely girl? That would mean spending time with her, allowing himself to become part of her disturbed family. And if they married – he almost gasped at the thought – they would have to create a home. To pay for it, to furnish it, to live together in it. And there might even be children. *What?*

But temptation and an unexpected feeling of openness and of spreading warmth overflowed. He stretched his arms around her, pulled her so near that her breath, soft and fragrant, touched his face, saw her closed eyes, realized she was offering herself, and was no longer able to deny himself her sweetness and innocence.

He bent his head and kissed her. Soft, warm lips; an eager intake of breath, and then she was returning the embrace, kissing him, giving herself. Joyously, Henry felt something grow inside him – a new awareness of what life could be if he allowed it to develop. Loving Loveday. Loveday loving him? And then the past engulfed him with cold, hard images, and at once he knew he must deny the pleasure of letting this kiss last and grow more passionate. For if he did what his body yearned for, he knew his ambitions would lose their power. Domesticity, he thought, grimly, families, responsibilities other than business ones. He couldn't accept that.

So, even though his blood raced and his body cried out, he stepped away, dropped his arms and said roughly, 'It's very late. I must get you home. Your Aunt will be worrying about you.'

Loveday stood quite still, not understanding, not wanting to believe what had happened. Memory taunted her, her mouth still tasting his; the hard prickle of his jacket against her throat still delighting her, the power of his arms around her waist banishing her fears. And, now, as suddenly as it had happened, it was all over. Henry had no feelings for her. He had just kissed her because she had expected him to. He had behaved like any other man and she had been forward, flighty, wicked. She had become one of the harbour girls, and now he was, quite rightly, rejecting her.

Rejection. Again.

A familiar feeling, but now, with it, came an unexpected turn of thought, a quick rise of burning anger, pushing away rejection and delighting in its new strength. All right, she would allow him to take her home – at a distance – and then say goodnight. But never again would she think of him in this loving, special way. A friend, he had said, so let it be. He would remain a friend, only to be called on if necessary.

And then, as together, in silence, with Floss padding behind them, they walked towards the ferry entrance to the beach, then down the road leading to Market Street, she knew something else which shone through her darkness like a light. Ned had promised more than mere friendship. He had held her very tight, wanted to kiss her, would have done so if only Ben hadn't come down the dark court. Well – Loveday lifted her chin and looked up at the velvet dark sky, to see a new, crescent moon shining through drifting clouds – Ned should have his chance of loving her. She would make it her business to somehow meet him within the next few days.

Uncle Davey opened the door to Henry's quiet rap. 'You're late,' he said, an eyebrow raised, but smiling at Loveday. 'Your aunt's no doubt up there in her bed counting the moments till you're home. Well, she'll sleep now. And you, Mr Long, can I make you a cup of something before you retire?'

Henry followed Loveday through the hall. 'No, thank you, Mr Jenkins. I'll see to Floss and then I'll go straight up. It's been a long day.' He looked at Loveday, standing at the foot of the staircase and wondered at what he had just done. Perhaps it was too late to apologize, perhaps another day things might turn out differently. The jumbling thoughts disciplined him, so that it was easy to say 'goodnight, Miss Hunt' and for a second watch her pale face reflecting his own thoughts. And then it was all over.

'Good night, Mr Long,' she said, and there was no expression in her voice as she turned away and went upstairs.

Henry followed in due course. It was a long, restless night, but with the morning light he knew had been right to act so honestly. Loveday would always have admirers. She would soon forget this foolish incident. She might even patch things up with that nobody, Ned Kerslake. And if the mere thought of that was like a bad taste in his mouth, he put it aside and concentrated on today's meeting with Kenneth Harvey's solicitor.

Independent. I must learn to be more independent, to live my own life, make my own decisions and not allow foolish emotions to control me. Loveday felt a new energy filling her the next day and managed to keep at bay the memory of last night's rejection by Henry. What did she care about him? Nothing. He was an autocratic man with ambition but no feelings and she had been foolish to even imagine he might care for her. So on with the work in the untidy bedrooms, humming to keep her spirits up and then, before leaving for dinner, telling Mrs Narracott that she would be late returning this afternoon.

'What? Where you off to then?' Mrs Narracott paused at the sink, sleeves rolled up to skinny elbows.

'I have to visit Mr Benedict in the hospital. He's very ill. I need to see him.' Loveday met the thunderous frown with a resolute smile. 'I'll make up the time another day. But this is important, so I'm going.'

'Well!' Mrs Narracott's explosive comment went unheard as Loveday left the kitchen and hurried back to Market Street. She was thankful that Henry didn't appear. 'Mr Long has several appointments today, so won't be back until after tea time,' said Aunt Janet. 'But he did wonder if you were going to see Frank Benedict. And he said, if you did, please give Frank his best wishes.'

Loveday's answer was carefully controlled. 'Yes, I will. I'm going as soon as we've finished the meal. I told Mrs Narracott.'

Janet looked across the table, her mind busy. Something had happened to the beloved child just lately. Of course, it had been hard, learning about Maggie, but something else – a new tilt of the head, a lively smile when she returned from those evening walks with Mr Long and the dog. Mr Long? Ah, thought Janet, spooning out fish stew and watching Davey butter his bread too thickly. So that's it, is it? Well, perhaps not a bad thing. He seems a gentleman, and a well mannered one. But, of course, he's older than her. Would it matter?

'You're spilling the stew, Janet – be careful' Davey's warning returned her to the intricacies of serving and she tutted as she cleared up the spillage, her thoughts racing. Glancing at Loveday as she did so, she wondered what had happened to Mr Kerslake, Mrs Sothern's cousin, who had called last week and seemed so nice. Now, he was a gentleman, too – and had obviously taken a fancy to Loveday. She sliced more bread, offering it around the table and said quietly, 'I understand that Mrs Sothern has invited Mr Long to dinner on Friday.' She paused, and then added, 'Maggie called in yesterday afternoon with a shawl that needs some stitches. She told me that Mr and Mrs Sothern are very interested in what Mr Long is doing down there in the shipyard.'

Loveday didn't look up from her plate. 'So it seems. Yes, I know he's going on Friday. I heard Mrs Sothern invite him at Labrador.' She slid a determinedly mischievous look at her aunt. 'Perhaps he's going to get Mrs Sothern to persuade Mr Sothern to put money in the old yard. Mr Long is a very ambitious man, you know.'

Davey nudged Janet's arm before she could reply and shook his head. She knew what he was silently saying – leave the child alone, let her live her own life. And deep within herself, Janet knew he was right. Of course he was. Yet Loveday had been their own child for so long – how could she not worry about her future? But she nodded back and then said lightly, 'Maggie will be having an evening off tomorrow. I invited her to drop in and see us.'

She watched Loveday look up and then back at her plate and she guessed what went on in the child's mind, but said no more And then dinner was over and Loveday helped clear away the dishes before she left to visit poor old Frank Benedict, while Janet hoped fervently that it wasn't too late to find him still alive.

The hospital was busy and Loveday stopped a passing nurse as she walked down the corridor towards the main ward.

'Mr Benedict? Yes, the last bed on the right.' The nurse looked at her intently, then added, 'Don't stop too long and don't bother him with anything. He can't last much longer. Just try and keep him happy, will you?'

'Of course.' Loveday's heart beat faster and a chill descended on her mind. She found Frank at the far end of the ward, where an open window allowed the faint music of the sea to enter the stuffy, highly disinfected room. He was seemingly asleep when she pulled a chair up to his bedside but he opened his eyes slowly and smiled.

'Ah, maid. Good of you to come. Somethin' I needs to say to 'ee afore I go.' Painfully, he tried to sit up and she helped him, pulling the pillows straight behind his head. He drew in a creaking breath, coughed and then looked towards the window. 'Salt. Salt of the sea. Lovely, better'n all this chemical stuff here.' A pause and then he turned his head towards her. 'What's the tide doin', my love? On the ebb, is it?'

Loveday's mind jumped. What had Henry said? Dying sailors wait for the tide to ebb. Somehow she managed a smile and took the frail, bony hand in her own. 'Yes, it's going out, Mr Benedict, but it's a lovely day. No wind to talk of, just quiet water and the fishermen bringing in a good catch, so I heard.'

He nodded and looked at her keenly. 'That ole scrimshaw,' he said, with a breath between each word. 'It's got a sort o'secret on it, see. I've given you the piece I were given in Newfoundland, and your mother – Maggie – has got another one. You must ask her for it.'

'I've got it, Mr Benedict. I saw my brother yesterday and I've borrowed the piece so that I can see them together.'

'Well, there's a third one, my lover. I saw it once and then – well, where it is now, I dunno. But when you gets it—' The old man collapsed into a wracking cough, bowed his head and seemed unable to go on. Loveday got up, called a nurse from the far end of the ward and watched while a drink was given and another pillow piled up behind the stooped back.

'Mr Benedict, don't talk if it's so difficult.'

Rheumy eyes looked at her again and she was struck by the spark of life suddenly shining on the thin, bony face. 'I ain't gone yet,' Frank croaked painfully. 'Jest time enough to tell you that when you finds that third piece of the ole scrimshaw, then you'll know it all and everything will be righted. Jest keep hopin' and waitin', my lover.'

Tight-throated, Loveday nodded. The words made little sense and all she could think of was that he was dying in front of her. She gripped his hand and with the other smoothed the few strands of grey hair off his forehead. 'Thank you, Mr Benedict. I'll remember what you've told me. And I hope I shall find the third piece eventually.'

He smiled at her. 'It all works out in the end, however bad it seems. Now then, maid, let me sleep. I've said enough and somethin's callin' me.'

153

Tears swam in her eyes as she gently put his hand on his chest, straightened the slipping coverlet, and rose from her chair. And then she remembered. 'Henry – Mr Long – said to give you his good wishes.'

'A good man. Thank him fer me.' Frank Benedict closed his eyes and Loveday knew she could stay no longer.

She walked back towards the Beach View Hotel, her mind busy, her feelings unhappily stimulated. On the esplanade, she stopped and looked down the beach. The tide was ebbing, just a few last waves receding slowly in a lace of froth and foam. Very soon it would be at its lowest and Frank Benedict could slip away with it. So Henry's words had been true.

What had Frank called him? A good man. Had Frank been right? So was *she* wrong?

During the afternoon's toil in the bedrooms at the Beach View Hotel, she thought constantly of Frank's words about the pieces of scrimshaw. There had been no time to look at them this morning, but as soon as she got home she would go to her room and really try to make out what the words said. Hope and wait, he'd told her. What on earth had he meant? Was it just an old, tired man's confusion, mixing the past with some dreamlike phantasies in his weary mind? Would she ever know?

But Loveday, with her new feeling of strength, refused to waste time on imagination. So, when she eventually returned to Market Street, three-quarters of an hour later than usual because Mrs Narracott, timing her, had said shortly that one of the attic rooms needed clearing before she left, she had almost forgotten the scrimshaw. In the forefront of her mind was Frank and the ebbing tide and the need to tell Henry all that the old man had said.

But Henry was still away.

'He sent a message from the shipyard. Apparently Mr Harvey's foreman is taking him around, showing him the state it's in. Said he would be late for tea, but not to bother as he would find a bite in the town if necessary.' Janet Jenkins frowned. 'I told Mr Briggs to tell Mr Long that there would be a good meal waiting for him here, whatever time he came back.' She sniffed. 'A lodger needs looking after – and Mr Long's a hearty eater. He wouldn't be satisfied with any of that café nonsense, I'm sure.'

Loveday smiled secretly. Her aunt seemed to have taken Henry into the family. Then the smile died. So what did Henry think about that? But she refused to give the idea any further thought. Quietly she told Janet about Frank Benedict and the ebbing tide.

Janet was silent for a long moment. Then she sighed, nodded. 'Poor old man. Those fishermen, full of superstition they are, always afraid of something. Mustn't go to sea on a Friday, mustn't wear green, oh, all sorts of things. But I'm sorry about Frank. Mind you, he was a good age.' Suddenly her face was swamped by memories. 'A good bit older than your dad, but I think they knew each other.' Abruptly she stopped. 'Well now, no need to go into all that. Why, I nearly forgot, there's a letter for you – here.'

Loveday took the envelope and examined it. Expensive, addressed to Miss L. Jenkins in a neat hand. 'Who brought it, Aunt Janet? It hasn't come by post.'

Janet smiled. 'Your friend, Mr Kerslake, delivered it. Said it's from his cousin, Mrs Sothern.' Her smile broadened and her voice grew softer. 'Such a nice young man. And he said he's looking forward to seeing you on Friday. Well, go on, child, open it.'

She watched Loveday's colour suddenly come and go, and revised her thoughts about Henry Long. So it was this Mr Kerslake, was it? Well, well, one never knew; girls of today had such secrets.

Loveday took the folded letter from the envelope and read it slowly. Isobel Sothern's invitation seeming almost rudely two-handed.

Dear Miss Jenkins

My cousin Mr Kerslake has suggested that you entertain us after dinner on Friday evening with airs on the pianoforte. I had envisaged that you would join us after the meal, but he is insistent that you accompany Mr Long, who is also dining with us. I have to admit that your presence would also make up my numbers. I look forward to your acceptance of this invitation at your speediest.
Yours sincerely
Isobel Sothern

'Well!' Loveday wasn't sure whether to be furious or amused – and then a small interior voice suggested she should rather be pleased. She chose the last possibility and handed the letter to Janet, who said quickly, 'Why, that's wonderful, child. What will you play?'

'What will I wear?' seemed a far more important question, and for the rest of the evening the conversation centred on whether the pale yellow dress might do, or whether MODES in the town could provide anything more elegant.

'You must write your acceptance note at once and hand it in tomorrow morning,' insisted Janet. 'And I'll see what I can do about your frock. Dear me, so little time – why it's Friday in two days! We shall have to hurry.'

It was getting dark when a rap at the door reminded the household that the lodger was still out, but that this was probably him. It was. Loveday opened the door and at once stepped back, not meeting Henry's eyes. She watched him tell Floss to sit before removing his hat, putting down his briefcase on the hall stand, and then turning to look at her.

Only then did words come to her. 'Has the tide turned?' she asked, and he looked surprised, but nodded. 'Yes, about half an hour ago, I reckon. Why?'

She put a hand to her mouth. 'Because Mr Benedict – I think he's finally gone. He asked about the tide when I saw him this afternoon.'

Beneath the spluttering gas mantle they looked at each other and she saw his taut expression soften into gentleness. He nodded. 'A good old man, let's hope he had a painless passing,' was all he said.

Tears pricked behind her eyes and swiftly she turned. 'Your meal is in the kitchen,' she said unevenly, and at once went up the stairs, away from him, knowing those keen eyes watched every step she took. She had no idea of his thoughts, but found herself uneasy and regretful.

In her candlelit room, she took refuge in the pieces of scrimshaw. She knew almost by heart the shape and carvings of the one Frank had given her, its blackened figure of a man carrying something, a woman's blurred face, and then the flowers and tiny carved, almost illegible letters. Her fingers ran over the patterns while her mind ran in circles. Who was the man? What did the letters say? Was there a message to be read or was it just the idle doodling of a bored seaman waiting for the tide? She picked up Maggie's piece and put it next to her own. Yes, the patterns repeated themselves, but, pulling the candle nearer, she peered through the shadowy light at the letters on the second piece and thought they seemed to carry on where the first ones left off. Was she imagining things?

Sighing, suddenly weary after the emotional reactions of the day, she put down the pieces and began undressing. And then other thoughts took over her bewilderment and frustration. Tomorrow Maggie would be calling in the evening. What would this meeting be like? Would Maggie show her resentment because of all the unkind things she had said last week? Would there be hostility still filling the air? Or perhaps more tears and stories of remorse, even more pleas for understanding?

In bed, with the candle dowsed and the new moon making a soft, brief appearance through the open window, Loveday lay awake, trying to sleep, but finding her thoughts too vivid, too demanding to do so.

Maggie, Jack wanting to go to sea and growing sullen and uncommunicative, Henry becoming immersed in his plans for furthering his ambition, and poor old Frank dying. Closing her eyes tightly, she demanded that all the worrying images vanish. Surely she could control her mind? And then a new thought came, why not imagine what it would be like, dining with the Sotherns on Friday? And yes, drifting off now, Loveday's smile curved her mouth and helped sleep to approach.

A new dress. Perhaps a dark red one . . . or even something green and floaty . . . the vague idea that Ned had liked her in the yellow dress lingered. Ned, with his smile and warm, insistent eyes, his irresistible charm. The image flowered into near reality and at last she slept.

Early next morning she wrote a short, polite note accepting Mrs Sothern's kind invitation, and saying she would be delighted to dine and to entertain the company afterwards by playing the piano. As she wrote she smiled wickedly. Poor Issy must be very cross with Ned for forcing her to invite such a low-class person, but Issy would soon see that the piano tutor was not only well dressed, but able to contribute sensibly to the general conversation. And Ned would be proud of her. And that, thought Loveday, sealing the envelope, and going down to breakfast, was all that she had in mind today. Everything else could be pushed back. This evening she and Aunt Janet would somehow contrive to find or make a dress which would outshine even Issy Sothern.

And if occasional uneasy thoughts about Maggie calling later on slipped through all this excitement, Loveday gave them no heed. Even Henry's low voice bidding her good morning was something to be ignored, after a hasty, polite nod of the head. She was in another world, and it was far happier than the one she usually inhabited. Suddenly, helping clear the table, she knew what was happening and caught her breath. Was it possible? Was another far land appearing, warmer, more exciting and more lovable and nearer than those far-off blue and green icebergs and sea monsters that Frank had told her about?

Such an extraordinary thought but it stayed with her as she left Market Street in good time to climb East Cliff and deliver her letter before returning to the Beach View Hotel And although she saw Henry and Floss following at a distance, she refused to look back, not wishing them to catch her up.

This new world was filled with thoughts of Ned, and she smiled as she approached Sothern House.

CHAPTER FIFTEEN

Henry met Owen Hutchins, Kenneth Harvey's solicitor, in the office on the first floor of the shipyard, having been given the key before he left the invalid the previous evening. On the long table were the piles of papers and drawings that he and Kenneth Harvey had been reading only yesterday. The accounts, which he had studied earlier, had been written up by Davey Jenkins, and appeared to be a model of copperplate writing and neat, legible figures. There were no problems there and his mind was relieved to think that at least the shipyard was still just about solvent, although neglected and run down.

Owen Hutchins was stocky, plump and grey whiskered, with keen brown eyes. Wide fleshy jowls broadened as he smiled and his voice was friendly. 'Good morning, Mr Long.' They shook hands and then sat down at the table. He drew a document out from his briefcase and laid it in front of Henry, looking at him assessingly. 'Well, my old friend Kenneth Harvey has made his wishes quite clear, Mr Long, and I must state that I consider him to be in complete control of his own mind. He wishes to appoint you as manager of the shipyard, which remains in his possession.' Fierce eyebrows raised warningly. 'Of course, you must understand that there is a board of directors which comprises Harvey, myself and Joshua Sothern, a local business man of whom you may have heard, and we shall have the final word about the decision.'

Henry nodded. How these legal men liked to draw out their briefs. He forced a check on his rising impatience. *Manager? Not partner? Well, that's something. At least I can get the business going again and then. . . .* He took a deep breath. 'I accept the position. And when will it start? As I see it, the shipyard is in urgent need of repair, restoration, and new contracts. I feel there's no time to be wasted.'

'Ah, you young men!' Owen Hutchins sat back and smiled. 'No time like the present, eh? Well, Mr Long, I shall be meeting with Kenneth –

Mr Harvey – and Mr Sothern in a few days' time and then I shall be able to answer your question. In the meantime, I would like you to read, digest and then sign this paper.'

Henry looked at it, swiftly read through his obligations and then signed his name with satisfaction. His new position was legally established, although a contract had still to appear. But he had no doubts that, in good time – and solicitors had plenty of that – all would be sealed and settled. This paper was enough to get him started.

He stood up and wished he had a bottle of whisky with which to seal the deal. He glanced around the room, at the shelves, cupboards and iron-bound sea chest and then gave up. No knowing where old Harvey hid his drinks. Well, for the time being words alone would have to do. 'Thank you, Mr Hutchins. I look forward to hearing the results of the board meeting and I would ask you to pass on my good wishes – and thanks – to Mr Harvey when next you see him.'

Owen Hutchins replaced the paper in his case, closed it, and then took a last keen look at the young man who was clearly eager to start work on getting the business going again. He nodded farewell, and then descended the stairs to the waiting gig, which took him back to his chambers in time for the next appointment, which just happened to be luncheon.

Henry, with Floss at his heels, lost no more time and at once strode down through the shipyard, looking around at each section of it, noting faults and making plans for its immediate repair. The store, with its long counter, gantries and shelves full of small drawers, was untidy. The painted labels of paints, nails, and oils were almost obliterated. Piles of unwanted rigging and rope lay in heaps in the corners of the long, low building and the smell of rubbish mixed harshly with the more familiar scents of resin, size, salt, timber and pitch which sent Henry's mind back to the Dorset shipyard of his youth and the long years of learning to build boats under his uncle's supervision.

He walked on to inspect the saw pit, where the two sawyers stood idle, watching his approach and then at once moving as if to resume their work. Henry's eyes narrowed but he said nothing. On then to the steamer where planks were steamed to the shapes required of them but there was no work progressing today. And so to the furnace with its huge cauldron of pitch. No bubbles or harsh, nose-clogging smell of coal tar – just a couple of apprentices hiding their playing cards and standing up as he appeared. One of them, Mick, who had rowed him round to Labrador, grinned uneasily and lifted a hand to his forelock. The other boy just stared.

Henry returned to the yard where a single boat keel had been laid down, looked around, nodded to the watching foreman and told him to gather the hands. He looked at them with a hard, cool stare as he said crisply, 'I'm the new manager, and my name's Long. Mr Harvey, who is sadly incapacitated, has delegated power to me and I'm going to get this old place working again. You'll all be kept on and I'll listen to any complaints you may have, but I warn you' – dull eyes were suddenly keener, staring back at him and showing new interest – 'I'll have no truck with slapdash work. We're going to make boats, and make money from them, just as the business did years ago. So – are you prepared to work with me, get Harvey's shipyard off the ground and remind the county of its past excellent reputation?'

A long moment's quietness, then slowly one voice growled 'yessir' and was taken up by others. Only Briggs, the foreman, kept silent and Henry looked at him pointedly. 'Well, Briggs? What've you got to say?'

Jesse Briggs sucked his teeth and met the new manager's eyes with a tight expression. 'Us don't want any newcomers tellin' us how to do our work,' he said slowly. 'Us do know more about boats and their makin' than people like you – so if I may, I'll ask what's your qualification – *sir*?'

Henry heard suspicion in the grudging title but kept his temper. 'Fair enough,' he said. 'I did my apprenticeship in my uncle's boatyard in Dorset, worked with him for ten years and I'm a qualified draughtsman. I plan to bring back some of the good old rowing boats that were made here a decade or more ago. Mine will be more modern. And you don't have to worry, Briggs, that I'll interfere where I'm not needed.'

They stared at each other and the watchers stood still, wondering. Henry's voice was clear and authoritative, his Canadian accent more marked as he made his stance for his new position, adding, 'But I'm the manager, I'm in charge and you'll do well to remember that.'

Silence again until a few quiet words of repeated *yessirs* brought the interview to an end. Briggs looked thoughtful and turned away, and Henry continued his inspection of the yard, Floss beside him, and his mind full of intentions and plans, knowing that this was a day he would remember for the rest of his life.

Maggie arrived after tea to find Janet and Loveday in the front room looking at material and old dresses. Davey, she imagined, would be hiding somewhere to get away from all this feminine fussiness, while the lodger, whom she had yet to meet, would probably be in the parlour or his own bedroom. Nothing to worry about there. But it was Loveday she did worry about. Meeting her daughter again after that horrible after-noon last week had been preying on her mind ever since and although she had forced herself to call in to the Jenkins's home this evening, now she was here, she wished fervently she had just gone to Carpenters' Row and spent the evening with Jack.

The two women looked up as she hesitantly said, 'Hello, not too early, am I? Mrs Sothern was good enough to let me come an hour before my usual time.'

Janet smiled. 'Come in, Maggie. Loveday needs a new dinner dress and we're just seeing what we can do with the bits we've got. This pale rose is pretty, don't you think?'

Maggie made a huge effort and looked at Loveday. Cool green eyes met her, but there was no smile and although the girl nodded, Maggie sensed the lingering hostility and felt herself quail. But then a thought came, helpful and supportive. 'I've got a dress would just about fit you, Loveday – given to me by Mrs Treveryan it was. She was always giving me things. This one's greeny blue, closed at the neck and a lovely rich silk.' She stopped. How much more must she offer before the girl decided to smile? 'I could go and fetch it and show it to you, if you thought—' Words died and she looked despairingly at her uncommunicative daugh-ter.

Loveday met the anxious, watery gaze and felt herself grow taut with the remembered rejection. She wanted nothing that this woman could offer. 'Thank you, but I don't like the idea of wearing a hand-me-down,' she said sharply and then was shocked at how Maggie recoiled, hastily leaning a hand on the nearest chair.

Janet's voice was cold and angry. 'Loveday, how can you say such an ungrateful thing?'

They looked at each other and Loveday realized that the dice were loaded against her; the sisters were on one side and she on the other. 'I—' she began, but Janet was off again.

'No hand-me-downs, indeed! And so where do you think that pretty yellow dress you wore when you went to the Wintergardens with the Sotherns came from? Not from Mr Rudkin's haberdashery store, because I only had a few spare shillings in my purse.' Her eyes flashed. 'Oh no, my girl, that dress was in the window of MODES when I saw it and knew that you must have it. Definitely a hand-me-down, so please don't offend your mother by saying such unkind things.'

The room was tight with silence and charged feelings and Loveday felt in turmoil. She looked at Maggie who stared back with a hesitant smile, and then at her aunt. Janet's face was unfamiliarly stern and she stood straight and implacable, her hand still resting on the length of material spread on the work table.

Loveday drew in a long breath. She knew she was in the wrong and that she should apologize, but it was hard. *My mother abandoned me and now she's just trying to make up for it. I don't know what to do.*

Then, unexpectedly, Maggie came forward and laid her hand on Loveday's arm. Her voice was quiet, so low that the words were almost inaudible. But they made sense. 'It was a gift, not something just thrown out. Mrs Treveryan was very generous, so there's a difference, you see. Perhaps you might like to look at it?'

Loveday stared at the pale, ageing face, took in her mother's stooped posture, and suddenly had images of what life must have been like in the years since Maggie gave her to Janet and Davey. The unhappy pictures brought a quick turn of mind. Leaving a young child, even in the protection of responsible relatives, must have been such a hard decision, even when prompted by the knowledge that another child was on the way and the workhouse the only escape. And although, as she rapidly thought, the reason for Jack's nurturing rather than her own was still not understood or explained, she felt a quick stabbing sympathy for the young woman who had made that extraordinary decision.

Of course she still felt wronged, abandoned and rejected. But still. . . .

The words tasted sour in her mouth, but she forced them out. 'Thank you, I'm sorry I was rude. And yes, I should very much like to see the dress.'

Like a shaft of redeeming sunlight, the atmosphere in the room lightened. Janet nodded, then turned, starting to fold away the length of material on the table, while Maggie stood straighter, her face uplifted by a delighted smile.

'Yes, of course. I'll go and fetch it straight away; it won't take me long. I know where I have it stored, upstairs, in the chest.' She opened the door and hurried out. Loveday exchanged glances with Janet and followed her mother. 'Wait, I'll come with you,' she said, surprising herself and then walking down the street at Maggie's side, not knowing what to say next, but understanding that something important and unplanned had happened; the first step towards a reconciliation had been taken.

Carpenters' Row was almost awash with a high tide, the water rolling and surging and often reaching the threshold of the row of cottages. Maggie exclaimed, pulled Loveday out of the way of the waves, and unlocked the door. 'This terrible place – how the landlord keeps it stand-ing I'll never understand. And he won't do any repairs – not for the rent I pay, he says.'

Loveday followed her into the small, musty smelling room and saw damp stains on the river-facing wall. She began to understand just how awful it must be living here – a good reason for Jack to want to leave and go somewhere else. And to Maggie – Mother, she thought quickly, but still couldn't bring herself to accept the name – after living in the comfort and opulence of Sothern House, even if the servant's quarters were in the attic, one night a week in this smelly little hovel must be quite dreadful.

Briskly, Maggie said, 'Sit down, won't you, while I go and fetch that dress,' and disappeared up the rickety stairs. Loveday heard bumps and scrapes on the floorboards as a chest was pulled out and opened, and then Maggie came down again, smiling, with the dress draped over one arm.

'Look,' she said, holding it up. 'It's so pretty and this colour would suit you well. Why don't we go back to Janet's and then you can try it on?' Her smile faded. 'I wouldn't want you taking your clothes off here, in this nasty place.'

The dress, which she held up against Loveday, was a startlingly vivid peacock blue-green, its thick silk murmuring as it fell against her body. Immediately Loveday guessed that the length was right, the ballooning sleeves which slid down into tight-fitting wristbands would suit her, and the severe bodice was surely redeemed by the whoosh of full skirt coming from the sides and falling to her feet. She fingered the high neck and pictured a lace collar from Aunt Janet's valued bag of pieces crowning the elegance of the dress.

She knew it would suit her; it was a foil to her auburn hair and pale skin and suddenly she longed to wear it, to look so good that Issy Sothern's prim mouth would fall open in admiration and even a touch of envy. Vanity, Aunt Janet had always told her, was one of the sins of which women must beware; but then Aunt Janet didn't share her own longing to step out of her humble, burdened life and become someone else, some-one independent and grown up who longed to be admired.

So – 'Yes, I'd like that. Thank you.' She gave no title to the small woman who was looking at her with pleading eyes and the suggestion of a smile. It was all too difficult and the sooner she got back to Market Street the easier she would feel, for being with Maggie brought with it something quite the opposite of what she wanted – a feeling of guilt. She was sure, though, that trying on this lovely dress would banish all such miserable thoughts. 'Come along,' she said eagerly. 'Shall I carry it?' and held out her arms but Maggie was already delving into a cupboard.

'Good gracious no, you can't just carry a dress out there along the street – what ever would people think? No, here's a bag, this will hold it nicely.'

So there they were, two women keeping an awkward distance between them as they hurried back up the street, both of them thankfully welcoming Janet's smile and interest as they returned to the front room, where the pier glass was already set by the window to catch the light, and Janet had her pincushion ready on the table.

And Janet had another surprise. 'I've found a pair of shoes which I haven't worn since I was a young woman. I think they'll probably fit you, child. And, oh yes, they'll look so good with that dress. Here, sit down and try them on.'

Glossy kid slippers with a small heel, decorated with mother of pearl. Dressed in the new ensemble and not finding anything wanting, Loveday looked at her reflection in the long mirror and could hardly believe what she saw. Her smile glowed as she thought that Ned must surely find this new, elegant creature irresistible.

Henry came home quite late, finding Jack in the kitchen with Davey. Toast was being made over the banked-up fire and Jack was tucking into large slices topped with cheese. Davey brandished the toasting fork as he introduced them, and then smiled as Henry returned from putting Floss to bed in the outhouse. 'Jack came along to find out where his mother had disappeared to – well, the ladies are busy,' he said, 'fussing about with dresses and what not. But I can give you a quick meal, Mr Long, if you're ready for it. Do you fancy toast and cheese? Oh, and this letter arrived by the last post.'

Henry opened it casually, his thoughts still focused on the shipyard and its demands. At first he only skipped through the contents, and then abruptly he read it again. Blankly he looked at Davey. 'I beg your pardon?'

'Your supper, Mr Long.'

'Thank you. Yes, cheese will do nicely. On toast. Sure, thanks.' He stopped and then pushed the letter across the table. 'Read this. Please – read it.'

Davey put down the fork, fished his spectacles out of his pocket and, slightly bemused, picked up the letter. When he had read and then reread it, he put it down, looked at Henry and said slowly, 'But this is amazing.

I can hardly believe—'

'Exactly.' Henry's voice was sharp and quick.

Jack looked up. 'What is it? What are you talking about?'

Henry looked at the boy; another relative, another member of the Jenkins family. Nothing really to do with him. He picked up the letter again, gave it another glance and then looked back at Davey. 'I think your sister must read this. Could you ask her to come in here? Alone?'

Davey nodded, made his way out of the kitchen and tapped on the front room door, putting his head around it and indicating to Janet, with a wave of his hand, that he needed her. She came slowly, looking back over her shoulder and saying, 'Take the dress off now, Loveday, and hang it up. I'll see to that hem tomorrow morning. And Maggie, will you have a cup of tea before you leave?'

Henry heard no more, for Davey closed the door firmly behind Janet as she walked towards the kitchen saying, 'Really Davey, what ever do you want at this time of the evening? I have enough to do already, you know—'

She stopped, saw Jack, and smiled. 'Well, how nice to see you here, Jack – and having a bite to eat. I hope your Uncle Davey is doing his best for you?'

The boy nodded, managed a smile, and reached for another piece of toast.

Janet looked at Henry who stood by the table, the letter in his hand. He pulled out a chair. 'Miss Jenkins, please read this.'

With an expression of surprise, she sat down and then accepted the letter. It took only a few seconds to read it. And then she looked up, staring first at Davey and then at Henry. Her face was drained of colour, her dark eyes even darker. She swallowed loudly and then, carefully, in a low voice, said, 'Loveday must see this. And, of course, Maggie. They are both in the front room at the moment, but I don't know. . . .' She shook her head, looked again at the letter. 'and then, of course, Jack—'

The boy's face was taut. 'What is it? What's it got to do with me? Tell me—'

'Be patient for a minute longer, Jack.' Thoughts flew across her face. She took a breath. Then, 'Mr Long, what do you suggest?'

He thought hard before answering. Once this amazing news was out the family would be – again – disturbed and in confusion and Loveday would have added worries. So, presumably, would her mother. And what price the boy? But he couldn't pretend the letter had never arrived. After all, he had told Loveday he would try to find out anything he could. And now the reply was here and of course she must learn the truth.

But, even as he paused, Janet had made her decision. 'Perhaps you would like me to tell everyone, Mr Long? After all, it's to do with my family and there's no need for you to become involved.'

She couldn't have used a more cathartic word. *Involved*, thought Henry wryly. Exactly what he hoped to avoid, being involved with Loveday's family. Even with Loveday herself. Surely it would be wiser to let Miss Jenkins read the letter?

As if she knew his churning thoughts, she said again, 'Give me the letter, Mr Long. I'll go and tell them.'

No, said a small but firm voice inside Henry's head. *She can be there to pick up the pieces if there are any, but I'm the one to tell Loveday what the letter says. All right, I shall be involved . . . but I can't just step away from all this. I've got to go on.*

Quickly, he smiled into her worried eyes and said, 'If you'll allow me, Miss Jenkins, I'll read the letter myself to your niece and your sister.' He turned, gave Jack a half smile. 'And your nephew, too. But please be there just in case. . . .' An image of possible dismay and overflowing emotions stopped him. '. . . in case they are very upset.'

Janet met his look with approval. She stood up and smiled, first at Jack and then at Davey.

'Come along, both of you,' she said. 'Quickly, before Loveday goes to bed and Maggie returns home.' Nodding, she led the way out of the kitchen and opened the door of the front room, taking Jack's arm and pushing him forward.

'Maggie, Loveday, and you, Jack,' she said unsteadily, as questioning eyes met her, 'Mr Long has received some news. Let's all sit down and hear what he has to say.'

Henry looked at Loveday, saw emotion colouring her cheeks, sensed that she was uncomfortable at having to face him after that kiss the other night, as he himself suddenly felt, but forced himself to open the letter.

Slowly and firmly, in a clipped voice, he began to read.

CHAPTER SIXTEEN

Amos stayed in St Johns for fourteen years. Money came and went, as did work. Lumbering, making barrels, mining, anything he could find to earn a living. He sometimes thought of Devon and the small girl and her mother but there was always another woman to banish the memories and not enough money to send back. Then there was Addie's daughter, but no son.

And now? Something had changed inside his head; the yearning for a son was still obsessive, but life had moved on. He was lonely and began to realize that over the years he had learned a gentler point of view. Don't judge. Don't seek revenge. Think about companionship, kindliness, loving.

Yes, he would go back to that misty, dreamlike far land. If Maggie was still there, if the small girl had grown up, he could find them, make his excuses, ask for another chance. Would they remember him? Sleepless one night, fighting nightmares of guilt and hopelessness, he looked into the blackness of his cold rented room and wondered for the first time if they might, somehow, even love him again. And if they didn't?

He wouldn't ever blame them. And what if nothing worked out, back there? What then? But every day brought the need for a decision nearer, made it more important, until he could think of nothing else.

He knew he must run the risk. Yes, he must go back.

'In reply to your enquiry re ss *Briganza*, leaving port in July, 1871, we can confirm that this vessel sank in the Atlantic Ocean after collision with a Norwegian collier in thick fog. There were nineteen survivors and we are able to name one of them as Amos Hunt, seaman, born in Devonshire, present whereabouts unknown.

I trust this information is sufficient for your needs.

Yours faithfully. Etc.'

Henry stopped reading, held out the letter and watched Loveday reach forward to take it in both hands and stare down at the neat, copperplate writing. In the silence that followed he saw her eyes become enormous sea-green pools, watched her face tighten and, with a stab of dismay, realized she was shocked and confused, and not, as he had hoped, intrigued and perhaps excited by the news.

Putting his spectacles back in his pocket, he said, 'I wrote a week or so ago and this is the reply. I knew you would want to know straight away.'

She said nothing, simply stared at the letter as if she couldn't believe what it said. He stood still in the little, cluttered room and slowly looked at the faces surrounding him. The silence was building up as emotions swelled, and he was aware of frantic minds debating whether it was good news or bad. He felt the room filling with a charge that was almost tangible.

Then voices began to explode.

'I can't believe it.' Loud and unsteady, Janet stared first at Davey, then at Loveday, and at last at Maggie who stood with her hand on Jack's shoulder. 'No, I don't believe it. He would have written. He would have come back. It's a mistake.' She shook her head then looked at Davey again.

'Can't be a mistake, Janet. This letter's from an Admiralty authority. They have lists and things. No mistake. But – I don't understand—' Davey's gaze turned on Maggie whose face was as pale as ash. 'My dear, I know how you must feel—'

'What?' Maggie turned her head, stared at him, mild eyes suddenly fierce, drowning in agitation. Words fell out, rapid and choked. 'No, I don't know how I feel . . . I mean, if he didn't drown, then where is he? Why didn't he come home? Why?' Tears fell then and she clutched at Jack, pulling his head to her breast, sobbing, calling out, 'Amos! Amos, why didn't you come back?' and then, with Davey's guiding hand around her, collapsed in the chair beside the table.

Jack kneeled at her side, long strong fingers stroking her arm. 'Don't, Mother, don't. P'raps he's still trying to come – p'raps he'll suddenly appear—' His voice broke and he coughed. Then he looked up, met Janet's eyes, looked at Loveday, and then back at his mother. 'He doesn't know 'bout me, does he? So when he comes he'll find he's got a son. And I've got a father.' Excitement filled his bony face.

Maggie's sobs quietened for a moment, Davey and Janet shaking their heads. Then he said, louder, sounding almost jubilant, 'A father! And I reckon as how he'll let me go to sea. But where is he?' Abruptly the excitement fell away. He coughed again, recovering enough to add hoarsely, 'D'you think he's still alive?'

Another, deeper silence.

Henry felt he shouldn't be here. This family must sort out its own sorrows and hopes. But then he saw Loveday staring at him, eyes troubled and colour burning her cheeks and knew, for good or bad, that he was involved. He had found the wretched news and in doing so had become part of them. Part of their troubles. He cleared his throat, looked at the pale, questing faces and said gruffly, 'If I can do anything to help any of you . . . please tell me.'

No one said anything. Eyes moved around from shocked face to face. Janet's breath was too loud, Maggie's face grey and trembling. It was Davey who at last put his hand on Janet's shoulder and said very quietly, 'I think a pot of tea would help us all to come to terms with what Mr Long has just told us. Loveday. . . .' He turned aside, smiled and finally broke into her sightless gaze. 'Be a good maid and put the kettle on, why not? And we'll all come into the kitchen where it's warmer. And Janet, I'm sure you've got some biscuits somewhere—'

Like the unexpected cessation of a winter gale, the atmosphere in the little room suddenly settled into a new, hesitant peace. Loveday nodded, went to the door as if she were walking in a trance, and one by one Maggie and Jack, Janet and Davey followed her.

Davey looked back over his shoulder. 'Mr Long, we don't wish to bother you with all this, but if you would care to have a cup of tea you're very welcome.' He paused. Then, 'After all,' with a wry smile, 'we're in your debt, whether we like it or not.'

Henry nodded, heard footsteps walking through the hallway and fading as the kitchen door opened and then shut again. Thank God he was alone now, and could put this whole bothersome matter out of his head. Floss was already in the back yard, so all he need do was light his candle and go to bed. To sleep and, if any dreams came, he was sure they would be of the shipyard and his forthcoming contract.

So why did he shake his head, and, instead, grudgingly accept that he must join the family in the kitchen? Why did he need to seek out Loveday's taut face and try to understand how hurt, or how pleased or even how fearful she was? Unable to deny this urgent demand, he sighed and then joined them, took tea as invited, and listened to the voices arguing, hoping, fearing, and not involving him at all. But he couldn't forget Loveday was there, sitting silently, pouring cups of tea and passing the biscuit tin, not looking at him.

When at last Maggie said a tremulous goodnight, leaning heavily on Jack's arm before leaving the house, and Janet and Davey lit their candles and disappeared up the stairs, only Loveday remained and he knew, with an uneasy certainty, that she wanted to speak to him alone.

They looked at each other in silence, she sitting at the head of the long scrubbed table, he perched on a hard chair by the door leading to the back yard. The fire shifted and embers fell into the grate. Henry waited. It was for her to either thank him, or perhaps invite him to share her sorrow.

She did neither. Suddenly getting to her feet, she came a step nearer, looked down into his upturned face, and said quietly, but in a voice full of slow, unsteady emotion, 'You shouldn't have done it. You've only given us new hopes, new expectations. Now we shall never know whether he's dead or not. At least before this letter came we thought he was gone, and even if we still grieved, we weren't going to spend the rest of our lives waiting for him to come back.' A moment's fast breathing. 'And you've hurt my poor mother so much – what will she be thinking now?' Her voice dropped. She bowed her head and almost whispered in a choking voice, 'You shouldn't have done it, Henry.'

He rose, completely taken aback. He saw her look away, ocean-green eyes wide and swimming, watched her fumble to find a handkerchief in her skirt pocket, saw the first tears running down her silky cheeks, and was lost.

'Loveday, Loveday—' God, he couldn't stand seeing her like this. He must comfort her. *Must. . . .*

She looked up, took a huge breath, let it out in a cry of pain, and then fell against him.

In his arms she felt like a small, trembling ghost. He breathed deeply, telling himself to take care. She mustn't be hurt any further. She was weeping against his jacket, her breath warming his already tensed body. She meant so much to him. If she lifted her head he knew he must kiss her.

She looked up, and even as his head came down towards her trembling mouth, she pushed him away. 'No! I'm sorry! I don't want to have any more to do with you! You've upset all our lives with your knowledge, your quick decisions and – and your unthinking suggestions.' She snatched a breath before her voice faded into almost inaudible, choked words. 'I wish you'd go away and never come back! No, don't touch me.' He took a step forward, arms reaching for her, but she moved very fast, towards the closed door. One hand on the latch, she looked back at him. 'I'm sorry, Henry. But you were wrong,' and she was gone, her light foot-steps racing up the stairs, waiting for a moment as she lit the candles on the passage table, and then on, up to the attic bedroom. The door closed with a faint bump and then the house was still.

Henry looked at the table with its empty cups and closed biscuit tin, at the few crumbs pale against the scrubbed board. He heard her words again, felt her body and her breath as part of his own, and then, with a racing, furiously disturbed mind, left the house, to walk along the seafront until his thoughts quietened down.

Later, he lay awake in the bed that had once held Loveday's warm, soft body, and tried to block out the images of her in the room above him, hurt, grieving, and angry. It was a long time before he slept.

Loveday let the tears fall, dampening her pillow, while her thoughts raged. Dead or not? If Father was alive, he had obviously not wanted to come home, which was terrible. But if he were dead, then nothing had changed. He was either a cruel monster, or no longer alive. Yet there was always hope in every despairing heart, and before sleep claimed her she had wearily decided to let the future arrange itself without any more tears and fears. If Father ever came home – *if, such a big if* – that would be wonderful. But if he didn't, then life would go on as usual and so she would forget the letter and carry on. Work, family life, music, the far land, wherever it now was – and Ned. With his name on her lips, finally she slept.

The new day was bright and the household at 6 Market Street strove to live it to the full. Janet and Davey treated Loveday briskly, but with even greater warmth and care, and smiled at the lodger, having mutually decided between themselves that what he had done was for the best, even though poor Maggie was all the more downcast.

Loveday said good morning very fast and had no smiles to spare. She helped with the dishes as usual, but set off for work five minutes earlier than she normally did, saying to Janet as she left, 'I shall have to walk to Sothern House this evening, Aunt. Please help me avoid Mr Long. I have no wish for him to accompany me.'

Janet looked doubtful. 'But that would be very rude of you, child. He's going too, you know.'

'I don't care. He can make his own arrangements. I shall go on my own and leave earlier so he won't know I've gone.'

But as the day progressed, so the arrangements changed, for she found Ned waiting outside the Beach View Hotel when she left at one o'clock, his smile welcoming, flecked eyes lighting up as she came rapidly out of the back yard.

'Lovey, I haven't seen you for at least three days – where have you been?' His voice was light, his expression hinting at amused pleasure, and she felt her heavy spirits lighten. She gave him a relieved smile. 'Don't be silly – I've been here all the time. It's you who has been somewhere else

– what have you been doing?'

He walked beside her down the street, close enough to see the bruised smudges beneath her eyes, hear a tremor in her voice. 'Oh, this and that.' He put a hand beneath her elbow, drawing her nearer. 'What's happened? Is something wrong?'

Loveday drew in a huge breath, met his eyes, and said slowly, 'Mr Long has found out that my father didn't drown at sea after all. He . . . he might be alive.' She paused, tried to laugh, and failed. 'The news has upset us all.'

'Trust that chap, Long,' Ned growled. 'Poking his nose into places that don't concern him. I'll tell him what I think of him this evening.'

'Oh no, please don't.' She couldn't bear it, not more animosity, more trouble. She clutched Ned's arm and looked at him appealingly.

He softened. 'Just a joke, Lovey. Course I won't say anything. But, tell you what, I'm looking forward to seeing you. Wearing that pretty yellow dress, are you?'

Suddenly the world grew a degree brighter. 'No, I have another one – dark greeny sort of blue, with balloon sleeves.' She smiled foolishly. 'You'll see it when I arrive.'

'And that's why I'm here, Lovey, to arrange to collect you in Joshua's gig. Can't have you traipsing all the way up East Cliff in your finery, can I? I'll be at your house about 7.15. Will you be ready?'

'Oh, I will, thank you, Ned.'

The delightful image of herself and Ned driving up to Sothern House in the smart gig stayed with her all during the hard working afternoon and with it came a resolute turn of mind. She would enjoy the evening and if Henry Long tried to bother her she would turn away. New strength brought renewed self-confidence. She had Ned to look after her now and she could rely on him. He was a kind man; well, look at that big smile and those twinkling eyes. He got on with people – here she told herself to forget his treatment of Ben and Daniel on Labrador beach; that had just been quick exasperation and annoyance – for he had soon changed again into the cheerful, reliable man she was becoming so fond of. Yes, with Ned seeking her out and escorting her about, Loveday felt that life was once again improving.

But a few shadowy thoughts still remained, haunting, hurtful and uneasy – until she rushed home, allowed Aunt Janet to help put up her hair and then step into the lovely dress. She told herself severely it was time to forget Henry. Forget that letter. Forget Father. She looked at her smiling reflection in the big mirror and thought, why, she had even forgotten the far land and its icy, dangerous enchantment.

Ned arrived, dressed in pinstriped trousers, a slightly overdone embroidered waistcoat and coat tails, driving the gig with the groom, Sharrow, beside him.

'You look wonderful, Lovey.' The words were for her alone, but he covered them by turning to Janet, waiting in the doorway. 'Miss Jenkins, have no fear – I will bring your niece safely home later this evening.'

His eyes gleamed as he helped seat her in the gig, his hand brushing hers as she stepped up. Sharrow was told to walk home, and Ned drove along the promenade, up the East Cliff and into the large gravel drive entrance of Sothern House. He handed her down with great decorum and then, taking her hand, led her through the enormous porticoed front door into the spacious, oak-panelled hall, and on into the drawing room where Mr and Mrs Sothern waited.

'Miss Loveday Hunt.'

She heard him introduce her with what sounded like pride, and suddenly she found herself feeling different, accomplished and almost well bred. Oh yes, she could hold her own with these people; she was a pianoforte tutor, she had good manners and an education. She smiled at the Sotherns, bobbed a curtsey, and said quietly, 'Good evening, Mrs Sothern, Mr Sothern. I hope Miss Eleanor is well?'

Isobel Sothern's eyes narrowed and a well-plucked eyebrow raised as she looked Loveday over from head to toe. But before she could reply, Joshua Sothern had already stepped forward, took her hand and bowed, saying with a welcoming smile, 'Your pupil is indeed well, Miss Hunt. She is supposed to have gone to bed, but no doubt she will make an appearance after dinner, when you have so kindly agreed to entertain us at the piano.'

Loveday was at once caught by the kindly expression on his side-whiskered and lined face and felt herself settling into the pleasant ambience of the evening. The drawing room was warm, with mirrors reflecting the flames of the dying sun filling the horizon, and huge bowls of flowers wafting their fragrance everywhere. Above, the gas lighting muttered in its elegant chandelier, and she felt relaxed and almost at home.

She sat beside Isobel Sothern, who was dressed spectacularly in a white, square-necked gown with a draped bodice and a sash of golden embroidered flowers flowing down its side, and tried to concentrate on the remarks directed to her.

'The weather is still very good. Let's hope it lasts.' Isobel looked again at Loveday's dress and managed a stiff smile. 'What a handsome gown, Miss Hunt. The colour suits you.'

'Thank you, Mrs Sothern.' Loveday hid her smile; *just suppose Issy discovered this was a gift from Maggie, her personal maid?*

There was a pause, while Isobel adjusted the jewelled pendant of pearls and rubies at her neck, waved her feathered fan as if suffering from the heat, and then said casually – too casually, thought Loveday warily – 'And when will Mr Long arrive, I wonder? No doubt he took a cab from the town.'

'I expect he prefers to walk. He is an energetic person.' Loveday had quick memories of Henry and Floss marching along the length of the beach, and then wished she could forget them. But almost at once the butler appeared in the open doorway and announced, 'Mr Henry Long,' and she was devastated to discover that the images grew more vivid and hard to discard.

She realized all eyes were on the man walking towards them. As Henry made his greeting, she saw that he was wearing an immaculate black evening suit over pristine linen. He looked even more imposing and eye catching than she remembered. His dark hair curled just above the stiff collar and his shoes shone beneath the gas light. No side whiskers like Mr Sothern sported, or even the hint of a sandy moustache as on Ned's freckled skin; just a clean shaven, sharply angled, strong jaw. Yes, she had to admit he was handsome, and far more appealing than Ned, in his slightly louche semi-bohemian evening clothes.

But, even as she watched him bow before Isobel, shake hands with Joshua, and glance politely – she recognized that cold expression – towards Ned, she held herself very straight and met his keen silvery eyes when they finally focused on her.

'Good evening, Mr Long.' Her voice was steady, her smile cool. She was very pleased with herself and at once caught Ned's approving glance.

And then he was turning again to Isobel, who gave him one of her big artless smiles. 'How very nice to see you again, Mr Long. Now do come and sit down here and tell me all that you are doing at the old shipyard. We're all so interested, you see.'

Loveday thought wryly that Issy's interest was not necessarily in business matters, but what did it matter to her if Henry wished to use his hostess as a lever to gain possible favours from Joshua? While the conversation ebbed and flowed around her, she sat like a statue in her chair and felt the abrupt onset of a restless disturbance circling in her mind and churning through her body. But she had no reason to feel like this – she had already rejected Henry's advances and made up her mind that it was Ned she loved. So why?

Now Isobel was on her feet, arranging her guests and leading them into the dining room where Henry was placed on her left, with Ned on the other side of the table, and Loveday seated beside him. She realized that it was going to be hard not to look across at Henry and was grateful for Isobel's continuing questions, and his quiet, considered replies.

But, when courses were being changed, Ned deliberately dropped his napkin to the floor and, bending down to retrieve it, whispered to her, 'So tedious, all this chat about the dreary shipyard. And he's a bore, this Long fellow – let's see if we can't upset him a bit.'

Before she could shake her head he was sitting up again, flicking a crumb from his sleeve, looking across the table at Henry and saying in a voice that was a degree too loud and slightly overbearing, 'I've heard a tale that you're planning to work in the shipyard, Long. Welding, is it? Or maybe the man at the bottom of the sawpit?'

Joshua Sothern put down his fork and leaned towards him. 'Ned, think what you're saying – Mr Long is hardly a labourer, you know.'

'Really? No, I didn't know. Well, perhaps his appearance is against him. Whenever I've seen him in the town he's just been a man with a dog – like most other working men.' Ned was smiling even more now and Loveday, with a knot forming inside her, realized this was his idea of fun.

Henry took his time to reply, finishing the last mouthful of his roast guinea fowl, wiping his mouth and taking a sip of his wine before finally meeting Ned's taunting eyes. He smiled lazily and said, with a deepening of his drawl, 'No, Mr Kerslake, I fear you've got it all wrong. Yes, I'm experienced in the practice of welding and have done my stint in the saw pit, but this particular job is quite different.' He stopped. His brief, quick smile flashed out and then was gone and Loveday saw determination and pride on his face. 'Mr Harvey and his board of directors – including Mr Sothern' – he bowed his head towards the top of the table – 'have agreed that I am to manage the shipyard. We signed the contract this very morning.'

He and Ned locked stares. Then Henry said lightly, 'Any more questions? Do ask them – I'm always glad to inform ignorance when it comes my way.'

A stunned silence swept over the table, until Isobel did her best to recover the proprieties by gushing, 'How very exciting, Mr Long. And so you'll be staying here in Teignmouth?'

Henry gave her a warmer smile. 'I will, Mrs Sothern. In fact, I shall be buying a house and making my home here. I've been wandering for far too long.'

For the blink of an eye, no longer, he looked across at Loveday and saw the pallor on her face, the surprise in her green eyes, and regretted his spontaneous words. But then he saw Ned turn to her, watched surprise being overtaken by gratitude, and knew his cause was lost. She wouldn't miss him. She was lost in that oaf's sly charm. She had made her decision. He finished the wine in his glass and nodded his head when a refill was offered.

Isobel was chattering on about the weather, the garden – 'The delphiniums are particularly good this year' – about the possibility of taking a holiday, and finally turned again to Henry and began asking questions about possible property hunting.

Somehow the meal progressed and at last she rose, catching Loveday's eye and saying, with a smile that centred on Henry and ignored everyone else, 'We shall leave you gentlemen to your port and walnuts, and then, when you join us later, Miss Hunt is going to entertain us with airs at the pianoforte.' She walked down the room, pausing at her husband's side, and saying, sotto voce, 'Don't keep him too long, Joshua. Plenty of time for business another day. At the moment I want to enjoy his company.' And then, louder, 'Come along, Miss Hunt.'

Back in the drawing room the minutes slowed until Loveday thought they had ceased passing all together. Isobel droned on about staying in London, and how she and Eleanor might be away for at least a month or two. 'So I shan't need your services much longer, Miss Hunt.' There was a satisfied smugness in the words and on the pretty face, as she added, 'But I believe you have other employment in the town, do you not?'

Loveday caught at her vanishing self-control and said very quietly, 'Yes, I do, Mrs Sothern.' She knew that only a few weeks ago the other, younger and less experienced Loveday would have flared up and told this petty woman what that work was; but maturity had brought wisdom. And then she thought briefly of Maggie – her mother – saying that she had much to learn, and realized it was actually happening.

At last the men joined them and Loveday was persuaded to go to the piano and 'play something pretty, something we can all enjoy, if you please, Miss Hunt.' She sat down slowly, feeling all eyes on her and wondered whether Henry was remembering that strange little musical episode in Mr Benedict's cottage. And at once her fingers sought out familiar tunes.

Father's tune. Then the jolly sea shanty which Henry and Mr Benedict had sung; but the memory was too vivid, and when it was finished she swung into a popular music hall song which had Isobel tapping her foot, and Ned beaming at her from where he stood not far from the piano.

When a small voice from the open doorway said, 'Miss Jenkins, can we play our duet?' she stopped at once, turned and saw Eleanor, in her nightgown and bed robe, waiting just inside the room, anxious eyes directed at her stepmama.

Isobel's voice was sharp. 'Eleanor – go back to bed at once, what are you thinking of?' But Joshua overrode her, getting to his feet and holding out a hand to his daughter. 'Come in, my dear. Just this once we'll allow you to stay, for I know you love your music. And I'm sure we shall all enjoy hearing you and Miss Hunt perform for us.'

They played a four-handed version of the Handel piece that Eleanor had been practising so assiduously, and the applause was loud and long, until Isobel banished Eleanor from the room and began looking around for fresh topics of conversation, her eyes focused on Henry. But Joshua was in a good mood. He stood with his back to the fireplace and looked around, swinging on his heels. 'Perhaps we could ask Miss Hunt for one more piece. Will somebody suggest it?'

And it was Henry's vibrant voice which said at once, 'May we hear again the tune you learned from your father?' He stopped, met Loveday's eyes as she half-turned on the piano stool, gave her the fleeting smile she knew so well and added quietly, 'You play it so well.'

Just for a moment her heart almost stopped as the old attraction returned and she knew she must accept it. She had felt it, on the first day of their meeting. Henry and Floss leaving the train. Henry, with his intelligence and quick understanding, his sometimes almost dictatorial manner, Henry in whose arms she had hoped to find security and love. But of course, she knew better now. He wasn't for her. He had caused even further disturbance in her family, and all he was interested in was his ambition. His shipyard. The house he planned to buy. And the fact that he shared her love of music was neither here nor there.

But her fingers found the familiar notes and again the sad little tune filled the room. And by the time she had finished, turning to face her audience, it was at Ned that she looked. Ned who gave her the warm smile that promised pleasure and, she told herself firmly, possibly even love.

CHAPTER SEVENTEEN

They drove home through the dusky, warm evening, with Ned allowing Sharrow to take the reins until they reached the gate of Sothern House, and then telling him to go home and have an early night. 'I'll bed the pony down when I get back. No need for you to wait up.'

His arm slid around Loveday's waist and he drew the cob into a slow walk. East Cliff was deserted at this hour, and when he halted under the shade of a big, overhanging oak beside the track, she knew why. She looked at him, saw shadows lightly masking the longing that filled his face, felt a quickening of her heartbeat, and allowed him to take her in his arms.

'Lovey, I've been wanting to do this ever since I first saw you. You're so lovely, so warm and soft so . . . *ripe.*' His mouth found hers and suddenly she was in a new world of sensation and pleasure. Another kiss. And it was Ned, of course it was, not Henry. But she let that particular memory go because she couldn't think about the past when the present was so exciting, so amazing, so wonderful. Her arms gripped him tightly. This was the man she could so easily love, give herself to, and it was all that she could think of this moment. No fears, no dreams – just now.

And then she heard, breaking into her joy like a small alarming wave of interference, footsteps crunching down the track behind the gig. At once she pulled away from Ned, glanced behind her, said anxiously 'Someone's coming,' and heard Ned's smothered oath and his quick reply, 'Never mind; it doesn't matter, come here, Lovey.'

But she had recognized the tall, powerful, black-coated figure now rapidly approaching and knew that her moment of joy was quite spoiled. Henry was here. He would see them. Did it matter? Instant images, voices and thoughts flashed through her mind. Yes, she had told him she didn't want any more to do with him, but something tight inside her was fiercely denying that, insisting that he mustn't see her in Ned's arms.

Instinct found words and she said loudly, 'Now the pony has recovered, Ned, we can go on.'

'What?' He looked at her, turned his head, scowled, realized who it was drawing near to them, and at once drew up the reins and clicked the cob forward. The gig moved just a pace or two ahead of Henry and then they were rattling down to the end of East Cliff, along the esplanade and into the town.

At the top of Market Street Ned drew rein and turned to Loveday, looking at her with an expression of annoyance. 'So what was that all about? Either you want me to kiss you or you don't – make up your mind. There are other girls much more willing than you, you know.'

Loveday was shocked. She felt an awful hollow growing inside her. Putting her hand on his arm she tried to find a likely excuse. 'I'm sorry, Ned. It wasn't that I wasn't enjoying it.' She paused because her mouth was dry. She mustn't upset him. Would he understand? 'But I didn't want anyone to see us. You don't know what it's like for a girl in my position. People talk and if they do Aunt Janet gets hurt and I don't want that.'

'Oh well.' He sounded mollified and slid an arm around her shoulders for a second. 'Yes, of course. Well, we'll try again another evening, shall we? When there aren't any Peeping Toms about.'

Relief flooded her. He was smiling again, looking at her with that cheery smile, that twinkle in his eyes. Dear Ned! He understood. 'Thank you – and yes, perhaps we can meet again .' She returned his smile and felt his hand press her arm before releasing her.

'That's my girl. And there'll be no perhaps about it. Just look out for me, Lovey – I'll arrange something very soon. And now – can you possibly give me a goodnight kiss? No one's looking.'

His quiet, mischievous laugh released her final fear and she lifted her face to receive his kiss, but something made her turn away at the last moment so that his lips rested on her cheek. And then she got out of the gig, waved and walked rapidly towards number 6. Thank goodness the door was ajar; she slipped inside without a backward look and heard the pony trotting away down the street.

Henry hadn't seen that embrace. Aunt Janet would never know. The evening had been a success and she had – almost – enjoyed it, apart from Henry and Ned's hostility, which she refused to dwell upon.

She heard voices in the kitchen and smiled. She was home and could go to bed and dream of her future with Ned, who, she was sure, was fast falling in love with her. Perhaps soon they would declare their feelings and start courting. Aunt Janet would surely be pleased? In bed, she lay reliving the dinner party. Everything was all right. So why was she not able to sleep?

Not until the door of the bedroom beneath hers opened and then quietly shut, telling her that Henry was back, did she turn over and close her eyes. And then her last waking moment produced a strange and unexpected question. Did she really love Ned enough to marry him if he asked?

Frank Benedict's funeral was first thing in the morning, and Janet accompanied Loveday to the church. They both wore dark clothes, Janet in an old-fashioned cape and ancient black bonnet, and Loveday putting on her shabby grey coat and winter hat. The church was half full, shadowy and unwelcoming, candles fluttering in the many draughts caused by the brisk westerly wind. Throughout the service the small congregation coughed, prayed and blew its nose. It was a sad, hushed time.

She saw familiar faces around her; fishermen and their wives, weather-beaten seamen who had perhaps sailed with Frank on those early, dangerous journeys to Newfoundland and back, and Loveday felt her emotions swelling. She had been fond of the old man; her dreams of the far land had all been built on his descriptions of icebergs, storms and whales upending enormous tails as they dived to the depths. And now she would see him no more. Did that mean the end of her far land, she wondered? Tears threatened, but she sought self-control; Aunt Janet was a strong presence at her side and after a few moments she was calm enough to look around for Henry. She had expected him to be there, but then imagined he would be far too busy with his new position at the shipyard. Yet a small voice in her mind insisted that surely he could have spared time to pay his last respects to the old man with whom he had obviously shared memories? Banishing it, she concentrated on the service, which was short, with no music, and only a few rough voices joining in the hymn of 'Nearer My God to Thee' at the end before the committal.

Following the cortege into the cold windy churchyard, Loveday became aware of a small, black-clad woman following the coffin, a stout, clumsy figure with grey hair wisping down from her dark hat. As they stood beside the open grave, listening to the final words of *ashes to ashes, dust to dust*, Loveday watched the woman throw a handful of soil down and could only wonder who this was. Frank Benedict had never spoken of his family, but she supposed this woman was a relative.

She was even more surprised when, as the little procession left the grave and headed for the churchyard gate, the stranger came to her side.

Intense small, berry black eyes looked into hers.

'Are you Loveday Hunt? I'm Mr Benedict's second cousin, Alfreda Parsons. I'm his only relative, y'see, and we hadn't met for many years, so we didn't know each other proper like. But, now he's gone, it's me who has to do all the business of clearing up his bits and pieces.'

The words were fast and full of annoyance and Loveday saw hostility in the unblinking eyes. Without thinking she took a step backwards, shocked and not knowing how to respond. 'Yes, I see.' How could this unpleasant woman talk so baldly about poor Mr Benedict, only just put beneath the earth? 'Yes, I'm Loveday Hunt.'

'I thought you must be. You're the only young one round here. And his will said something 'bout you being young.'

Loveday looked at Alfreda Parsons as she stood, tightly bundled up in her shabby black mantle, and thought it was clear that this Parsons woman imagined that Frank had died merely to inconvenience her. Quick anger kindled. She glanced at Janet who was pulling at her arm, whispering, 'I must get back, child. Are you sure you'll be able to return to work, after all this?'

'Yes, Aunt. I'm all right. I can manage, thank you.'

'Then I'll leave you.' Another nod and Janet was gone.

The moment's pause had brought a new feeling of self control, and now Loveday looked more calmly into Alfreda Parson's impatient face. 'His will, you said? And he mentioned me? But I never thought—'

'As he had two ha'pence to rub together, eh? No, nor me. And it seems we was both correct. Just the cottage and its contents, and I shouldn't think as they're hardly worth my train fare down from Manchester.' The piercing eyes narrowed. 'But you might as well know. He left you his shell collection and his harmonium, proper dusty, all of 'em, and not up to much, I'd say. But as they're yours now you've got to arrange for them to be moved. And I want them moved proper fast. I gotta be back home by termorrer, so just get them out, Miss . . . er—'

'Hunt.' Words deserted Loveday for long moment. His shells. His harmonium. Dear Mr Benedict. Suddenly the tears that she had managed to control during the service broke free. Searching for a handkerchief, she turned away, saying unsteadily, 'Yes, of course, I'll see to it. As soon as I can.' She stopped, looked again at the hard face so close to hers, took a deep breath and said firmly, 'Very well, Miss Parsons.'

'Mrs if you please.' The all-important retort brought a quickly hidden smile to Loveday's face.

'I'm so sorry. *Mrs* Parsons. Where are you staying? I'll make arrangements

181

and let you know as soon as I can.'

'Number 13 Buckland Road. I'll be there later this afternoon. There's so much to do. Trust that stupid old man to put it all on my shoulders—'

It was too much. Loveday smoothed her face, lifted her head an inch higher, and said crisply, 'Please let me correct you. Mr Benedict was an intelligent man, and not at all stupid. Everyone in Teignmouth knew him and liked him. He was a lovable and friendly old man – you've just said that you didn't know him, so you have no right to say such unkind things. And now I must go. Goodday to you, Mrs Parsons.'

She marched down the promenade proud of herself, and suddenly aware of how amusing Mr Benedict would have found this strange encounter. How lucky he was that the frightful Alfreda had stayed at home in Manchester and never bothered him. And then she found she was smiling as the truth took over. He had left her his shell collection – and the harmonium.

The shells would find a loving home with her own, up in the attic bedroom. She had no idea what she would do with the harmonium, but as she reached the Beach View Hotel, she knew that something good and amazing had happened; of course she would never forget him, but now, with the harmonium in her possession, there would always be a warm and vivid memory of his gnarled fingers teaching her the notes and his croaky voice saying, 'Keep goin', maid. You'm doin' well.'

Yes, he would always be there, in the music.

Henry left the church quickly, ensuring that Loveday didn't see him. Not wishing to embarrass her by his presence, he slipped away as the mourners processed into the churchyard. He had joined in the service with kindly thoughts of Frank Benedict, but now he must return to the reality of life and all the work awaiting him at the shipyard. As he strode down the esplanade and into Northumberland Place he tried hard to banish the image of Loveday, slim and grey-coated, her glorious hair tucked away beneath the big hat, standing beside her aunt as the service had progressed. Her clear, true voice had risen above the rough murmurings of the small congregation in the final hymn, and for a disturbing moment he had almost wished himself by her side, his own voice joining hers in remembering Frank Benedict.

Now, as he walked, he recollected that the old man had told him things Loveday and her family had never known. That Amos had survived and even sent Frank a message after the shipwreck. 'Oh yes,' said Frank resignedly, 'he were a bigamist all right, coupling with women wherever he went; he had an obsession about siring a son, see; I know as he were difficult to live with. But I didn't want to hurt his family even more, so I never said.'

Henry frowned, remembering. And yet Frank had insisted that Amos was a man who loved deeply and truly. 'One day,' he'd said wheezily, eyes half shut as the images played themselves out in his head, 'he'll come back, see if 'e don't, b'y. An' then it'll be all right.'

But Frank's optimism had never communicated itself to Henry's younger and more realiztic mind. Of course, he'd been foolish enough to allow his unexpected feelings for the girl to offer to find out about her father's possible survival – and look where it had landed him. Now he swung through the shipyard entrance and knew he was thankful to have something else to think about; a work plan to put into action; a new life to lead. But, despite all his resolution, she stayed there, at the back of his mind, strong and upright, with a gleam of unshed tears in her eyes as he had seen her, looking her way before leaving the church, and he had unwillingly to accept that Loveday Hunt was a woman whom it was going to be hard to forget.

Once in the shipyard he was glad to hear and see evidence of work starting again. Old stored and seasoned timber had been hauled to the sawpit at the end of the shed and now there was a steady rhythm of push and pull adding to the roar of the furnace in the steamer. Heat radiated through the shed and on to the wharf, and the smell of pitch permeated the whole yard.

Henry smiled wryly to himself. No longer was there any opportunity for Floss to be petted and played with. As he moved from bench to gantry and on to where the new keel had been laid down, he watched her wandering from man to man, head lifted, eyes full of expectancy, but being ignored as routines reasserted themselves and the old yard became newly alive.

Walking through the yard, he looked everywhere, saw everything, felt jubilant at the rebirth of the neglected business. When Floss suddenly disappeared and paid no attention to his summoning whistle, he followed her, turned a corner at the very end of the yard and found her sitting happily beside a crumbling wall which had broken through the rotting wood of the yard boundary. Here, on the sandy foreshore of the river beach, were a couple of children stroking Floss and offering scraps of mussels which filled a tin can beside them.

His voice was sharp. 'How did you get in here? This is private property.'

The peaky-faced, shabbily dressed girl jumped up and stared defiantly back at him. 'Not doin' any harm, mister. Jest talkin' to the dog. What's wrong wi' that?'

Henry looked at her keenly. He'd seen her around the town, a small version of a trouble maker, he thought. 'Two things,' he said shortly. 'My dog doesn't need your titbits and you shouldn't be here in my shipyard. What's your name?'

'Daisy Marten. This 'ere's Joe, my l'lle brother.' She scowled as she pulled small Joe by the arm, backing off with the tin can in her hand.

Narrow eyed, Henry assessed the damage. This broken entry into the yard must be repaired at once. 'Well, Daisy,' he said crisply, 'I don't want to see you or Joe here again. So off you go.' He watched them climb over the rocks but before they disappeared around the corner of the beach, Daisy raised her hand put fingers to her nose and shouted something back at him.

Kids, thought Henry dismissively. Always up to mischief. Then he looked down at Floss, still nosing among the sandy earth for forgotten scraps, and fondled her ears. 'You're a wicked dog. Stop eating rubbish and come here.'

Together they walked back through the shed, Floss looking suitably chastened and Henry already dismissing the encounter once he reached the office. *His* office. He sat in Kenneth Harvey's old leather chair and turning it, looked out over the Point where a choppy sea with white waves raced over the bar. And for a long moment he stayed there, in his imagination seeing the boat, already under construction in the yard, with his new designs and ideas being implanted into the traditional crafts-manship.

Life was good, he thought. Easy now to forget those disturbing thoughts of Loveday Hunt who, he was quite certain, was setting her cap at that Kerslake oaf, a real Lothario if ever there was one. Well, women were strange creatures, and none more so than Loveday. He was fortu-nate not to have wasted any affection on her.

Then he forced himself to forget everything as, once more, he began sketching out the next new plan, already taking shape beneath his care-fully sharpened pencil.

Loveday looked and looked but saw no sign of Ned. Never mind, he was probably off somewhere with his photograph equipment – after all, that was his livelihood. So she thought, instead, of the new problem about housing Mr Benedict's harmonium. Alfreda Parsons would be waiting for information about the instrument's move, so she must think hard; where was it to go?

At tea time Aunt Janet frowned. 'Well, very good of him to leave it to you, but there's no room here.' She looked across at Davey. 'Wouldn't go in the outhouse, I suppose?'

'No!' Loveday's voice was sharp. 'It's got to be somewhere warm and with enough room for me to sit there and play it. No, certainly not the outhouse.'

'Well.' Janet met Davey's quizzical eyes. 'Have you any idea of who might kindly store it?'

Slowly he nodded, then looked at Loveday. 'There's an old shed at the bottom of the yard where nothing's ever put. Roomy enough for it, I reckon. Dry, because it backs on to the steamer, and you could put a lock on the door. Might do.'

Loveday considered. It sounded a possibility. But in the shipyard? That meant Henry must be asked. She smiled persuasively. 'Uncle Davey, what a wonderful idea. Do you think Henry . . . Mr Long . . . would mind?'

'Don't see why he should. You could keep the key, visit when you want. No, I don't think he'd mind. Why not ask him?'

'Oh, I think it would be much better if you asked him, Uncle. I mean, he knows you so well, working there.' Something knotted inside her at the thought of facing Henry again.

Janet said quickly. 'No, child, I see no reason why your Uncle should have the bother of it. Ask Mr Long yourself. He'll be in for his tea very soon. Ask him then.'

Loveday left the table, face very sombre. Aunt Janet was right, of course, she was. But Henry was no longer a friend; in fact, she had told him she wanted no more to do with him. *Did I really say that? How terrible. Did I really mean it?*

When Henry arrived she braced herself, following him through the kitchen and into the yard where he was feeding Floss and putting fresh straw in the outhouse. 'Mr Long—' Her voice was unsteady, but she met his questioning eyes as he straightened up and looked at her.

'Yes, Miss Hunt?'

She heard the wry crisp note and tightened her mouth. 'I mean Henry.'

'That's better. Loveday.' He came a step closer and looked down into her chastened face. 'Something wrong?'

'No, no, of course not.' She had forgotten the power of those flinty eyes, the charm of the casual, low-voiced drawl. 'Just that . . . well, I want to ask you—' Her cheeks were hot, the words too rapid.

Henry stood silent for a few moments. 'Can we talk about it over tea?'

he asked. 'I'm pretty hungry, you know.'

His impatience was obvious and at once she felt more confident. Clearly he was in no mood to be friendly again. Well, she was pleased about that. So, standing still and looking coolly at him, she said quickly, 'Mr Benedict has left me his harmonium and his cousin said I must move it by tomorrow. I . . . I wondered if you might kindly let me put it in a shed in the yard. Uncle Davey said there was an empty one.'

He made no reply, but she watched a frown slide across his face and then retreat again. He stepped towards the door and held it open for her. 'So the old man left a will, did he? I suppose he got Gus, the accordion player, to write it up for him. And you're to have the harmonium. Well, sure, if you can't find any one else to house it for you – one of the Sotherns, perhaps?'

She heard the darkness in the words and flushed, but held her head very high. 'I wouldn't dream of asking Mrs Sothern.'

'Or that charming cousin of hers?' He followed her into the kitchen and closed the door behind him.

Loveday felt her anger growing. She turned, frowning. 'If you mean Ned Kerslake, why not say so?' Her voice was sharp and she had the pleasure of seeing Henry shake his head and open his arms wide, as if in apology.

By the range, Janet turned quickly, looking anxious. 'Loveday, I'm sure Mr Long wants to have his tea in peace. And shouldn't you be out arranging for someone to collect Mr Benedict's harmonium?'

'Aunt, it's my harmonium, and I am waiting for Mr Long to give me an answer about the possibility of storing it – for a short while – in the empty shed in his shipyard.' She saw Janet's face drop, knew she was behaving in a way that was distressing her aunt, but knew too that she was a grown woman now, no longer the obedient and amenable child.

Henry was looking at her very straight. 'The answer is yes, Miss Hunt,' he said flatly. 'Tell your carrier to bring it first thing tomorrow morning. I shall be there and arrange to have a lock fitted. You alone will have the key. Now—' His eyes were dark and she sensed something hidden behind his familiar, brief smile. 'If that is all you want of me, do you think I could have my tea? In peace?'

Loveday turned and marched out of the room, aware that Janet was watching with an expression of dismay and confusion. Why was Henry acting so strangely? Even though they were no longer friends, surely he could have been less aggressive? And had there been a hint of amusement in his last words? Well, he could have all the peace he wanted. Once again

– I want no more to do with him. She slammed the front door behind her and went in search of Mrs Parsons and then of Ossie Mead, the carrier who was usually to be found outside the station. First thing tomorrow, he must collect the harmonium, and then deliver it at the shipyard. She would be there to oversee the transaction, but Henry Long needn't worry – she would bother him no more once she had the key to the shed in her pocket.

She would work as usual at the Beach View Hotel, and then look for Ned, who surely would be wanting to spend the evening with her. He would probably be waiting for her when she left in the afternoon. With her head in the air and a determined smile on her face, Loveday walked towards the lodging house where Alfreda Parsons was staying. And as she walked, she thought about her life, which suddenly seemed to have become more hopeful. Mother had returned. Father might still be alive. She had been given a musical instrument of her own. And even although Mrs Sothern had said she would no longer need her services once she and Miss Eleanor were away, the harmonium would be there, for her to play whenever she wanted to.

And Frank's shells: her smile increased. And even though Mrs Parsons merely nodded impatiently when she learned of the removal of the harmonium tomorrow morning, Loveday, walking towards the station and the carrier, still felt that happiness, that rare and precious commodity, was somewhere in sight, even within her grasp.

CHAPTER EIGHTEEN

The late afternoon was breezy, but the sharp morning wind had moved around and allowed the clouds to disperse. Sunlight filtered through the trees bordering the road, and as Loveday walked she was more than usually aware of nature's beauty. Perhaps it was having time to look around, no longer worrying about rushing to see Frank Benedict, or watching the clock so that Mrs Narracott wouldn't shout at her. Perhaps it was because she had learned to accept life and not rail against it as once she did. Or – a smile lifted her lips – could it be knowing that she believed that Ned loved her?

Her mind was elsewhere when a voice called from behind and, turning, she saw Maggie not far away. 'Loveday! Please wait.' The voice wasn't strong, and as Loveday stopped and began retracing her steps, she saw how Maggie's body wilted beneath her efforts to hurry.

'What ever are you doing here, Maggie?'

'I've just delivered a note' – a pause to recover breath – 'from Mrs Sothern to Mrs Gray at Gorway House. And then I saw you, and I thought—'

'Yes?' Loveday was intrigued. Beside her mother, she slowed her steps and looked into the ageing, suddenly intent face.

'Well, I need to talk to you. You're my daughter. There's things you don't know, things you ought to learn about. And I never see you alone, so now—'

Loveday's heart sank. Was this going to be another variation of her mother's story, more excuses about abandoning her? Another plea for forgiveness? She said, more sharply than she intended, 'I'm only going as far as the station. And then I must go home.'

'It won't take long. We'll just go down Barn Park and then I'll leave you. I'll go back up East Cliff to Sothern House. Mrs Sothern'll be waiting for me, so I must hurry. Please – *please* – listen to me, Loveday.'

How could she refuse? 'All right. So what's this all about?'

They walked slowly, their arms occasionally touching, Loveday bending to look at Maggie's face as she began to talk. 'I know I left you and you think it was wicked of me.'

'I—'

'No, just listen.' This was a Maggie Loveday hadn't encountered, a small, almost timid woman who suddenly had a strong voice and a forceful expression on her lined face. 'I want to tell you about Amos. About your father. It was because of him that I left you with Janet and Davey. Not that I didn't love you.' For a moment Maggie met Loveday's gaze, nodded her head, and allowed a smile to soften her taut features. 'How could I not love you, you're my daughter. But you don't know about love, do you, not yet. You're young, you don't understand what it does to you when you love someone. Like I loved Amos.'

They were approaching the railway bridge and had to keep to the side of the road as a pony and trap rattled past them. Maggie was breathing fast and slipped her arm into Lovedays crooked elbow.

'Amos loved us, you and me, of course he did. But he wanted a son, you see. Wanted it so badly that when I didn't give him one he couldn't help himself – had to go off and try to find another woman who might give him one. And then, when he'd gone, I found I was with child again. I didn't know where he was, so I knew I must just wait until he sent a message, or a letter, or something. But he didn't. Four months and no word of him.'

Loveday was caught up in Maggie's passion. Suddenly she knew how terrible those four months were. She had been happily taken in by Janet and Davey, but Maggie – Mother – had been alone, worried out of her mind, and then finding herself again with child and the prospect of the workhouse her only future. 'Did Aunt Janet know?' Surely there must have been comfort somewhere.

'No. I didn't tell her. Didn't want her to know why he'd gone and left us. She was happy to take you in – poor Janet always wanted children, but never had them.' For a second, Maggie smiled again, but then went on in the same hurried, breathless voice. 'I moved away because I didn't want people to be sorry for me. I found a good position back in Cornwall, and I prayed that the child would be a boy.' She stopped, her hand to her chest, and looked at Loveday with smiling, almost triumphant, eyes.

'And he was. My Jack. Oh, I knew how glad Amos would be, so I just kept quiet and waited.'

They had crossed the road, Loveday persuading her mother to lean against the parapet of the bridge for a moment's rest. Maggie sucked in great breaths, and looked at Loveday with memories filling her face. 'I thought he'd come back. I knew he loved us. So I just waited.'

'But—' Loveday had to be careful with her words. 'He didn't come back, and you thought he was drowned. So how did you carry on, waiting like that?'

Maggie was silent for a long moment. Then she let out her breath in a sigh and said, slowly and quietly, 'I loved him, you see. That's what I'm trying to tell you, child. When you love someone, you never give up.'

'But you thought he was dead?'

Maggie paused, then nodded. 'As the years went by, I did. But I never stopped loving him. I still love him, today. I still hope he might be alive.'

They started walking again, going through the town and reaching the promenade, where once more Maggie rested against the wall. 'I just wanted you to know. To understand that I never stopped wanting you back, but I knew, for Amos's sake, I must look after Jack. I didn't have much money, but I did the best I could. Jack's always been delicate, you see – that cough of his. I had to take more care of him than I did of you. And Janet has looked after you like a mother, hasn't she?'

Loveday felt herself caught in a circle of abounding thoughts and conflicting emotions. It had been hurtful to hear Maggie's story, to remember once again that she had given her daughter to her sister. But through all that, one fact was slowly, strongly, overwhelming the others. Love, Maggie had said, was what it was all about. Loveday remembered Maggie telling her, weeks ago, that she had much to learn. And now she was learning – fast.

So she smiled down into the anxious eyes looking up into hers, and said quietly, 'Yes, she's been a real mother to me because you weren't here. And that's why it's so hard to think of you, now, as my mother. But thank you for telling me, Maggie, because I needed to know.' She stopped as the old rejection stabbed through her. 'I'll try to understand why you gave me to Janet and Davey.' Tears pricked behind her eyes and she swallowed hard. 'But, you see, the hurt is still there.' She felt it, like an iron knot inside her, hard and intractable and knew that, somehow, she must get rid of it.

Maggie nodded, tried to smile. 'I want to make up for it, Loveday, if you'll let me.' Then she turned away before Loveday could see how her face crumpled. 'But I must go now – we'll see each other again soon, I hope,' and quickly she began walking towards East Cliff.

Loveday watched the small figure trudging up the hill and then retraced her steps to the station where she gave Ossie Mead his orders to collect the harmonium early next morning. She would be waiting for him, and they would take it to Harvey's shipyard.

She walked home slowly, emotions swamping her. It wasn't just that she was stuck in the agonizing rut of rejection, knowing that Maggie had left her, it was today's problems, too, that filled her. She knew that she must meet Henry tomorrow and thank him for providing a home for Frank's harmonium. She was still grieving for Frank, and then there was the shock of thinking that her father could be alive. And, of course, her dreams of Ned. But where, oh, where, was Ned?

Walking helped to calm her, but it was very late when she reached the end of the esplanade, for something had prevented her going straight back to Market Street. What was she waiting for? Why was she here, in the dusky half-light, searching the tide line as if expecting something – someone – to be there?

She saw them, Henry and Floss, dark shapes walking rapidly up the beach towards the steps; felt again the strange disturbance within her that seeing him always brought. She wondered at it, but was suddenly too weary, too emotional, to try and sort out her feelings. Almost running, she headed for home.

Would there ever be a time, she thought despairingly, as she slipped into the house, when she knew what she was doing with her life? When things would settle down? When, once again, she could concentrate on the far land of her dreams? And it was only when she reached her candlelit bedroom and prepared to sleep, that she was face to face with a sudden, shocking truth. Where, now, was the far land?

In the shipyard, Henry stood impatiently watching Ossie's horse and cart bringing in the harmonium. There was a good deal of backing up and shouting, but finally, with the help of one of the apprentices, and Ossie's own hard-muscled strength, it was taken off the cart and manhandled into the empty shed which stood in a line of derelict outbuildings stretching away from the busy centre of the yard.

'It's next to the steamer.' He caught Loveday's eye. 'No fear of damp getting in – and you'll be warm, too.'

She wanted to smile, to tease a bit and ask if he would charge her for the shared heating, but his face was cold, showing how keen he was to see the back of all this intrusion into his busy day. It wasn't the time to try to engage the brief, friendly smile that had always charmed her. His voice was sharp as he added quickly, 'Here are the keys. The bigger one is to the main entrance, Miss Hunt, so you can come and go as you wish without disturbing anyone.'

Without disturbing you. Her face tightened and she nodded politely. 'Thank you, Mr Long. And now we'll leave you. I do hope all this hasn't taken too many vital moments from your working day.'

Their eyes locked and she felt the reverberation of a mental clash. Well, it was better this way. He was a businessman with no thoughts other than how the new boat was shaping up, while she had her whole life, full of dreams and opportunities, before her. Thanking the apprentice and nodding to Ossie, she went into the shed and sat down on the piano stool. Yes, the shed was warm and fairly light; a small window had been cleaned and let in enough light to see the keys. She wondered if Henry had ordered this to be done, and then found herself trying to feel warmer to him, but the old sense of disturbance was too much and at once she sought distraction.

Her fingers found the keys and played a few familiar tunes. The sound was homely and brought back memories of Frank Benedict instructing her. She was smiling as she rose, left the shed, locking it safely behind her, and then walking out of the shipyard and heading back to the Beach View Hotel where, no doubt, Mrs Narracott would tell her off for being half an hour late.

Dusty rooms and all the same everlasting routine work until one o'clock, when thankfully she sped home, looking up and down the esplanade with the hope of seeing Ned. There was no sign of him, and her heart sank. The usual holiday makers, with their children, their parasols and their dogs chattered and crowded around her and then, suddenly arriving at her side from nowhere, was Daisy Marten with a grin on her grubby face.

'Take one o' these, will 'ee?'

Loveday looked at the small, crumpled piece of paper that was pushed into her hand. 'What ever—?'

'Mr Moore gives us a couple o' bangers if we gets rid o' twenty o' they – go on, take un.' Daisy, followed by a small boy still unsteady on bow legs, rushed off, leaving Loveday to decipher the poorly written advertisement.

MR MOORE 1 FORE STREET.
13 BEEF SASUAGES FOR A SHILLING

She smiled, and then laughed and the world brightened around her. Well, young Daisy, for all her known sly ways and gossip mongering, would have no problem earning her living if she carried on like this. Yes, the child was nosey and dirty, but she seemed to have a gift for business. Loveday remembered that Madame Chance had agreed to the child's offer of advertisement. Ned had said that Daisy was giving advice about good photographic sites, and now it was Mr Moore's sausages. What next, she wondered?

She reached Market Street in a calmer frame of mind, knowing that several of her problems had been resolved; the harmonium was safely stored, and Frank Benedict's shell collection, which she had fetched from the cottage when the harmonium was moved, was soon unpacked from the shawl holding it and spread over her bed, awaiting the opportunity to look at it more thoroughly and allocate it space somewhere in the room.

When Henry came back for dinner, she avoided his brief glance, and managed to get through the meal by discussing Mr Moore's butchery and Daisy Marten's quick mind with Aunt Janet and Uncle Davey.

'Well, they're a decent enough family,' Aunt Janet said thoughtfully, 'although that Daisy has always been wicked. And what about Ben; do you ever see him now?' She looked across the table at Loveday with an eyebrow raised.

'Not very often. I'm too busy.' Loveday knew what her aunt was thinking: about Ned, about Henry – and only dropping Ben into the conversation because she needed to know what Loveday felt about each of them. So she merely smiled at her aunt and then changed the subject by saying that very soon Mrs Sothern would be going away and so she would no longer teach Miss Eleanor.

Janet frowned. 'But what a pity. And I had great hopes that Mrs Sothern's friends might well have taken you on.' She sighed. 'At least you still have your situation with Mrs Narracott.'

Rapidly, and without proper thought, Loveday said, 'But I'm so tired of being a chambermaid. I shall look for something else, I think.'

There was an immediate silence as Janet and Davey exchanged shocked glances, Henry folded his napkin and Loveday knew she had committed something of a family crime. One didn't talk about oneself before strangers. So did Aunt Janet really think of Henry as a stranger?

She was never to know, for Henry stood up, pushed his chair towards the table and said slowly, 'Well, as we're talking about changes, I fear I have another one to make, Miss Jenkins.'

Something in his tone made Loveday turn as she prepared to leave the room. His voice was expressionless. 'I regret I shall be leaving you quite soon.'

Janet put a hand on the nearest chair back as if to steady herself. 'Really, Mr Long? Well, I'm sure we shall all be sorry to see you go.' She paused, a frown puckering her brow. 'I do hope that you don't feel you've been uncomfortable here? Ill fed, perhaps? Not enough privacy?'

Loveday, just inside the hall, waited with held breath for his answer. Of course, he had told Isobel Sothern that he was looking for a house – she had almost forgotten. But this was definitely a shock.

'No, no, nothing like that, I can assure you.' Now his voice was warmer, full of concern that Janet might be upset. 'I've been more than comfortable – and happy – here. It's just that, with a permanent position at the shipyard, I feel I must settle down.' He paused, flicked a glance towards Loveday, before looking again at Janet. 'And I've been fortunate enough to find just the right place.'

There was a moment of silent expectation, until he added rapidly, 'Frank Benedict's cottage is for sale, and I've decided to buy it.'

Loveday let out her breath, not knowing what to say or even to think. She saw Aunt Janet relax and smile slightly, although surprise filled her voice. 'Well, Mr Long, that is really unexpected. But, of course, you know what you're doing.'

'Yes,' said Henry tightly, but with enormous certainty. 'I'm going to turn the old place inside out put in a few comforts and spend time there, in my own home.' He stopped, turned and looked at Loveday's amazed face. 'I haven't had a real home for years, and I think it's about time I settled down.'

Another silence, until Janet started collecting empty dishes and said over her shoulder, 'Well, we can only wish you well, Mr Long, but we shall miss you.' She turned, looked directly at Loveday, still hovering in the hallway. 'Shan't we, child?'

And Loveday could do no more than nod slowly, avoid his keen stare, and mutter, 'Yes, of course.' She couldn't stay, although questions were piling up in her mind. What was it to her if Henry Long had made such an extraordinary decision? He was not part of her life. Determinedly, she picked up her shawl, jammed on her hat, and fled. At least, in the upstair bedrooms at the Beach View Hotel, she would have work to do which would stop all the worries and uncertainties – wouldn't it?

By the time she reached home again she felt weary. Not physically, because all that dusting and sweeping and preparing veg when the kitchen maid was away had been her life for the last four years since leaving school. Domestically she was experienced and strong. No, it was the images that began hovering in her mind once she left the confines of the hotel.

The street seemed empty because no Ned was there, with his big bag and folded tripod. People passed her, horses picked their way elegantly over the cobbles, and children screamed as they played their hopscotch and skipping games. But in her mind she saw only desolate pavements and looming, empty houses. And houses – ah, yes, that brought Frank's cottage back into focus. So Henry was buying it. He would clear it up, furnish it, live in it. He and Floss. And no doubt one day before too long he would find a wife with whom he would – what did he say? – 'settle down'.

Loveday's jaw tightened and she blanked out those images. Well, she too had come to a change in her life – she would find a new path. Make a new journey. In fact – the idea lessened her tension as she reached Market Street – she would discuss these ideas with Aunt Janet this evening. Henry could do what he liked, but after tea, she, Loveday would have time and peace to sort out Frank's shells, and then spend time with Aunt Janet in her sewing room. Yes, she was looking forward to it.

And then, like a flash of lightning, the idea grew broad and vivid; this was the time to find a new far land. Forget the icebergs and monster waves of her childhood dreams, think instead of somewhere easier, a place where she could be herself, the grown woman, could settle down – even Henry's remembered words held no pain now – and grow into a life which she knew instinctively would bring happiness and enormous satisfaction. All she had to do was wait for it to happen.

When tea was finished, Henry late as usual, and Loveday gratefully disappearing upstairs before he had time to even pass the time of day with her, she closed her bedroom door and spread out all the shells that had come from Frank Benedict's collection. A motley of – what had he called them – a *proper ole conglomeration*. She smiled, recalling his wheezy voice and his gentle manner. She arranged them all on the dressing table, setting aside her brush and comb to give them room. They would be the first things she saw when she awoke in the morning. The cowries were supposed to be lucky, and the scrimshaw pieces were extraordinary and intriguing. Taking them in her hand, she knew she should have returned Maggie's piece to Carpenters' Row, but somehow it seemed right to keep it here with her own bit of bone. At the window, catching the final fading light, she stared at the strange carvings. Pictures, and letters – if only she could make out the details more clearly.

And then she went downstairs, knocking on Janet's workroom, taking the scrimshaw with her and smiling at her Aunt, busily sewing buttons on a grey wool shirt. 'Aunt, can you help me make out what all this is about? These carvings, these squiggles, that look like words, but are so tiny.'

Janet looked at her, smiled and put down the shirt. 'Well, there's a magnifier somewhere – I use it sometimes when the buttonholes are very small. Look in that drawer, child.'

It was a large, square piece of glass worked to make things look larger. Loveday pulled up a stool and sat down, the scrimshaw on her lap. 'There's a picture of a big man. He's carrying something, but I can't see what it is. And there's a smaller figure running ahead of him, and then there are the flowers and the spirals and the writing, and then what looks like a woman's head.' She peered, holding the bones first one way and then another. 'One word looks like *family*, but I can't really see.'

Janet watched her. She peered through the magnifier. 'I can't see any clearer than you. It's all very worn and indistinct, isn't it?' She watched Loveday, still frowning at the pieces of bone in her hand and her thoughts spread. Perhaps this was the time to draw out the child; ask her what she meant about finding a new situation. Was Loveday at all attached to any of her friends? Ben Marten? Mr Long? Here Janet shook her head, thinking that was highly unlikely because he was such an ambitious and self-sufficient man. Could it be – she raised a dark eyebrow – that handsome cheerful Mr Kerslake? But Loveday had made no mention of him lately. Dare she ask the question?

Instead, she picked up the shirt again. 'If you've got a few moments to spare, child, you could help sew the buttons on the other sleeve. The vicar really needs new shirts, but you know how parsimonious he is – said this one will do a bit longer.'

Loveday put down the scrimshaw pieces and began sewing. The evening wore on, warm and dusky and the gas popping as it filled the room with light. Now, thought, Janet, now.

'So, if you leave Mrs Narracott, have you any idea of what new situation you will try to find?' she asked in as casual a manner as possible.

Loveday went on stitching. 'No. Not really. I must try to think. I'm sure there's something better I could do.'

Janet focused on the last button on one grey sleeve. 'You would make a very good companion,' she suggested quietly. 'Perhaps to some elderly lady living on her own; you're kind and very domesticated. You read well and you know something about sewing. Or even an elderly gentleman? A widower, perhaps with motherless children to bring up?'

Loveday pricked her finger. 'Ow!' Her voice was sharp. 'No, Aunt, I don't want an elderly widower, thank you very much. I want someone young and—' She stopped abruptly as she met her aunt's wide eyes. 'I mean, I'm young, I need young company—' Suddenly her heart was beating too fast, the colour rising in her cheeks. 'I want to love someone – and him to love me back. I want him to care for me.'

Oh Henry, why did you say those words? I can't get them out of my mind.

They looked at each other and a deepening silence grew. Loveday stitched on grimly – *what had she said?* – and Janet allowed her thoughts to wander even further. Until there was a loud double knock on the front door when Loveday got up, put the shirtsleeve on the work table, and said 'I'll go. Who ever can it be at this time of the night?'

The hallway was dark and she turned up the gas before opening the door. A dark shape loomed up in front of her and for a moment she stepped back. She saw a heavily built man with a full-bearded, weather-scored face. He was looking at her out of clear blue eyes, almost hidden by folds of creased tanned skin, and he was saying huskily, 'Does Janet Jenkins still live here?'

'Yes.' Something turned her stomach over and for a second thoughts flashed – *he's as tall as Henry* – but then everything was knocked aside by shock as she heard the big man's next words.

'I'm Amos Hunt. Tell her I'm here, will you, maid?'

CHAPTER NINETEEN

For a moment time stopped. She was shocked into a mixture of bewildering emotions until disbelief took over, and then, even as her body stiffened and her heart raced, joy swept her forward.

'Father!' Breathlessly, she stared up into his face, into blue eyes that looked down at her, half frowning; at the grey, shaggy brows raised as if in matching disbelief.

He said nothing, but stepped into the hallway and, without turning, closed the door behind him, putting out a hand, drawing her closer, turning her wondrous face up to the spluttering gas light.

'Loveday?'

The years vanished and here she was, a child again, standing beside this man, smiling up at him, as he played the last notes on his scraping fiddle, her voice finishing the little tune he had made. And then that one word, her name spoken by her father, home from the dead, became a magic talisman, banishing the doubts, the problems, the ongoing worries and the fears.

'Father! Have you still got your fiddle?'

He smiled, craggy face softening, lifting his mouth to show tobacco-stained teeth, his hand still on the side of her face. He stroked her cheek, caressed her 'I've got it, maid. So you remember me?'

'Yes. Yes! Oh, Father—' She belonged to him. He was here, after all those years. In those ecstatic moments, with no more said between them, just the warm, close contact of their bodies as he put his arms around her, the smell of him, salt, tobacco, dirt, nothing else mattered. Even the hurtful memory of him leaving them was beyond her thinking now.

The door beside them opened and Janet stood, staring. Her voice rose. 'Who ever—?'

Amos released Loveday, stepped aside and looked at his sister-in-law. 'I've come back, Janet.'

Loveday held her breath, instinct sending the joyous moment flying for now trouble had returned. She went to her aunt, standing so rigidly in the doorway. What to say? How to behave?

As she paused, Janet took command of the situation. 'Yes, I see you have, Amos. And at a very inconvenient time of the night. We are just about to go to our beds. Where will you be sleeping?'

Loveday felt the air chill. She looked from her aunt to the tall, stooping man and realized from his expression that he was a match for Janet.

His voice hardened. 'Thanks for your welcome. I've got a bed at the Seamen's Mission. But I had to come before I slept. Had to see if—' For a second the thick words wavered. 'I had to find Maggie.' He glanced down at Loveday, and gave her the flash of a smile. 'And the girl.'

Davey appeared in the parlour doorway, yawning, his face abruptly registering amazement. 'Well!' He stared at Amos, then took a step forward, holding out his hand and smiling. 'So the wanderer has returned? Good to see you alive and well, Amos.'

Loveday let out her pent-up breath. Thank goodness for sweet-natured Uncle Davey. She smiled at him and remembered the usual placating words that had always worked in the past. 'Shall we make a pot of tea and discuss things?' Without looking at Janet, she turned and led the way into the kitchen.

Henry was late returning from the usual evening walk. Paperwork had piled up and he had sat in the upstair office long past his customary day's end. Plans to copy, to amend, to compare with some of the old records. Worksheets to check. Notes he'd made in the yard as work proceeded. Would the new boat be all he dreamed of? Were the men working with enthusiasm? Briggs was constantly at his elbow, almost daring him to introduce new methods, but Henry felt that slowly they were getting used to each other.

It was only Floss's impatience that told him, as dusk filled the room, that the day was over. They took a brisk walk down the length of the beach, beside the incoming tide, rounded the Point and then marched back down Brunswick Street, through Northumberland Place and on into Market Street. He thought he'd seen a shadowy small figure running around corners and out of alleys and had waited, suspiciously, but apart from the distant noise of children's voices, there was no one and nothing to worry about. He strode down the narrow street, unlocked the door of number 6 and entered.

A light in the kitchen and raised voices. He looked at his watch.

Unusual for the Jenkins to keep late hours. He hesitated. Taking Floss to her sleeping quarters in the back yard meant going through the kitchen and interrupting the company talking there. Perhaps – a smile touched his mouth – it might be permissible, just this once . . . he took Floss by the collar.

'Up you go, and don't dare make a sound.' The stairs creaked, but safely in his room with the door closed he grinned as the dog settled down on the bedside rug.

Tomorrow he must be up and out early; he didn't fancy facing Miss Jenkins's indignation if she discovered that Floss had spent the night in her lodger's bedroom. Wry amusement emptied his weary mind of all else, until he got into bed and heard the quiet rise and fall of voices just below him. And then, as if to startle him back into full wakefulness, thoughts of Loveday came and refused to go away. It was some time before he slept.

In the kitchen the teapot was refilled and cups emptied as the voices wove in and out. There was so much to learn, to know, to discuss. Janet's back was stiff, her voice sharp as she told Amos Hunt just what she thought of him abandoning his wife and daughter. 'You are a selfish man,' she said angrily, disregarding Davey shaking his head and Loveday looking down at the table top. 'You did what you wanted and never thought of your family left behind. And now, what do you expect of them? To forget all the pain and worry and take you to their hearts again? I can't believe that you do.'

He cleared his throat and sat up straighter, a brooding, eye-catching figure in the rusty dark pea jacket, sea cap on his knee. 'But that's just what I do want. I've lived a hard, dangerous life on the rock. You, Janet, with your comfortable home, can't even start to imagine. Ice, hardship, starvation, loneliness to beat all else. Well, I've learned lessons about people, and about myself. I've had this dream, see, all the years I was out there, of coming home, but something always stopped me. Until now.' His voice quietened and he hunched back in the hard chair, part of the semicircle of family, but not quite within it. He looked aside at Loveday, reached out, touched her hand. 'No, she's right, little maid, I don't deserve your understanding. Or your love. But there was a reason I went. Why I stayed.'

Loveday knew. 'You wanted a son.'

He turned towards her, frowning, a sudden light in his eyes. 'By God, yes. How do you know?'

'Maggie – Mother – told me. She said you wanted a son so desperately that you'd do anything – go anywhere – to have one. Yes, she told me.' Her voice drifted away. This was the hardest part of the meeting. He had to know about Jack. Who should tell him? Surely, it must be Maggie? But Maggie was at Sothern House, and not likely to come to Market Street until next Sunday.

Silence fell and eyes avoided one another. Until Loveday felt something urging her to make the next move. To get things going forward. To arrange for Father to meet Mother. She rose from her chair and looked at Amos. 'It's very late and we all need sleep. Go to bed, Father, and in the morning – early—' She felt Janet's eyes on her, met them, felt a new strength and then steadied her voice. 'Early in the morning I'll meet you and take you to Sothern House where Mother is. You can talk to her, explain—'

Another silence, until Amos pulled himself out of the chair and got up, breathing heavily, watching Loveday as she went to the door and opened it. A moment's pause, while he looked at Janet, at Davey and then back at Loveday before following her out of the kitchen into the hall. He stopped as she opened the front door. Outside darkness had fallen with only a glimmer of a distant street light. 'You're a good maid. Got a warm heart, you have. My girl.' Clumsily he bent down, encircling her with strong arms. 'You understand. Well, I'll watch for 'ee tomorrow then – early.'

He was gone in a second, heavy footsteps fading, his black shape disappearing from her intent gaze, watching him go. Slowly she returned to the kitchen where Janet was washing cups, Davey drying them. They both looked up, met her gaze and then returned to their duties.

Weariness suddenly immersed Loveday. She must rest, sleep, stop thinking, stop planning, stop worrying. 'Goodnight,' she said unevenly and left the room without waiting for a reply.

It had been an extraordinary day. And tomorrow would probably be even stranger. What would Maggie say? How would Amos react to the news of Jack?

Too tired to think any more, she was asleep the instant her head rested on the pillow and no dreams disturbed her.

She was up before dawn had properly arrived. The sky outside her small window was pearly grey, just showing the first glow of pale apricot. Quickly she washed and dressed, then crept down the creaking stairs, found her shawl, and was out in the street without anyone in the house knowing it.

Along the harbour, a tall figure walked up and down outside the Mission and at once Loveday felt strength flow inside her. She wasn't alone. 'Father.' He put a hand to his salt-stained cap and returned her smile. 'You're good and early.'

'Yes. This way.' She led him away from the harbour and along the deserted esplanade, towards East Cliff. 'I hope Maggie – Mother – will be able to come down and talk to you before Mrs Sothern is awake. She's a lady's maid, a good situation, and she likes it.'

He nodded, but said nothing, slowing his steps to match hers. The tide was turning, the waves splashing against the wall, fishing boats already bobbing over the bar, and his eyes locked on to them. 'Reckon I'll find a job somewhere here – an old hand like me.'

Loveday said quietly, 'When you went away I used to think of where you had gone – Newfoundland, such a long way away. And then Mr Benedict—'

'Old Frank?' His voice lightened and there was the hint of a smile on his rugged face.

Loveday smiled back. 'Yes. He taught me to play the harmonium. And he told me tales of the icebergs, and the whales and the bears, and the dangerous journeys. I began to think of it as a place I wanted to go to.' She paused hesitantly. 'It was my dream – the far land I called it.'

Amos stopped in midstride. He looked down at her. 'The far land? So you had one, did you, maid? Well, so did I. And it was here – back in this warm, gentle place, with the monstrous sea acting quiet for a change. And, tell 'ee what—' He reached out his hand and took hers in it. 'That's what brought me back. The far land, and the people in it. Maggie, and you . . . and . . . well, hopes that I could make up for all me bad ways.'

At the entrance to Sothern House Loveday halted, looked up at him and said, 'I'll go to the kitchen and ask for a message to be given to Mother. Why don't you stay here, in the garden? Somewhere private where you can talk – perhaps over there, in the gazebo.'

He nodded, said again, 'You're a good maid. I'll just wait,' and walked down the path.

The words ringing in her ears, she felt close to tears. Did she deserve his praise? She was only doing all she could to help. He was her father, a man she had never truly known, and now, suddenly, he was part of her life. She could understand his thinking, his reasoning, his excuses. If only Mother would feel the same. Heart in her mouth, she approached the closed back door and knocked.

She waited for close on five minutes, until Maggie came out of the

202

door, looking round, seeing her, and then coming quickly to where she stood under the shade of the lilac bush. 'What is it, Loveday? Not Jack, is it? Oh, don't tell me—'

'No, Mother.' Realizing that this was the first time of using the title, she wondered for a moment at how her feelings were changing. 'No, not Jack. And it's nothing to worry about. Just that—' She stopped, tried to smile, saw the anxiety in Maggie's eyes and was silent for a second. What should she tell her?

'Maggie.' A rough, husky voice full of emotion, loud enough to make Maggie turn her head, look towards the distant gazebo at the end of the garden and see the big man striding towards her.

Loveday stood like a statue, watching, listening, overwhelmed with feelings, and knowing she must go. She stayed long enough to see Maggie's face lift into an expression of amazement and then, like a butterfly taking flight, smile, so that all the wrinkles, the creases, the folds of ageing flesh disappeared and a younger, more passionate woman stood there. But then no longer stood, but ran to meet him, flew into his open arms. And then standing still, the two figures as one, tears and laughter mixing with voices and embraces.

Loveday turned her back, and fled.

She had hardly reached the gate leading into East Cliff when a voice called her back. 'Lovey! Wait! What on earth are you doing here? I haven't seen you for days, and now, suddenly, you're here, of all places—'

'Ned!' She could hardly believe it, but there he was, rapidly coming closer, his eyes twinkling, his hair brushed up by the errant breeze off the sea; and he was smiling. 'I couldn't sleep, came out here instead.'

Overwhelmed by emotions, both those she felt herself, and those of her mother and father which she had just witnessed, Loveday lost all control. She threw herself into his arms, felt his body stiffen with sudden surprise and then relax, drawing her tightly against him, his mouth finding her throat, her cheeks, and then her mouth, until, breathless, abruptly aware of what she was allowing to happen, she pulled away.

'Oh Ned . . . I don't know . . . I mean, I shouldn't.' How could she not kiss him back, wanting so much to find her own source of love, warmth and safety.

But his voice was suddenly rough, 'For God's sake, girl, make up your mind, can't you?' And again his hands strayed down her back, his face stooped to her throat, then down to the brief showing of warm breast pushing out of her dress, and she knew this was wrong. Not because of the physical lovemaking but because it came to her, like a stabbing pain, that Ned had no use for a shared mind, companionship and loving, which was what she longed for. He was just playing games.

She ran, her mind in a turmoil, breath hastening as her footsteps crunched down the track away from the house, towards the sea, towards home and safety. She didn't see Henry and Floss walking rapidly along the promenade, not yet able to walk on the beach because the ebbing waves still pounded so fiercely, rolling back the sand and shingle and denying human access. Not until Henry stepped in front of her, his open arms a barrier to her flight, did she think of anything other than Ned's betrayal and the end of her dreams.

'Loveday – where are you going? What's happened? Tell me.' His voice was crisp and clear, his eyes looking down into hers with an expression of dismay.

She couldn't speak for a moment, so just stood within his loose embrace, staring at his face and thinking how different he was from Ned. 'My father has come back,' she said at last, hearing the quiet, unsteady words as if in a dream; 'He and my Mother are together again. And Ned—'

A huge sob erupted and she bowed her head, choking on words that she knew she mustn't say, but needed so badly to expel.

Henry's arms drew her closer: not as Ned had done, but like someone offering comfort. 'That's great news about your father,' he said crisply. 'But what's this about Ned? That wretched Kerslake fellow been upsetting you, has he?'

Loveday heard the hostility, heaved a great sigh, looked into his grey eyes and told herself not to be so foolish. She didn't want any trouble between them. Ned loved her in his own way, of course he did. She had just been ridiculously old-fashioned in not wanting his lovemaking to go any further. Next time they met she would explain, and he would smile in his old cheery way and they would go on from there. Next time. . . .

She managed a watery smile. 'Nothing's wrong, Henry. Just a small misunderstanding. And now I must get back for breakfast. Aunt Janet will be wondering where I am.' She stepped away, one hand giving Floss a brief stroke, and then hurriedly went on her way back to Market Street telling herself that all would be well once she and Ned met again. Soon. Very soon.

Henry watched her go, his hand on Floss's collar, his thoughts raging tempestuously. He had a good idea of how Kerslake was behaving. He knew that sort of fellow – smiles, eyeing the girls, too ready with warm arms and demanding kisses. And Loveday was too young, too naïve to know how he was treating her. Well, perhaps it was time for he and Kerslake to meet. To thresh things out. And to tell him, once and for all, to play his promiscuous games with other girls. To leave Loveday alone. Forgetting about breakfast he went straight into the shipyard, got the apprentice to boil water for coffee, go out and buy him a sandwich, and then started the day's work. But for once his concentration was disturbed. Kerslake had better look out.

Loveday told Aunt Janet that her father and mother had met. 'And of course, she will have told him about Jack.' They looked at each other, minds visualizing the scene, imagining what Amos had said, how he had felt. What he and Maggie were doing now.

As she left for work, Loveday saw them, walking slowly along the beach, the tall stooping man and small woman looking at each other as they talked. So much to say, to regret, to forgive, to declare – even to plan for.

'We'll go straight to Jem Brown's and ask to see Jack,' Maggie said radiantly. 'He's probably somewhere around the town, working. We'll find him. Oh, Amos, I can't wait to see his face when he knows who you are.'

Amos nodded, his own thoughts almost bewildering him. A son. The boy he had wanted for so long. What would the lad think? How would he feel? Would he forgive his errant father, or harbour angry feelings of abandonment? Amos took Maggie's hand. 'I don't ask for too much,' he told her humbly. 'Maybe he'll not want me after this long time.'

The idea was terrible, but it was there, quietly knotting itself inside him. And as he and Maggie made their way to Jem Brown's workshop, the disquiet grew worse. 'You go in and ask,' he said roughly. 'I'll wait here.'

She came out a few minutes later, her bright face clouded and tense. 'He's gone – oh, Amos, he promised he wouldn't – but he's gone. No more work, Jem said, just a note saying he was going out in the Marten's fishing boat. They went this morning, with the tide. I can't believe it. Jack, oh, Jack!'

Amos put his arms around her, 'Quiet now, Maggie, quietly. The boy's not gone for ever. Fishing boats come back in the evening and we'll be there when they get in. Stop crying – you can't blame the boy, can you? The sea's in his blood, of course he wants to go. Come now, take my arm, we'll walk around a bit until you feel better.'

Loveday saw them again as she hurried back from the morning's work, her thoughts centred first on Ned and then on her mother and father. And brother. What would she find when she got home? And Henry – who had missed breakfast and had seemed so angry when she let Ned's name slip out in between her tears. What would Henry think of all this family upset?

Dinner was a quiet meal, with Aunt Janet spooning helpings of mutton stew and heaping Amos's plate. Maggie was subdued, hardly picking at her food, and only speaking when Janet asked how she had managed to get time off today.

'I told Mrs Sothern that my husband was home after a long time away and that I needed to be with him.' Maggie's quiet voice grew louder and she smiled at Amos, beside her. 'And do you know, she said all right. But that I must be back after tea as she is going out to dinner and needs me to dress her.'

'Very good of Mrs Sothern,' said Janet drily. 'But perhaps she can at last understand how ordinary people live, and the problems they often have to deal with. But what about Jack? You'll be back at Sothern House before the Martens get into harbour.'

'I'll be there.' Amos looked Janet in the eye and noted her grudging approval. 'I'll meet the lad. Tell him who I am. See what he says.'

'I'll come with you, Father.'

He smiled across the table. 'You an' me together to greet your brother. That's good, maid.'

When the meal was finished, Janet took Loveday aside. 'All this is very well, but I'm worried about Mr Long. No breakfast and what if he decides there's too much family talk going on to come for tea? Please, will you call in at the shipyard on your way home and tell him I'll give him a hot meal in the parlour, by himself?'

'No. I mean . . . well—'

Janet gave her a steely stare. 'And why not, pray? It would be only good manners to tell the man that we haven't forgotten him. And he'll need a proper meal – no breakfast and goodness knows what he found for his dinner. Yes, child, you go, as I ask, and deliver the message.'

Loveday's thoughts churned and finally settled. Aunt Janet was right. And – a quick stab of pleasure – she could go to the shed while she was there and see if the harmonium had settled in all right. Was it in tune? She could just play a few notes, no need to stay long, or to even let Henry know she was there, once she had delivered the message.

She gave Janet a wry smile. 'All right, Aunt, I'll go.'

Janet nodded, watched her leave the house, and told herself that although this was a very disturbing time for the child, at least she seemed in control of her feelings. She was behaving very well. In fact, everything seemed to be turning out for the best. Who would ever have thought that Maggie and Amos would be reunited? And now Amos was at long last to meet his longed-for son . . . how strange life was. One never knew what would happen next.

Loveday gave Henry Janet's message and quickly left again, hardly hearing him, getting up from his chair and following her to the door. 'Please thank Miss Jenkins. I'll be there. And Loveday—'

But she was gone, running through the now-empty yard, opening up the shed door and finding the harmonium quite safe and welcoming. She sat down and smiled at the stained ivory keys, and as she began playing, thought how pleased Frank Benedict would be if he knew about Father and Mother. And his old harmonium, safely housed, and played.

The fire was only a small one. The children had waited until the men had gone home, then sneaked in over the still broken down fence, and opened the furnace door in the steam room to roast the sausages Daisy had earned from Mr Moore. They stuck them on bits of driftwood already collected from the beach, held them up to the embers and sat on the floor, enjoying their treats, flushed with the heat of the open fire, and not noticing when a coal spat out and ignited bits of shavings lying beside them. Until suddenly flames shot up.

'Oh, c'mon, Joe!' Daisy grabbed the boy's arm and yanked him up, pulling him over the fence and out of danger, rushing along the beach and looking back to see if the fire was getting a hold of the yard. But only a wisp of smoke crept out and as they watched, so it disappeared. ''Tis all right,' said Daisy stoutly. 'Jest a bit o' smoke. That Mr Long'll never know.'

But he did. Loveday's arrival had unsettled him and her rapid disappearance was even more disturbing, arousing his emotions. He had wanted her to stay; he wished he could have invited her to look over his new plans and designs. Even taken her into the yard and shown her the new boat, growing so fast now. He would explain how the planks were steamed and then nailed together. How it grew from the keel upwards. How it was slightly different from the old design, but still held the potential of sail and oars. But he hadn't done so, and it was past tea time so he supposed he must go back to Market Street and eat Miss Jenkins's meal in solitary splendour in the parlour while her family – and Loveday – talked and ate in the kitchen.

Feeling decidedly unsettled, he tidied his plans, locked the office, went down the stairs and whistled up Floss, who came looking guilty, licking her lips and with her black hair slightly stinged along one side. Henry stopped dead, heard music coming from the shed, recognized the sad little song that Loveday played so well, and for once in his life was undecided. Should he join her? But did she want to see him? Her flight just now wasn't encouraging.

But then abruptly another sense assailed him and Floss's singed hair and the smell that drifted from just beyond the shed made sense, urging him into action.

FIRE!

It was only a small patch of burning shavings, with some brown, charred bits lying beside it, which Floss at once seized and hastily ate. Henry took off his coat and flung it down on the embers, sending up a plume of acrid smoke. Coughing, he found a bucket of water and doused the smoking pile. No more flames, just that creeping, harsh smell of burning hanging about. Slamming the furnace door shut he assessed the damage and sighed with relief. Nothing to worry about. No doubt those wretched children had come in again. He looked through the space in the fence. No, it still hadn't been mended. There would be recriminations tomorrow when he called Briggs to explain.

Then, undermining all the worry and fear, in his head he heard the harmonium's music singing through the noisome fumes and instantly and terrifyingly his mind took flight. She was still there. He ran towards the shed, filled with one thought alone. *Thank God she was safe.* But she might have been killed had the fire ignited even further. If the fire had taken hold, these old wooden buildings would have gone up like a newly lit gas jet. He closed his eyes, denying the vision, but the truth hit him with a hammer blow and he could only think of what life would be without her.

Breathlessly he reached the shed but found the door locked. She had gone, and, as he stared bleakly at its scarred, flaking, wooden panels, he understood at last what it was to love so deeply that his heart almost stopped beating, and his whole world began to crumble.

Turning away, he knew himself to be a different person, letting loose all his thoughts, his feelings, his hopes and his love.

CHAPTER TWENTY

Loveday left the yard, vaguely aware of an unpleasant smell but so full of her own thoughts that she paid no heed to it.

She must find Father and take him to the quay where the fishing boats moored. She must be with him when Jack returned. Her worry grew. Would Jack greet his long-lost father as a son should? Would he welcome him, or revert to being once more the sullen and unfriendly youth who so often appeared? She frowned, then sighed. What if Jack, too, after suffering the pain of rejection, just as she had done, refused to accept his father?

Oh no. No more problems, please.

And then, hurrying towards the harbour, it was Ned that crowded out everything else in her mind. Was she wrong to still believe that Ned might love her? That he just had a temperament that quickly erupted when he was annoyed? And why had she been so foolish as to anger him, once again, when he kissed her? Shaking her head, she knew now that all she longed for was to offer her love and have it returned. How childish of her, then, how ignorant, to spoil all the chances of affection that she was sure Ned had been giving.

And then, so unexpected that she stopped in mid step as she reached the river beach. *No*, declared a sudden strong voice inside her whirling mind. *You are an independent woman. So behave like one. Decide what you want, and then go and find it.*

She was smiling, a new purposeful expression on her face, as she reached Amos's side, her head clear and the path ahead inviting. She must find Ned, tell him what she felt for him, and wait for his answer.

'Here's the *Lucy Ann* now.' Amos's voice was tense as he watched the boat swing around the Point and enter the calmer water of the harbour. He looked down at Loveday. 'Your mother said as how the boy's always been delicate – a cough, so she told me.'

'Yes. But he's big and strong, for all that. And I think he made the most of his colds and coughs, just to annoy Mother because she won't let him

209

do what he wants.' Loveday surprised herself with this instinctive knowledge.

'An' what's that, then?' Amos's blue eyes were fixed on the boat slowly making its way to the quay where they waited.

'To go to sea. Like you, Father.'

He nodded, sighed deeply. 'If I'd known, I'd have been back long ago. But, like your Aunt Janet says, I'm selfish, an' it's hard to change a lifetime's habit. But I'm trying.'

'Evenin', Loveday.' Ben Marten's voice rang out over the water and the boat came to a stop as he leapt out on to the quay, rope in hand, looking back at his father, handling the tiller. 'Slowly, Dad. An' Jack, tie us up, b'y.'

Loveday felt Amos stiffen beside her, watched as he stared at the slender figure of his son jumping off the stern, coiling and knotting the rope to the mooring post. He moved forward quickly, stopping as he reached Jack, and she heard the emotion in his rough, husky voice.

'I'm your father. I left you but I'm back here now. And you're my son.'

Ben shouted about unloading as he bent to pick up the first of the baskets of fish, Daniel shouted back, a breeze tinkled the rigging and the gulls screamed as they flew above the boat, but a silence built between Amos and Jack and Loveday, holding her breath, prayed for something happy and wonderful to happen.

Jack straightened up, stared at the heavy, ageing man standing so close to him and at once stepped back. His thin face tightened into a grim frown and he said nothing for a moment. Until Amos shook his head, tried to smile, and, as if forced by some inner strength, opened his arms.

There was a moment when Loveday could hardly breathe. She knew that sullen expression, that held-back attitude. She knew what Jack was feeling. The rejection, the old pain. But – *Oh Jack, forget the past, just be thankful Father's here.*

And then he was caught in the wide, strong arms; caught in a bear hug that must have almost squeezed the breath out of him. *He smiled.* He smiled and said excitedly, 'I knew you'd come! Tell me about the sea, tell me about the ship you were on. I'm going to sea, too, I don't care what Mother says.'

Loveday turned away. Her eyes swam and she just nodded as Ben shouted after her, but couldn't reply. It was all right. It didn't matter that she wasn't there with them. They didn't need her; they had each other. Jack and Father were together – at last. She walked slowly back to Market Street and found Aunt Janet waiting up for her.

'Well? What happened?' Janet's voice was tense, her face unsmiling.

Loveday took a huge breath and sat down by the kitchen table. 'They're together,' she said unsteadily. 'Jack looked awful at first, but then, well, he changed.' She smiled. 'He and Father were talking, so I left them to it. Jack was going on about going to sea and Father was listening.'

'And will they go back to Carpenters' Row? Both of them? Thank the Lord. So now we can all go to bed.' Janet's face lost its stiffness. 'And tomorrow is a new day. Goodnight, child – and bless you. You've been so helpful. So good. So strong.' Bending, she kissed Loveday's brow and then left the room.

So strong. Loveday nodded, alone in the warm, gaslit kitchen. Yes, she had grown up at last. All the recent events, both happy and difficult, had helped her to leave behind the innocent, simple girl. Without doubt, she was a woman now, and knew about life and love. Maggie's words rang through her mind. 'You have a lot to learn.' Well, she had learned. But maybe there were still more lessons ahead of her.

Slowly, she turned off the gas, lit her candle and went up to her bedroom, wondering where Henry was, and when he would be coming back. She had half hoped that he might have heard her playing the harmonium at the yard and come and found her. She missed their early friendship, but it was she who had ended it. Henry meant nothing to her. It was Ned whom she must find and talk to. Ned whom she loved.

Henry was up earlier than usual. He couldn't face breakfast with Loveday, not after that sudden and unexpected revelation of his feelings for her last night. He and Floss slipped out of the still sleeping house and walked, as usual, from the harbour around the Point and along the beach towards East Cliff and Frank Benedict's cottage – now his. Henry grinned and felt his spirits rise. It was soon in sight and he stopped and looked at it. Yes, shabby, in need of renovation, but it was going to be his home. The longer he looked the more he thought he might move in even while it still needed doing up. Staying at the Jenkins's home was becoming increasingly difficult. Amos Hunt, his wife and son were reunited and settled, and he felt himself no longer to be part of the family. So, yes, he would move in to the cottage very soon. Living in a state of disrepair wouldn't harm him, and he would be his own man.

As he turned back, he saw a figure on the beach ahead of him – bending over, doing what? – he wondered curiously. Approaching he saw that letters were being cut into the newly washed beach. What did they spell? SORRY – and then the stretching arm formed another word. LOVEY.

He had now reached the writer, at once recognizing Ned Kerslake, and feeling his anger already rising. What was this oaf doing? He paused behind him, for suddenly it was vital to know the rest of the message, if that was what it was.

SORRY LOVEY. GOODBYE, NED.

Henry heaved in a huge breath, reached out and swung Kerslake round to face him. 'What the hell d' you think you're doing?'

Taken aback, Ned stumbled before regaining his balance. Then he stood and glowered at Henry, wiping his hands of sand. 'That's my business, Long. So push off.'

'You're wrong. It certainly is my business. And I'm not pushing off, thanks very much. You and I have certain matters to talk about . . . and, sure, they all concern Miss Hunt.'

'Really?' Ned's face tightened into a grinning sneer. 'Things between Lovey and me – Miss Hunt, of course, to you, but she and I are on more intimate terms, you see, and I always call her Lovey – are nothing to do with you.'

Henry's voice was deep and strong, his Canadian accent marked, giving extra power to the words. 'Wrong again. Anything to do with Loveday Hunt is my business. She's the niece of my landlady and I have a duty to look after her.' His fists tightened and he took an involuntary step nearer Ned.

'Oh yes? So you have games with Lovey, do you, just like me? So she's more a good-time girl than she lets on, would you say?' But Ned backed off, sneer disappearing and an anxious expression filling his face as he assessed the powerful body before him.

'Take that back, you great oaf,' Henry snarled, hands bunching.

Ned retreated again, but held on to his courage. 'And what if I don't?'

'I'll break your bloody neck.'

'You and who else?' But now Ned's voice was unsteady, and he eyed the heavy shoulders and huge fists with alarm.

Henry shook his head, a fierce grin lifting his face into anticipated pleasure. 'Just me,' he said, and hit out.

Loveday finished her breakfast early and left the house. She had no idea why Henry wasn't there, but of course she didn't really care. She would get to work early because when she was sweeping, making beds and dusting, even doing the slops, her real life managed to hide away. She hadn't slept well and needed an escape from all the emotions of the past few days. So, as she walked along the promenade, looking at the fast ebbing tide, suddenly she stopped short, then hurried to the seafront. Two men on the beach below, fighting. Letters in the sand, one of them strangely familiar. LOVEY – the word before it made illegible because of the men's footprints scuffing the sand, and then – GOODBYE, NED.

She gasped. Goodbye? He was going away ? But he hadn't told her – why not? And that was Henry and Ned down there. Why were they fighting? This was terrible. Shocking. What should she do? Already a few passers-by were gathering, watching the scene below them. Someone shouted, 'Go on, hit him back,' and she saw Ned holding his face, bending down and then straightening up, head butting Henry, who merely tottered back a few steps, then came into the attack again.

Unable to just stand there and watch, Loveday rushed down the nearest steps and ran towards the two men. 'Stop!' she shouted. 'Oh please, stop.' And then came to a halt as Henry half-fell, going down on one arm. 'Henry! Ned!'

Her shouts had no effect at all. Henry got up and felled Ned with an almighty uppercut, before standing, breathless, looking down at his victim. Only then did he glance aside and see Loveday, standing wide eyed and horrified just behind him. He smiled at her, not one of those quickly disappearing flashes of humour she was used to, but a large, proper, slightly grim, smile. 'It's all right,' he said, 'it's all over. I've won. He won't bother you any more.'

'Bother me?' She was shocked into silence and could only stare at Ned, brushing sand off his knees, nursing a swollen jaw, and already heading towards his distant escape route to East Cliff. 'Ned!' she shouted but he didn't turn. 'Ned, come back – please come back.'

Henry put a restraining arm around her shoulders. 'Let him go,' he said roughly, pressing a handkerchief to his bleeding nose. 'He left you a message – you can't make it all out now, the sand's so scuffed up, but I'll tell you what it said, then you'll understand.'

She looked into his deep set eyes, saw the glinting warmth in them and wondered at it. 'What? What did he say?'

SORRY, LOVEY. GOODBYE, NED. The words were clear and bare, hanging in the silence that grew between them.

'Goodbye? But what . . . what did he mean? He didn't say he was going away . . . not last time we were together.' It was so hard to believe.

Henry raised a dark eyebrow and smiled at her. 'Hurtful of him, but that's the sort of man he is. I'm afraid he's deceived you, Loveday. He's a man who plays with girls and then leaves them. I knew it at once, but I couldn't—'

She turned, the pain making her eyes spark flames, her anger instantly needing to find an outlet. 'Couldn't tell me? Why not? Why leave me to find out like this?' Her voice rose and shook. 'You should have told me, Henry—'

'No.' A decisive shake of his head as he rubbed his left arm, grimaced, then pressed the handkerchief against his nose once more. 'You told me in no uncertain terms that I shouldn't interfere in your life. You said I was wrong in finding out about your father, so of course I knew you wouldn't believe me if I warned you about Kerslake. I'm sorry, Loveday, but you wouldn't let me help. Try and understand.'

She sighed, felt the warmth of his arm as it came across her shoulder and slowly nodded her head. It was all so clear, so dreadfully hurtful. But, of course, the truth often was. She had been obstinate, unthinking, and where had it got her? So Ned had only been playing games; just as she had suspected, but then her stupid vanity had prevented the truth from being more obvious. *I thought he might have loved me. All my dreams, all gone.*

At the point on the beach where steps led to the promenade, directly opposite the Beach View Hotel, she came to a stop. 'I must go to work.' She knew she must make some sort of apology – she didn't want him to think badly of her. 'Henry, what can I say? I've been so stupid. I thought – well, I hoped that Ned might be more sincere than he was.'

'And he's hurt you.' Grey eyes, silvery in the sunlight, catching at hers and making her wonder as her already troubled emotions rose even further. Unexpectedly her heart beat quickened, and she wanted to say – what? But before she could sort out her thoughts, he looked away and the moment was gone.

She was left with regrets. 'Yes. Of course. I thought . . . he loved me—' Her voice broke.

Henry stiffened, removed his arm and remembered that Loveday Hunt would never allow a scene to be enacted before the watching population of her home town. So this wasn't the moment to declare himself. He must let her go, even though his heart swelled and everything in his mind denied what he was doing.

'Go and have a cup of tea and tell Mrs Narracott all your troubles, Loveday,' he said roughly. 'Then you'll feel better.'

She flinched. Was that all he could say to her? Even bleeding and sore as he must be after that awful encounter with Ned, surely he could have said something warmer, something more helpful? She caught her breath, lifted her head, and said sharply, 'Yes, that's what I shall do. Goodbye, Henry.' And then, as she walked away, realized that he *was* being helpful, for yes, Mrs Narracott would listen, would advise, and be sympathetic, and then there was work, that great escape from these overpowering, tremendous emotions and memories that seemed to be alive inside her.

Henry watched her, wondering how he had ever found the strength to let her go. Then, with Floss following, he strode on towards the shipyard. Work, he thought bleakly, was the answer to these painful knots winding up in his mind and his body.

Henry was absent at dinner time. 'I do hope Mr Long eats properly in that old office of his; I don't understand why he can't come back – it's only a step, after all.' Janet fussed about the meal, insisting on keeping a helping for the lodger's tea. 'I can easily warm it up for him.'

Loveday knew why he didn't come back. He was keeping out of the way of all the family upset that had happened so recently. Henry Long, she now knew, was a man who preferred to keep himself apart from other people's lives. Well, he would be moving out soon and – she told herself vehemently, indeed, quite fiercely – that would be a good thing. She could go back to her old bedroom, and there would be no Floss in the outhouse, a fact which constantly worried Aunt Janet who, despite her contrariness, often asked if the dog was warm and well fed.

The days dragged on. Jack, Maggie and Amos were all together at Carpenters' Row, and only occasionally called in to see Janet and Loveday. They smiled, they talked, and Jack had high hopes of getting his own way about going to sea. Maggie was a different woman, Loveday thought: she was more upright, full of smiles and chatter. And she brought some news.

'Mrs Sothern and Miss Eleanor are leaving for London this weekend. Well, I shall have some time off, but she says she wants me back when they return. And thank goodness that Mr Kerslake has gone already. My word, what a fuss, what with his camera and all those bags and trunks and things. Told Cook he had to go back to his main office to get his plates – or whatever they're called – developed and then he'd be off somewhere else. Egypt, I think he said. Oh, and he never left any tips.' She made a comic face. 'But we were happy to see him go, I can tell you! Not a nice gentleman at all.'

Loveday didn't answer and Maggie looked enquiringly at her. 'I expect you'll miss him? I mean, we did wonder—' She stopped abruptly.

'No. I shan't miss him.' Loveday left the room, knowing that there was little truth in her words. She did miss him, even though she now knew how badly he had treated her. The days seemed increasingly dull with no possible meetings with Ned to look forward to. After work, she walked slowly along the beach, trying to get her life into balance again, even though she recalled her positive decision only a few days ago. To be strong and determined. But it was hard to deal with shattered dreams.

She wondered if she should consult Madame Chance again, but then no words could ever heal the empty feeling inside her. And it was only at the end of the week, when Henry was making arrangements for the carter to collect his bags and take them to his new home, that a new pain surfaced. Henry would no longer be at home. Yes, of course, he had annoyed her, intrigued her, even excited her at first, but the fact that he was going was a quite different feeling. It made her turn round at the Point, and retrace her steps towards East Cliff, and the cottage.

She was just passing the bathing machines when Ben shouted from the esplanade.

'Loveday! Wait fer me.' He jumped down and raced towards her, his broad smile comforting and making her return it. Thank goodness for friends.

'Ben! I thought you'd be on your boat.'

' 'Tis Friday. Us don't sail on Fridays, 'tis unlucky. No, Loveday, it's jest that I got something to tell you. 'Bout the fire.'

She stopped. 'What fire?'

'At the shipyard. Last week. Me Dad on'y got it out o' our Daisy yesterday. Oh, she's a shocker, a'right, that maid. She an' Joe bin in the yard again – slipped in through the fence, she says – an' was cooking the bits of sausage the butcher gave them – opened the fire door in the steamer room, see – when the fire spat out and things started burning. Not bad, but they ran – an' she's bin havin' nightmares ever since.' Ben stopped and frowned. 'An' I wondered whether your Mr Long had said—'

My Mr Long? Something inside Loveday began to tremble. 'What about Mr Long?'

'Well, he were there, I reckon, and so he must ha' smelt the fire and put it out.'

Smelt the fire. Was that what she had smelled, locking the shed door and leaving the yard? Loveday tensed. Henry had still been there? But what if the fire had been worse? If it had taken hold of all those old sheds and dry timber – if it had gone up in roaring flames? Images and sounds escalated in her terrified mind and she put a hand on Ben's arm to steady herself.

What if Henry had been caught in it . . . burned . . . killed? Life with-out Henry?

She gasped, threw Ben a last glance and then ran as fast as she could towards the cottage. She must know if he was all right. What had Ben called him? *My Mr Long. Oh, why had she ever thought loving thoughts of Ned Kerslake who clearly had no affection for her at all? How could she have been so foolish, so full of ridiculous dreams when the truth had been hiding inside her?*

The distance between the pier and East Cliff had never seemed so long. Her boots filled with sand because she ran as fast as she could, her breath became quick and heavy, and all the time her mind was circling, the pictures vivid and terrible. The fire . . . Henry trapped in his office. . . .

Then common sense prevailed. But of course, he hadn't been trapped. Why, only the next day he had given Ned the hiding of his life and was now probably resting, treating his bruised arm, and his bloodied nose. So why was she full of this overwhelming feeling that she must find him, must talk to him, must say – what?

On the beach below the cottage she came to a breathless halt, staring up at the little building, seeing the open door, and suddenly becoming full of indecision. She approached very slowly, reached the road and then walked towards the wicket gate. A huge black head looked over the top of it, and a handsome black tail waved a welcome. Floss, in the garden. So Henry must be there – inside.

At the open door she paused again, heard his voice humming a tune which she at once recognized. It was the sea shanty that Gus had played on his accordion, the jolly tune which they had all joined in, even Mr Benedict, and which Henry had sung with her. Now she listened to his warm, easy voice and felt something begin to fill her with a new hope-fulness. When the first verse ended, she waited for the second one, and then, as the last line came into her head, she joined in.

Come safe home to me. They were singing it – together.

Loveday had no more thoughts, just a burning need to find him, to tell him. She went to the foot of the stairs, took a deep breath, and called, 'Henry.'

217

CHAPTER TWENTY-ONE

Henry had been at the cottage for a good hour and a half, leaving the yard early for once in order to buy paint on his way home. He had already cleaned out the bedroom and now was slapping paint on the newly plastered walls, making the one room habitable. His bags were stacked downstairs and he was suddenly unexpectedly happy. Forget all the problems, both with the yard and the new boat, and with Loveday and her difficult family. Here, he was in his own home. True, a small voice in his head had at first whispered that he might be lonely here, but he concentrated on the paint and pushed it away. And then he grinned – Crystal, Frank's cat – had come home again. No, he wouldn't be lonely.

When he heard Loveday's voice joining in with the shanty he was singing to himself – the rhythm of painting needed music to help it along – he lifted his head sharply and let the brush fall, drips running down his clothes. Her pure voice and the words of the old song caused an extraordinary and almost alarming disruption inside him. And then the one word – calling to him from below.

He raced down the stairs, found her standing in the doorway, wide green eyes smiling, lovely face a little uncertain, and told himself not to be a fool any longer, for God's sake get on and tell her how he loved her.

'Loveday.' He stepped close, opened his arms and then shook his head, saying helplessly 'I'm covered in paint. It'll get all over you.'

Uncertainty left her face and her smile was radiant. 'I don't care about paint, Henry,' she said, and flew into his arms as if drawn by a magnet.

He held her to him, cherished her warmth, her quick, nervous breathing, and felt everything dissolve around him. Then he said, very low, 'I'm not sure what's happening. I thought you didn't care.'

She nestled closer. 'I thought so, too. All that foolishness with Ned. And then Ben told me about the fire and I knew I had to find you. To see if you were safe.'

218

Wondering, he looked into her eyes. 'But you knew I was. You saw me with Kerslake the day after the fire.'

She looked down, colour rushing into her cheeks. 'That was then. Things are different now.'

'Tell me.' His deep voice vibrated through her body, his arms held her lovingly, safe and warm.

She felt his heart beat through the linen shirt, knew she had come home at last. All she had to do was to tell him. A deep breath helped the words come out. 'I love you, Henry. I've loved you right from very first time I saw you walking down the platform and smiling at me.' Her voice was muffled, but he heard and knew no answer was needed. It was enough that they were together – at last.

He cupped her face in his hands, raising it until their lips were very close. Looking into her wide, longing eyes, he whispered, 'Of course I love you. I always knew it. So kiss me.'

Loveday had never known such joy. Her whole body was aroused, radiating with wonder and happiness, and when she stepped back from the fierce embrace, breathless, she was laughing. 'Henry Long, I'll never let you go again!'

'Just try, my love.' His voice rose, the flinty eyes gleamed silver as he took her arm and pulled her towards the stairs. 'Here, come and look round the old house. The bedroom's good enough for us to sleep in and tomorrow evening I'll get the downstairs into shape. And you can bring your harmonium home, by the wall, just as it was before.'

On the landing upstairs she stopped, waiting for him to reach her side. Then, suddenly hesitant, she said very quietly, 'Yes, but you've forgotten something, haven't you, Henry?'

'Have I?' Again his arms were about her, his face bending to hers. It was hard to draw back, to say what had to be said, but old-fashioned values were important.

Her voice was husky. 'Something about getting married, perhaps?'

'Oh! My God, how could I forget?' And then he was on one knee on the dusty floorboards, his hand taking hers, his face looking up at her, and a smile overflowing as he said, deep and resonant, 'Miss Hunt, will you do me the honour of accepting my hand in marriage?'

Yes please! Without any more hesitation she pulled him up, flinging her arms about him and kissing him with abandon. Then, as they finally drew apart, she sang the little song again, 'Come safe home to me' and knew that, at last, here she was, at home, with her love.

*

Amos Hunt sat on the bed in the small upstairs room at number three Carpenters' Row and looked at the scrimshaw pieces that Loveday had given back to him last night. She had come, a great smile of joy on her face, with Henry Long, who said very politely in his deep, Canadian voice, 'I'm asking for your permission to marry your daughter, sir. I love her – and I will care for her.' Well, what could any father say except, 'All right, boy – and I wish you both much happiness.'

So, that was all right. Long seemed a decent enough fellow, and he was going to make money at the old shipyard. Amos had been there, seen the new boat rising from its wooden keel, recognized the old design, but was intrigued by Long's new ideas, and wondered if he might not apply for a job here. All his experience might be useful. But then the other, urgent, still obsessive need had turned that on its head. Jack, his boy, needed to go to sea. He needed to be with Jack. They could sail together.

The nightmares still came, but the present was slowly banishing them. He and Jack had begun to understand each other and Amos prayed it would lead to love. The boy had a delicate constitution, so his mother said. Well, a voyage in clean, windswept air would help him recover.

Already Amos had made enquiries. Yes, there were ships sailing from Plymouth to Portugal, transporting fruit. It wouldn't be a long voyage, but enough to bring father and son together and to form a lasting bond. But what would Maggie say? Well, he would have to persuade her when she came this evening. Tell her he would be back this time; but he and Jack must be together before they returned to make the family complete again – and for good.

The family. He fished in his pocket and pulled out the third piece of scrimshaw, putting it in a line with the other two. Frank Benedict's piece, Maggie's piece, and now the one he wanted to give to his daughter. He looked at it for a long moment, before taking his pocket knife and, bending over the scrimshaw, started carving. A new figure appeared, and the words were made clearer. He hoped she would understand, and be pleased.

Her wedding day. Loveday gave a last look in the pier mirror and thought how wonderfully Aunt Janet had enhanced the primrose-coloured dress made for her visit to Sothern House. Now a new small bustle lifted the short train of ivory sateen, and a huge bow of golden ribbon emphasised her waist. Her hair, swept upward, was crowned by a wreath of artificial orange blossom holding a short Honiton lace veil, which Maggie had brought from Mrs Sothern. 'She said as she'd heard of Mr Kerslake's bad behaviour and hoped you would accept this as a wedding gift. I think she was ashamed of him.' Maggie had added, quietly, 'I mustn't gossip, but she's with child – and so much nicer now.'

The dress fitted perfectly, emphasising her curves at breast and hips, and was embroidered down the front of the bodice with tiny pearl flowers which Maggie had helped stitch on. Loveday looked down at her kid slippers with the mother of pearl buckles and wondered how she would manage to walk along the esplanade to the church. True, Mrs Sothern had offered the use of the gig, but it held unhappy memories, so she had decided to walk.

The fragrance of sweet peas, gathered by Maggie from the garden of Sothern House, enveloped her as she stood in the hall with the posy in her hands, and suddenly she realized that this house held all her youthful happiness. She looked at Aunt Janet bustling down the stairs, resplendent in her best lavender-coloured dress with a small straw hat trimmed with pansies, and then at Uncle Davey, standing beside her in his dark suit, smiling with his usual warmth.

'You look beautiful, child.' He bent, kissed her cheek, looked at his hunter watch and then said, 'Time to go, I think. You don't want to keep Henry waiting, do you?'

Loveday's heart was too full to reply, but she smiled her answer, put her hand on his arm and stepped out into the sunshine, where the neighbours gathered to see her go and wish her well. Voices raised. 'God bless you, Loveday,' and 'What a lovely bride.'

In the church porch, Floss sat with a huge satin bow tied around her neck – Aunt Janet's doing, of course. Inside the lighting was dim with candles flickering, and the organ playing a soft accompaniment to the wedding party as Amos met them at the door, then led Loveday down the nave and to the altar where Henry waited. Her eyes feasted on him, so tall and handsome in his black coat and pristine white linen, dark hair falling smoothly over his high collar – waiting for her.

It took so little time to marry them. Prayers, solemn promises, and then the ring placed on her finger. 'You are now man and wife,' intoned the vicar, and Henry bent his head to kiss her – so carefully, so delicately, only his deep eyes showing the passion he was having to keep in check.

Out into the sunshine again and the walk through the town to the Jolly Sailor Inn where a table of ham sandwiches and bread and cheese, with dishes of mussels and shrimps, waited beside the jugs of ale and cider. There was mirth, congratulations, loving wishes – how long before they could be alone, wondered Loveday?

Only another hour or two. She returned to Market Street, changed from the wedding gown into her best summer dress, and then joined Henry, who waited in the kitchen, chatting to the family gathered there. Maggie was in tears, Aunt Janet's eyes swam, and Uncle Davey kept blowing his nose. Only Jack seemed normal. 'Good luck, Loveday,' he said, adding quickly, 'I might not be seeing you for a bit – just wait and see.'

But before she could ask what he meant, Henry took her arm. 'Time to go home, Loveday,' he said firmly and they walked quickly up Market Street, down on to the beach, and along the strand of lapping lacy-topped waves, until they reached the cottage.

'Home at last,' she whispered, as he swept her into his arms and carried her through the open doorway. He kicked the door shut behind him, and at last they were alone and together.

Amos and Jack, with their bags, waited by the quay for the ketch from Plymouth to come into harbour, to pick up some cargo and the two new hands who were to come aboard and work their passages to Portugal and back. All the Jenkins family was there to see them embark and leave. Maggie, now accepting the fact that this last voyage was a deeply necessary one, sighed and knew she would, once again, be waiting. But this time there was a promise from Amos to return. 'God willing,' he said, put his arms around her and knew she would be praying for them both every night.

Janet and Davey stood together, closer than ever in the knowledge that Loveday was now in the care of someone else. A good man, they both thought. But they would always be there – just in case. It would be hard to have the house to themselves – no young feet running upstairs, no useful hands in the kitchen. No pure voice singing as she went about her life. 'Bless her, she deserves all the happiness she can get,' said Janet in an unsteady voice as the ketch lined up along the wharf side. And then, more loudly, told Amos to be sure to take great care of that boy and his delicate chest.

Amos bade them all a quiet farewell. When he came to Loveday's side, he put his hand into his pocket, pulled out the three pieces of scrimshaw and gave them to her. 'It's finished now,' he said just loud enough for her alone to hear. 'I needed to come home, to find you, before I could add the last bit. Take it with you, maid, and try to understand what it means.' He paused, cleared his throat, and added huskily, 'I give it you with my love.'

There was no time for any more. The boat moored, and bustle and noise ended the emotions and last words. Amos and Jack went aboard with their bags, looked once more back at the family on the wharf, waved, and then disappeared below deck. The cranes alongside began creaking and wheeling as cargo was stowed, and the small gathering dispersed, Janet and Davey returning to Market Street, Henry walking rapidly towards the shipyard with Floss at his heels, and Loveday wandering along the beach towards her new home.

Maggie stayed where she was, handkerchief pressed to her eyes, but her body upright and strong. She would remain until the loading was finished, and then she would watch the boat slowly leave the harbour and start on its journey. How long would it be before they both came home again? Well, she had waited once, and she could do so again. When the freshening wind began to blow into her face she turned and walked back to Market Street. At least she could live with Janet and Davey until that wonderful day came along. And she had her daughter who now called her Mother and had begun to love her. Yes, thought Maggie, life was very complicated, but sometimes things worked out.

Loveday and Henry, with Floss at their heels, walked along the beach for their usual evening stroll. The days were busy for both of them, Henry watching with delight how the new boat was growing and planning its launch when the autumn regatta came along, while Loveday polished her new home and worked at being a good cook. Her shell collection stood beside a sleeping Crystal on the sunlit windowsill, pride of place being the three pieces of scrimshaw. She had looked for a long time at the final piece her father had given her, and it wasn't until the three were lined up that the message became obvious.

A tall man carrying something was Amos and his fiddle. The woman's face was Maggie's. The small figure running so far ahead was, of course, the longed for, unborn son – Jack. And a new carving filled the little space left – a girl's figure, with some red paint etched into the curling hair – herself. As the message revealed itself, she found it easier to decipher the scratched words and make sense of them at last. 'My family.' Just two words, but they explained everything, just as Frank Benedict had said they would. Loveday put down the pieces and went across to the harmonium. The little air Father had played on his fiddle suddenly became happier and sweeter. She wiped her eyes, and then remembered the potatoes cooking on the range – hastily she ran to remove the boiling pan. Henry must never have a burned supper.

223

The sun was going down, the calm sea reflecting its warm and peaceful palette of colours. Henry's hand clasped hers and they didn't need to say anything. Until Loveday stopped, as something came into her mind; something important that she had just learned.

'I used to dream about a far land,' she said, turning to look at him. 'It was Newfoundland, of course, because Frank Benedict had told me about blue and green icebergs and whales diving deep and polar bears and people wearing skins and living on cod. I used to want to go there. And then Ned came along with his stories of deserts and camels, and that was another far land.'

'We all have our own dreams,' Henry said quietly, swinging her hand. 'Our own personal far lands. Mine was to build a boat that the world would acclaim. And your father, from what he's said to me, had his dream of coming home here for his far land. Now he's got a different one, of course. And so have I.'

Teasingly, she smiled at him. 'And what's that?' As if she didn't know.

'Being with you. Short and simple. But it's all I need. And, tell me, have all your own youthful and innocent dreams changed? Been answered, perhaps?' His voice was low and she heard the warmth of his love.

She nodded, stared out to sea, then turned and looked all around her. The town – her town – enclosed the curving bay and lights were beginning to flicker in windows. Coming out of the waves, Floss shook her long coat and spattered them with water so that, laughing, they had to jump aside. In the distance a seagull mewed.

Loveday pulled Henry's arm closer to her side. 'No more whales, and icebergs, thank you. Not even camels and deserts. I'll go along with your boat dreams, but I have no more of my own. You see, I've found my far land.'

She stopped, raised her head and kissed him. 'It's here – with you.'

Then, as a large, wet, hairy dog pushed past her skirt, she added, laughing, 'And Floss.'